M000034585

SIMON SAYS

ALSO BY BRYAN THOMAS SCHMIDT

NOVELS
The Worker Prince (Saga of Davi Rhii 1)
The Returning (Saga of Davi Rhii 2)
The Exodus (Saga of Davi Rhii 3)
Simon Says (John Simon Thrillers)
The Sideman (John Simon Thrillers-forthcoming Feb. 2020)

CHILDREN'S BOOKS
Abraham Lincoln Dinosaur Hunter: Land Of Legends
102 More Hilarious Dinosaur Jokes For Kids

NONFICTION
How To Write A Novel: The Fundamentals of Fiction

ANTHOLOGIES (AS EDITOR)
Infinite Stars: Dark Frontiers
Joe Ledger: Unstoppable (with Jonathan Maberry)
Predator: If It Bleeds
Infinite Stars: Definitive Space Opera and Military Science Fiction
The Monster Hunter Files (with Larry Correia)
Maximum Velocity (with David Lee Summers, Carol Hightshoe,
Dayton Ward, and Jennifer Brozek)
Little Green Men—Attack! (with Robin Wayne Bailey)
Decision Points
Galactic Games
Mission: Tomorrow
Shattered Shields (with Jennifer Brozek)
Raygun Chronicles: Space Opera For a New Age
Beyond The Sun
Space Battles: Full Throttle Space Tales

SIMON SAYS

By

Bryan Thomas Schmidt

Ottawa, KS

BORALIS BOOKS
Ottawa, KS 66067

"Mr. Roboto" by Dennis DeYoung © 1983 Stygian Songs (ASCAP)
admin. by Wixen Music Publishing, Inc. All Rights Reserved. Used
by Permission.

ISBN-13: 978-1-62225-7508 hardcover
ISBN-13: 978-1-62225-7515 paperback
ISBN-13: 978-1-62225-7522 ebook

First Edition: October 2019

Printed in the United States of America

10 9 8 7 6 5 4 3 2 1

Interior Design and Layout by Guy Anthony De Marco
Front Cover Design: Kent Holloway
Cover Layout and Additional Design: A.R. Crebs
Author Photo: Bryan Thomas Schmidt

Dedicated to

KCPD Training Officer Gilbert Carter,

With thanks for his friendship, guidance,

Advice, and letting me intrude on so

Many work days over the four years

I did ride-alongs to research this book.

He's one of the best out there,

And I'm grateful for his service.

CHAPTER 1

THE TWO-YEAR-OLD BROWN 2027 Ford Explorer Interceptor drove slowly along Woodsweather as its two occupants checked the numbers on the various buildings, primarily brick warehouses. Like most recent models, the car was fully capable of driving itself, especially to such a simple location, but its driver was a seventeen year veteran of the Kansas City Police Department and a huge skeptic of all the latest gadgets. He refused to even use the car's video monitors for backing up or its automatic parallel parking function, which had proved to be highly more efficient than any human driver.

Fuck that, he thought. He wasn't trusting his life or his partner's to a machine no matter what. It was bad enough the machines were taking over—taking jobs from humans, controlling paperwork, cars, and spying on everything these days. Cops like himself were fast becoming relics Simon knew, but some things were still best handled by humans.

Forties, former star running back at K-State, divorced with an estranged teenage daughter—ex-everything really, Master Detective John Simon drove as his younger partner, Blanca Santorios, read the numbers off the buildings. Dark-skinned with beautiful black hair that ran down to the middle of her back and stunning brown eyes, her beauty belied the tough cop underneath. She was pushing thirty now but didn't look a day above college-aged, and at the moment, she had that special glow that pregnant women always had. Few people knew about the pregnancy, though, as Santorios refused to notify the department until she had to so she could avoid desk duty, every detective's dread. She was just starting to show, so they both knew it wouldn't be long until she had no choice. Sergeant Becker was smart and very observant, and female cops never missed these things like their male counterparts did.

Santorios squinted through the fading daylight toward the front of the grungy building obscured by shadows. "Two-five-five-six," Santorios checked a slip of paper in her hand. "This is it."

The warehouse had been built in the 1940s along the Missouri Riverfront between Mulberry and Eighth on Woodsweather Road. While much of the Missouri West Bottoms area had become run down over time, historic preservationists and revitalization funders nostalgic over its history and not wanting its prime location in the heart of downtown Kansas City to go to waste had fought and won. From the early 2000s on, the West Bottoms had thrived again.

"Who the hell makes these cars," Simon grumbled, sliding around on the leather that had become one with his ass. "I think I'm stuck to this seat."

"Keep it. It matches your eyes," Santorios grinned as Simon pulled the car to a stop by the curve.

Simon groaned as she chuckled and began unbuckling his seatbelt. "Tell me again why we've wasted three evenings on this?"

"Because Peter tipped me off," his partner reminded him. "Relax, will you? Do you want to just wait in the car?" Her soft eyes met his and she meant it.

Simon chuckled. "Ever since Andy knocked you up, you've been scolding everyone like a parent. What are you—practicing?"

"Not everyone. Just you," she replied. "The whole reason Becker made us partners was for me to keep you in line."

Simon scowled. "Don't get cocky. It never lasts."

"Look, I'm just going to look around like before," his partner said, moving on. "See if there's any activity. Seriously. Wait in the car if you want." But she knew he'd never do that. They were partners and hell or high water he had her back.

They opened their doors and got out—Simon on the street, his partner on the curb—just as a big rig rolled past, sending muddy water from the morning's rain flying up under its wheels to splatter Simon's slacks. He'd just had them dry cleaned and pressed. "Fuck!" he cursed as he slammed the door and looked down at himself.

"To protect and to serve," Santorios teased.

"Seventeen years and they still have the same stupid slogan," Simon muttered. A cool breeze blew in over the river, rustling the nearby oaks and made him shudder a moment.

"God's wrath for your bad attitude," she replied with a laugh.

"You getting religious on me?"

"They came door to door on a rough day," she quipped.

Simon chuckled. Best partner he'd ever had. Gave as good as she got. She led the way as Simon came around the car and they started up a double wide sidewalk toward the double glass front doors of the warehouse office.

Santorios reached up and tried the doors. Locked. Just as expected. "Let's go around to the back," she said.

As they turned to head west, they both noticed the tractor trailer backing in behind the warehouse.

"I thought you said nobody's here," Simon said, shooting his partner an inquisitive look.

"Except for those nights where they get strange deliveries he told me," she replied. "Unusual activity after hours. Probable cause." And a possible lead on some of the burglaries they'd been investigating the past few months. Santorios picked up her pace now, headed along the front of the warehouse toward the side where they'd seen the truck.

"Our lucky day," Simon said and followed, bursting with pride. When they'd first partnered up for Simon to train her, the newly promoted detective had been about as by-the-book as they come. Afraid to push any boundaries and risk her detective status or alienate her superiors. But her older, more jaded trainer had worked on her, and after six years, now she was the one fudging the rules.

"God being good to us," Santorios said.

"Remind me to find those missionaries and shoot them, will you?" She shushed him with a glare and a dismissive motion as they moved around the side of the building toward the rear dock. Truth was his partner's renewed interest in her Mexican family's traditional Catholic heritage was also part and parcel of her forthcoming motherhood, and Simon knew the more frequent religious references in their banter were a result of that.

A group of a half-dozen or so men waiting a yard back along the rear dock swung into action as the big rig pulled to a stop with the usual repeated annoying warning beeps as it backed up and settled against the dock's edge. Two

Hispanic-looking men rushed the doors, one resting a hand on the handle as the other knelt to unlock a padlock at the base with a set of jangling keys. He worked quickly and efficiently, like one who'd done the task many times before, then stood and stepped back as his partner worked the latch-lever and swung first the left door then the right wide open with barely a squeak.

The rest of the group swooped in then and began unloading crates off the truck, some using handcarts, others crawling into the trailer, while one or two retrieved forklifts and drove them forward with the same annoying beeps as the big rig had produced moments before.

The men were so busy, none of them noticed the two cops cautiously approaching the metal side door just below the dock to their right which led into the building. Santorios jiggled the handle. Unlocked. She pulled it open slowly, trying to be as quiet as possible, and stepped inside. Simon followed.

They were in a dimly lit corridor with old vinyl flooring that looked right out of the Seventies. The long fluorescent fixture overhead had two bulbs, one flashing on and off sporadically to create shadows up and down the passage's length. At the far end was some kind of counter in an alcove in the wall, facing down the corridor. Guard station, most likely. But there was no sign of any guard.

They exchanged a silent look and moved ahead cautiously, taking in the walls. Halfway down on one a larger cork bulletin board held the usual assortment of workman's government warnings: notices about work injuries, regulation of work hours and overtime, safety rules and procedures, etc. All stapled up by their four corners in a neat row along the right hand side of the board. The other half of the board contained assorted notices of birthdays, official holidays and chaotically posted notes for fellow employees, many half-covering parts of each other.

The corridor smelled of dust and sweat and industrial cleaning solutions. The ceiling overhead was unfinished and raw with concrete and steel beams showing through high above and the light hanging by a wire at least ten feet down from them. They heard the sounds of hydraulics from behind the wall to their left — the warehouse floor — and voices as the men worked.

"Show me," a baritone voice growled.

Wood creaked as someone pried open a crate, Simon guessed. Metal clanking. A dropped crowbar perhaps? Then there was rustling and the baritone spoke again. "Good shit."

"It's good," another, higher pitched voice insisted. "Just pay up and I'm out."

Simon and his partner exchanged a knowing look. Probably drugs.

"Pay the man then," they heard the baritone say as a forklift engine started up again with a whine.

They reached the far end of the corridor facing the counter. A door to their right seemed to lead into office space, while another opening to their left led into the warehouse workspace. There was a knocking sound, then the metal click of latches. Maybe a briefcase opening?

Santorios nodded to the left and Simon nodded agreement. They both reached behind their jackets to loosen the straps over their weapons, then moved cautiously toward the opening. They could see the warehouse's concrete floor beyond, stained with oil, dirt, and various substances. Stacks of crates lined a wall in the distance with a row of basic wood-frame shelves lining the area to their right, the warehouse's west end. Smaller crates and boxes filled the shelves. "Hold it!" The higher pitched voice said. "The price was two hundred. You're fifty short."

The partners entered the warehouse floor behind a huge row of crates and moved silently along toward the dock opening, seeking a better view of the proceedings.

"Take the money," the baritone ordered.

"I answer to people," the other insisted. "Pay me what you owe me."

"There were complications," the baritone said, his voice cold. "Not possible."

"Bullshit!" the other replied.

"May I help you?" It was a male voice from behind the detectives, a little tinny, not quite firm.

The partners whirled around, hands instinctively heading for their shoulder holsters, but they stopped when they saw him: tall, bald, a black man in his late twenties, perhaps. Bright blue eyes, a neatly pressed security uniform and badge. He was unarmed except for a taser that hung off his belt on a hook. And he was smiling at them, not threatening at all.

"Master Detective John Simon," Simon said, relaxing and keeping his voice down with hopes the men near the truck might not hear.

"Detective Blanca Santorios," his partner said, smiling back at the guard.

"This is a restricted area," the guard said. "May I see your identification?"

"Sure," Santorios said. "And maybe you could answer a couple questions?" Both detectives pulled their wallets and flashed their badges and IDs.

"You are police officers?" the guard said as if he wasn't sure. Not the usual response.

The voices out by the truck went silent and there was a shuffling. Simon tensed. Had they overheard?

Without warning, a large, scruffy bearded man with tattooed arms swung out from behind the row of crates, ten feet back from the guard, wielding a Barrett M4-Carbine automatic rifle and opened fire. The first rounds cut through the guard's shoulders and back and knocked him to the floor, moaning.

Simon and Santorios both reached for their weapons— Santorios a Glock 22 and Simon his trusty Glock 37—as they simultaneously dove aside and aimed them at the gunman. Simon headed right and Santorios left, up against the crates.

In moments, they returned fire, snapping off several shots as the gunman turned his rifle on them and fired off a stream of rounds.

He jerked as he was hit in the shoulder, knocking him to the right, and then the knee, causing him to cry out and buckle. Simon put one in his forehead and he went down, silenced.

The iron smell of warm blood joined the scents of oil, dirt, sweat, wood, and more as Simon looked at his partner, neither clear entirely whose shots hit where. Both had aimed for center mass, per training, but diving and rolling never helped one's aim.

The crates beside Santorios exploded then with the sound of automatic and machine gun fire. Hundreds of bullets a minute as the men behind them, who were unloading the truck, opened fire.

"Shit!" Santorios dove toward her partner as Simon looked around for cover. Dust and splinters flew from the crates as the fire cut through them but only a few bullets made it through to strike a narrow cement beam near Simon's head. The only thing solid to protect them. His partner landed beside him in a crouch.

"Just relax. Wait in the car," Simon mimicked his partner's earlier words, then asked, "You okay?"

"No. They're trying to kill us," Santorios cracked.

"I noticed," Simon replied. The beam was too narrow for adequately protecting one of them, let alone two. He jerked his head toward the dead gunman, lying just outside the opening through which they'd entered from the corridor. Santorios nodded back and they both jumped to their feet and ran as fast as they could as gunfire continued tearing apart the crates.

They both dropped and rolled, coming up aiming back toward the dock, feet apart in firing stance.

"Police! Drop them!" Simon yelled. They could see some of the men now, armed and reacting to the two detective's appearance in their line of sight.

The men swung their rifles as one called, "Fuck you!" Then they opened fire again, along with several others Simon couldn't see.

Again, they split up, ducking and rolling as they dodged the bullets then fired back. One of the gunmen went down, hit in the chest by Santorios, his machine gun spraying a barrage of bullets into the air as he fell.

Simon landed between two of the wooden shelves and sought cover behind a loaded pallet jack. Bullets ricocheted off it as he took aim and fired back at the two Hispanic men, who had left the unloading and were firing Barret M-4s from close by.

A man in jeans and two more in suits were firing automatic pistols from the shelter of the stacked crates behind which the two cops had encountered the guard earlier, while two men on forklifts fired Uzi semi-machine guns from their cockpit seats, and others scattered around the room ran for cover. The man in jeans had several days old stubble on his face and wore cowboy boots and a flannel shirt—Simon made him as the truck driver. One of the two suits was wearing white Armani like a 1980s Miami Vice throwback, with slicked back short brown hair and green eyes that shone with arrogance and command. The one in charge perhaps? The other suit was cheaper, polyester, and the stereotypical gray with matching slacks, a white button down shirt and bland tie rounding out the ensemble. He was dark-skinned with dark black hair, military cut, and looked Hispanic except for his light blue eyes. The rest of the men, including the other two Hispanics, wore khakis or work pants and Polo-style shirts.

Santorios fired at one of the forklift drivers, but her bullets bounced off its metal frame with a clang, deflecting into boxes. The driver aimed his machine gun at her as she dove behind another concrete beam near the wooden shelves—this one wide enough to hide her.

Simon took aim at one of the forklift drivers, raising his Glock at a slight angle and firing off three shots in a row. The first two deflected like his partner's had off the machine's steel frame, but the third hit the driver in the neck. He screamed, his machine gun falling from his hands as he grabbed at his bleeding neck and tried to move the forklift one handed.

As the other men returned the two detectives' fire, the

forklift's servos whined and it turned in an arc, accelerating. But then Santorios got a clear shot at the driver and took it. His head jerked back as he fell forward on the controls, and the forklift accelerated even more toward one of the other men, who shouted and tried to dodge. Too late. He was pierced by one of the forks through his stomach and slammed against a row of crates. The forklift kept rolling then, pushing him back into the warehouse's north wall near the opening for the guard station. Blood shot from the corner of his mouth as he moaned and struggled to free himself.

Amidst the distraction, Santorios ran and dove into a roll, headed for cover beside her partner behind the loaded pallet jack.

"We need a better angle," she said as she landed in a crouch behind him. Simon nodded. "We need backup and better weapons, too."

"You got a cell," she reminded him. Radios left in the car, no bodycams—working undercover had disadvantages.

For a moment, he thought about calling but they'd already broken procedure following a hunch, and he wanted to know more before calling backup; make sure they were covered. He noticed a double row of crates nearby, stacked in front of some kind of conveyor. "You stay here and cover me."

"Where are you going?" Santorios asked, but Simon ducked under the bottom of a nearby shelf and took off running without answering, and she opened fire again, shifting her aim between the various men, trying to keep them occupied. Bullets ricocheted off the pallet jack into crates and nearby shelves as others sent straw, splinters and dust raining down on her from overhead. She threw an arm over her head and crouched down into a ball for cover.

Simon landed free of the shelving and rolled across the floor on his side, coming up just short of the conveyor crates, pulling himself quickly behind them as some of the men turned their weapons his way. The conveyor stretched off through the shelves and up to a higher level. Scattered stacks of two or three crates were piled along it, and most didn't appear very well balanced. Simon grabbed the black plastic handle of a control lever and flipped the conveyor into reverse then jumped onto the belt. He landed sideways, pain lancing his shoulder from an old football wound. He ignored it and pushed his arms out to the side facing the gunmen, gun aimed and ready.

The belt rolled with a loud humming whine and some of the unbalanced crates tumbled off as it moved, others falling off the far end.

The gunmen reacted turning to look for the cause of the commotion. A couple fired randomly but hit only the stacked crates between them and the conveyor.

Then Simon's head and arms came clear and fired, hitting one of the gunmen in the groin. The man screamed and squeezed off a couple shots before dropping his weapon and falling to his knees.

Simon fired at another, who sprayed the stacked crates with a machine gun stream as he arced his aim toward Simon. Bullets bounced off the metal conveyor below the belt as Simon rolled over and off the far side, needing cover again.

He heard shots and when he looked up again, the gunman who'd been shooting at him was dead with a hole in his chest. Santorios? The other men had disappeared though, except one who was racing his forklift as fast as it could toward the back of the truck.

"Where'd they go?" Simon shouted, looking over toward Santorios.

"I don't know," she called back, rising up to peer at him over the pallet jack.

"Duck!" Simon shouted then and fired straight at her.

She shrunk back into a ball, her eyes surprised and pissed at the same time.

Simon's round tore through the chest of the gunman who'd appeared behind her and taken aim with his M-4. The man fell without a sound, blood sprouting from his wounds as Santorios stuck her head up again, glaring at Simon.

Simon shrugged. "Found one."

"Thanks for telling me," she said.

They heard the sound of the big rig motor then, and the soft hum of another engine, this one electric, starting outside. At least one of these guys was environmentally conscious. And escaping!

"Shit!" Simon ran toward the dock doors as the man on the forklift opened fire from the back of the trailer.

Santorios stood and took aim, firing six shots in a row straight at the truck. Two hit the forklift guy in the face, one leaving a red hole through the center of his forehead. He stopped firing and slumped in his seat.

"Jesus, you've been practicing," Simon muttered and shot his partner a grateful glance as she moved from behind the pallet jack and raced toward him.

"We've got to stop them," she shouted.

They both fired at the big rig, but hit only the trailer doors and some crates inside as it pulled forward, accelerating.

Then they could see a blue BMW racing up the ramp outside ahead of the truck.

"Damn it! Get the plates!" Simon said, aiming his gun past the truck at the BMW as Santorios aimed at the truck. Together, they ran toward the edge of the dock, firing at the two vehicles as they tried to catch the license plates. "The goddamn truck's blocking the Beamer."

Then the BMW was gone, tires squealing as it spun around a corner and out toward the street. The truck turned right behind it, moving slower as the driver fought the sharp angle with limited maneuverability. Simon and Santorios both fired off shots at the cab, blowing out a window and putting holes in the door and side panels but then it too was moving past, turning again onto the street outside.

Simon turned and ran back toward where the guard had fallen, hoping he was still alive and could answer some questions. He pulled his cell phone as he ran, calling for crime scene, back up and relaying information on the two vehicles.

"Semi's plate is Missouri EWE726," his partner called and Simon relayed the information over his cell.

Simon reached the place where they'd left the fallen guard. Crates had fallen around it but he was nowhere to be found. Simon saw a pool of greenish liquid there and knelt, feeling it. It was cold, not warm and sticky, nothing like human blood. "What the fuck? Where did he go?"

Santorios ran up behind him then. "I thought he was surely dead."

"I wanted to at least check. We need someone we can question at least."

"I think we shot them all."

Simon growled and stood again, shaking his head. "Sergeant's not gonna be pleased about this." His eyes panned the warehouse—chaos and destruction left in the shootout's wake. Shattered crates, the wrecked forklift, bullet ridden shelves and beams... It was a mess.

"Next time I will wait in the car," he threatened.

Santorios simply laughed and soon he joined her as he caught his breath from the adrenaline rushing through him.

CHAPTER 2

PETER GREEN LEFT the Ashman Gallery in Kansas City's thriving Crossroad Arts District just after seven and headed down Main for the nearest street car stop at 20th Street. He'd been working at the gallery now for five years as assistant manager and loved the job. In addition to excellent pay and benefits, the manager, Stacey Soukup split weekend duties with him, so they each got every other weekend off. It was something few other assistant managers at any other gallery in Kansas City received.

This was actually his first night free in a week as he'd been helping inventory the gallery's stores in preparation for another exhibition. That meant time spent at the warehouse in the West Bottoms. And he'd stayed after hours there a couple of times trying to get through all the items Benjamin Ashman and Stacey had acquired and stored there but not yet displayed. They had some real hidden treasures, and he'd enjoyed the task, except for some odd activity he'd witnessed involving a semi-truck unloading crates one night after all the warehouse people had gone home. It had been just Peter and the guard when the warehouse supervisor, Wayne O'Dell, and some other unfamiliar men showed up. Peter had stayed in the shadows and not asked questions. But then he'd seen the Degas—one of the master's best pieces, proudly on display prominently at the gallery ever since Peter had worked there. For some reason, it had been taken down and shipped to the warehouse.

After the men had left, Peter had searched and searched for that crate, but never found it. What were they doing with it? Even stranger, when he'd gone back to the gallery the next day, the Degas had been there in its usual spot, well-lit, proudly displayed. That's when he'd casually mentioned the weird activity to his friend Blanca at their aerobics class. He liked Mr. Ashman, but he'd never liked O'Dell. If the man was doing something shady behind the boss's back that might hurt the gallery, then Peter wanted to stop it. But he wanted to be sure. Blanca was a Kansas City detective with robbery/homicide. And she'd been asking him about a series of commercial and industrial burglaries with similar M.O.s, so he'd figured she could check it out, and either bust O'Dell or tell Peter it was nothing to worry about. Either way, no one would know he'd been involved and Mr. Ashman would be protected. Peter could keep his awesome job and everybody won.

He stopped beside the bus stop, waiting with a line of people. The street car stop was just across the way in the middle, but he'd wait 'til the bus passed to make his way out there. He could see the driverless bus coming up the block and the street car would be a few more minutes. Driverless buses had become common within the past few years and Lucas still found the idea disturbing, even though their track record for safety was actually quite impressive. The computers were expensive and sophisticated but as more and more bus drivers retired, the city had begun gradually switching them over.

He stood back a little, out of the way of the bus crowd, listening to them chatter about the weather, their jobs, families, etc. and just kept to himself. Peter was single, his last lover having cheated on him with another man and left him six months before. He'd been pouring himself into work to get over it, but one of these days he did need to get out and try meeting men again. Not tonight, though. Tonight he had aerobics and he wanted to see Blanca; find out how things had gone at the warehouse.

The bus slid to a stop with squeaking hydraulic brakes and the doors opened, as people poured off the back and on the front. Peter appreciated the city's all-electric buses a lot. No more exhaust fumes, less noise. In the five years since the city had made the total switch to electric, the street had become a lot more pleasant outside the gallery. Main Street was a busy route for several, not just the street cars.

The whole loading and unloading took under a minute and Peter was alone on the corner as those exiting the bus scattered for their various destinations, moving up the street in both directions. Some were probably even headed for his gallery. With Stacey and the girls working tonight they'd be in good hands.

As the bus pulled away, he stepped toward the curb preparing to cross, when a red Mercedes SL300 pulled up and stopped, blocking his path. Peter fought back an annoyed comment as the driver rolled down his tinted window and Peter got a good look at his face—Miles Ross, one of O'Dell's goons—early thirties, flashy dresser, got all the girls until they discovered his personality. What did he want?

Then he saw the black shiny muzzle of the automatic pistol. What was going on?

"Next time, shut the fuck up," Miles muttered and fired twice into Peter's chest.

Peter stumbled back, mouth open in shock as the air rushed from his lungs and blood poured onto his hands from the holes in his chest. A woman nearby saw him and screamed, but Peter couldn't breathe. Why had he been shot? He fell to his knees, gasping.

"Somebody call nine-one-one!" someone shouted.

Then Peter's eyes were hazy. He had to lie down, just until he got his energy back. As he slid toward the pavement though, his world went black.

LUCAS GEORGE LAY there stunned on the warehouse floor for what seemed like minutes but he discovered later had been mere seconds. One minute he'd been questioning two intruders who claimed to be cops, doing his duty as security guard, then he'd been lying on the floor. It took him a bit to process what had happened to him. The sounds of gunfire, yelling, and the two detectives chattering, then racing past him went virtually unnoticed as he considered the fluid leaking onto the floor from three holes in his body. *I've been shot. Must get help!* He had to get to his maker ASAP.

As the others disappeared behind the shredded stacks of crates, still vibrating from the projectiles they'd been assaulted with minutes before, Lucas raised himself up with a push of his arms, looking down to inspect his wounds. The bullets seemed to have gone straight through. But given the amount of fluid pooling where he'd lain, he didn't have much time—maybe an hour or less—to get help, if he wanted to survive.

And Lucas very much wanted to live.

Few knew he was an android. His kind had only reached the present level where they could almost pass for human in the past two years, and only the wealthiest clients, people who didn't want obvious androids involved in their business, could afford his model line. The detectives had never noticed he wasn't human. Not that they'd gotten a very good look at him in the shadows, of course, but still, that pleased Lucas a great deal. His maker would be pleased as well. He supposed Mr. O'Dell knew, and Mr. Ashman, of course, but the other warehouse employees paid him little regard. He was just the strange, quiet, black dude who came in late afternoon and stayed all night alone. No one envied that job, and he was not involved in their work, so Lucas tended to blend into the background, and in some ways, he suspected that was why Benjamin Ashman had given him the job.

He had limited skills and training to actually guard anything. His job was to report and intercept intruders; chase them off with a stern confrontation if he could, but nothing physical—no fighting, no violence. He had only a nightstick and that was just for show. His cameras recorded everything he saw and heard. And he had a direct connection to the VOIP systems to call Police or anyone else he needed to notify should anything happen.

In his last year at the Gallery Warehouse, he'd only had occasion to use VOIP once. The place was usually deathly quiet. It had been the first time men showed up late, after hours, with a truckload of art. Until that day a few months past, it had never happened. And so when the men refused to stop their activities at Lucas' instructions, he'd called Mr. O'Dell. O'Dell had told him it was authorized and not to worry about it. After that, O'Dell showed up with the men a lot, and Lucas just kept to his patrolling, ignoring the activity.

But tonight he'd been shot. He wondered how it felt for humans. Should he be in pain? Perhaps he was fortunate he wasn't. Either way, as he pulled himself up off the floor and looked around, there was still gunfire and human chatter coming from behind the crates. But he realized he had a clear path out through the opening that led to the office and the corridor beyond, so he dialed Steven on his VOIP and quietly headed for the corridor and the back door waiting beyond.

Steven answered after five rings. Lucas informed him he needed emergency maintenance. And Steven told him to wait at the curb for a car, no further explanation required. No questions about leaving his duties. No instructions besides to wait. Lucas found it odd. After all, leaving his duties at the warehouse was a serious breach of his programming. Perhaps Steven, the maker's assistant, was confused? But then again, the Police and Mr. O'Dell were there. Surely that meant the warehouse would be watched. And if he didn't go, Lucas wouldn't survive. So he went, hoping his maker could not only fix him but sort things out with Mr. Ashman later.

The car arrived in fifteen minutes and Lucas climbed into the back, staying silent the entire ride to his maker's lab across town in Leawood, a nearby suburb.

AS HE STEPPED back onto Woodsweather and approached the Interceptor, Simon heard a buzzing in his ear and turned. A small, black media drone was floating along beside him.

"Detective Simon, can you tell us what's happening please?" a female voice said, emanating from the box. Some producer monitoring it at the nearest TV station or bureau. Welcome to the modern world. Instead of sending reporters first, many media outfits used drones controlled by producers back at their offices to get the first footage and interviews at crime scenes. In many areas, the drones could arrive much faster than ground vehicles because of their ability to approach in the air at higher speeds. It was like a new wave of electronic paparazzi, and it drove Simon nuts.

He swatted at the drone like it was a fly. "Get the fuck away from me. No comment."

"Has there been a shootout? Can you tell us what happened?" the voice continued, undeterred.

Simon reached up and grabbed the drone with his palm over the camera, swinging it around like a Frisbee with all his might so it pointed away from the scene.

"Hey!" the voice complained.

"I said no comment. Get back behind the line!" Simon ordered and left it behind, hurrying on.

Before leaving the warehouse, Simon sat in the car and ran the thumb prints of each of the dead men through PRINTZ, the KCPD's new digital finger printing system. He simply had to pull up the app, press their thumb or a finger against the screen, and search and PRINTZ did the rest. It was connected to the KCPD's own database, IAFIS, the FBI database, and several others. Each of the men came back with criminal records, unsurprisingly. Most were minor offenses, but a couple had felonies and had done time. With two clicks, Simon emailed it back to his office computer so he could print it and add it to the case file later.

SIMON HAD INHERITED his grandmother's house on a quiet street in Fairway, Kansas a decade before. While the department requirement that all officers to keep a residence in the Kansas City, Missouri limits meant Simon had to keep an apartment down south on the border with Grandview, the Fairway house had now become where he both spent most of his time and kept most of his things. 5516 Canterbury was a quiet brick, two bedroom, H-shaped home with an attached garage built in the fifties. When he'd inherited it, the interior looked like it had been stuck in the seventies so he'd remodeled it with the help of friends and fellow officers. The old shag carpet and browns and oranges had been replaced with subtler, modern shades like ocean blue, off white, and even tan, fresh Wallpaper trim in the kitchen, hardwood floors in the bathrooms and basement, and new runners, trim, and doors throughout. Now it looked far more modern than old school and that suited Simon just fine.

Although his Sergeant knew he was technically violating the department's rule, as long as he kept his Grandview address on file as his main residence, no one objected. After all, he had lived in that area most of his seventeen years on the force. The renovations had only been finished on the Canterbury house two years before, and Simon rarely had anyone from the department over besides Blanca and Andy and a few close friends, so only his closest circle even knew that. In any case, the State of Missouri, which owned the Kansas City Police Department, had loosened its enforcement of the policy in the last five years after repeated loss of their best, most experienced officers. Everyone knew stubborn old timers like Simon wouldn't hesitate to quit if pressed. So now, as long as it was kept quiet and off-books, the most senior officers could get away with it. Simon wasn't about to rock that boat.

He parked his classic 1985 Dodge Charger in the driveway just after midnight and headed up the sidewalk to the front door. Someone was in the house. Several lights were on in the kitchen, living room, and his daughter's bedroom, a bedroom she rarely used these days, and Simon wasn't expecting anyone. Some idiot was having a very unlucky night, but when he got to the door, he found it double latched as usual. Had they broken a window?

Loosening the strap over his Glock 37, he inserted his keys as quietly as possible and turned first the deadbolt and then the lock in the doorknob itself, swinging open the door, and pulling his gun. He saw no one immediately inside the door, so he took up a cautious stance and moved inside, arms extended, pistol leading the way.

The living room was lit only by a lamp beside his favorite recliner, the lamp he always kept on when he was home. Music was playing from one of the bedrooms to the left, but first, he turned right to check the kitchen and then the dining room behind it, looking for any intruders who might be in that part of the house. The back door and door to the garage were closed and locked. And he saw no sign of anyone inside nor out on the screened in back porch. No open windows or broken glass and nothing looked disturbed. That meant whoever it was had gone to the bedrooms.

As he circled back to check the bedrooms and bath at the other end, the faint whiff of a flowery perfume tickled his nose. *What burglar wears perfume? Am I being robbed by a fucking chick then?* He moved down the hallway, quietly and saw the bathroom door wide open, the interior dark. His own bedroom door was also open, just as he'd left it, and he saw no sign of movements in the shadows. The music was coming from his daughter's room, but Emma hadn't visited in months and she was currently mad at him, so he wasn't expecting her. Who'd broken in—some teenager?

Reaching his left hand out in front of him as his right steadied the gun, he pushed on his daughter's door and it swung open. A familiar face bounced into the light, dancing to the music.

"Emma?" He lowered his pistol even as he raised his voice. For just a moment he thought he was staring at Lara, his ex-wife, the love of his life, only not Lara now but Lara when they'd met back in high school. Then it hit him.

His fourteen-year-old daughter stopped spinning and whirled to face him, eyes widening as she saw the gun. "What the hell, Dad? You gonna shoot me?"

"What are you doing here?" he demanded as he holstered his gun.

"Mom had a last minute business trip. She left you a message. I'm here all week."

"What?" He hated when Lara did this to him. Especially with the current tension between him and Emma. Emma and her mother lived across town in Independence. How was he going to get her to school and home and deal with her dance lessons, piano, and after school activities on no notice whatsoever? He sighed.

Lara dreaded talking to him and avoided him accordingly. She had ever since their marriage fell apart. He'd never loved anyone in his life the way he loved Lara, and they were great together. Until she got sick. Bipolar disorder destroyed everything. It often did. He'd stayed and fought but after years of verbal and psychological abuse and watching what it did to Emma living with fighting parents, he'd walked away. One of the hardest days of his life. And

Lara had been punishing him for it ever since.

"What the fuck, Dad? You deaf?" Emma scowled, hands on her hips and glared at him. "Don't you check your messages."

"Don't use that language with me!" He scolded, glaring back. She looked so much like her mother it hurt and he winced. "When did she call?"

"This morning," Emma said, as if that made all the difference.

"I am just getting in from work, and no, I had no time to call and check messages today," he replied. "She could have called my cell."

Emma rolled her eyes. "You know how she loves talking to you." This was true but dropping Emma off for a week with no warning was bullshit, and it pissed him off.

"Welcome home, honey. It's good to see you, honey." Emma growled, scowling again.

"You haven't exactly been my biggest fan lately," Simon replied, not even bothering to broach the subject of her being up so late on a school night.

Emma shrugged. "You have to earn it."

Simon turned and headed back to close the front door. "Turn the music down so we can talk," he ordered. No point asking. She'd just defy him. Instead he used a tone even Emma knew better than to argue with.

The compact stereo clicked off as he closed the door tightly and set both the locks for the night.

"What did you think—I was a thief dancing around your daughter's room?" Emma said loudly, startling him. She'd snuck up behind him.

"Don't do that," he growled and turned to face her.

"Never sneak up on a cop," she mimicked—a warning he'd given her a thousand times for sure.

"It's a good way to get shot," he fired back.

"Apparently right up there with coming to stay with your dad," she said, smirking.

"I didn't shoot you...yet."

She laughed. "I'll bet you were tempted."

"You have no idea," he said.

She threw him a smug smile as she turned and headed back for the kitchen and he followed.

"You eaten?" he asked.

She waved dismissively toward the kitchen. "Pepperoni and sausage. I put it on your card."

"Oh sure. Any other charges I should know about?" He always kept a credit card under his silverware holder in a drawer in case she needed something sometime when he was stuck at work. She always managed to take advantage, too, but then he'd never kept much around that would interest a budding, hungry teenager.

He got a better look at her as he flipped on the kitchen lights and went in search of some pizza. She was wearing more makeup, a sight that made him automatically tense. And she'd laid the perfume on heavy. What else was her mother letting her do without discussing it? He pulled open the fridge with a hiss and a waft of cold air hit him.

"I bought a grand piano," Emma said, answering his question. "Steinway delivers. It's coming tomorrow. Oh, and the Porsche is for me. You can look, don't touch."

Simon shook his head. "You gonna stop hating me long enough for us to get along this week?" He flipped open the cardboard Domino's box and grabbed two slices with his right hand while cupping the stems of two Coronas with his left and pulling them all out toward the counter in one smooth turn.

"He's a nice boy," she whined. "Everyone likes him. Mom loves him! You had no right to embarrass me like that!"

"You're fourteen," Simon replied, hating that they were revisiting the same argument again. Simon had found Emma sitting on the porch, holding hands with a boy when he'd come to pick her up. He'd simply said the same thing in front of the boy, he found himself saying now, "We've always told you no dating until you're sixteen."

"You have. Mom says she's fine with it." That was a change. Lara and Simon had agreed on that rule before Emma was born.

Simon snorted as he opened a cupboard and pulled down a plate and a beer glass bearing the Sporting K.C. logo in shiny fluorescent blue. The pizza was still warm and smelled delicious. Perfect for his mood. "Your mom's fine with a lot of things I'm not. That's why we got divorced."

Emma scoffed. "Maybe she just loves me more."

Simon shook his head. "No, ma'am. No trying that old trick. You're too old for that b.s. and you know better." He slammed open the silverware drawer, lifting the plastic holder quickly to double check that she'd put his MasterCard back—right where he left it. Then grabbed a fork and spun it shut, grabbing his pizza and beers and headed for the living room. Manipulating parents by playing them against each other was an age old trick for children of divorce and Emma had gone through that phase. With the baggage between he and Lara, it had been brutal, too, but he thought they'd put that behind them.

Emma groaned. "You're such a dick. No wonder she left."

"Language!" he scolded again. It hurt every time she said it, but Simon tried not to let it show. He knew better. His problems with Lara had developed over many years, most of their twelve year marriage. They'd never been a perfect fit—two very different people. But at first, love had overcome the obstacles. After ten years married to a husband who was gone at all hours for long periods at a time, in and out of dangerous situations he couldn't always talk about, Lara started to get fed up. The fact that he preferred time at home when he was off to going out to symphonies and fine arts like his wife just fueled the fire. But then she'd been sick and she was an angry manic. Brutal. At least with him. She treated Emma much better but Emma didn't parent her. Simon had tried to take charge, take care of his wife and that just pissed her off.

"I'm not a child!" She'd whined so often it became like a refrain. The end had come when she started having spurts of violent anger. Between having guns in the house and gun safes she knew the combos to and not wanting Emma exposed to that ugliness, he'd finally surrendered and filed for divorce. He had long ago accepted it. Was learning to live with it. But hearing his daughter throw it at him so casually when she'd been the one most hurt during the actual divorce—that stabbed his heart more than he wanted her to ever know.

"Okay, so fill me in. What you got going on this week that we need to coordinate?" He changed the subject gladly as he settled into his favorite recliner and set his beers on the side table then begin cutting into the pizza with a fork.

Surprisingly she had practice two nights that week right after school and then one dance lesson that Thursday. It was a lighter than usual schedule. Either Simon or Santorios could swing by and pick her up as needed. Luckily, they had no major pressing cases that would suck up all their time at the moment. Truth was Emma hadn't stayed with him for three months and being pissed, had hardly spoken to him. The couple times he'd gotten her on the phone, she'd hardly said three words until he'd hung up in frustration. His only child was the center of his world, and she knew it. He'd do anything for her. And he was thrilled to finally have time with her again.

Once they settled the schedule, he asked, "What time do you have to be at school in the morning?"

"Usual."

That meant eight-thirty. To get to Independence in rush hour, they'd have to leave at least by seven forty-five latest. So an early start was in store. "Then off to bed. It's late," he urged.

Emma sighed. "You think for once you'd be so glad to see me you'd cut me a break."

"Sure, baby. Come cuddle with me for a bit and tell me how much you missed me," he motioned toward the couch as she made a horrified face.

He laughed then turned serious again. "I'm thrilled," he said, locking eyes with hers in a sincere look he hoped conveyed the truth. "But if you fall asleep during class, your teachers won't be. So get to it."

Her shoulders sank and she spun, marching away to let him know he'd let her down again.

"I love you, Emma," he called after her, then went back to

his pizza. As expected, he got no response. A few minutes later, her door shut quietly and he didn't hear another peep from her that night. At least she gave him that much respect, he thought.

Then his mind turned back to the mess at the warehouse and the hours they'd spent after the shooting, processing the scene. The sergeant had been out for an event tonight. He was going to get the riot act tomorrow. Oh well. All in a day's work.

CHAPTER 3

LIKE MANY OF her fellow officers, Blanca Santorios and her husband Andy Harris lived south of the city, on the border with Grandview, Missouri, a few miles below the slummier areas around Troost, Holmes, and Prospect just to the north. Their house had been built in the forties but renovated by Andy, who owned his own building company specializing in restoring older houses. The home of the eight years of their marriage was a three bedroom ranch in a cul-de-sac off East Red Bridge Road. Light blue with old fashioned working shutters, Blanca had fallen in love with the place the moment she saw it, and with a few tasty renovations, her husband had modernized it to be just perfect for them.

Blanca had grown up in the projects, her dad working three jobs to keep food on the table and her mom fiercely supervising her kids' every moment to be sure none of them fell victim to the local gangs and other problems that kept barrio kids locked in that lifestyle. Her parents' sacrifice hadn't required any deficit in the love or attention they lavished on their kids. They'd been poor but it had been a happy home, and Blanca still fondly visited her mother there every weekend—after her husband's heart attack, Maria Santorios had still refused to move. "This is home, and I'm staying!" she insisted.

Glancing at the bright red LED of the clock on her bedside stand, Blanca saw it was six a.m. as she quietly slid into the straps of her shoulder holster in final preparation for her day. She'd gotten a message on her cell about Peter Green being involved in a drive-by the night before near the Ashman Gallery and wanted to get in early to read the reports and talk with the officers. Andy snored gently on the far side of the bed and she smiled. *Sounding like a daddy already.* Warmth filled her. God how she loved that man—her blonde, blue-eyed farmboy knight, who'd ridden in on a proverbial horse and carried her off to a dream life.

Walking around the bed, she leaned over and kissed him gently on the cheek.

He stirred, moaning and reached up to pull her face close again and kiss her on the lips. "It's early, baby."

"Someone shot one of my snitches last night," she said. "Gotta head in. Go back to sleep."

He mumbled. "Sorry, babe."

"I love you. See you later, 'kay?" And she stood upright again, smiling down at him.

"You, too," he answered sleepily as he rolled back over and drifted off again.

Blanca made her way down the hall, stopping as always to examine the new nursery they'd just finished the previous weekend. The colors, cute animal wallpaper, and brand new shiny crib made her heart patter inside. She could almost skip to the car now, but she fought the urge, patting the door instead, turning, and heading on her way.

She grabbed a plastic 16 oz. orange juice and two energy bars on her way out the door, then headed for the garage. Punching the opener button as she exited the kitchen, she double checked that her badge was secured to her belt and her gun fastened securely in her holster then clicked the unlock on her key fob and grabbed the driver side door as the garage door slid upward with a hum behind her. If she got there early enough, she could make it up to Simon for the mess at the warehouse by getting a big head start on the paperwork. She owed him that much.

As she turned to get behind the wheel of her 2019 Ford Taurus, there was a sharp pain in the back of her head and her knees weakened as she fell into blackness.

PROPERTY CRIMES DETECTIVES worked out of squads at each of the KCPD's stations. The Central Patrol Division, where Simon and Santorios had desks, was an elongated, white brick monstrosity with blue interior walls built in the early 1990s at 1200 E. Linwood and remodeled a bit in 2023 to add interrogation and conference rooms and update wiring, lighting, and detention facilities. The property squad room was a couple key-carded doors past the desk where two admin clerks and the Desk Sergeant dealt with paperwork and the public, as well as vehicle signout. The room itself was a cubicle farm of eight tan and limestone cubes with black, rolling chairs, computer terminals, file cabinets, bulletin boards, and a large office for the unit's Sergeant. It tended to buzz on and off all day from ringing phones to chattering detectives, suspects, and victims. It also had inconsistent air conditioning which Simon had come to believe was aimed at keeping the already skeptical detectives near the edge of pissed off as well.

After dropping Emma off at the Middle School, Simon

arrived ninety minutes late. He'd have to do better the rest of the week but they both had needed the sleep, and he'd make the excuse that his daughter's stay was totally unexpected, because it was the truth.

As he made his way into the squad room, he noticed that Santorios' cube was empty. Unusual because she always beat him in. He began winding through the hectic maze, when Detectives José Correia and Art Maberry intercepted him. Correia was Brazilian in background—late twenties, slick dresser, good looking, a ladies man. Maberry, on the other hand was mid-thirties, overweight and a nerd, with facial hair he often let grow too long between trims, and a never ending collection of Hawaiian shirts. Simon guessed the man hadn't dated in years, but really, he didn't care. The two guys were annoying with their constant razzing of everyone, but they were also two of the unit's best and they'd earned Simon's respect.

"Hey Simon," Maberry started in, "Congratulations on that warehouse you guys rousted last night. That was some massacre you guys made."

"Yeah," Correia added, "Did you ever try questioning the bad guys before you shoot them? You might actually solve a case."

"We can't decide whether to shoot 'em or just do it your way—run 'em over," Simon answered.

The two fellow detective's amusement changed to embarrassment.

"The brakes went out, man!" Correia insisted.

"Tell that to the widow," Simon replied. "I'm sure she'll feel a lot better." He left them behind with a chuckle and moved on toward his desk. The car had needed new brakes, he knew. But a few weeks back they'd run over a witness while peeling out from a curb after getting an urgent call. The guy had simply hurried out to tell them something he'd forgotten and Correia didn't see him. It was an accident and the guy had lived, despite suffering a broken leg. Besides, Simon had just run over a guy with a forklift himself. And Simon and the other detectives loved giving the insecure Correia shit about it daily.

Detective Anna Dolby, thirty-five but still looking as hot as she had in college, former track star, chocolate skin and beautiful long hair shook her head as he moved past. "You're amazing, Simon."

"Been reading the women's room walls again, Dolby?" he replied.

The others laughed as Dolby glared and Simon pulled out his chair, sinking into his desk. The neatest in the room, Simon kept it very organized. He liked to know where everything was so he could work quickly. Santorios' desk, on other hand, facing his, looked like a tornado had hit it twice. He had no idea how she could work like that.

"That was a good line, pal," Detective Martin Oglesby said from a cleaner-than-most desk nearby, as he shot taunting looks at Dolby. A fifteen year fellow veteran detective, he and Simon had served together most of their careers. Oglesby was chubbier and taller than Simon, also divorced, kids off at college, but he was solid, and they were old friends. He also had a slipped disk in his back and worked a lot standing up instead of sitting, his computer elevated on the desk using an old wooden magazine rack from the lobby that had since been replaced. "Oh, we had another shooting last night," he said, sobering up.

Simon looked up and their eyes met. "In Kansas City? I'm shocked."

Oglesby smiled. "Yeah, yeah." He read from a report on his desk. "A Peter Green, on file as your partner's snitch. Someone blew him away down the block from the Ashman Gallery while he was waiting for the light rail."

Simon turned somber. *Shit.* "Does she know?"

Oglesby shrugged. "Haven't seen her yet."

That was odd. Where was she? "Any I.D. on the shooter?"

Oglesby shook his head. "We've got three people coming in this morning to look at pictures."

Simon grunted his thanks as Oglesby offered another slip of paper across his desk.

"Crime Scene ran some of the numbers on those nanochips," Oglesby said. "Came up part of a stolen batch I've been searching for all month."

Simon grinned as he stood and reached for the paper. "Glad to be of help."

Oglesby leaned back as Simon took the paper and sat back down. "Oh, and I'd avoid the Sarge if I were you—"

"Is Simon here yet?!" a shrill female voice demanded from across the room.

Simon looked up to see his boss, Sergeant JoAnn Becker, early forties, one tough cop who looked like a tough school principal, standing in the doorway of her office where she could clearly see him.

"My office! Now!" she demanded as their eyes met.

Simon groaned and stood, heading her way. He'd been dreading this since the warehouse.

"Where's your partner?" the sergeant asked.

"Not in yet," Simon replied.

"It's eight-thirty! What makes you two think you can show up late for your shift and still work here?" Becker scolded.

"Union rules?" Simon joked as Becker scowled to let him know she was less than amused.

The other detectives chuckled and smiled, watching with enjoyment.

"Probably out celebrating—" Maberry joked.

Becker whirled and glared at him. "You're not funny, Maberry. Take the Junior Driver of the Year and go solve a crime for once!"

Maberry's face fell, flustered. "Yes, ma'am."

"Damn, boss. That shit's cold," Correia complained.

"That's 'sir' to you guys. Now get!" Becker ordered, turning to Oglesby. "Oglesby, get Santorios on the phone and find out where she is. Now!"

As Oglesby picked up the phone, Becker turned back and led Simon into her office, slamming the door behind her.

IF IT HADN'T been for the stacks of files and paperwork covering every available surface with the exception of the center of her desk, Becker's office would have been as organized and neat as Simon's. A row of three-drawer, black file cabinets lined the wall to the right of her large Oak desk, its surface, at least what was showing of it, worn and scratched from years of use. The half of the desk that was clear of stacks held an LED monitor and mouse. A keyboard sat on a tray that slid out from underneath in front of the black leather chair, which JoAnn Becker quickly moved to occupy, motioning for Simon to take one of two plain wooden ones opposite her desk.

The office actually smelled nice. Cleanest, most pleasant place in the building, he figured. He noted some kind of air freshener plugged into a socket in the corner. Whatever it was she'd shown good taste. Plus, despite the stacks, no dust. Every surface was wiped clean and fresh—like some kind of sterile medical room. Even with her temper, he'd always loved that about her.

As Simon sat, he said, "I know what you're going to say—"

She frowned, her brow creasing with irritation. "Don't start with me. Six bodies. Illegal search. Destruction of private property—"

"We had probable cause and a tip from an informant," Simon countered. "The M.O. resembled our burglary string, too."

"A warehouse owned by one of the most prominent men in town, a good friend of our Police Chief and the Mayor," Becker said. "You had to know the suits would pay close attention. You fucked up bad."

"We found six cases of stolen nanochips from Ogleby's investigation," Simon said. "Crime Scene ran the numbers. And maybe stolen art, too. We only went there to look around anyway—"

"You didn't follow procedure. No report filed on this before you went in. Now the city's facing a potential lawsuit. The Mayor just chewed my ass off."

Simon shot her a sympathetic look. They'd known each

other for years. "And it was such a nice ass—" Sometimes he couldn't help himself.

She stiffened, slamming a fist on her desk. Not amused in the slightest. "I'm not in the mood, Sergeant! This is serious. The Mayor and Deputy Chief Keller both want you two off this case."

"Come on, Sarge," Simon said. "It was a solid lead. We just went up to take a closer look, see what was happening, and they started shooting at us. We had to defend ourselves. It's a clean shoot."

"That's what I told the Deputy Chief. He wants me to review all your files. Make sure everything is being done right."

Simon sighed and leaned back in the chair. "You know it is."

"It doesn't matter what I know!" she snapped. "Your ass is in the hotseat. And I am not going to offer my own to join it."

Simon nodded. "I'm sorry, Chief. We'll clear it up with the Shooting Team, I promise."

"Yes, you will," she said. It was an order. "And I want the paperwork on my desk by one o'clock, and files on all your cases. Up to date."

There was no way. They had so much to update. A new file to open. "You've got to be kidding!" He stood and headed for the door.

"Where are you going?!" she demanded.

"To find my partner," he replied, turning back, his hand on the doorknob. "We have a lot of paperwork to do."

"And why were you late?!"

"Emma showed up last night. No warning. Lara went out

of town for the week. I had to take her to school. Plus, I got home after midnight so she needed sleep..."

Becker relaxed, her face warming a little. "That's the first thing out of your mouth today that didn't piss me off. I like that kid. Sorry about your ex."

He smiled. "You know how it is."

She chuckled. "Mine's an asshole, too." She waved dismissively and he opened the door. "John."

He turned back, raising his eyebrow in a question.

"No more funny stuff." It was a warning.

He shrugged. "Wasn't any to begin with, Sarge. What can I do?"

With that, he marched back toward his desk, not really caring if she believed him or not.

BLANCA AWOKE IN a dark room on a hard chair, her feet tied to the legs, hands tied behind her back, alone. She coughed as her eyes tried to focus. "Hello?"

No answer.

She called louder. "Hello?"

The room was large enough she couldn't see the walls around her, but she didn't see anything else either, and it simply smelled like a dusty, old room. No distinctive scents or sounds. Where the hell was she?

A bright, blinding hot spotlight flicked on somewhere nearby, pointed straight into her eyes. She winced and looked away, eyes stinging. "Hey!"

Then he was there—a tough kid who looked barely out of high school, a cocky grin frozen on his face and an odd look in his brown eyes—like he wasn't altogether there, at least not in the way most people are. This guy wasn't normal.

He extended an arm and whirled around, whacking her across the left cheek with all his might. Her head rocked to the right so hard, she feared snapping her neck. Then he struck her again, the same way on the right. And he snorted.

"You like that, bitch?" he asked in a country drawl similar to what the local farm boys all used. He sneered, showing a mouth as holey as a golf course. What had someone so young done to lose so many teeth? Too many fights, she figured.

"Who are you?" she said, almost a whisper. Her mouth was dry and she couldn't seem to muster enough saliva to wet it.

"None of yer fuckin' business, bitch!" And he hit her again. The next half hour it was the same thing over and over until Blanca swore if she ever got free, she'd kill his ass.

Then three other men showed up. Two she recognized from the warehouse—one with slicked back, styled brown hair and green eyes in some sort of throwback 80s Armani thing. What the hell? The other was Hispanic, dark, military cut hair, with a cheap gray suit. She didn't know which was worse, but both clearly thought they were the coolest. Morons. The third man was white and wore a modern Armani, very hip and contemporary. Not as good looking as his *Miami Vice* wannabe counterpart, and his eyes held a meanness that scared her even worse than the country kid.

"How's it going, Helm?" Modern Armani asked the country kid.

"She ain't talkin'...yet," he replied, continuing to glare at her. He hauled back and slapped her again—left then right. Her head snapping back and forth again, feeling like it would fall off. "Like that, baby? Was it good for you?"

"Fuck you," she said and spat blood onto the floor at his feet.

Helm sneered and Modern Armani joined him. The other two chuckled softly.

"Perhaps what Officer Santorios needs is an example of what we do to people who disappoint us," Modern Armani said. He nodded to the cheap suit Hispanic.

In moments, the country boy had stepped behind and grabbed the guy by both arms, shoving him roughly forward into the light, beside Blanca.

"Get the fuck off me, puta!" the Hispanic complained.

"You failed Mister Ashman," the modern Armani guy said.

"It's not my fault, Miles," the Hispanic replied, shaken. "It all went bad. We were lucky we got out."

Modern Armani nodded with faux sympathy. "We can only excuse so much."

"Give us a chance to see what we can recover," the Hispanic said. "O'Dell and I got a plan."

In one fluid motion, almost faster than the eye, Modern Armani had a Sig Sauer aimed right at the Hispanic and shot him through the forehead twice, dead center.

Without a sound, the Hispanic's corpse fell back, blood pouring down his forehead, thumping on the floor beside Blanca. *Miami Vice* guy looked totally stunned.

"Not his problem anymore," Modern Armani said and

glanced at *Miami Vice.* "You better handle it."

Miami Vice gulped. "I will. I have a plan, I promise."

"And buy a better suit. You look like a moron." Modern Armani—did the kid call him Miles?—chortled. Helms joined him.

Miami Vice said nothing, sliding slowly back deeper into the shadows as if to be less noticeable.

Miles holstered the Sig Sauer under his jacket and turned to Blanca. "Okay then. Let's talk."

Blanca's body tensed from instinct as an incredible urge to get away overcame her, only she couldn't free her legs from the chair. Miles and Helm continued to stare, and she couldn't remember the last time she'd ever been so scared.

SIMON'S HAND HURT from grasping a pen as he signed yet another stack of reports and then went back to his computer to type again.

Oglesby wandered over with a cup of coffee. "Made some fresh. Want a cup?"

Simon sighed and shook his head. "No thanks. I'd just spill it. Gotta get these done."

"Still no sign of Santorios, eh?"

"No. She's still not answering her phone." Simon and Oglesby had both tried. Probably the Sergeant, too. This was not like her. He was getting worried.

Dolby hurried over to join them. "Some witness is coming in from the warehouse."

Simon stopped typing and looked up. "What witness?"

"Some security guy, I think," she said with a shrug. "He's supposedly being brought in by some doctor. Someone who patched him up."

"Let me know as soon as they get here," Simon said, turning back to his screen.

"Boss wants us to handle it," Dolby said. "You know, case there's any issues with the shooting."

Simon frowned, tensing and fought the urge to curse. Wasn't Dolby's fault. "I need to be there."

Dolby looked sympathetic but shook her head. "Orders." And she started walking away, motioning for Oglesby to join her.

"Sorry, John," Oglesby said as he turned away and Simon's phone rang.

Simon picked it up on the third ring. "Yeah?"

"John Simon?" a strange male voice said.

"Yeah, this is him. Who is this?"

"Your partner says, 'hi.'"

"Blanca?" Simon heard shuffling on the other end, muffled chatter, then a deep breath.

"John?" It was Santorios.

Simon stiffened, snapping to attention in his chair. "Where are you? What's going on—?" Dolby and Oglesby rushed back and joined Maberry and Correia gathered around his cubicle.

"Just listen, John," she cut him off. She sounded strange— timid, scared. Totally unlike her usual self. "Don't give them what they want," she said then, speaking faster, strong again.

"Fuck them, John!"

Simon heard a slap and Santorios cried out.

"Give what to who—" he replied but go no answer. Instead, he heard the sound of her moaning moving further away from the phone.

"We'll be in touch," the male voice said again and then hung up.

"Son of a bitch!" John yelled it as he rose hurriedly from his chair and raced across the bustling cube farm toward Becker's office.

"What is it?" Maberry called after him.

"They've got Santorios!"

"Who?" Correia asked from his cube nearby.

The other detectives rushed toward him as Simon tried to breathe. Where the fuck was his partner and what the fuck was going on? The Sergeant came out of her office and he began describing the call as they all listened.

CHAPTER 4

SIMON AND THE other detectives gathered around Becker's desk, discussing Santorios' kidnapping.

"Oglesby and Dolby, you're on this," the sergeant ordered.

"She's my partner!" Simon objected. Property detectives didn't have official partners but they did work a lot in pairs for interviews, field visits, etc. And Simon had trained Santorios and been tight with her since. They called each other 'partner' despite the lack of official designation.

"Exactly," Becker said. "You're too close to this. You know Martin and Anna will do good work."

Simon heaved a sigh and rubbed the back of his neck. "I want to be kept informed of everything," he insisted.

Oglesby patted his shoulder. "You got it, pal. We've got your back."

"John, you start thinking about the men at the warehouse," Becker continued. "Get with a sketch artist and get us drawings and any other details you can recall— overheard names, etc."

Simon nodded. "I know the drill."

Becker turned to the others. "You four—on the phones. Call around to people you know—find out if anyone's seen her, and get over to her house for a look around."

"Should we call Andy?" Dolby asked. "He's probably at work."

"He probably doesn't even know yet," Simon said.

"You let us worry about it," Becker reminded him. She looked at Dolby. "Find out and if he needs to be notified, I'll go in person."

"Don't let Correia drive!" Simon quipped, joking to hide his anger and grief.

"Hey!" Correia objected as Maberry chuckled and elbowed him in the ribs. Breaking the tension with humor came naturally to cops, but this time Simon almost felt bad for the effort.

Dolby nodded. "Okay, Sarge."

A clerk poked a head in—young enough to look like a high school escapee, files tucked under her arm as she looked at Oglesby and Dolby. Simon didn't even remember her name. "Oglesby and Dolby, that guard from the warehouse and some scientist are in interrogation six."

"Thanks," Dolby nodded and the clerk disappeared.

"Let's get to it," Oglesby said as he and his partner turned for the door.

"Anything else?" Dolby glanced back at the Sergeant.

Becker shook her head. "You know what to do." Then she glanced at Simon as the two left. "You stay here with me."

"Can I at least listen—"

She shook her head. "We need to talk first." She motioned to Correia and Maberry. "Go!"

"Yes, sir," the duo said in unison and also headed for the

door, closing it behind them.

As the door clicked shut, Becker sunk into her chair. "I know how you feel, John. But we have to handle this the right way. We will find her. We will get her back."

"You expect me to just sit on my hands?"

"I expect you to do your job," she scolded. "You have cases. Work them. And I still need that paperwork. You'll be busy. Let others worry about Santorios. That's their top priority."

Simon pinched his lips together, biting back a retort. Then, "Fuck. If something happens to her—"

Becker's eyes softened. "We all love her, John. No one wants that. I just need you not blowing up and making things harder. You've been here long enough to know how it works."

"It's never been my partner before," he growled. But yes, he knew the regs. He didn't agree with them this time. This pissed him off. But the regulations were explicit—no detectives working cases where they had personal involvement.

"Shooting Team should be here soon anyway," Becker added. "Unpack you about the warehouse last night."

"Like I want to talk to those pricks!"

"You don't have a choice," Becker snapped back, glaring at him. "Now drop the attitude and get your ass to work!"

Simon knew better than to say anything else. God forbid she sent him home and the Shooting Team came there. He wouldn't be handing them reasons to fry his ass. He raised his hands in surrender. "We done?"

She waved the back of her hand toward the door and he

headed back for his desk.

SIMON LASTED AT his desk all of two minutes, until Becker left and disappeared out into the hall. Simon headed for the coffee and then took a u-turn, heading for interrogation instead.

The interrogation rooms were down the hall from the detective's squad room. Simon slipped into the observation booth of room three, only slightly bigger than the interview room itself, set up with chairs for several observers as needed. He ignored them and stood beside the one-way glass, which made up most of the room's fourth wall, staring into the room. Behind him the room smelled of dust and sweat. Too many people spending long hours in here meant the janitorial staff got less access to these rooms. The only light came from the bright LEDs high in the interview room ceiling, leaking through the window. But that suited Simon just fine. He wanted to see everything clearly and less light in here made that easier. It also kept him focused on the activity behind the glass. Two small black speakers in the corners above the one-way glass allowed him to listen in. The signal was clear and at a comfortable volume. The microphone and camera were in clear view in a back corner of the room in compliance with Missouri State law.

Besides Oglesby and Dolby, there were two people in the room. A white female with long dark hair, skinny—almost too skinny—and short but very intense and focused. Beside her, in another chair, sat a man with chocolate skin and bright blue eyes Simon recognized. The guard from the warehouse. Taller and younger than the woman, he was bald, head shaved clean, and had the kind of immediate looks that made Simon suspect he was popular with the ladies. Yet there was something off about him, something not quite fluid about his movements, a tinniness to his voice. The woman introduced him as Lucas George and herself as Doctor Livia Connelly. She was a former brain scientist turned inventor, and Lucas was one of hers.

It took Simon a moment to realize what she meant, then it clicked. Lucas was an android. *Holy shit.*

After the introductions, Oglesby started the interview, looking at Lucas. "Tell us about the men at the warehouse. Who are they?"

"First of all," Connelly interrupted, "he can't tell you everything."

"Why not?" Dolby asked.

"His programming," Connelly said.

"What do you mean?" Oglesby asked.

Connelly's voice filled with passion and she sat up in her chair, like this was a topic that utterly fascinated and thrilled her. "Are you familiar with Asimov's Three Laws of Robotics?"

The two detectives shook their heads, exchanging a confused look.

"Not really," Dolby said.

"Isaac Asimov?" Oglesby asked.

Simon chuckled. That much had seemed obvious. Leave it to Martin to be clueless.

Connelly nodded. "Yes. Isaac Asimov invented these three laws of robotics in some early science fiction stories. They have generally been widely accepted as the key basis for all A.I. programming."

"Artificial Intelligence?" Oglesby asked.

"Yes," Connelly nodded, continuing, "First, a robot may not injure a human being or, through inaction, allow a human being to come to harm."

"That sounds like a good thing," Dolby commented. Oglesby clearly agreed.

Connelly ignored them and went on, "Second, a robot must obey orders given it by human beings except where such orders would conflict with the First Law."

"Any human?" Oglesby asked.

Connelly nodded. "Yes, unless there are restrictions in special programming."

"Like what?" Dolby asked.

"Because of the nature of Lucas' work, he has a slight modification," Connelly explained. "A robot must obey orders given him by his Maker, his owner, and any authorities they assign to be in authority over him provided they don't conflict with the First Law. It prevents sabotage by criminals, competitors, or other mischief makers.

"Third, a robot must protect its own existence as long as such protection does not conflict with the First or Second Law."

"Do police fall under authorities assigned to authority over him?" Dolby asked.

"Yes," Connelly replied.

"Okay, so why won't he tell us everything?" Oglesby said.

"He has an NDA," Connelly said. "Non-Disclosure

Agreement. When certain people buy these androids to work for them, they sometimes want to protect proprietary information. Lucas' model is equipped with full video and audio recording capabilities, and if those feeds were to be misused or fall into the wrong hands—"

"So he tapes everything?" Dolby interrupted.

"It's on a loop really. He only saves what is deemed important for his records."

"And how does he determine that?" Oglesby said.

Connelly shrugged, leaning back in her chair. "Well, it could be requested by an employer, in fact. It's not entirely up to him. But generally he doesn't save anything unless there is a good reason."

"So like footage of the events at the warehouse the other night—"

"My programming forbids me from sharing events that occur in my place of work with outsiders," Lucas said. He'd let Connelly do all the talking so far, so both detectives and the doctor turned to him, surprised.

"There was a crime committed," Oglesby said. "We need to see it. We can get a subpoena—"

"I am afraid my recording loops reset every morning as desired by my employer," Lucas replied.

"What does that mean—he erased it?" Oglesby said.

Connelly nodded.

"Shit." Oglesby let his frustration show.

"Well, what we need to know first are the names of the men at the warehouse," Dolby said. "Can you tell us that?"

"Mister Wayne O'Dell, warehouse manager, was there,

and his assistant Garcia," Lucas said.

Oglesby and Dolby exchanged a pleased look. Now they were making progress.

"Does this Garcia have a full name?" Dolby continued.

Lucas looked puzzled. "I have only ever heard him referred to as 'Garcia,'" he said.

"Ok, that really narrows it down," Dolby mumbled. "Did you recognize any of the others?" she asked full voice as she looked at the android again.

Lucas shook his head. "No. I did not know all of them. One is a driver who regularly brings his truck there."

"Do you know his name?" Oglesby asked.

"I do not remember," Lucas said.

"So you might have recorded it at some point but you have no record?"

Lucas nodded. "Yes. I suppose that could be."

"This driver, does he bring his truck only at night, after the warehouse is closed?" Dolby asked then.

"I don't know," Lucas said. "I only work there from five p.m. to eight a.m."

"So you've seen him several times, but only during your night shift?"

Lucas thought a moment. "Yes, I believe so." He continued sitting up in his chair like he was highly focused or at attention, even when they had been talking to each other or Connelly. It made him look all the more inhuman, Simon thought. In normal interviews, the subjects always shifted in their chairs, leaning forward and back, sometimes slouching, looking distracted, tired, even irritated. Lucas' face and posture hadn't changed a wink since the interview started.

"We need you to tell us more," Oglesby said. "What you remember of that night, the men, what happened."

Lucas hesitated for a moment. "I believe these activities are restricted by my NDA."

Dolby looked at the doctor. "Should we start treating him as a reluctant witness?"

"What does that mean?" Connelly asked.

"We have ways of handling people who are uncooperative," Dolby said.

Connelly frowned. "What are you going to do—beat him? He's built to withstand that. And he has no physical feelings. It won't work."

Dolby leaned forward, eyes imploring. "Can you help us here?"

Connelly looked at Lucas. "Lucas, I think what they are wanting are generally details of what you remember, nothing specific. That kind of thing shouldn't be a violation. Just don't tell them any business secrets."

Lucas nodded. "Yes, proprietary information is forbidden."

"Exactly," Connelly agreed, her eyes locked on his with an encouraging look. "Please. Go ahead."

Simon tensed, clenching his fists and releasing them. His shoulders were stiff and aching. This was taking too long, and Simon was getting frustrated. All this dancing about while Santorios was in danger meant that much sooner until something bad might happen to her. He wanted to rush into the room, shake some sense into the robot. *Resistance, my ass. I'll make you talk.* But then again, he realized that might not exactly make it any better, especially in this case. They weren't dealing with a normal witness.

"How about this," Oglesby continued, looking at Lucas again. "Were you the only guard on duty at the warehouse?"

"Yes," Lucas replied.

"How many nights a week did you work?"

"Seven."

"No days off?"

"I do not require rest like the human employees," Lucas said.

"Is that a yes?" Dolby asked.

"Yes. No days off," Lucas clarified.

"What about Wayne O'Dell and this Garcia—what hours do they work?" Oglesby asked.

"I believe they are in and out," Lucas said. "I am not there from eight a.m. to five p.m., but I do see Mr. O'Dell many nights when I arrive for work and some mornings as I leave."

"Some mornings. Not every morning?"

"I don't think so, no."

"So he doesn't keep regular hours?" Dolby interjected.

"I do not know," Lucas replied.

"What kinds of things are stored at the warehouse?" Dolby asked.

"Artwork, I believe, and other products manufactured by Mister Ashman's companies," Lucas said.

"You don't know for sure?"

"It is not within my duties to examine the items," Lucas

said.

Simon growled, body heat rising. He'd had enough. Whirling, he hurried to the door and out into the hallway. Moments later, he burst into the interview room and glared at Lucas.

"Enough of the games," Simon said. "My partner is kidnapped. Men are dead. You need to tell us what you know, right now!"

"Who is this man?" Connelly demanded.

"John—" Oglesby started.

Simon shook his head. "No. I've had enough. All he does is give wishy washy answers. He knows more than he is saying."

"He has rules to follow in his programming," Connelly said, shooting Simon and angry look.

Dolby gave a look of surrender and said, "Master Detective John Simon, Doctor Livia Connelly and Lucas George."

Simon leaned both hands on the end of the table nearest the android and leaned forward, eyes on Lucas. "People are dead. Others may be murdered. We have stolen merchandise we found being unloaded from that truck. We need to know what you know so we can stop this. It is against the law for you to lie to us or withhold information."

Lucas looked puzzled. "I cannot lie. It is against my programming."

"Omission is almost the same thing," Simon said, continuing to glare at him. "Look. You have two minutes until I climb over this fucking table and throw you into the wall, pal. Talk!"

Connelly looked exasperated. She turned jerkily toward the other detectives, her jaws clenched, eyes narrowing. "I want this guy out of here. You cannot treat one of my androids like this. It is abuse."

"We're all a bit tense," Dolby explained. "One of our detectives was kidnapped. We think by the men responsible for the stolen items at the warehouse."

Connelly shook her head. "I'm sorry about that, really. But Lucas is following his programming. Trying to force him with violence is not going to solve anything."

Simon whirled, tense, furious energy radiating from his eyes as he met hers. "My partner is pregnant and they took her! If she dies, you two will be responsible! So I want some answers." His pulse pounded and he realized he was sweating, his body flushed with heat. Connelly simply looked back at him with fear in her eyes.

"I cannot refuse to provide information that is relevant unless it violates my NDA," the android said matter-of-factly.

"I don't give a shit about your NDA!" Simon yelled. "You better start talking."

"He's doing the best he can, believe me," Connelly said, glaring at him.

Oglesby stood and put a hand on Simon's shoulder. "John, this isn't helping."

"The Sergeant wanted us to handle this, Simon," Dolby added. "Why don't you let us do our jobs here—"

Simon spun his glare on her. "Fuck doing your jobs. I'm doing mine." He grabbed Lucas' arm and pulled him from the chair, dragging him toward the door.

"I am fully capable of self-motion," Lucas objected.

"Where are you taking him?!" Connelly demanded, pushing back her chair with a loud squeak as she stood. She looked almost ready to leap at Simon, her eyes narrow with her own anger, shoulders tense, and legs apart. Dolby and Oglesby stood as well, all three staring at Simon.

Simon shoved him out the door. "We're going to talk to some people. See if that jogs his memory. Don't worry, he'll be back."

"John—!"

Simon cut Oglesby off by slamming the door.

SIMON WAS TURNING right off Forest onto Lindell before Lucas spoke to him. He'd been so angry he hadn't wanted to stop and check out an official unmarked car, so he'd taken his own instead. Since this wasn't officially his case, it was probably better anyway.

"Where are you taking me?" Lucas asked.

"To talk to Benjamin Ashman."

"Oh, that will be most fascinating. I have never met Mister Ashman."

"You said he's your employer."

"Mister Ashman owns me, yes," Lucas replied.

Simon shot him a puzzled look as he pulled the Charger to a stop at a red light. "He's your 'owner' and you've never met?"

"Yes. Mister O'Dell handled the warehouse and was the one who instructed me at work," Lucas said. "But I was purchased to work there by Mister Ashman."

"He purchased you sight unseen?"

"The capabilities of my line are clearly stated, besides the customized programming we may receive for any particular assignment. There was no need."

Simon accelerated again as the light changed. He couldn't believe he was driving around with a freaking robot. So lifelike that he and Santorios had mistaken him for human at the warehouse. Of course, they had been distracted and all of them had been standing in shadows. Still. *What kind of fucking cop are you, Simon?*

"I will be most pleased to meet him," Lucas said again.

"This isn't a social call," Simon replied. "This is Police business. Official. I'll do the talking."

"Then why did you wish me to accompany you?"

"I need you to tell me if you recognize anyone from the warehouse after hours," Simon said.

"I believe this would not violate my NDA. Okay."

Simon bit back a scolding curse. He couldn't give a shit if it violated an NDA. He was going to find his partner and save her life, no matter what. But that was not likely a productive argument to engage in with the android at that moment, so he just focused on his driving.

"You drive very erratically," Lucas observed.

"I what?" Simon shot him an annoyed look.

"You are exceeding the posted speed limit of twenty-five and weaving in and out of traffic. This is most dangerous statistically."

"You know what else is dangerous?" Simon asked.

Lucas raised an artificial brow in question.

"Pissing off a guy with a gun. Shut the fuck up."

Lucas obeyed. They drove the rest of the way to the Gallery in silence, hitting only one more red light, and Simon found a spot on the curb almost directly out front.

"Let's go," he said as he climbed out of the car.

Lucas climbed out of the passenger side and followed him across the sidewalk without a word.

They stopped outside the door and Simon looked the android in the eye. "You just look around and see if you recognize anyone," he instructed.

Lucas nodded and started to speak but Simon cut him off.

"Don't say anything until later. Just remember, okay?"

Lucas nodded again. "I follow instructions well."

Simon chuckled at the odd syntax. "I'm going to take that as a 'yes.'"

"It most definitely is," Lucas confirmed.

"Just...try to act normal in there," Simon added, knowing that was hopeless.

"What is your definition of normal, Detective?" Lucas asked with absolute sincerity.

Simon almost laughed, then thought better of it. "Just say as little as possible, okay?"

"Okay," the android agreed.

Simon took a deep breath and reached for the door. *God, please let this idiot not fuck things up.*

CHAPTER 5

THE ASHMAN GALLERY was a large two-story open space with a double-wide glass staircase up the middle of the room to the second floor, part of which opened above like an atrium with railings and circled the lower room, the other of which couldn't been seen from below and extended with a full floor toward the back. The place smelled of cleaning fluids and the floors and walls shined like they were regularly kept spotless. Simon also caught the scents of colognes and perfumes, perhaps employees and visitors mixed, and speakers overhead piped in soft classical orchestra music—Bach or perhaps Beethoven, at the moment.

Paintings, sculptures of various mediums, and drawings covered all the walls, many lit with special spotlights for emphasis. Just beside the stairs, an L-shaped black desk had phones and brochures about the collection on a stand. Several employees with name badges stood behind it watching the few people browsing the room.

"Have you ever been here before?" Simon asked Lucas, almost at a whisper as they both took in the room.

"I have not," Lucas replied. "It is fascinating."

"Just remember to look for anything...or anyone familiar and tell me later," Simon said.

"Of course," Lucas agreed.

"I'm going to take a look upstairs," Simon said.

As Lucas began examining the art along one wall, Simon headed for the stairs, passing a life-sized sculpture of four nude, different colored men—none of them human skin tones—intertwined awkwardly.

"It's a representation of how all men are brothers," said a lilting female voice.

He turned to see a tall, beautiful brunette with long curly hair and tan skin flashing him a killer smile.

"Looks to me like these brothers are a little *too* close," Simon replied, shaking his head as their eyes met.

"Their nakedness symbolizes a release from the walls we hide behind. Total openness," Stacey added.

"Well, that's more open than most people can handle, I'll give 'em that," Simon said and smiled.

Stacey laughed. "Exactly." She extended her hand. "Stacey Soukup, I'm the manager here. Can I help you with anything?"

Simon shook her hand, her flesh soft and gentle in his calloused grip. "No. I'm just looking around."

"And your friend?" she nodded to Lucas.

He watched as another employee greeted Lucas and offered him the similar "insights" on a nearby work.

"Fascinating," Lucas said with a nod.

"He's looking, too," Simon said, shaking his head. "He's never been to a gallery."

"Wonderful!" Stacey looked delighted.

Simon motioned toward the stairs. "Is there more up there?"

"A few special pieces, including our star—Degas' 'Springtime Dance.' It's delightful," she said, meaning every word, yet still coming across like a saleswoman.

"I'll take a look," Simon said and headed for the stairs.

"Sure you don't want me to come along? I can get us a glass of wine? Some brie?"

Simon shrugged. "Not just yet. It's my first time here, so I just want to get a feel for the collection."

Stacey stepped back, shoulders lowering in gentle surrender. "Of course. Well, I'll be right over there if you need anything. Just holler." She indicated the black desk.

"Thanks," Simon said, meaning it and headed up the stairs. In truth, he'd been tempted to stay and talk to Stacey all day. She was exactly his type. And he felt a strong attraction to her. But this was business, and Santorios needed his help. Besides, who knew who all was mixed up in the shady business at the warehouse or his partner's kidnapping? This wasn't the time.

The stairs were opaque, despite being glass, shiny but lending a foggy view of the ground beneath. Simon could see vague colors and shapes of employees or patrons passing by but nothing clear.

The second floor was laid out in an H pattern of sorts, with half the H being the atrium stretching from above the stairs to the front entrance. Rails lined both legs of the H and the walls were covered with paintings. At the center, in front of the stairs, hung a large Degas with special lighting that made it clear: this is the gallery's prize piece. The other half of the H was formed by two hallways leading down from the two balconies and back into a hallway with doors off the center. Simon guessed they were offices and perhaps a conference room and employee break room. First, he looked at the art a bit, taking it in. The atrium really was stunningly appointed with gold painted trim and rails and crystal lighting.

Then he spotted a sign with an arrow pointing to the right hallway that read: "Offices. Employees only."

He decided to start there and began walking down the corridor. As he turned past the Degas into the hall, a man with slicked backed brown hair in a pastel old school Armani suit was walking toward him. As soon as their eyes met, the man turned and dodged into a nearby office. Simon barely got a look at his face but the man looked familiar. Someone from the warehouse?

The first doors he passed were marked as men's and women's restrooms, so he skipped those and went to the one he'd watched the man enter. The door was locked and there was no window but the sign outside said: "S. Soukup, Manager."

He knocked. "Police. Official Business."

There was no response. He spotted an open door at the end of the hall and heard voices. It appeared to be an office with large windows overlooking the street. As he walked toward it, he saw the sign reading: "B. Ashman, Owner." Benjamin Ashman!

Simon picked up his pace, glancing back over his shoulder quickly to make sure the man hiding from him hadn't come out of Stacey's office. The hallway was clear.

Then Simon neared the door of the large office. Two men were talking and as he peered in, he saw Ashman—mid-sixties, full gray hair, often mistaken for everyone's grandfather—sitting behind his neofuturist glass desk in a leather chair big enough to rival a throne. Simon recognized him from the society pages on media sites. Across from him, standing, was a man with a long, blond ponytail, broad shouldered in a nice black designer suit that was tailored for his body but still couldn't hide the fact he was in good physical shape.

Both men looked over as Simon strolled confidently into the office. "Mister Ashman?"

"Yes?" Ashman said, puzzled.

The blond man frowned. "Who are you? You can't just barge in here!"

Simon flashed his badge. "Master Detective John Simon, Central Division. I'm investigating the incident at your warehouse."

"You can make an appointment—" the blond said, stepping angrily in his path and glaring.

"Lay one hand on me and I'll break your fucking arm, pal," Simon warned.

"Do you have any idea who you're talking to?" the blond said, grabbing Simon's arm anyway.

Simon whirled, twisting the man's arm and pulling until the man yelped and fell to his knees. Simon held him there, just short of breaking his arm. "Down, boy."

The blond snarled, "Fuck you!"

Ashman raised a hand to silence him. "Paul, please."

The blond reacted with frustration, then sighed, his body relaxing in surrender as Simon stepped around him and faced Ashman at the desk.

"What can I do for you, Detective?" Ashman asked,

offering a warm smile as he turned his chair slightly, still leaning back comfortably relaxed in it.

"You can tell me why armed men were moving stolen art and nanochips at your warehouse?" Simon said. They hadn't confirmed the art was stolen but might as well shake things up.

Ashman shook his head. "That whole incident is regretful. There was no excuse for those men firing at you. Even if you didn't, as I understand it, have a proper search warrant." He said it calmly, with no accusatory tone but his eyes raised the question.

Behind Simon, Paul rose to his feet, wincing as he rubbed his arm and straightened his suit. He stood near enough to react again if needed but didn't attempt to block the detective from Ashman or remove him.

The office smelled almost as clean as the display areas near the entrance, but there was also the scent here of paper dust, printer ink—a working office. Not unexpected.

"We had probable cause," Simon said. "A witness reported unusual after-hours activity at your warehouse, and we thought perhaps a crime was being committed. We appear to have been right."

"Those nanochips are manufactured by one of my companies, and the art is part of our overflow collection," Ashman said, unperturbed in the slightest. "A gallery like this cannot adequately display all of our works at once for various reasons—limited space, security, restoration..."

Simon scoffed. "Nice story. Except the serial numbers on the nanochips matched a batch reported stolen a month ago."

Ashman shot Paul a concerned look, brow creased, but continued to lean back, relaxed in his chair. "I know nothing of this. Paul, find out immediately."

Paul nodded and started for the door, shooting Simon a warning glare as he passed.

Simon smiled and wiggled his fingers at him like a wave. "Go play nice with the others, Pauly."

Paul's nostrils flared but he continued on his way without another word.

Ashman nodded. "I can assure you we did not steal our own nanochips and if one of my employees has been involved somehow, we will investigate fully and it will be dealt with. We will cooperate fully with your investigation, of course."

Slick, confident, and totally calm. The guy wasn't rattled at all, and that pissed Simon off.

"You expect me to believe that with all the people you know and interact with—including some of the city's most notorious criminals—and with machine guns guarding your warehouse?"

Ashman frowned, irritation in his voice for the first time, "I do not associate knowingly with criminals, Detective. I meet a lot of people because of my various businesses and long support of the arts, of course, but that does not make them close personal connections. If you suspect someone of something, I am most disappointed to hear of it."

"So I am to believe that one of the smartest, most successful businessmen in the city interacts with known criminals and is totally unaware of it?" Simon chuckled. "Bullshit." He didn't buy it for a second. And Ashman's reaction showed clear understanding. "Machine guns. Isn't that overkill?"

"Detective, I would expect men in your line of work have

a natural suspicion," Ashman said. "But we have quite valuable assets to protect. I will speak with my warehouse manager about more appropriate weaponry, but we need security. I assure you again, I have nothing to hide."

"Prove it," Simon said. "I'd like access to a full inventory of the contents of your warehouse and a list of employees and their contacts."

Ashman leaned forward, elbows on his desk, his tone calm and polite again. "There are, as I'm sure you can understand, privacy and security concerns to consider. Do you have a warrant?"

"Your being totally legit, of course, I was hoping I wouldn't need one," Simon said.

Ashman thought a moment. "Well, perhaps. Though my lawyers might be most unhappy with me. Perhaps you can give me a little time to talk with them and consider this?"

"Look, Ashman! I know you have friends like the Mayor and the Police Chief to hide behind, and I know you have already tried to get them to stop the investigation," Simon said, his voice a warning. "Let's stop playing games. If you're really as innocent as you say, you have nothing to fear from letting me see the files. Your excuses just make it sound like you are hiding something. And I warn you, I will find out what it is."

"Is that a threat?" Ashman asked as their eyes met.

"You bet your ass," Simon said, raising his voice in anger now. "Your men killed an informant and now they've kidnapped my partner! I want her back, right now!"

Ashman looked shocked. "I know nothing of the sort. I'm so sorry to hear this. I do hope you find them."

Hands grabbed at Simon's elbows and arms then, as three

security men rushed in and surrounded him. Paul stepped forward, shooting Simon a smug look.

"So much for cooperating, eh?" Simon snapped, looking at Ashman.

"You barge into my office unexpected and make accusations and threats," Ashman said. "I really don't have to tolerate such rudeness. It's time for you to leave now." He waved dismissively and the men started dragging Simon toward the door.

Ashman raised a hand to stop them as they reached the doorframe. Neither man let up their grip on Simon in the slightest.

Ashman's eyes softened. "I'm sorry it has to be this way, but you really should be more professional. I do hope your partner is okay. And I am most sorry about your informant. We lost two of our employees recently as well. My sympathies."

Simon looked in his eyes and knew Ashman meant Peter Green was one of the employees. He wondered who the other was.

Then the men started dragging him down the hallway.

"Get the fuck off me!" he demanded, struggling to free himself in vain.

"We're just going to see you to your car," Paul said quietly as he followed along behind. There was thinly veiled delight behind his eyes.

"I can walk," Simon said, struggling again.

As they reached the top of the stairs, the men released him but stood in a line, blocking his way back.

Paul motioned toward the front door below and ahead.

"After you, Detective."

Simon turned, straightening his jacket and started down the stairs. Paul followed close on his heels with the three security men walking behind, shoulder-to-shoulder like a wedge. They barely fit side-by-side on the stairs.

As they reached the floor, gallery employees and the few patrons turned to stare.

Simon hesitated, looking around for Lucas. The security men grabbed at his arms again.

Simon jerked free and leaped ahead. "I said, stay the fuck off me!" He spotted Lucas turning at the commotion from a corner nearby. "We're going, Lucas," he said, then headed for the door.

Beside Lucas, staring in shock at him was Stacey, who looked very disappointed.

As usual, thrilling the ladies wherever you go, nice work, Simon.

Simon stopped at the door, waiting for Lucas to catch up and glared back at Paul and the security men, who stood several feet away, blocking the stairs.

"Have a nice day," Paul said in a sing-song, smug tone, offering a fake smile.

"Fuck you," Simon said, and a few employees and patrons gasped.

Lucas approached and Simon opened the door. The android followed him out.

"You know, perhaps if you spoke to people more kindly, they would not get so angry with you," Lucas said.

"Shut the fuck up and get in the car," Simon said.

"You are fortunate I have no emotion chip," Lucas said. "I think I would not like you much either."

Simon clicked the fob to unlock the Charger and hurried around to the driver's side as Lucas climbed in the passenger side seat in silence. As he opened his door, Simon looked back to see a disappointed Stacey and two other employees staring out the front window after him. When they saw him looking, they turned back and disappeared into the gallery.

Simon sighed and crawled into the car, slamming the door.

SIMON PULLED THE Charger out into traffic and headed south on Main, ignoring his passenger. As he drove he typed Paul Paulsen into his cell uplink and ran it through the KCPD's main database like he had O'Dell, Garcia, and Ashman before him. The man had a few minor violations, one juvenile arrest for smoking pot—nothing major. But that probably just meant he'd been good at concealing his activities. This guy was dirty. He reeked of it.

The android sat quietly past the first couple lights then asked, "Why are you so angry?"

"Angry? What do you know about it, 'Mister No Emotion Chip?'" Simon snapped.

Lucas cocked his head a moment, thinking. "It is true. I have no such chip. But none exists that I know of."

"Then shut the fuck up."

"I do know that anger often manifests in humans as

aggression," Lucas said.

"Is that right?" Simon rolled his eyes, wondering if it would break his fist to punch an android.

"Yes," Lucas said, missing the sarcasm totally. "And you speak this way with everyone. I'm surprised you could get along with a partner."

Simon turned and glared at him. "Don't talk about my fucking partner, robot. You know nothing about it."

"I know that most human relationships would not be affected positively by telling each other to 'shut the fuck up,'" Lucas said plainly.

Despite himself, Simon laughed, his shoulders shaking as he shifted on the car seat.

"This is funny?" Lucas asked, puzzled.

"Yeah," Simon said, laughing harder.

Lucas' brow creased and he sat in confused silence.

"Yeah, my partners never liked that," Simon said. "But Santorios says it to me all the time."

"Your current partner? The one who is missing?"

"Yes, Blanca Santorios. That's her name," Simon said.

"A beautiful name. I would never tell her to 'shut the fuck up,'" Lucas said.

Simon grinned. "It's not meant as mean when we do it."

Lucas turned to look at him. "This expression can be kind?"

Simon shrugged as he pulled to a stop at another light. "The way we use it." When Lucas didn't respond, he added, "Partners banter back and forth. We tease each other. Kid around. It actually comes out of our fondness for each other."

Lucas thought a moment. "Hmmm. Fascinating. You do this with all partners?"

"Only the ones I like," Simon said.

Now Lucas laughed.

"You find that funny?"

"Why, yes. Is it not a joke?"

"Dead serious," Simon said.

"So, we should banter?" Lucas asked.

"You're not my partner."

"We are spending a lot of time together investigating," Lucas said.

"We have been to one place."

"And where are we going now?"

"An apartment. Of a guy who got killed. It's down in Hyde Park."

"Gotcha, partner," Lucas said and winked.

Simon frowned. "What was that?"

"Banter. It was in a video I saw. I believe it was cowboys."

Simon shook his head, chuckling. "No. If you want to banter like a cop, you'd better study up. That is not how we talk."

Lucas seemed disappointed. "Study what?"

"I don't know. Listen to cops."

"Okay, I will try," Lucas said.

Simon waved a hand dismissively. "Whatever floats your

boat, pal." He slowed, flipping on the turn signal and waiting in a turn lane to turn left on 38th Street.

"Shut the fuck up," Lucas said.

Simon glared at him as he made the turn. "You shut the fuck up."

"Did I not do it correctly? You seem angry again?" Lucas asked.

"We don't have that kind of rapport, C3PO," Simon said.

"C3PO? I don't know the term," Lucas said.

"Yeah, whatever. Shut the fuck up." Simon grinned.

They drove the next few blocks to the apartments on Gillham in silence. But inside, Simon chuckled to himself. The android could be quite amusing. *Gotcha, partner. Who programmed this dork?*

BENJAMIN ASHMAN HAD trusted Paul Paulsen to handle details of his business, including personnel, for fifteen years now. And this was the first time he'd ever questioned if he'd made a mistake. Paul Paulsen had always carried himself like a man with a mission, and that had earned him his boss's admiration and respect. Ashman had never once questioned if Paulsen was on the right mission either. Until angry cops came bursting into his office and gallery unannounced after a shootout at his warehouse with thousands in damages, confiscated shipments. Ashman didn't know all the details, but by the time Paul returned from showing the detective out he was fuming.

Ashman slammed his palms on his desk and stood as Paul returned and closed the door behind him. "What the hell is going on at my warehouse?!"

Paul raised a hand in reassurance. "Garcia and O'Dell made some bad decisions. It's been handled. Garcia is already gone."

Ashman wasn't sure what he meant by that. He didn't want to know. But he hoped whatever solution his aide had found would keep that troublemaker away for good. "And how are we handling it?"

Paul shrugged. "I thought you didn't want all the details."

Ashman sighed and returned to his chair. Those had been his orders. And for almost two decades, he'd always considered himself better off. But then he'd never had trouble from the Police. His carefully cultivated relationship with the Mayor and Chief were supposed to help with that, but not even they seemed able to control this Detective Simon.

"I don't," Ashman replied. "But you find out everything and make sure we don't have any more trouble with overzealous cops. We are a legitimate business. And we do things the right way."

Paul nodded. "Of course, Mister Ashman. As always."

"Find out who has the cop's partner," Ashman said. "And if we can help, do it."

"Do you really think we should get involved in that?" Paul asked. "He's already accused us. Maybe we should stay clear."

"I want him off our backs," Ashman said. "If we can provide a tip or some other good faith gesture, do it. Get him looking somewhere else."

79

Paul nodded. "Of course."

"I want it handled properly, Paul," Ashman said, shooting his aide a warning look.

"As always, of course," Paul said without hesitation, holding Ashman's stare.

Ashman urged with a wave. "And get my paintings and nanochips back. The Police have mistaken them for stolen. We don't need the press getting a hold of that."

"Who do you want me to call?"

Ashman frowned, annoyed. "The Chief, of course. Whomever it takes. And I want that warehouse repaired and cleaned up. Yesterday."

"That is already in the works as soon as the crime scene is released."

"Good."

Suddenly, there was anxious knocking at the door. Paul turned and hurried to answer. Wayne O'Dell rushed into the room.

"I think that cop recognized me," he said, in a panic.

Paul put a hand on his shoulder. "It's being handled."

Ashman glared at O'Dell. "If you were doing your job right, that wouldn't be a problem."

O'Dell winced and looked at his feet. "I'm sorry, Mister Ashman. They caught us by surprise. We were just trying to protect—"

Ashman waved dismissively, cutting him off. His eyes narrowed as he said, "Machine guns. I should just fire you now." His voice was flat, indifferent.

O'Dell's eyes pleaded. "Please, Mister Ashman. It won't

happen again. My family—"

"Get out of my sight!" Ashman spat, motioning to Paul.

Paul pushed O'Dell toward the door. "Wait for me in my office, Wayne."

"But that detective—"

"Now!" Paul ordered, and O'Dell wilted like a dried flower and hurried back out into the hallway.

Ashman remained silent until his aide closed the door again. "He's done, too. Wrap up his duties and find a replacement. I've had enough."

Paul nodded. "Of course."

The phone on the desk rang and Ashman glanced at the caller ID. "Time to work. Go." And he picked up the phone, turning away—a signal for Paul to go do his job. The aide left without a word, shutting the door behind him.

"Benjamin Ashman," Ashman said into the phone.

CHAPTER 6

P ETER GREEN'S APARTMENT was on the third floor of a five-story Art Deco building facing the northwest section of Hyde Park. Simon parked on the street, watching chirping robins grabbing worms and bugs for their young off the park lawn as he came around the car to join Lucas. The symphony of bird and insect song blended with a gentle whistle of leaves in a soft wind as they walked up the sidewalk and entered the building through the double glass front door. Surprisingly, it was unlocked in late afternoon and Simon saw no desk or attendant on duty. An elevator was facing the front doors, but Simon thought a moment and chose the stairs. Lucas followed.

The stairs and lobby smelled stale and old—a mixture of years-old paint, industrial cleaning products, and aged wood common to most older buildings in the city. The lighting fixtures were cracked and clouded over a bit with residue but it was obvious the place had been restored at least once since its glorious opening. The elevator was too modern, and the lights now ran energy saving LED bulbs.

Lucas turned a puzzled look at him. "You think I do not speak like a human? I function ninety percent like a human being in most respects."

"What?" Simon asked. What was he babbling about now?

"You said—"

Jesus, were they back to this again? "Yeah, and at least ten percent is how you talk," Simon said. "No normal human uses the cadence you use."

Lucas looked disappointed. "Well, I hope you will assist me to do better. I am designed to blend in with humans and wish to learn."

"If you want to blend in, stop saying things like 'in most respects' or 'I am designed,'" Simon said, shaking his head. "You sound like a machine."

Lucas hrmphed. "I will remember."

They reached the third floor and Simon hurried ahead of Lucas, looking for the apartment labelled '6.' They found it at the end of the hall. Yellow Police Line tape had been pulled free and hung in pieces on either side. But that could mean cops as well as anyone. Once a scene had been processed, there were all kinds of reasons why investigators might return there looking for more answers, etc. So Simon paid it no mind and tried the door.

"We probably have to get the super," he said, but then he turned the knob and the door slid open slightly.

"It appears to be unlocked," Lucas commented.

Simon frowned. Detectives would have locked it. And the building was still nice enough the super would have checked. Was someone in there?

He loosened the strap on his weapon and motioned for Lucas to be quiet.

"What is the matter?" Lucas asked more softly.

"Just let me go first, quietly," Simon said and pushed softly on the door.

The door swung open into a living room that looked like a tornado scene. Papers, CD cases, books, candles, cushions and more littered the floor randomly. There was a recliner and two love seats facing a TV in an L-pattern, but most of the shelves had been rifled through, their contents just tossed wherever it landed. Although the windows remained unbroken, the cabinets of the kitchen across a bar to the left had been left open, cans and boxes shoved hastily aside in a search. And the fridge door had been left ajar.

"This man Peter was not good at house cleaning," Lucas said.

Simon shushed him, whispering, "Someone else did this."

As Simon slowly turned, scanning the room, hand hovering near his Glock as he looked down a short corridor to what he assumed was a bedroom and bathroom, Lucas also turned, taking it in. The place smelled of incense, dust, and human sweat at the moment, but from the looks of the shelves and bar, Peter had kept things regularly wiped down and clean. Who had done this?

Then a familiar man with short brown hair and an old Armani suit appeared from one of the back rooms and headed up the hall.

Lucas saw him first. "Mister O'Dell?"

The man looked up as Simon slid back out of view.

"Lucas? What are you doing here?" the man asked.

"We are looking for evidence."

Simon recognized the man as the one who'd dodged him at the gallery, and then he remembered Lucas telling him an O'Dell ran the warehouse. This man had been shooting at Simon and Santorios.

O'Dell's face showed concern as he stopped approaching and shifted his weight, seeing Simon. His face fell and he turned around and ran back to the room he'd come out of, slamming the door.

"Police! Stop right there!" Simon shouted and drew his weapon, racing after the man.

He reached the door in seconds and tried it. The knob barely turned—locked.

"O'Dell, don't make me come after you," Simon said.

A burst of automatic fire tore through the door and Simon dove clear. The bullets left holes in the door and tore into the opposite wall.

"That wasn't smart. Now you've pissed me off!" Simon warned as he got back to his feet.

Then he heard wood scraping and sliding—a window opening?

Simon fired three shots through the door for cover and braced himself, then turned as he ran and shoved his shoulder against the door. It bent under his weight but didn't open.

"Shit!"

He waited a moment, stepping clear to see if there would be any return fire. Then he lifted a leg and kicked it full force with the bottom of his foot against the knob. The door went crashing inward, banging against a wall and swinging back.

By then, Simon was through the door, gun raised and panning the room for O'Dell. A nearly made queen bed was centered against the wall opposite the door with a nightstand packed with books and a lamp up top and a bureau filling out the small room. Clothes hung neatly in a closet with shoes organized in pairs on a rack below. A window in the back right corner was open and the room was clear. Simon caught sight of painted metal bars just outside, hanging off the building. A fire escape.

He ran to the window and ducked his head out then back. O'Dell fired back from the landing below, bullets ricocheting off the metal and bricks. Simon jumped clear, then waited a moment. He leaned his gun arm out and fired straight down, three shots, at where O'Dell had been.

When there was no further response, he looked out. O'Dell was running south down the alley below.

"Stay here, Lucas!" Simon called, then climbed out the window and fired a couple more shots toward O'Dell.

The man stumbled as one grazed his shoulder, cursing as his Sig Sauer fell from his hand and skittered across the alley. O'Dell left it, recovered his footing, and kept running.

Simon raced down the fire escape to go after him. He got to the ladder leading down from the second landing and slid down it like a fireman, his hands pressing the sides, landing with his feet spread on the cement square at the bottom then racing out onto the gravel and down the alley the way O'Dell had gone.

He couldn't see the man ahead but saw the Sig Sauer and considered picking it up, then decided to leave it, instead picking up his pace, hoping to catch O'Dell.

Simon was thankful he'd kept in decent shape since his football days. He could still run fairly fast when he pushed himself with no injuries or aches to contend with. Not every cop of his years on the Force could say that. In fact, very few. He'd been lucky, he knew. And so he reached the end of the alley fairly quickly and stopped at 37th, looking both ways for O'Dell.

After a few seconds, he saw O'Dell crossing northbound Gillham toward the park and set off after him, quickly accelerating again.

O'Dell made it across before a light changed but Simon was cut off by traffic. He tried to dodge out and zigzag, but no one was slowing down, despite the gun in his hand. He flashed a badge, "Police business!" But got only a flipped bird and muttered curses in response.

"Yeah, fuck you, too, assholes!" he called after them. The traffic here was one-way, two lanes. He had to wait.

Then he heard tires squeal and an odd pounding and whining like servos to his south. He turned to see Lucas racing across the street, dodging cars, jumping over a Volvo hood, headed for the park, without regard for the traffic. The smell of burned tires and exhaust filled the air as Simon realized Lucas was chasing O'Dell.

"Lucas, stop!" he called.

"Sorry," Lucas called back to one of the drivers.

He hit the sidewalk on the far side and raced diagonally across the lawn to catch O'Dell in less than a minute, turning around and running backwards beside him as he raised a palm.

"You must stop, Mister O'Dell," Lucas said. "Detective Simon has questions for you."

"Get the fuck away from me!" O'Dell yelled.

The light changed and Simon raced across the crosswalk as the last northbound car hurried through and the others slid to a stop at the lines, staring.

"It is important to respect the authorities," Lucas reminded O'Dell.

"Go away!" O'Dell said, panting as he shooed Lucas with a dismissive wave.

Lucas continued keeping pace with him backwards as they crossed the park toward southbound Gillham on the other side.

O'Dell looked both ways, checking traffic, even though the street went only southbound, and Lucas grabbed for him. Instead, the warehouse manager dodged between two parked cars and raced into the street. Lucas and Simon shifted course to intercept him, with Simon now only ten feet behind them and gaining.

Then a red Mercedes SL300 swerved out of the far line straight at O'Dell, causing a box cargo truck to skid and honk as the driver slammed on the brakes and others to change course behind him. The Mercedes accelerated, smashing into O'Dell with the crack of bones. O'Dell cried out as he flew up and slammed into the car's hood, limp, then rolled back off as the car kept accelerating and sped away, leaving O'Dell in a heap on the ground.

Simon and Lucas raced to him, Simon checking for a pulse. The cargo truck slid to a stop nearby and the driver climbed out, hollering, as other cars slid to a stop as well.

"Shit! He won't be talking now," Simon said. The irony scent of warm blood now mixed with that of the oil and debris on the street as blood pooled around O'Dell's crumpled form.

"Is he okay?" the trucker called.

Simon just looked at Lucas. "He's dead."

Lucas looked sad. "He was a nice man. I am sorry."

Simon stood, grunting. "Nice men don't run from cops and shoot at them." He glared at Lucas. "What were you thinking?"

Lucas shrugged. "I was trying to assist you. Be a good partner."

"We're not partners. You're a civilian and I told you to stay put," Simon scolded. "You could have been hurt."

"I feel no pain and have chrome parts that withstand projectiles better than human flesh," Lucas replied. "I also can run fast."

"Yeah, I noticed." Simon shushed him. "But now he's dead and can't tell us anything."

Lucas looked puzzled. "I am responsible for this?"

Simon scoffed, shaking his head. "I gotta call this in." He pulled his cell from his pocket and hit speed dial to call Police dispatch.

MILES ROSS PULLED the Mercedes into a gas station and took out his black cell phone, the one with the secure line, untraceable. It had cost him five times what he wanted to pay for a phone but it had been worth it. Switching towers, carriers, and even call waiting information was as easy as a couple key punches. He just felt safer knowing he had a way to dodge traces, even those by the sophisticated computers cops and Feds used these days. Miles left the electric engine running, enjoying the vibration but turned the rock station down low as he made the call.

Dialing in the memorized number, he waited while the phone connected to South America, then routed through three towers—a function the person he was calling had set up for safety—with only a click and a beep to indicate each change. Outside his window a vagrant approached the car, waving at him to signal washing the window. Miles scowled and flashed his Sig Sauer, sending the frightened toothless bum scurrying away.

Miles chuckled as the phone finally rang. A familiar scratchy voice spoke Spanish on the other end. "Si?"

"Kansas City 76513," Miles said the familiar code. "Royal Blue."

"I am hearing too many rumors down here," the heavily accented voice said then.

"It's being taken care of. Nothing to worry about," Miles replied.

The man grunted. "There better not be. Too much is at stake. Don't make me send my own people."

Miles scowled, bristling at the insult. "We'll fucking take care of it. I told you." He'd tensed and leaned forward in his seat, then realized the station attendant could see him through a window and sat back quickly, relaxing and changing his expression. With cops nosing around, he couldn't be too careful. They'd seen his car today, too. Now he had to dump it. He loved this Mercedes.

"Don't use that language with me!" The man yelled so loud Miles had to yank the phone away from his ear 'til he finished. "Remember who you're talking to!"

When the man had finished, Miles put the phone back and added, "I just finished one now. Give me a week and it'll all be over."

"A week may be too long with all this heat," the man answered, still irritated. "I want that cop dead. And her partner, too. Then we find another warehouse."

"Already got that handled," Miles said. "We've never failed you. Have some trust."

"I trust no one," the man replied. "That's why I am still alive." He hung up, loudly, and the line went dead, then a dial tone came through.

Miles closed his phone and slid it back into his jacket pocket. "Stupid foreign motherfucker." Working for the guy hadn't been his idea. He'd do his job but he didn't have to like or respect his bosses or their crazy mission, whatever it was. They talked about it a lot, but he rarely listened. It bored him. He liked their money, though. He smiled at the thought of it. Miles couldn't give a fuck about all their talk of "saving the world," but he fucking loved their money.

He slid the SL300 back into gear and checked his mirror, shooting out into traffic like a demon as two other cars swerved, tires squealing, forced to avoid him. With the flick of a switch, the license plate rotated to a different number, the old one retracting inside. He'd dispose of it later with the car. For now, he'd be harder to trace until he did.

He cranked the radio back up and sang along to some Wolfie Van Halen. The kid was better than his father, he was quite sure. Breaking out on his own had been the best thing he'd ever done.

DR. LIVIA CONNELLY was on Simon as soon as he and Lucas entered the squad room, the usual cacophony of ringing phones, chattering detectives, and clicking keyboards thick in the air.

"You had no right to take him anywhere!" Connelly yelled, examining Lucas like a doting mother. "If any harm came to him—"

"Maker, I am fine," Lucas insisted.

"Simon! My office! Now!" Sergeant Becker's voice cut through the chaos like a blade as Simon looked up to see her motioning from her office.

"This isn't over!" Connelly warned. "Let me look at you," she continued, turning to Lucas and walking around him like a tailor or a dress shop sales clerk, examining every inch.

"You should learn not to yell at cops, lady," Simon said, with a smug smile, and marched toward the Sergeant's office.

Becker slammed the door behind him as he entered.

"Taking a civilian, someone else's property, without permission into dangerous situations..." she started in.

Simon rolled his eyes. "He's fine, Joann. Give me a break."

"You have a dead suspect. You were shot at. A damaged crime scene. Witnesses claiming you threatened them."

Simon scoffed. "I threatened no one. I did my job."

"As combatively as usual, no doubt," Becker said as she slid into her chair behind the desk and stared up at him.

"Blanca is in danger, Joann. I'll do whatever it takes to find her and get her back safe," Simon said. "So should you."

Becker slammed a fist on her desk. "You know damn well, I will do whatever it takes to save my officer! Don't fucking start with me! Ashman complained to Deputy Chief Keller. He's been all over me. You're lucky he hasn't called you down personally." Her eyes were tight, her nostrils flaring, as she motioned with sweeping arms. "He still might."

"I can handle Keller," Simon said. "Been there before."

"Not when he's this pissed off, you haven't."

Simon sighed. "It's not my fault the suspect tore apart a dead guy's apartment," Simon said. "In fact, we should have expected it, had someone on watch."

Becker shook her head. "This is not on Oglesby and Dolby. And don't you try to put it there."

"I am not blaming anyone," Simon said, raising his hands in surrender. His chest tightened and he clamped his jaw to hold back a curse. "The guy was there when we showed up."

"And you let a civilian chase him down," Becker scolded.

Simon waved his arms dismissively. "I told him to stay put while I chased the guy. Next thing I know, the android is running backwards beside him, trying to talk the guy down. He can run faster backward than we can forward, Sarge. It was unbelievable."

"He shouldn't have been there," Becker said and glanced through her window into the squad room where Connelly was still examining Lucas, inch-by-inch.

"He's fine, Sarge. Not a scratch on him."

"And you took him to Ashman's Gallery and burst into the man's office—"

"I did not burst. The door was open. His aide was all over me and I put him in his place," Simon said. "No threats. Just questioning."

"Which is why they threw you out into the street," Becker said.

"I walked, actually. They just helped me find the stairs," Simon snapped.

"This is not funny, Detective." Becker glared.

"Well, if you could have seen their faces it was," Simon said with a chuckle.

Becker's face twisted, her lips tightening and eyes cold.

"Lucas recognized a couple men there from the warehouse," Simon said, face serious again. "There's something going on with Ashman. I just need more time. I ran all PRINTZ on the guys at the warehouse and O'Dell. He's hiring some ex-cons, felons. A few have minor offenses, but most have a history of illegal activity. Even O'Dell—"

"It's not your case," Becker said. "Oglesby and Dolby are on it."

"Lucas is the only witness," Simon said.

"If he has to look at pictures, they will handle it," Becker said.

"Fine!" Simon growled, turned and glaring out the window at Connelly. "Any news on Blanca?"

"Not as of—"

There was movement as Oglesby approached outside and knocked on the door. Becker waved him in as both she and Simon looked up, expectantly.

"Sorry to interrupt," Oglesby said as he opened the door. "A maid just found a body over at the Admiral Motel. First responder thinks it's Santorios."

"Fuck!" Simon's chest tightened and he fought to breathe, starting for the door, but Oglesby was in the way. He hoped the uniform was wrong. He closed his eyes, offering God a silent plea.

"Where are you going?!" Becker yelled, standing and moving around her desk.

"I gotta ID her," Simon insisted, turning back again.

"Oglesby and I can do that," Becker said. She looked at Oglesby. "Did you call homicide?"

Oglesby shrugged. "Dispatcher has them en route already."

Becker pulled her own Colt from the desk and slid it into her shoulder holster. "Okay, you're driving. Everyone else stays here."

"Come on, JoAnn!" Simon spun, fighting back another curse. "It's my partner!"

"Exactly why I don't want you anywhere near this."

"You going to tell Andy?" Simon said, knowing that Blanca's husband was the type to take the news with great emotion.

"My officer, my job," Becker said.

"I should do it," Simon insisted. His eyes pleaded with her.

Becker locked eyes with him a moment then sighed, relaxing a bit as she stepped from behind her desk. "Fine. But let us check out the scene first, and we'll fill you in, okay? I still need that paperwork."

Simon groaned and nodded. "Yes, sir."

Everyone in the squad room had quieted when they stepped out of the Sergeant's office, and many were staring at them.

"You all have work to do," Becker said firmly. "Oglesby and I are on this." She and Oglesby weaved hurriedly through the maze toward the door as Simon headed for his desk, his head lowered.

"God, John, I'm so sorry," Dolby said, putting a hand on his shoulder as he passed.

Simon ignored her and pulled his chair out roughly with a loud squeak of wheels, then sat down hard and stared at the paperwork sitting just where he'd left it.

"Fingers crossed that they're wrong," Correia offered.

Maberry nodded. "We know how you feel, John. It's not your fault."

Simon glared at them all. "Whose fault is it then, Maberry?"

The others looked away, silence their only answer.

Simon turned back to the paperwork and flipped open a folder with a yank, trying to concentrate.

SIMON TRIED TO focus on the paperwork. He really did. But thoughts of Santorios and the case just kept filling his mind.

The case had been messy from the start. Santorios believed she had a solid tip—from a friend in her aerobics class, a nice, law abiding, decent guy, the kind who wouldn't harm a fly. But the tip had caught her by surprise when they were just wrapping up another heavy case—a burglary on Lumberman's Row in Hyde Park. The prominence, wealth, and connectedness of the victim had made that all the more complicated and sensitive. Plus they'd had to reassure neighbors, increase patrols, appease the press. All things which took time away from the actual investigation and kept the case dragging on longer than a typical burglary. Only a few items had actually been taken, and if it weren't for the scene's location in a historic, rich, semi-private cul-de-sac of huge houses—mansions with servant's quarters, stables and other outbuildings often occupying other parts of their huge lots—it might have been quick to process. They got a great lead on the thieves after a few weeks and managed to recover several stolen items from a private collector and a few others at two pawn shops off Prospect Ave.—a silly place to dump such high class items since none of the people living in the worst, crime ridden area of Kansas City that made up the Prospect Avenue district would ever buy such things. Their money went for guns, drugs, bribes, and other necessities.

So when Blanca got the tip, she hadn't even started paperwork. They'd had a quiet day and decided to check it out and then things went all to hell. Now, one of the city's most prominent businessmen, well-connected himself, was putting heat on the department, and had excuses to explain everything it seemed, even possibly the evidence. Simon wondered how long it would be until that went away, too. Only the ties to Oglesby's case and the shooting were locking that up for now. But how long? Guys like Ashman always found a way around such obstacles.

It was a good find for Santorios, Simon thought, a potentially major case. Now her last legacy. Fuck if he'd let them take that away. She deserved to be honored for it, not killed and dumped in some crappy motel.

Finally, he gave up and headed down to the crime scene.

THE ADMIRAL MOTEL had a long history of hookers, drug

dealers, and murders. Located on the corner of Admiral Blvd and The Paseo, about a mile from Police Headquarters, it sat on the edge of the Independence Avenue corridor just west of Prospect Avenue, the north end of an area stretching south almost to I-435 that composed the worst, most violent, gang infested, poverty stricken neighborhoods in all of Kansas City, Missouri and had for decades. The Prospect Avenue corridor, as it's often called by media and the cops especially, had once been the birthplace of Kansas City's Civil Rights movement, and was an area of fine suits and respectable businessmen through the 50s and 60s. But in the 70s it began to change significantly and went downhill from there.

Now, cops and civilians risking passing through at night might be randomly shot at, robbed, or killed. The frequency of murders, drug busts, prostitution and more left the area with the worst statistics in the entire Metro area. It was a place to be avoided, escaped from, not sought out. Sadly, all too many never managed to escape.

The current owners of the Admiral Motel had repainted and fixed up the rooms into something far more respectable that belied the Motel's past history, but it was still a dangerous neighborhood and not a prime location for tourists, despite its advertising as such. The cops were still called out here several times a year, and there had still been murders and other incidents, particularly with solicitation, that continued to give the place a seedy reputation and Simon figured always would.

The Parking Lot was filled now with black and whites, two undercover cars, a crime scene van, an ambulance, a coroner's van, and two media trucks, all centered around a room at the far west end of the first floor. Simon flashed his badge and was admitted to park behind the yellow crime scene barrier that had been set up in the parking lot and was guarded by uniforms. Then he got out and hurried toward room 125.

As he crossed the parking lot, he heard a buzzing in his ear and whirled to find another small, black media drone racing toward him. "Detective Simon, can you tell us what's happening please?" a female voice said, emanating from the box.

He pulled his Glock 37 and swung it like a club, bending one of the drone's propeller blades and sending it diving against a nearby tree where it whined and fluttered, trying to recover its bearings.

"Violation! Violation!" A computer voice whined.

"Stay the fuck away from me!" Simon warned as he ducked under the yellow crime scene tape and hurried on. As he went, he saw other drones hovering around, only some respecting the lines established by officers with yellow crime scene tape. *Goddamn media.*

Room 125 was packed with investigators and crime scene techs processing evidence, Becker and Oglesby looking on with two homicide detectives. The wall behind the bed was bright blue, while the two side walls were lime green, matching the bathroom tile at the back end. It smelled clean, if musty, like a typical hotel room. Except for the bed, everything looked clean and undisturbed like it had been left ready by maid service for the next customer.

Santorios lay on the bed like she'd been thrown there, and she probably had—nude, with bruises on her legs, arms, face, and neck where she'd been beaten. There were cuts and contusions too, likely acquired when she struggled. But the cause of death was clearly indicated by a single bullet hole in the center of her forehead, the back of her head slightly collapsed into a bloody mess. Blood had poured out onto the sheets, bedspread and floor in a pool. Her brown eyes wide and staring at Simon as he moved in for a better look.

He'd been angry and sad before, but now he was overcome. The world seemed to slow down and he felt like he'd been punched in the gut, his throat scratchy and his eyes gummy and clouded.

Becker spotted him and turned, frowning. "John, I told you to stay in the office."

"I had to see," he choked out, then his stomach lurched and he almost lost it, managing to choke it back a moment before running outside and vomiting on the end of the sidewalk.

Becker and Oglesby followed him out of the room.

"I'm sorry, John," Oglesby offered quietly.

"Fuck!" Simon said and spat. "Those bastards. She was pregnant. Those fucking bastards."

Becker's brow creased. "She was pregnant?"

Simon nodded and turned away, fighting back tears welling at the corners of his eyes. "She was about to tell you. It had just started to show. She wanted to put off desk duty as long as she could, Sarge."

Becker grunted. "I can't blame her for that. Not the first time."

"I want who did this," Simon said, whirling back to meet her eyes with a fierce glare. "I want them dead. Make them pay."

"And this is why I didn't want you here," Becker said, sympathetic yet stern. "Homicide has this one and you know they will put extra effort on it like any officer-involved. But it is not yours to run. You need to stay away from it."

"What the fuck am I going to tell Andy? He'll be devastated." Simon clenched his fists and looked down, turning away again.

"Do you want me to go? Someone to go with you?" Becker asked softly.

Simon shook his head. "Who's running it?"

"Bailey and Tucker," Oglesby said.

"You know they're the best at this," Becker added.

Simon nodded. "I want to read the daily reports."

Becker hesitated, watching him. She clearly wanted to just say "no." Finally, she replied, "We'll see. Okay?"

Simon glanced at his watch. "Shit. I gotta go pick up my daughter from school." It was 2:45. He had just enough time to arrive only a few minutes late. He could take Independence Avenue and skip the highways.

"Good," Becker said. "Best for you to keep busy."

"We'll make sure everything is done right, John," Oglesby assured him.

Simon could hear traffic whizzing by on I-70 nearby and on nearby streets as if it was a perfectly ordinary day, as if nothing unusual had happened. But for John Simon, this day changed everything. Things would never be the same and it pissed him off that those people didn't care, let alone notice.

Simon looked at Oglesby. "Shit, Martin. I want my fucking partner back." It was the one thing no one could give him. But he knew that, so after a few moments, he turned and walked back to his car, leaving Becker and Oglesby to watch him sadly. He felt the grief in their stares even as he climbed into the Charger, started the engine, and headed off. He didn't permit the tears to flow until he'd pulled into traffic.

CHAPTER 7

MILES HAD PARKED the BMW he'd swapped with his Mercedes in a shadowy corner of an alley just across Forest Avenue from where most cops parked their cars. He sat there, reading a magazine, radio playing in the background, waiting until he saw Simon's Charger leave the station and pull out onto the street.

Turning on his engine, he slipped the car into drive, waiting until Simon was a block down the street before easing it out into traffic after him. Then he pressed a bluetooth button on the dash to dial his phone. It rang three times before Paul Paulsen picked up.

"Yes?"

"I'm on him. He just left the garage."

"Does he know about his partner?"

Simon was driving angrily, fast, quick turns, aggressive. Which probably wasn't that far off from his normal but still made Miles suspect he already knew about Santorios. "From the way he's driving, I'm guessing yes."

"Are the cops at the Admiral?"

"Swarming like wasps."

Paul grunted. "Good."

Simon was driving fast enough, Miles had to accelerate to keep up, despite his intention to keep his distance for now. He followed the detective down an on ramp onto the I-70/I-35 loop north of downtown, headed east.

"What do you want me to do?" he asked.

"Hold off. Mister Ashman has something in the works that may make it a moot point."

"So you want me to let him go?"

"Nah. Follow him for a bit. Learn his routine. See who he talks to, but don't engage...for now," Paul said.

Miles sighed. "Will do, boss."

Paul hung up without further comment and Miles turned up the radio to another favorite song—a new one by Syzygy, a trio made up of the sons of Styx's Dennis DeYoung, Journey's Steve Smith, and daughter of Foreigner's Lou Gramm. It was a mix of contemporary rock and old school trappings from their fathers' influences.

God damn, I love rock and roll, he thought as he sped up and changed lanes, beating out the drum beats on the steering wheel with his fingers. He was still several cars back from Simon but keeping him well in view. Stalking prey for future hits was one of his favorite things. Today would be fun.

NOWLIN MIDDLE SCHOOL was located near 31st Street and South Hardy Avenue in Independence. Simon took I-70 on the loop East out of downtown then took exit 7A to 31st Street and followed it over. Emma stood waiting for him in front of the school, her purple backpack slung over one shoulder, on the driveway that led past the East side of the connected buildings. The area where students came out of the building and north was all red brick, but in the south half, the outer wall had brick on the bottom and white cement making up the top half. The line of parents' cars turned in at the north end of the drive and circled back south.

Simon leaned over and flipped open the door for his daughter as she made a show of glancing at her watch.

"Forget about me as usual?" she said, feigning irritation that Simon easily saw through.

"Nope. You know how it goes. Had to leave a scene to come here," Simon replied. "Sorry I'm late."

Emma shrugged then pulled the passenger seat forward and casually tossed her backpack on the backseat before shoving the seat top back and sliding in. "What kinda scene? Something exciting?"

She closed the door and slid her seatbelt in place as she waited for him to answer. Simon just sat in silence wondering how to break it to her. Emma loved Blanca Santorios. They'd hit it off from the moment they met. She always told him, "She's good for you, Dad. Making you less macho and misogynistic."

Her perspective surprised him. Simon hadn't considered himself anti-women at all. Maybe a little old fashioned about opening doors and carrying in groceries and lawn work and stuff, but he'd grown up respecting strong women in his life like his two grandmothers and his mother. They would not have tolerated any misogyny. They'd kept his father in line, too.

As he eased the car back away from the curve and headed south toward the street, Emma looked at him. "What?"

She looked right at him, but Simon couldn't bring himself to meet her gaze. Instead, he made a show of being the ever conscientious driver as he turned right onto South Hardy and headed back toward 31st.

Emma frowned. "Dad, come on. You're scaring me now."

This time he did look and saw the worry on her face. She bit her lip and looped several hairs around a finger, gently tugging at them as she watched him. Then her eyes widened and she stiffened. "Oh God. It's not Mom, is it? Is Mom okay?!"

Simon swallowed and nodded. "I'm sorry, honey. Yes, your mother's fine. This isn't about her."

Emma released her hair and rubbed her hands on her jeans. "Okay, then tell me."

Simon cleared his throat. "Blanca was murdered to today."

"Oh no!" Emma looked away as tears welled in her eyes and began pouring down her cheeks. "Why? Why would someone do that?"

Tears bunched in Simon's eyes now, too, and he hurriedly wiped them away, wanting to be strong for her. "I don't know, honey. I've been asking myself that since I found out."

"How long ago?" she asked.

"They found her an hour ago, at the Admiral," Simon said. He actually had no idea about the time of death yet.

"Ewwww, the Admiral Motel? Gross."

"How would you know? We've never taken you there." Simon looked at her, brow raised in question.

"I've driven by. Kids at school talk about it. I just hear bad things."

She spoke with too much authority and Simon found it unsettling but stayed silent, tipping his head to one side as he fought off another question.

Emma scowled, reading him clear as day like always. "God, Dad. It's not like that. Ewww."

Simon chuckled. "Like what? I didn't say anything."

"You have a dirty mind," she scolded, clearly thinking he'd been wondering if she'd gone there with a boy. The thought had crossed his mind, but he had already dismissed it. Her horrified reaction amused him. "Why would Blanca even go there?"

"We think they took her there or dumped her," Simon said, immediately sobered again by the thought of what he had to do next. "I have to drop you off and go tell Andy."

Emma sniffled and wiped the tears on her sleeve then put a hand on his arm. "Do you want me to go with you?" Her eyes brimmed with sympathy.

This time, her dad met them with his own. "That's sweet, baby, but no. It's official, and it's going to be hard. I should do it myself."

Emma stiffened the seat, staring straight ahead again and gritting her teeth. "I hope you find the fuckers who did this and kill them."

"Jesus, Emma," Simon was taken aback, even embarrassed that his kid was talking like that so much these days. But then, he wanted that too, though he sure wasn't going to tell her.

"What? They deserve it," Emma said, eyes changing from sadness to conviction, even a flash of anger. It reminded him too much of her mother and he looked away.

"Don't talk like that, please," he said.

"You know you cops say that stuff all day," Emma whined.

"That doesn't mean I want to hear you doing it," Simon said.

She pulled her hand away and sighed. "Was it someone you're investigating? My God, she's pregnant! Oh, that's so much sadder!" As she realized it, she started crying again. "Poor Blanca. Poor Andy. I really liked her."

Simon nodded, choking back his own tears again now. "Me, too, kiddo. Me, too."

For the rest of the drive home, they hardly spoke. Instead, Emma flipped on the radio and tried to find cheerful pop music she could sing to. Simon just let her, even though he hated her music, and drove in silence, brooding over what had happened to his partner, thinking of how hard it would be to tell her husband, and wanting so much to do as Emma said: find the fuckers and kill them all.

SIMON LEFT EMMA at the Fairway house and drove south on I-35 to Grandview, promising her he'd bring dinner when he returned while making her swear she'd get to work on her homework. He had little confidence she actually would, but at least he'd tried. Parking at the curb in front of Blanca and Andy's house, Simon sat there trying to gather his words as the engine shut down. There was no easy way to say what he had to say. He was about to speak with a man who'd just lost everything that mattered. For the first time he wondered why he'd volunteered for this.

"Because you loved her, too, chickenshit," he mumbled, then reached for the door.

Sliding out, he shut the car and clicked the automatic lock on his key ring, then headed slowly for the door, ambling, and wishing it was all a dream, that Santorios would meet him at the door and tell him it had all been a mistake. Losing his wife, the love of his life, was the most painful thing Simon had ever been through to this day. Having to watch a friend going through the same thing was hard to face, but he had to and marched on.

The door opened before he got there and Andy's eyes met his, immediately ringed with worry. Cop spouses always knew—their loved one's partner showing up alone and unannounced was never good. Blond and blue-eyed, Andy Harris was of Scandinavian stock, hardy, hardworking, he'd built his own construction company from scratch and made enough to do what he wanted. These days, that included building low cost houses or remodeling in neighborhoods most people never cared about. This guy was as much about service in his own way as his wife had been. And that made what had just happened to her all the more tragic.

"What's going on?" Andy asked.

"Let's go inside and talk, Andy," Simon suggested as he climbed two steps onto the cement stoop.

"Where's my wife?" Andy demanded, eyes searching behind Simon for any sign of her. Then their eyes met and he knew. He shuffled back a step, stiffening, his eyes squinting as he gasped. "No." He turned back in the doorway. "No!" his voice was rising in pitch and timber both now. "NO, you son of a bitch! Goddamn it, no!"

He marched back into the house, swinging the door shut behind him, but Simon caught it gently with a palm and followed him inside, softly closing it behind him.

"What the fuck happened, John?" Andy demanded as tears flowed freely down his cheeks. "Where is she?"

"I'm sorry, Andy," Simon struggled for words. What could he say?

"How?" Andy insisted.

"Gun," Simon whispered.

Andy's head came up as he locked eyes with his wife's partner. "Who?"

"We don't know for sure," Simon admitted, looking down because he couldn't bear to look Andy in the eyes. His throat tightened, his belly fluttering.

"But you think you know, don't you?" Andy kept his eyes on Simon. "I was expecting her home in an hour or so. Figured you guys were swamped with the Shooting Team and evidence. She hasn't returned my calls all day."

Simon took a breath, searching for words.

"Tell me. Fucking tell me, John! I need to know," Andy said, fists clenching.

Simon nodded. "She never showed up at work."

"What?!" Andy sniffled, wiping his eyes free of the tears with a sleeve.

"I haven't seen her all day and she didn't return my calls either," Simon said. "Then they called."

"Who?"

"We don't know for sure," Simon replied. "It was before noon. We've been looking for her all day. I was out asking questions. Trying to find her."

"And no one thought to fucking call me?!" Andy slammed a fist against the sofa's armrest.

"Against policy," Simon said. "If we hadn't found anything in a few hours, I would have called or the Sergeant. But we didn't want you to worry. The whole case has been Fugazi from the start." Old Vietnam War military slang, the term meant "Fouled Up, Got Ambushed, Zipped In."

"She's fucking dead! What good does worry do now?" Andy demanded, but his eyes said he realized it was illogical even as he did and he looked away again, leaning back into the sofa.

Simon sighed and went on, "It was her informant. It was solid, but they started shooting at us."

Andy nodded. "Yeah, I saw the news. And she told me some."

Simon shrugged. "I think they took her. They were trying to get to me—"

"This is your fault?!" Andy was yelling now. "My wife and baby are fucking gone because of you?!"

"It's not that simple," Simon added.

Andy raised a hand to stop him. "Whomever they are, I want them, John. Find them. Make them suffer. Kill them if you have to. But I want them!" His eyes locked on Simon's again.

Simon nodded this time. "You know I'll do everything in my power—"

Andy wilted like a flower then, stepping back and falling to his knees. Before Simon could get to him with help, he managed to crawl back and flop onto a leather sofa. Simon rushed to his side anyway.

"I lost everything. Everything that mattered. Fuck! What am I supposed to do?" The tears were flowing now as Andy gasped for breath like his lungs had stopped working. His face was creased with panic, his eyes sunken and narrow.

"I'm so sorry, Andy. God, if I could—"

"Don't say it!" Andy snapped. "Don't patronize me. Don't pity her. It just makes it worse."

Simon shut his mouth and closed his eyes, understanding, and just stood there in silence for the moment.

"Do you want me to call someone?" he finally asked.

Andy raised his hands in bafflement. "Who?"

"If you want me to stay awhile, grab some dinner—"

"I just want to be alone," Andy whispered.

"That's not a good idea right now. Let me at least call your brother—"

"Get the fuck out! Now!" Andy's brow was creased, his eyes shiny with anger as he stared at Simon.

Simon backed away, slowly. "If that's what you really want."

"I want it. Get out." Andy looked away again.

Simon turned for the door. Andy said nothing before he reached the door and remained silent as his wife's partner opened the door and stepped outside, closing it behind him. Then Simon realized he didn't even have Andy's brother's number. He'd have to look it up. Someone should know.

He went back to the car and shut himself inside, then dialed information on his cell.

MILES HAD PARKED his BMW two houses down after following John Simon from his daughter's school to the house on Canterbury. The detective hadn't stayed long but he'd left without his daughter. The girl, a middle schooler, was home alone, and Miles now knew a whole new way to get to Simon if he needed to.

But Paul had told him to hold off. He wondered what this plan of Mister Ashman's was that would supposedly fix everything, as Paul had implied. For a moment, he considered taking the girl anyway. It seemed simple enough, especially since her dad was on duty for a couple more hours and likely wouldn't be home soon with his partner kidnapped. The detective would want to be close to the center of the investigation where he could get the latest updates, for sure. Cops tended to be intensely loyal to their partners. Something about facing life and death together and having each other's backs.

Miles had never had a partner, and even his bosses he didn't trust as far as he could spit. They needed each other but when that usefulness ended or one became threatened, anyone was disposable. That was the way it worked in the dog eat dog underworld. Everyone knew that going in, it didn't really have to be explained. Even if some tended to forget it. The only ones stupid enough to complain about it were idiots not fit for the life, and they never lasted long at it.

Miles' chest felt light, his senses heightened, even as a rush of adrenaline flowed through him. He'd been doing this since he dropped out of high school. Almost twenty years now. Only life he wanted. Only life he knew. And he delighted in imagining the things he might do to hurt Simon or his little girl. There was nothing worse for a father than knowing his child had suffered any pain, even the slightest. It could drive a man wild. Miles had always counted on that in doing his job and exploited it whenever the opportunity arose.

This would be no different.

He thought a moment. Maybe he could just go up and scare her a little bit. As a warning. That would certainly give Detective John Simon pause. Not that he had any hesitance about taking or hurting the daughter. He'd just killed a cop, a cop he'd snatched right in front of her own house the day before. Fear was not a handicap he entertained in himself. Fear was a weapon he used on others.

He shut the radio off and pulled his keys from the ignition. At the very least he should check out the house, scope it out in case they needed the info later on. So he'd go walk around while he decided what to do. He chuckled. John Simon would freak to know his partner's killer was so close to his house, right outside while his daughter was alone inside.

As he shut the door and loped toward the house, the idea of Simon's discomfort and fear caused him great delight and he cackled.

EMMA WAS ACTUALLY doing her homework. In between dancing around her room to a new Carnie Hayes CD and trips to the kitchen for snacks, that is. Carnie Hayes was a third generation country pop star whose music had struck a chord with Emma the first time she heard it. Her singles like "Born To Be Lonely," "Secret Crush," and "Walk Away From

Me, No Run" provided the perfect narration to her teenage life.

Ironically, her dad didn't hate it either, although he pretended he did. He hated lots of her other music for sure, but she'd once caught him singing along to Carnie in the kitchen when he thought she was in her room ignoring him, so she knew. Carrie Hayes at least was growing on him.

Right now, with her dad on her mind, it was like comfort music. Thinking about Blanca being dead, shot and killed by thugs who might also be after her dad, really scared her. She was nervously awaiting his return and hoping he didn't get called to anymore "official business" tonight but would instead come home and be with her. She'd feared that he'd go looking for it, wanting to be near the center of the case and stay informed; that he'd go back to the office tonight instead of coming home. So she'd made him promise with a pinky swear like they used to do when she was a kid, just to make sure.

Yeah, it was childish, but her dad kinda liked to think of her as still a little girl anyway, so he never noticed when she used that trick to charm him. It was her secret. Her mom saw right through it, though, but mom wasn't here. And tonight, she was glad. She wanted to be here with her dad, not far across the city at home. Her dad needed her right now, and she needed to know he was okay.

The doorbell rang and she flipped a switch on the remote to listen until it rang again, making sure.

Who could that be?

Then she thought maybe her dad had called ahead and ordered a pizza or something for dinner. He was lazy like that. Emma and her mom liked to cook together, but not dad. He liked it the easy way, and she supposed she understood, given the demands of his job. She didn't care much what they ate as long as they were together and everyone was safe, so she hopped up off the bed and danced her way to the door.

Peering through the peephole she saw a strange man, no one she recognized. No pizza either. Maybe he'd set it down to ring the bell. Lazy ass. Or maybe it was Chinese or something else. Whatever.

Her mouth watered at the thought of food. She was safe at her dad's home. Didn't even occur to her for one moment to worry. Instead, she slid back the deadbolt and opened the door, smiling and hoping her dad had already paid.

CHAPTER 8

SIMON STOPPED AT Subway for two foot-longs and then grabbed a case of bottled Pabst Blue Ribbon and two Diet Cokes at the Seven-Eleven next door. He popped the cap off a Pabst in the parking lot, drinking it down in a few gulps. *God, I needed that.* After he drained the bottle out the window of any remnants, he slid it back into the case behind his seat before starting the car and heading for Fairway.

Talking to Andy had been harder than expected. He knew Blanca had fallen for him because of his passion, but the fury took Simon by surprise. Not that he didn't understand or share it, of course. But he was a cop. He knew how to channel that energy. What might Andy do? God forbid if they needed someone to watch him and keep him out of trouble. The last thing the man needed now was legal problems.

Simon figured he'd check on him as often as he could. And if it became a concern, he'd deal with it then. In the meantime, he wanted to get home to Emma. Leaving her there alone after breaking the news felt wrong to him. Besides, she really seemed worried when he left and their time together was precious. She'd want him home with her at a time like this. And truth is there was nowhere else his heart wanted to be.

For a moment, he did toy with going by headquarters for an update. But instead he called Becker on his cell. Crime scene was still working the scene and there were no significant updates. No witnesses had turned up that saw Santorios brought into the hotel. The room had been rented in the office by a regular who raised no hackles. They had a name and description and homicide would track him down. She refused to give Simon the name.

"Go home and be with your kid," she told him, less an order than a warning, but he got the message.

By the time they finished talking, he was turning off the highway into his neighborhood, a few blocks from the house. He took a few deep breaths and thought about drinking another beer. No, he'd wait 'til he got to the house. No good could come from getting pulled over by local cops on an open container rap.

When he got to his driveway, there was a strange car there. Some kind of mix of station wagon and SUV. He got closer and saw it was a Mitsubishi Outlander, in obnoxious chrome coloring, too. Who the hell? Then he thought about Santorios and his breath caught in his throat as his chest tightened and he sat up straight. Shit. Had the killers found his secret home?

He pounded the accelerator and raced into the driveway, squealing to a stop beside the Mitsubishi. He was out, armed, and racing for the door before the engine even died, eyes scanning, full on assault stance. Who cared if he alarmed the neighbors, his little girl was in there.

At the door, he tried the knob as softly as it could. It

turned all the way. Unlocked. Fuck. He readied himself and then pushed hard with his shoulder, swinging the door inward even as he turned his body, raised Glock 37 leading the way as he went inside, calling, "Emma! Sweetheart, where are you?!"

He heard laughter from the kitchen and a male voice saying, "Come with me if you want to live."

In seconds, he'd crossed the floor and stood at the kitchen doorway, gun raised.

"You gotta say it tougher," Emma said. Her voice turned gruff, as macho as a fourteen year old girl can manage, "Come with me if you want to live."

"Come with me if you want to live." The man tried it again, this time with a bit of a growl. What the fuck?

Simon leaped forward into the kitchen and found Emma there, laughing...with Lucas.

Emma's eyes widened. "Jesus, Dad, why are you always trying to shoot me?"

Simon let out the breath he'd been holding, his shoulders sinking, and let the gun fall down into his right hand at his side. "There was a strange car in the drive," he said, then glared at Lucas, who had turned with a surprised look, both the android and Emma facing him now. "How the hell did you get here?"

"I drove," Lucas said simply, as if it were obvious.

"He has a car, dad, a robot with a car. Isn't it awesome?!" Emma high fived Lucas as she said it, her voice lilting with joy like some cheerleader or fangirl.

Simon holstered his gun.

"What did you think—some intruder busted in and I was

trading lines from *Robocop?*" Emma asked, as if it were the most ridiculous idea in the world.

"I am learning banter—cop talk," Lucas said, sounding pleased.

"Oh for the love of God," Simon moaned.

"I gave him all the cop movies we could find to upload to his memory," Emma said. "He's going to study them, the cadence, inflection—stuff he said you told him he doesn't do well."

"Yes," Lucas agreed, smiling at her.

Simon frowned. "Why are you doing this?"

"Because I want to help you," Lucas answered.

"And you thought coming to my private home was the next step? How'd you even get this address?"

"It was in a file on your partner's desk at the station," Lucas said. "I didn't have time to tell you how sorry I was to hear of her death before you left earlier. Before my Maker left for her lab, I explained to her I'd been helping you. That you need me. And that I wanted to stay.

"Everyone was scattering, busy, and so I wanted to find you," he concluded.

Simon sighed. "There are better ways."

Emma glared. "Stop being so whiny, dad. He's a friend, and we've been having fun. He helped me with my homework, too."

Simon scoffed. "You used a computer to cheat on your homework, great."

"I am much more than a computer," Lucas said.

Simon cut him off. "Yeah, I know, I know. But that's

beside the point. Anyway, we're not friends. He's a witness in a case."

"Well, he's my friend," Emma said, shooting him a disappointed look "He didn't give me the answers, dad," she added. "But he did help me understand the problems. I swear."

Lucas nodded. "Yes, she is very smart. It did not take much effort."

Simon grunted, "Well, let me go grab the beer from the car and shut the front door, which was unlocked, by the way." He shot Emma a look.

She blushed. "Oh shit, dad. I'm sorry."

"For the hundredth time, dammit, stop using that language," Simon scolded as he turned and headed for his car again.

"I forgot," she called after him. "When Lucas told me who he was, it was so exciting to meet a real android!"

Simon cursed to himself as he went out and pulled the case of Pabst from the back seat, the Subway bag from the front passenger side, and then locked the car with the clicker and turned on the alarm.

As he started back for the house, his eyes met a very scared looking Audrey Willis, his elderly next door neighbor, who was standing on her stoop in a bathrobe, watching Simon's house. "Is everything okay, John?" she called.

Simon smiled. "Yeah, Audrey. Sorry for the scare. Kid's here for the week and invited someone over without telling me."

Audrey shot him a funny look. "I've heard of over protective fathers, but—"

Simon chuckled as he turned and hurried toward the house. "It was a hard day at work. I'm a little on edge."

He glanced back as he stepped inside and saw Audrey finally shrug and disappear back into house. *Great, just what I need: neighbors thinking I've lost it.* He shut and locked the door, deadbolt, too, then headed back for the kitchen, anxious for a sandwich and more Pabst.

Lucas had relaxed into a chair at the table.

"I only bought two sandwiches," Simon said.

Lucas chuckled. "I do not need one."

Emma covered her mouth, stifling a giggle. "No, see, say something like, 'No thanks. I'm fine.' Or 'That's okay, I'm not hungry,'" she explained. "It sounds more natural."

Lucas cocked his head and repeated, "No thank you, I'm fine. That's okay, I'm not hungry."

Emma nodded, pleased. "Yes, that's better! You're starting to get this."

Lucas smiled back. "I will keep practicing."

Simon set the case on the counter and grabbed another bottle, popping it open as Emma took the sandwich bag and hurried toward the table. She already had an open Coke sitting there.

"I am so hungry," she said as she sat and dug into the bag.

"There's a meatball and a ham and turkey," Simon said.

"Meatball!" she said, raising her hand and opened each sandwich 'til she found the right one. "Mine!" she said greedily as she tore into it.

Simon shook his head and took a big swallow of the Pabst, then joined them at the table. Emma slid the other sandwich across to him.

"How did you think you could help me, Lucas?" Simon asked, curious what the android would say.

"Well, we have not yet identified all the men from the warehouse," Lucas said.

"Yeah," Simon said as he bit into the sandwich. That certainly was true.

"And perhaps some of the stolen art will look familiar, if you want to show me," Lucas said.

"What about your NDA?" Simon asked between bites as he paused for another sip of beer. A typical teenage food monster, Emma was too busy chowing down to chat at the moment.

"The NDA will affect some things, yes, but not everything," Lucas said. "Your partner is dead. If I can help find who killed her, it is the right thing to do. As I told my Maker. She was not happy with me, but I have freewill, and she agreed to let me choose what I want."

"That's very big of her," Simon said, still trying to wrap his mind around AI with freewill, human appearance, and so much more.

"I also feel indebted to Mister Ashman for creating the nanochips which make life possible for me," Lucas added. "Without the technologies Ashman Industries has created, I would not exist."

"This Ashman is the bad guy?" Emma asked, her face filled with realization. "Did he kill Blanca? I know an Ashman at school. What's his name?"

Lucas started to answer but Simon cut him off. "No. We don't talk about this in front of her. It is police business." He glared at Emma. "You stay out of it. You know better." The last thing he needed was his daughter accosting Ashman's kid. "We don't know for sure who the suspects are yet. That's what Lucas was saying, why he wants to help."

Emma looked disappointed as she took another bite of her sandwich and uttered a ho-hum grunt.

"I'm sorry," Lucas said.

Simon nodded. "Look, I appreciate the effort you put in, and I'm glad you could help entertain my daughter. She actually needed that tonight. But it's getting late and we've had a long day. Can we pick this up again tomorrow at the station?"

Lucas nodded and scooted back his chair, standing. "Of course. Police Headquarters. What time shall I meet you there?"

Simon thought a moment. "Well, I have to drop Emma off early—"

Emma scowled. "Dad—"

He cut her off, "—to get back on this case as soon as possible. So let's say any time after eight."

"Eight a.m.," Lucas nodded again. "I will be there. Yippeee kayay, motherfucker." He smiled.

Emma exploded with laughter as Simon frowned.

"Don't say that in front of my kid, okay? Anyway, that's not how it's used."

"I got it wrong?" Lucas looked disappointed. "I must work on this."

Simon nodded. "Yes, go do that. Good night." He wasn't sure it was a good idea to have his daughter get too fond of the android. After all, he was a witness. Simon had no intention of keeping him around for long. He'd only get in the way. Civilians always did.

Lucas bowed slightly to Emma. "It's been a pleasure meeting you, Emma Simon."

"You, too, Lucas George," Emma said, still giggling.

"My friend," Lucas added and grinned, pleased, then turned and headed for the door. Simon got up to let him out.

As he shut the door, he turned back a moment to Emma. "You two are a bad influence on each other," he said, hiding his own amusement under a scolding tone.

Emma shot him an innocent look and shrugged. "What? He wants to talk more like a cop because you asked."

Simon rolled his eyes. He had to learn what not to say around the android, he decided, but this time he was amused.

LUCAS MET SIMON at the security desk in the lobby of Central Division and they headed together for the parking lot and Simon's unmarked vehicle. Simon needed to find a Confidential Informant who could be hard to find outside a certain window so he figured Lucas could ride along and chat with him in the car.

Simon turned left out of the lot and headed for the West Bottoms again.

"What is your plan, Detective?" Lucas asked.

"There's a guy I want to talk to. They call him Mister Information. Knows everything that's happening with shipping in this town, because everyone talks to him."

"So we're going to see this Mister Information?"

Simon nodded. "Well, it's probably best that you wait with the car while I go see him. He's usually at the BNSF yard this time of day."

"He works for a railroad?"

Simon chuckled. "No, he sleeps there. This is his night."

Lucas looked puzzled. "Humans have odd habits."

"Some of us do, yes." Simon grinned.

All good investigators spent years developing their own team of HUMINT—Human Intelligence. CIs, Confidential Informants known on the street as snitches or just informants, usually played a core role in any successful investigation. Seventeen year veterans like Simon had CIs who came and went, often several times. Good CIs always went through background checks and intensive interviews to determine their motives, usefulness, and trustworthiness before entrusted by any detective. Some got killed. Some went to jail or prison. Some overdosed, because many were drug users. And others disappeared from time to time. Simon had seen it all. But Mister Information was not one of those. The former Gulf War vet, now in his late fifties, had been around as long as Simon had been a cop and played a key part in solving some of his best cases.

Mister Information was a vagrant with a Meth habit, who slept in an old abandoned boxcar that had been on the tracks at the Burlington Santa Fe and Northern Railroad yard of I-670 in the central bottoms, Kansas side, for over a decade at least. The yard itself, off 670 and Kansas Avenue, was a memorable sight for tourists and those passing through the city on the highways. In its busiest days, passersby could see trains coming in and out at all hours, loading and unloading freight, getting maintenance, and even repairs. Here, dozens of tracks converged into one and towers that resembled airport control towers rose into the air just off 635, from which controllers and others could route and reroute the various arrivals.

Simon got off 670 at Swartz Road and turned left on Argentine, taking an immediate left at 42nd Street, headed for the service road that led through the middle of the yard. Mister Information's favorite haunt rested on a short span of tracks to the south side of a cluster of many tracks in the middle—one of those spurs formerly used to change cars back and forth with incoming and outgoing trains.

The car itself was brown, like most boxcars, mostly faded dark paint with several ever-growing rust spots at various corners and the sides, including one that was starting to obscure the white Santa Fe RR emblem painted decades before on its side. Simon pulled the Interceptor to a stop on the side of the Service Road and looked for the red rag Mister Information hung on one of the car's ladder rungs every night to signal he was in. The rag looked as raggedy as the car itself—torn, remnants really, smeared with oil and dirt— it flapped in the light morning breeze as Simon grunted.

"He's in. I'll be back in a bit."

Simon climbed out and headed for the boxcars. The railyard smelled like oil, dirt, diesel and chemicals, as well as coal and dust—lots of dust. Lucas caught up with him as Simon climbed over the rails and headed for the far side of the boxcar.

"I told you to wait in the car," Simon said annoyed.

"No, you suggested I wait with the car, but I wanted to see the railyard," Lucas said. "It's my first time. I will stay back and only observe."

Simon was too tired to fight so he continued on, Lucas following. Mister Information used the door on that side because it was often shielded by other cars parked for the night. But tonight, the next two tracks to the north were clear, and the door stood half open as the two approached. Inside the car was dark, in shadows, with just a thin arc of sunlight lighting a few feet in from the open door. But Simon knew its usual occupant would be there, as always.

The first thing he saw as he climbed the short ladder beside the boxcar's door were two scruffy, worn tennis shoes. Then he saw legs and the cuffs of jeans and stepped inside. Mister Information was asleep beside a half-spilled bottle of Absolut Vodka—how the vagrant afforded it was anyone's guess. He had a dirty, holey t-shirt with a dirty, worn flannel shirt over the top and a scraggly beard and long, unkempt brown hair. His face, hands, and neck, the only exposed skin, was appropriately dirty and his head was cocked to one side on a stack of newspapers he used as a pillow as he lay atop an old army issue sleeping bag, snoring.

Simon chuckled and moved to one side as the car shook a little and Lucas stepped in beside him, staring down. Simon shot him a look and held up a palm, motioning for him to stay back.

"Is that him?" Lucas asked as he stopped in the doorway.

Simon nodded. "Yep. He's more useful than he looks."

"He's the disease and we're the cure," Lucas said sotto voce.

Cobra, an old Stallone cop film. Simon groaned. "Just let me handle this. Get the door." He stepped forward and lightly kicked on of the vagrant's shoes. "Wakey, wakey, sleepy head!" Simon grinned as he stared down at one of his best CIs. Sunlight filled the car as Lucas loudly slid back the car's metal door behind him, and Simon kicked Mister Information again.

The man's eyes flickered, then opened, and he immediately called out, covering his eyes with a forearm and sleeve. "Get that damn light outta my eyes, man!"

"Come on, Denny, I got some questions."

"What else is new?" Mister Information whined as he struggled to scoot back and sit up, still shading his eyes as best he could. "I need a drink."

Simon nodded at the Absolut. "Looks like you've had plenty."

"Hell, I'm just getting started." The vagrant grinned.

Simon gave a polite laugh and turned to Lucas. "Man's got all the info. Don't ya, pal?"

"That's right," Mister Information said proudly. "I'm an information specialist extreme!"

"He's got a b.s. and everything," Simon added.

The vagrant scowled. "Hey respect."

Simon raised an appeasing hand. "Oh, so sorry."

"What's the jig?" the vagrant asked as he slid to one side and angled himself so the light shining in behind Simon and Lucas wasn't directly on his face. Simon was thankful the breeze coming in dissipated the man's stench. He didn't shower more than twice a month at best and often got very ripe. "Can you shut the door, man?" the vagrant said, looking at Lucas.

Simon nodded to the android, who turned and slid the door back to the position in which they'd found it—partially closed.

"Nanochips and art," Simon said, returning to the vagrant's earlier query.

"What about 'em—I can't afford either one," the vagrant said and grinned a grin checkered from missing or damaged teeth. He grabbed a bar above his head, part of the closed door on the south side of the car and pulled himself to his feet. "Got a smoke?"

Simon shook his head. "No."

"You?" the vagrant looked at Lucas.

"He doesn't smoke either," Simon said.

Mister Information frowned. "Well, shit, I got some around here." He began patting himself down from upper shirt pocket down to his socks, stopping when he reached his right ankle. "There."

Pulling the jean leg up, he pulled a pack of Marlboros from his sock. "I know you hate the smoke, man." He pulled a lighter from the pack before shoving the pack back and releasing his pant leg as he moved to stand beside the door. After he'd lit the cigarette and taken a deep, long drag, he blew the smoke outside and asked, "What about 'em?"

Even in the sunlight, the vagrant's skin was so dirty, Simon couldn't tell his ethnicity. White? Asian? Hispanic? Given the texture of his hair and features, the only thing Simon knew for sure was that he wasn't black.

"Who's moving art and nanochips together? Using an old diesel rig? Could be passing through the yard or not," Simon said. "Surely you've heard something."

Mister Information shook his head. "No. Doesn't sound familiar."

"We think Benjamin Ashman might be involved," Simon

added. "We discovered some crates in his gallery's warehouse."

"Ashman? Why would he steal art or nanochips? He owns plenty of both. Makes the chips." The vagrant blew out a stream of smoke and shook his head multiple times. "Crazy."

But something wasn't right in his eyes.

"Wayne O'Dell? Paul Paulsen? A Garcia?" Simon threw out the names.

With each name, the vagrant's head shook more and more vigorously. "Not me, man. Ask someone else," he insisted.

"We both know you wouldn't be saying that if you didn't know," Simon said.

Suddenly, Mister Information leaped for the door and slid down onto the tracks, racing away.

"Son of a bitch!" Simon said as he followed. "Stop, Denny! Freeze right there!" Of course the vagrant ignored him and kept running, already three sets of tracks ahead.

He turned right to run between two more parked sets of boxcars. Lucas passed him before he got there. "Let me handle it!" Simon scolded but the android had already disappeared between the boxcars after the vagrant.

Simon pushed himself, breathing heavier as he forced his muscles to their limit and began catching up with both men. A train whistle tooted somewhere in the distance, signaling an approaching train.

Simon turned right, less than twenty feet behind Lucas now and saw Mister Information a few feet further ahead, climbing up onto a boxcar and then taking off across the top. Lucas followed on the same ladder, but Simon turned where he was and instead climbed atop the nearest car, allowing him to arrive even with Lucas and make up some slack. They both took off after the vagrant again.

Simon saw the light and fuzzy movement of the approaching engine now, headed down the track they'd just crossed between Mister Information's home and right next to the boxcars they were running on. The tracks began vibrating beneath them, the cars rocking gently back and forth as the train approached.

The android was managing to catch up now, almost in range where he could tackle or even grab the runner by the collar, but then the vagrant disappeared into a boxcar ahead. Lucas disappeared moments later.

Simon caught up in short order and saw the top bay had been left open. Below him, Lucas had cornered Mister Information.

"Don't touch me!" the vagrant shouted.

Simon bent his knees and jumped down to land behind Lucas, pausing to catch his breath a moment as he assessed the situation.

The android grabbed the vagrant and lifted him off his feet. The side door was open now, the wind snapping at them as the other train soared past, apparently not stopping here. The cars blurred by at over sixty miles per hour at least.

"Lucas—" Simon started to object but his voice was muffled by the thunder of the passing train.

Lucas swung the vagrant and hung him out of the car, a foot away from the passing cars. The vagrant screamed as Lucas asked, "When was the last time you picked your feet?"

"What the fuck are you talking about?! Let me back in!" the vagrant yelled.

"You ever been to Poughkeepsie?" Lucas asked.

Mister Information's frightened, wide eyes focused on Simon. "He's crazy! Help me, man!"

Simon recognized the quotes from *French Connection* and stepped up beside Lucas. "I told you to let me handle it."

"He was not cooperating," Lucas said plainly. "In the movies, this calls for good cop, bad cop."

The vagrant began kicking and struggling to free himself.

Lucas leaned out further, pushing the man closer to the passing train. "Go ahead, make my day, punk!"

"I can't talk," Mister Information said, his eyes pleading. "The word's out. Anyone who talks is a dead man!"

Simon grabbed at Lucas' arm trying to pull it and the vagrant with it back into the car, but the android was too strong.

"Someone threatened you?" Lucas asked.

"Who was it?" Simon said, amazed at the android's control. "Talk about what?"

"I can't, man! Please!"

"You want me to let him drop you?" Simon asked, taking advantage of the opening. He yawned and started turning away. "I'm getting bored fast."

The android pretended to lose his grip and allowed the man to swing closer to the passing train. His head now seemed mere inches from the side of each passing car. The wind ricocheting off the metal blew his hair.

"Hasta la vista, baby," Lucas said in a surprisingly good imitation of *Terminator*.

Mister Information screamed, "Jesus Christ! I'm not jiving

you! I don't want to die!"

"I thought you couldn't cause harm to human beings," Simon said, putting a tense hand on Lucas' arm. He was actually starting to worry himself now. His heart raced as his throat constricted.

"I have not yet," Lucas said matter-of-factly.

"For God's sake!" the vagrant called and Simon crinkled his nose, stepping back as the man shat himself. His face and hands glistened with sweat now.

"Jesus, Denny..." Simon said and scowled. Then he pulled Lucas' arm. "Pull him in. Now!" It was an order.

Lucas obeyed, setting the vagrant loose to fall in a heap at their feet, inside the boxcar.

"You made him crap himself," Simon said.

Lucas pursed his lips. "Then I am thankful I cannot smell."

"Yeah, lucky you," Simon turned to the vagrant. "You better start talking."

Mister Information nodded, taking a breath, then it all tumbled out, fast, jumbled. The CI didn't even look up, staring at the floor. "They wanted information on the rails. Connections with customs. Other stuff."

"Give me a name, Denny," Simon said.

"Hooked them up with this guy I know—Koslo," the vagrant replied.

"Who's running front, though?" Simon asked, referring to the warehouse crew. The chirping of birds and insects filled the air again as the last car of the passing train slid past and it moved on.

"O'Dell and this guy in a suit," Mister Information said.

"With a long, blonde ponytail. I don't know him."

"Paulsen," Simon said.

The vagrant shook his head. "I never heard his name."

"That all?" Simon asked.

Mister Information nodded, his eyes still locked on the floor.

Simon hopped down onto the ground between tracks where the train had just sped past. "Go clean yourself up, Denny. Wash those clothes." He tossed a couple twenties back on the floor beside the man as Lucas also climbed down from the car.

Together, they left him there and walked back across the tracks toward the waiting car.

"Wait! When I agreed to help you, you promised me protection, man!" the vagrant called after them.

"You wanna be safer, disappear for a while," Simon called back.

"But these guys are dangerous! You can't leave me."

Simon laughed. "You're not riding in my car smelling like that. You'll be fine." He kept walking. In truth, he knew there'd be no way for Paulsen or anyone else to know they'd even talked, unless the vagrant ran his mouth off. And he hadn't told them much. After a moment, he looked at Lucas. "I thought you had laws that prevented you from harming humans?"

"I do," Lucas said. "I did not harm him."

"Still, you can't do stuff like that."

"Threaten people?" Lucas asked.

"Scare them, yeah," Simon said. "I could arrest you."

Inside, he was rather impressed the android had gotten the information. Denny would get over it.

"But I am helping," Lucas said.

Simon shook his head. "It's against department policy for civilians riding along to interfere with official duties. But threatening a witness? My Sergeant hears about it, she'll have my badge and you will go to jail."

Lucas frowned. "I will remember."

They walked in silence for a bit, moving around the cars where Mister Information lived, the Interceptor back in view.

"But he did talk," Lucas said. "Did I sound like a cop?"

Simon rolled his eyes. "Yeah, you got a couple of 'em right. But that *French Connection* stuff was crazy."

"What is picking feet?" Lucas asked.

"Hell, they didn't even know that when they shot that film," Simon said as he punched the clicker and the car alarm beeped off, then he opened his door as Lucas went around to the other side.

CHAPTER 9

A S SIMON DROVE, he asked, "What did you do—
stay up all night watching cop movies?"

"I don't sleep," Lucas replied matter of factory.
"They are very entertaining to pass the time."

Simon grunted. "Yeah, but not always so realistic. Cops
can't really threaten or even endanger witnesses."

Lucas shook his head. "There was no danger. I knew I
would never drop him. He did not."

Simon laughed hardily. "He sure as shit didn't. What a
mess."

Lucas laughed, too.

"But let me be the cop from now on. Please," Simon
quickly added.

"You were angry with me." It was less a question and
more of an observation. "I do not understand," Lucas
continued. "I did what Policemen in movies do."

"Yes, but real cops have rules to follow," Simon said. "You
aren't a cop. You don't know. That's why you need to let me

do my job."

Lucas shrugged. "I will respect your wishes, of course."

"Good," Simon said as he pulled to a stop in an alley behind Ashman's gallery warehouse, just outside the dock entrance and settled in to watch a moment.

"What are we doing?" Lucas asked.

"Dropping by your old workplace," Simon said.

"The warehouse?"

"Yeah. I want you to see if you recognize anyone."

"They will not be happy to see you."

Simon shrugged. "I'm a cop. No one's happy to see me." He climbed out of the car and Lucas followed, moving down the alley behind him as they stealthily approached the warehouse.

"I think the best way in is just to act like we belong here," Simon said.

"I belong here," Lucas said.

"You still have a job?" Simon had wondered, since Lucas had shown up at his house the night before when he'd normally be on shift.

"My days off after the incident have now expired," Lucas said. "I return tonight."

Simon hoped it would be safe for him. "Maybe you should stay here then and watch. I'll try and lure as many as I can to the dock so you can see them. If they see you with me, it could be trouble."

Lucas shook his head. "I will be fine."

Simon stopped and locked eyes with the android. "Are

you sure?" Simon wasn't at all.

"Around here, I am just some robot. Invisible. No one notices me."

Simon shrugged. "Yeah, well, that could change real quick, pal. Let's be careful."

They started along the side of a box delivery truck backed into the dock, headed for a set of stairs leading up one end of the loading platform.

"Let me do the talking," Simon added.

Lucas just nodded and kept following.

As they drew nearer and got a better look at the dock, Simon saw the bullet-ridden wood frames and cement pillars. They were probably awaiting release of the crime scene status to do repairs. He imagined Ashman didn't like that one bit and grinned. *Tough shit.*

Simon led the way up to the dock and Lucas followed. The sound of electric forklifts and hydraulics mixed with the slamming of pallets and cracking of crates became a loud drone. A couple men looked at them and one smiled at waved at Lucas but most paid them little attention as they walked across the warehouse floor, dodging pallets and forklifts toward the shelves on the far side.

As Lucas hung back, examining faces, Simon continued on. A black man in a gray one-piece jumpsuit rounded the corner from the hallway Simon knew led to the security desk and offices, almost running into him. He gave Simon a measured look, examining them and stopped. "Can I help you?"

Simon was ready and badged him. "Crime Scene follow up."

"Shit. You guys are killing me. We can't even do repairs until you release us. What more could there be to do? Everyone was dead, you took the crates..." Evidence of the shootout was all around them—from damaged crates and cement pillars to shelves, the conveyer, and the forklifts.

"Just a few more questions," Simon said faking a friendly tone. His look told the man he had a job to do. It's all routine. Luckily no one recognized him from the other night.

"Look, my guys don't know anything about that," the man said, with the assurance of authority—a supervisor of some kind, Simon guessed. "Those people O'Dell and Garcia brought in don't work with us. We almost never see them."

Simon nodded as Lucas caught up from scanning the men and warehouse back by the dock. The supervisor's eyes filled with recognition.

"Lucas! Are you back tonight?" he asked, smiling.

Lucas smiled back and nodded. "I believe so, Mister James."

"Good," the supervisor said. "We need you. Maybe things can finally get back to normal around here." With that he shot Simon a glare.

Lucas stepped up beside Simon, like a partner, comfortable, appropriate spacing. The supervisor noticed and looked back and forth between them. "Wait. You two are together?"

"He's a witness verifying a statement. Seeing if he recognizes anyone," Simon said. "You the boss?"

James scoffed. "Yeah, I just can't afford better clothes."

Simon grunted. "I know the problem." He was wearing one of his usual affordable suits, grayish tan. "Mister James is it?"

James nodded. "Yeah, Harry James, but look. We don't want any trouble. We have strict instructions to not talk to police."

"My questions are basic and simple," Simon said, ignoring his last statement. He motioned toward the pallets being moved by a forklift nearby. "What's in those crates?"

James shook his head. "Nah, I know you need a subpoena for that."

"Can't fault me for trying," Simon said. "We're just going to look around a little and see if anyone from the other night is around, okay?"

"I thought they were all dead," James said.

"No, a few got away," Simon said.

"They're dead now, too," the supervisor said then realized what he'd done and cringed.

"Garcia's dead? The truck driver?"

James sighed but he didn't relax. He looked tenser now than when they'd arrived, his eyes weary, his body stiff. "Look. I can't be talking to you. Garcia and O'Dell. Don't know about the driver." He motioned dismissively. "You have ten minutes to go through the building. That should be more than enough. But I hear one word of trouble or hassling my people, I will have to revoke that until you get a warrant. Got it?"

"You're telling me stolen nanochips and art were passing through here and no one on day shift had a clue?" Simon cocked his eyes and mouth in a way that clearly communicated disbelief.

"I'm not telling you anything," James snapped, anxiety mixed with irritation as he shifted uncomfortably on his feet.

"Neither will my people." His hard stare made it clear no further questions would be welcomed.

He locked eyes with Simon, who raised his hands in surrender. "Yeah, okay. They don't know anything."

"Not if they want to keep their jobs," James mumbled and hurried off onto the floor to whatever task he'd been heading for.

It wasn't like Simon had expected cooperation. If Mister Information had been warned off, these people were probably scared shitless. But sometimes, people couldn't help themselves—the right question, the pressure of a cop asking, and they'd spill stuff they never intended to. It was his job to try.

Simon lowered his voice and looked at Lucas. "You recognize anyone?"

The android shook his head.

They walked together through the rest of the warehouse floor, down every aisle, employee break room, men's room, skipped the women's since there had been no female suspects, and then went out by the security desk and through the office. The security guy and a couple clerks stopped them once or twice, a few others smiling with recognition at Lucas while regarding Simon only with suspicion. Simon flashed his badge and kept going. The few he stopped to chat with wouldn't answer any questions about the night of the shooting. Their answers were always very general.

Finally, after Lucas hadn't recognized anyone, Simon led him back past the security desk and down the corridor to the back door. They left, heading for headquarters.

THEY WALKED UP the ramp into the station and climbed the stairs to the second floor in silence. A few uniforms and clerks nodded at Simon as he passed, while suspects handcuffed to chairs or being questioned checked him, some glaring. Simon ignored them as always. Unless he knew them, the less interaction the better.

"Simon, Deputy Chief Keller's looking for you," Correia called from his desk as the two entered the property squad.

Maberry turned from the desk facing Correia's. "Yeah, he sounded pissed, too." Keller had had a hard-on for Simon ever since they'd clashed a decade before when Keller was his boss. It usually amounted to nothing. He shrugged it off.

"You guys are enjoying it too much," Simon quipped as he and Lucas weaved their way toward Simon's desk. Simon saw Oglesby at his desk and nodded. "Oglesby, any progress on those nanochips?"

Oglesby shook his head. "We haven't been able to get anywhere with them."

"I thought you had the numbers—"

"The list is fuzzy," Dolby said from her desk nearby.

"Surely they have the information in a database," Simon said.

"But we need a subpoena to search it," Dolby said. "No probable cause."

"Probable cause?! We're trying to help identify items in a theft they reported!" Simon protested.

"Proprietary data, trade secrets," Dolby said.

"They say we don't need to access the database if we have the list," Oglesby said.

"That is bullshit!" Simon replied, and saw the others knew it as well. The standard run around. If the nanochips were legit, there wouldn't be a problem. Just another reason Simon was convinced they had something to hide.

"Simon!" the Sergeant's voice cut through everything.

Simon smiled. Ah, the sound of a normal day. "Morning, Sergeant."

"Get in here!" she said loudly. She was tense, unfriendly. Something wrong.

Simon shot her an innocent look. "What?"

"What is *he* doing here?" she demanded as she saw Lucas.

"He was helping me try and ID some suspects," Simon replied, motioning for Lucas to stay behind as he headed for the Sergeant's office.

"You're off the cases he witnessed," Becker said, brow creased in frustration. "What suspects could that be?"

"Have a seat at my desk, okay?" he said to Lucas and nodded.

Lucas said nothing as he headed for Simon's desk. Simon just turned and walked toward the Sergeant.

"The rest of you get back to it!" she scolded, glaring at the detectives and others staring at them now.

Simon said nothing, moving past her into the office as she shut the door behind them.

"You're late," she said.

"I clocked in before eight," Simon said. "Check the log."

"Then where you been?"

"Out gathering information and driving the witness around," Simon said.

"Just like you did the other day when you went to roust Benjamin Ashman at his own gallery?" she asked, as she sunk into her desk and leaned forward, elbows resting on her desk, eyes meeting his.

"I was merely asking questions. It's his thugs that got rough."

"Given your usual personable manner, I shouldn't be surprised."

Simon grinned. "Not my fault he wouldn't shake my hand, Sarge."

"This isn't funny," Becker scolded, staring. Simon stopped grinning. "How'd it go with Andy?" she asked, softening a moment.

Simon shook his head. "He wants revenge."

"Shit. Just what we need."

"He just lost everything," Simon added. "He needs time."

"We better have someone watching him just the same," Becker said.

"He'll calm down in time," Simon said. "I can take him to the shooting range. Help him work it out."

She shook her head. "I'll get the psychologist on it."

"I thought that was just in house," Simon said.

"He'll recommend someone."

Simon shrugged. "Probably a good idea."

"What the fuck are you thinking taking a civilian out on a

roust?" she said.

"I wanted to see if he recognized anyone, any of the art."

"Did he?"

"Yeah, a couple."

"Keller is furious with you," she said. "You already knew he was tight with Ashman. Same social circles. He's been asking for you."

"I can deal with Keller," Simon said, and he meant it. He'd been there before.

"Not if you act like the same smartass you are with me," she said.

"What is it this time—"

The office door slammed open and a shorter man in his early sixties with a round face, growing paunch, and graying hair stormed into the office. Deputy Chief Kenyon Keller was pure politician, who'd come to the force from the military and worked his way up over twenty-five years, many thought by doing the minimum necessary to keep his nose clean. As an administrator, though, he'd proved quite competent, even if his manner didn't inspire morale in his men, he was a superstar at paperwork.

"I've been looking for you, Detective," he said angrily.

"I was out in the field, working," Simon replied nonchalantly.

Becker walked over and closed the door behind the Deputy Chief as he squared off to face Simon, looking him over.

"Don't give me any of your lip, Officer," Keller said, deliberately leaving off Simon's rank this time in an attempt to irritate him. "You have been harassing citizens in pursuit of a case that you were instructed not to work. And we've had multiple complaints."

Becker returned to her desk and sat. "Why you don't we sit down and discuss this?" she suggested, smiling at the Chief, but he ignored her. She motioned to Simon but he just stared back at the Chief.

"This whole case has been bullshit from the start," Keller continued. "You went to that warehouse looking to find something, shot it up, killed a bunch of men, and now you're trying to frame Ashman."

"I'm trying to find out who's involved and who might have kidnapped and killed my partner!" Simon snapped back, his patience thin. "A cop is dead!"

"And you really think one of the most important men in the city, a great philanthropist and supporter of the arts is responsible?" Keller looked incredulous. "He has an art gallery and his company manufactures those nanochips."

Simon shrugged. "They checked out as stolen. Serial numbers were on a list for an open case. Ask Oglesby and Dolby." He looked at Becker for support.

She shook her head. That just pissed him off. She had always backed her people up in the past when they deserved it. Whose side was she on here?

"What evidence besides their presence at the warehouse and manufacture links them to Ashman?" Keller demanded. "Finger prints? Witnesses?"

"There were a few partials on the frames of the artworks," Simon said. "Nanochips were clean. But they are usually handled with gloves due to risks involving static electricity. PRINTZ showed all the men at the warehouse had criminal pasts."

"But you didn't connect them to Ashman?" Keller added.

"Not directly, yet, no. We don't know who hired them, but—"

"Someone wrote the numbers down wrong," Keller continued, jabbing Simon in the chest with a finger. "And the art belongs to the gallery. They don't have room to display the entire collection at once. They switch it out from time to time."

Simon stopped back, shoving Keller's finger away and shot him a confused look. "Evidence confirmed those serials. And if the art was routine, so be it, but we had to check it out. We had a solid informant."

"A man we can't even interview," Keller snarled.

"Because he's dead! Come on!" Simon looked helplessly at Becker, who gave him a look that said her hands were tied. Simon's stomach tightened as he reached up to rub his aching jaw. "We did this one first. They fired at us. We had to protect ourselves."

Keller shook his head. "Those confiscated crates are being returned to Mister Ashman tomorrow morning. The case is closed for you. And you are not to go near Mister Ashman, his gallery, warehouse, or employees again. If I find out you do, I'll have you up on charges."

"Sergeant—" Simon looked at Becker, surely she'd back him.

"This comes from Chief Weber," Keller said. "It is settled." He poked Simon's chest again, hard.

Simon whirled his head and glared. "Keep your hands off me, Keller!"

Keller stepped forward, their chests almost touching and looked up, locking eyes with Simon. "That's Chief Keller to you, *Detective*!" He said Simon's rank like a curse word.

Becker stood and stepped between them. "Both of you! That's enough." She looked at Keller. "I'll be calling to verify this with the Chief myself."

"Go right ahead!" Keller snapped and glared at her, then turned and stepped around her moving toward the door.

Simon held his hands to each side and backed away. "*Deputy* Chief Keller."

Keller exhaled loudly, annoyed by the jab, then stopped at the door and nodded to Becker. "I don't want to hear about this again, Sergeant."

"I'll handle my men, sir," Becker said with a nod.

Keller glared at Simon one more time, then whirled and marched to the door, swinging it wide with a loud squeak and slamming it behind him. Eyes turned to stare behind him as he stormed angrily through the squad.

Becker sighed and returned to her chair. "Asshole."

"And then some," Simon agreed.

"For now, you need to step back and wait 'til I call the Chief," she said.

"Come on, Sarge! That was a good bust!"

"A good bust the suits have nullified," she said. "I have to follow orders, too. I'm sorry."

"God damn it!" Simon slammed a fist against the back of a chair facing her desk and turned away, knuckles white.

"Do you want to take a few days off? Get yourself together?"

He shook his head. "No, I need to be working."

"Well, it can't be on this," she said plainly. "Bailey and Tucker are working it hard. We have to wait and see what they find."

"Fine. Can I go?" Simon turned back, impatiently meeting her eyes.

She examined him a moment, reading him. "Where are you going?"

He shrugged. "Gotta give the witness a ride home, and then I guess I'm back here working that paperwork."

Her face suddenly took an apologetic look. "That'll have to wait. First, Shooting Team's in interview two. They've been waiting to talk to you for three days."

"Son of a—"

"It's procedure, and you know it," Becker said, not buying his enraged act. "Get it over with. You did nothing wrong. Forget Keller. It has to be done."

Simon let his arms drop limply at his sides in surrender. "Yeah, yeah."

She smiled, sympathetic. "That time off's available if you need it. After this. I'll get someone else to drive your wit home."

Simon gave a curt nod of agreement. She grabbed a folder off her desk and waved dismissively. That was it.

Simon turned, opened the door, and stormed toward his desk, knowing he wasn't about to do any such thing as stop looking for Santorios' killer. He'd just have to try and do it off the radar. Call in some favors.

He motioned for Lucas to stay put as he moved past his desk, the other cops and residents of the squad room watching him go. He turned down the hall and headed for the second interrogation room in silence.

CHAPTER 10

SHOOTING TEAM INTERVIEWS almost always took place in the same interrogation rooms officers used to interview subjects about their cases. In this instance, Simon wound up in the room next to the one where he and Oglesby and Dolby had questioned Lucas George two days before.

Sitting around the table, waiting for him when he arrived, were two Shooting Team members—Bahm and Beebe—an odd pairing officers had taken to calling "the BBs." Given the department's fondness for acronyms, officers often found themselves making humorous acronyms of their own. They referred to all kinds of things, in this case, the two detectives were females in their fifties who often worked together on such interviews. Marge Bahm, a fellow property detective from another division, had her hair in a bun, was slightly older and had the grandmotherly, school marm look. She dressed in older suits that she'd clearly had for years, out of fashion shoes, and button down shirts with ruffles like something out of the 80s. Lena Beebe was younger, just having turned fifty, wore her hair cut short and straight. She wore dark glasses and inexpensive but comfortable modern suits and shoes. Her expression was always stern. In fact, the rumor was she never smiled. Simon had certainly never seen it in seventeen years. She'd served alongside him in fraud for two years before Simon left for pleasanter surroundings, but he'd had many encounters with her over their mutual time on the force.

The other occupant of the table was the Police Union rep, Sergeant Anthony Raymond, who was one of the few gay officers on the force, a good friend of Bailey, the homicide detective working Santorios' case. He was a former career street cop, now finishing his twenty years on desk duty, but he loved cops, was intensely loyal to the boys in blue, and was personable, kind, and unfailingly trustworthy. The best kind of union rep—one even tough, suspicious IAD investigators had trouble finding fault with. And they found fault with everyone by nature.

Simon sat next to Raymond across from the two shooting investigators, a digital recorder sitting on the desk between them. Technically they were his peers and on his side, but while Baum was fair, he just couldn't trust Beebe.

"I think we're ready," Raymond said as Simon shook his hand in greeting. He didn't bother offering to shake hands with the Shooting Team. Neither of them showed much interest. They had a job to do.

Bahm nodded to her partner. She, at least, seemed friendly. Beebe was thoroughbred bitch. She reached out and flipped the record button on the recorder to "on."

"Wanna tell us why you've been out working the street for three days and unavailable for this interview?" she demanded.

Simon shrugged, leaning back in his chair. After seventeen years, he'd been through enough post-shooting interviews for them to be routine. "My partner got kidnapped and murdered. Frankly, I was working on paperwork the first day and then got busy trying to find who did it. I forgot." And that was the truth, he had.

"We're sorry about your partner," Bahm said, her face sincere with sympathy.

Simon nodded to her. "Thanks."

Beebe showed no emotion. "You've been a cop what— sixteen years?" The mistake was deliberate, an attempt to piss him off.

Simon didn't take the bait. "Seventeen. Three longer than you." He returned her stare.

"Then you've been on long enough to know policy," Beebe said. "Officers stay out of the field until officer-involveds are fully investigated and cleared."

"Yeah, I know the policy," Simon said, this time allowing annoyance into his voice. "My fucking partner was murdered."

"Watch your language!" Beebe scolded.

Bahm put a hand on her partner's arm. "We know you've been through a lot. And this should be routine."

"Master Detective Simon is not under suspicion?" Raymond asked, wanting to confirm, as was his job.

"No, we understand the suspects shot first and forced the detectives to engage," Bahm said. "That's not in question."

"Then why the hostility?" Simon said, staring at Beebe.

"We have a job to do," she replied coldly. Undeterred. "You should have stayed at your desk."

"When someone shoots your partner, you do that," he snapped, then looked at Bahm. "I hope that never happens."

She nodded. "Thanks. Of course."

Beebe shot her partner an annoyed look, then turned back to Simon. "Okay, I wanted our objection on the record. Were you involved in an officer involved shooting two days ago on Monday, October 15th?"

Simon hated the standard questions but he knew they were just following rules. "Yes. With my partner, Detective Blanca Santorios."

From there the interview continued routinely, with no further press from either Shooting Team officer. Simon answered all of their fairly usual questions and they concluded the interview in around forty-five minutes. It was like any other officer-involved incident interview, thankfully. After his encounter with the Deputy Chief, he'd half-expected them to be looking for an angle they could use to make trouble for him, but despite Beebe's usual coldness, that didn't happen.

Afterwards, he went back to the squad but found Lucas gone as expected. He wondered who had driven him home. Sitting at his desk writing up routine reports on the morning's activities with Lucas, he remembered what Keller had told him about the evidence from the warehouse. He wanted to go take a good look at it before it got released, so he decided to head over to the property office on Holmes and take a look.

As he approached the Interceptor, still debating about taking his own car, a tinny voice startled him. "We're not gonna fall for any banana in the tail pipe."

He turned to find Lucas standing nearby, smiling. Clearly he was trying to lighten the mood. Everyone in the squad room had probably heard Keller and Simon yelling through the walls earlier.

"I thought you left?" Simon asked, clicking the unlock on

the keyring for the Interceptor.

"They offered, but I told them I took the bus," Lucas said.

"You lied?"

"I ride the bus sometimes," Lucas said. "I wanted to talk to you."

Simon grunted as he climbed in behind the wheel. Lucas got in on the opposite side.

"I heard the Chief."

Simon sighed. "Yeah, well, he's never liked me."

"What are you going to do?"

"Right now?" Simon asked as he shut his door and started the engine. "Go look at the evidence before they release it. Do you need a ride to your car?"

Lucas shook his head. "No. Can I come along?"

"You heard my Sergeant. She wasn't happy with me taking you."

"I know, but it was my choice," Lucas said.

"That doesn't matter. It's not a good idea." And Becker's frustration with him aside, she always had her people's back, a fact he'd just been reminded of when she stood up against Deputy Chief Keller. It would be foolish to push her, though.

"Okay, but I was wondering if you could show me some of the items from the warehouse. I might recognize something and be able to call up visual memories," Lucas said.

"Visual memories?" Simon shot him a puzzled look.

"My digital cameras record everything I see," Lucas said.

"Great," Simon frowned. He hated life in the fishbowl of

modern surveillance technology, no matter how much it came in useful at times on the job. "Big brother always watching us. I thought you said you erased all the warehouse stuff under orders from the boss?"

"Except when they want it saved for some reason. I just thought if I saved any memories with pictures, I might also have images of faces you'd recognize—"

Fuck. No matter how much he hated it, if it led him to Blanca's killers, he'd never regret it. Becker would just have to understand. "You know, maybe you looking at the evidence isn't a half-bad idea. See if you recognize any of the paintings."

Lucas looked pleased and shut the passenger door. "Of course. I have an excellent memory."

"Yeah, lucky you, your head is a computer."

"Welcome to the party, pal," Lucas quipped.

"*Die Hard,*" Simon mumbled.

"You really do know those movies," Lucas said.

Simon grinned. "I like action. What can I say?"

Lucas laughed as Simon backed the car out and headed for the exit.

THE KCPD'S PROPERTY AND Evidence Section was a few blocks from headquarters in a rectangular, brick building that took up an entire block at 1525 Holmes near East 16th Street. The street entrance was framed in white cement surrounding a metal door with a shatterproof glass window half-covered in informational flyers—rules of access, hours, warnings, etc.

Simon parked the Interceptor at the curb out front and led Lucas to the door. Pushing the buzzer, he badged the security camera and waited for the buzz signaling the lock had been released by someone inside. Then he opened the door and led Lucas in.

The lobby consisted of a few tables and chairs along the front wall where evidence boxes could be pulled and reviewed, and a counter on the opposite wall, caged, with an opening behind it leading into a large warehouse-like room filled with row after row of wood plank shelves. The shelves were each numbered on the end as were the aisles, with big numbers on the cement floor, and then the individual shelve slots also bore numbers. This way, evidence boxes could be stacked and logged with a number coded system.

A black female evidence offer met Simon at the counter. "Can I help you, Sergeant?"

Simon pulled a slip from her pocket and handed it to her. "Looking to examine evidence on a case I'm working." The tile floor beneath his feet was shiny, reflecting the old fashioned fluorescent bar lighting overhead. The place smelled of industrial cleaning products with a faint remnant of dust.

"R-917004," she said and typed it into a computer. "Some of that evidence has been scheduled for release tomorrow."

"Yeah, that's why I wanna get a look at it before it goes," Simon said.

The evidence officer raised an eyebrow. "Wow. There's a lot."

"I'll just be skimming a few boxes randomly, I think," Simon said.

The evidence officer looked at Lucas. "Can I see your badge?"

Before Lucas could answer, Simon shook his head. "He's with me. Witness. Security officer from the warehouse where we impounded the crates. May need his help for some identification."

The evidence officer looked Lucas over for a few minutes, then apparently decided he looked harmless and nodded. "Sign the log."

She pointed Simon to a tablet resting on a stand facing him across the desk from her. He flicked the screen with a finger and a screen came up asking for his badge number and finger print. He scanned his badge number by holding it against a small glass screen then held his right index finger on it as flat as he could. A green LED moved up and down, registering the print before the screen clicked and a record screen popped up listing his name, rank, unit number, badge number, and time of sign in. It also had the picture from his official ID. He looked younger, he thought, and realized he probably needed to update the photo after a decade just so it was more accurate. You never knew when someone would make an issue of it.

After the pad beeped, the evidence officer pushed a button and a gate at the north end of the desk buzzed. "Come around."

Simon led Lucas over and pushed through the gate, holding it as the android did the same.

The evidence officer met them near the opening to the backroom. "Probably easiest to set you up back there. Take forever to pull them all down and you said you only need a few."

Simon nodded. He wanted to do this quickly in case word

got back to his Sergeant and Captain or the Chief. "Can I borrow tools to open them?"

She nodded. "I'll get you what you need."

She led them down aisles in a winding pattern that seemed random, but Simon knew she knew exactly where she was going. The cleaning fluid smell disappeared behind an overwhelming smell of old cardboard, dust, and various evidence from drugs to gunpowder to a variety of things. Some of the smells were dampened by evidence bags, others were quite prominent, and together they mixed into a cornucopia that wasn't awful but certainly nothing pleasing.

As she turned the corner on another aisle, Simon spotted dust and tape cracked with age on some of the older evidence boxes and crates. Those were the ones which had been there, untouched, for many years. Since evidence was processed and stored in order of receipt, evidence from cases of all kinds was mixed on the same shelves. So the older stuff was all together and as they approached their destination, the evidence containers got more modern and cleaner, as if they'd been freshly examined.

Finally, several aisles and rows in, she stopped and pointed to a familiar looking set of crates stacked on a nearby shelf numbered 8601. "Here."

Simon nodded. "Thanks."

She looked at Lucas again. "He doesn't touch them, but you can pull items and show them to him, okay?"

"I know the rules, yes, ma'am," Simon said.

She motioned to a toolbox at the end of the aisle. "Crowbar, screw drivers, box knives, etc. Put back what you use."

"Yes, ma'am. Thank you," Simon replied.

With that the evidence officer nodded to them each in turn, then whirled and headed back the way they'd come, moving much faster on her own than she had leading them.

"She was suspicious of me," Lucas said.

"It's her job," Simon said. "Don't take it personally."

"No. I found it curious."

Simon examined the crates for a minute, a few with splintered holes from the shooting still in their sides. Then he stepped up and began lifting them down and setting them on the floor. Looking at Lucas, he said, "Get me a crowbar, hammer, flathead screwdriver, and box knife, will ya?"

Lucas nodded and went down to the end of the aisle, retrieving the requested tools from the toolbox, then came back and offered them to Simon.

Simon had pulled a half-dozen crates of two different sizes down and stood looking at them.

"May I assist you?" Lucas asked.

"No." Simon shook his head. "Let's start with these." Taking the proffered crowbar, he bent down and pried at the lid of a large crate. Jiggling it back and forth, up and down, he managed to pry open the lid with the squeak of nails and then set the crowbar down and set the lid aside. The crate was filled with art wrapped in bubblewrap over brown paper and foam.

Using the box knife next, he carefully slit the sides of one of the art pieces and pulled the wrapping aside until he could pull out the frame. The painting was large, about 18x24—a landscape. Showing it to Lucas, he asked, "Do you remember seeing this at the gallery?"

Lucas stared at it a moment, thinking. "Not that one, no,

but it is quite lovely. Surely I'd remember."

"No doubt, computer brain," Simon cracked. He repeated the process with several others, but Lucas didn't remember them either.

Noticing a much taller, thinner crate, Simon opened it next. Inside was a larger painting, and Simon went through the same process of unwrapping it from shipping and pulling it out. This one he recognized himself. "Springtime Dance," the Degas—prized possession of the gallery. In an intricately carved frame, painted gold, it was 24x30 and heavy enough that lifting it out had caused him to shift several times for balance.

"I remember that one from the top of the stairs," Lucas remarked.

Simon nodded. "Except we impounded this evidence Monday, and we saw it at the gallery after that. So what's it doing here?"

Lucas frowned. "That is a very good question."

Next, Simon opened another smaller crate, and this time Lucas recognized three of the works.

"Why would they have two of these paintings—one for display and one here?" Lucas wondered.

"Because they're forgeries," Simon said.

"They are fake?" Lucas asked.

"Either these or the ones at the gallery," Simon said.

"But they are identical." Lucas shot him a puzzled look.

"Designed to look that way, certainly, but not exactly. There will be subtle differences. If we show them to an expert."

Lucas sighed. "Ah, but they are being released. So we don't have time."

Simon shook his head. "I can't take that chance. Wanna do me a favor?"

Lucas smiled, pleased. "Of course."

ELIZABETH DOMS HAD worked evidence at the KCPD's Property and Evidence section for over a decade. It was quiet and boring at times, but there was a rhythm to it, and details mattered. She prided herself in her organization and adherence to procedures. It had been rare occasions on her watch when evidence went missing or misfiled. Keeping it straight was her job and she would do it well. And she was lucky enough that at least on day shift, her key co-workers felt the same or stayed enough out of her way that she could do it her way.

As she sat at the desk, logging in newly arrived evidence boxes, the sound of scraping and banging caught her by surprise. Someone was disturbing her evidence warehouse. She tensed, frowning, and stood from her stool, hurrying toward the door. She hoped it wasn't the Master Detective and his odd companion. They'd had so much to review, she'd chanced leaving them alone so she could get back to her work. She had a heavy load today. Now it sounded like she'd regret that decision.

"What the hell is that?" Corey Satterfield, another evidence officer, older with gray hair, asked from down the counter as he processed evidence requests on his computer.

"I don't know!" Elizabeth replied, not hiding her irritation, and hurried back toward the warehouse.

As she raced through the aisles looking for the source of the disturbance, she spotted movement a few aisles ahead. Picking up her pace, she raced around a corner to find the detective's companion, a dark complected, tall bald man—he'd called him a "witness"—removing crates and boxes at rapid fire pace from shelves, dusting them with some kind of blower, and putting them back.

"What are you doing?!" she demanded as he put a crate back.

"Dusting," the man said, shaking his head. "It is very dirty in here. How do you breathe?"

The dust had never bothered Elizabeth. "I use my lungs, stupid. You stop that right now."

"But they must be cleaned before someone gets sick," the strange man said, his voice oddly tinny. And he kept right on lifting and dusting and replacing.

Elizabeth raced forward, trying to interfere and stop him.

SIMON HID IN an aisle near the front, waiting until the evidence officer was drawn by Lucas' distraction, then he dodged up front, let himself through the gate, and slipped out the metal gate. A gray-haired white male evidence officer glanced up from the far end of the counter.

"I have to get something from my car," Simon muttered.

The man said nothing and turned his attention back to his

computer screen as Simon slipped out the door, walking nonchalantly to the Interceptor and climbed in. Starting the engine, he pulled the car forward, turned right into the parking lot adjacent to the Property building and headed back toward the rear of the building and the double doors he'd left unlocked there.

The doors were alarmed. So once he opened them, he'd draw the attention of everyone on duty. But he'd checked before finalizing his plan. The officer who usually guarded the dock was on lunch break. And Simon had found a few plastic bags and slipped them quickly over the dock cameras before going to retrieve his car. He figured the chances were no one sat around watching the cameras. They only looked when they had reason to. So hopefully, no one would notice the dock images had clouded over until Simon and Lucas were long gone.

Parking his car outside the dock doors, which were level with the ground, he paused in the car a moment, considering what he was about to do. He would be risking his entire career if he followed through with the plan. Then the image of Santorios' dead body lying in the Admiral Motel flashed into his eyes and he opened the door and climbed out without a further thought. He had to do this.

He raced up and put his ear to them listening. He could hear Lucas and the black evidence clerk talking loudly. If he did this right, he could grab the painting he'd stashed close by and get it into the back of his car before anyone made it back to the door.

He took a deep breath, visualizing his steps, then smiled. Ready. Time to initiate phase 2.

He placed his hands on the doors and swung them open.

THE ODD MAN was being very difficult. Elizabeth was about to draw her service weapon and threaten him, something that would make her feel foolish, but no matter what she said or did, the damn fool wouldn't relent and stop his stacking and dusting in her property room.

Then the dock alarms sounded. *Shit.* She saw Corey enter the warehouse and glance that way, then hurry toward it and decided she should stay here before this man did more damage. Drawing her weapon, she shouted, "Freeze!"

The odd man stopped and looked at her, eyes widening in shock. "You wish to shoot me for cleaning?"

"I've asked you to stop several times, now do it!" she said. She heard the sounds of voices and feet running as other staff headed to check out the breach. It was under control, good.

The man raised his hands and backed away. "I was just trying to be of service. Someone has neglected their duties."

"I don't dust," Elizabeth replied, angrily. "Now you get back out of here, right now."

"But the detective—" the man protested.

"I will find him and throw him out when I'm done with you!" Elizabeth said. She took a moment to examine the shelves he'd touched. They actually looked cleaner and more neatly stacked than before. No obvious harm. That almost irritated her more. *Damn fool!* She waved her Glock 37. "Go!"

The man nodded and began walking back toward the front of the building with Elizabeth following behind. She wondered if the detective had just been too lazy to watch his charge or if this was some kind of corrupt plot and the breach was connected. Why anyone would go to so much trouble was beyond her.

She holstered her gun and shoved the odd man forward through the door to the front. "Get out of here!" she ordered, then turned as Corey returned from the dock. "What's going on?"

Corey shook his head. "The alarms must be malfunctioning. We're checking the tapes. Doors were locked and sealed. No sign of anyone." He looked puzzled as he hurried back to his terminal and went back to work.

Elizabeth watched as the odd man exited through the metal gate with a clang and continued on toward the door. He gave her no more trouble and she smiled. "This one was disturbing shelves."

"Disturbing?" Corey looked up, curious. "What was he doing?"

She rolled her eyes. "Dusting."

"Dusting?" Corey looked both surprised and confused.

"Yeah," she said. She knew it sounded crazy because it was. Who came to a police evidence warehouse to clean? Nutjob! She'd have to look up the name of that Detective and file a report. She'd do that after she finished logging in the new arrivals. First things first. And she went back to her own terminal and set to work.

SIMON AND LUCAS chortled as soon as Lucas climbed into the Interceptor again out front and they drove away.

"She was quite confused by me," Lucas said.

Simon grinned. "I'll bet. Probably thinks you're crazy."

"Won't she report it?"

Simon nodded. "Sure. And I'll claim you wandered off when I went to get something from my car and got interrupted by a call. Next thing I know you were out at the curb. I couldn't take you back in, so we left."

Lucas smiled. "You are very clever."

"Thanks," Simon said, pleased with himself.

"Did you get what you wanted?" Lucas asked.

Simon nodded, motioning behind them to where the Degas lay, wrapped again in the shipping materials, lying flat across the folded down back seat of the Interceptor all the way to the rear door. A couple smaller paintings lay on top of it. "Enough to make the case I need to."

He'd also taken a few nanochips, tucking those in his jacket pocket. He'd resealed all the crates, so chances were no one would notice anything missing until Ashman's people opened the crates on the other end. By then, the report of the evidence warehouse breach would become the focus, Master Detective John Simon and his crazy witness forgotten in the embarrassment of property owned by a prominent citizen, friend of Chief Weber, having been stolen right out from under them at the property warehouse.

It was hard to believe it had gone so smoothly. Simon chuckled and turned up the radio to Blake Shelton's latest, singing along. Lucas smiled beside him.

CHAPTER 11

AFTER DROPPING LUCAS off at his car, Simon spent the afternoon working his contacts. He wanted a bit more information before they took action on the evidence he'd confiscated. He and Lucas were meeting at the City Diner on Grand Blvd. early the next morning and would go to the gallery straight after, just as it opened, before the evidence was released to Ashman's people. Simon wanted to see if any of the paintings they'd found in evidence were still at the gallery. It would help confirm his hunch about the forgeries.

He also called a forger he'd once arrested, who now occasionally worked as an informant and set up a meeting for the following day. He did the same with a chip expert he'd also arrested, who worked for a lab that made custom motherboards and other products involving special chips. They were one of Ashman Industries' best customers.

Next, he called Bailey and Tucker, the homicide detectives working Santorios' case, who were based at Police Headquarters off Locust in downtown Kansas City. Although they wouldn't tell him everything, they were following leads to Ashman's men. No one else was a suspect at the moment.

"What can you tell us about the husband?" Bailey asked.

"Andy?" Simon replied, confused by the question.

"Yeah, he seems very hostile."

"He just lost his family. He's pissed. Like anyone."

"More than normal."

Simon shrugged, even though he knew the homicide detective couldn't see it over the phone. "He's emotional. So was his wife. Made them a good fit. Want me to talk to him?"

"Nah. Someone's keeping an eye just in case."

"He's good people, Tom," Simon said. He'd always liked Andy. And he knew his word would go a long way with the two detectives. Tom Bailey and Jerry Tucker had been around for fifteen years, almost as long as Simon. They'd been partners most of that time. They were experts at what they did. He trusted them. But that didn't make him any happier to be sidelined. And knowing they were keeping stuff from him set him on edge. "You have any trouble, call me."

Bailey agreed and hung up. He hadn't revealed much, but Simon knew he couldn't expect much more. They probably had orders from the fourth floor—Administration—to keep him away from it.

Not wanting to be overheard by Becker or any of her sources, he was making the calls from a booth in a Denny's off Broadway. Not the best food, but cheap and open 24 hours, so they were used to cops and gave them extra attention and service, while still keeping enough distance not to eavesdrop, at least most of the time.

Next, he called an old friend, also a Deputy Chief, named Greg Melson. Melson was one of those guys who'd started out a few years before Simon and worked his way up through sheer determination and hard work. Not overly political, instead he was one of the few administrators who got promoted on sheer skill and extraordinary competence. He and Simon had worked a few cases back in the day, and there was no one in Administration Simon respected more.

"Hey, John, how ya doing?" Melson asked, tone sympathetic as he thought of the detective's recent loss.

"Okay, Greg. Day to day, you know," Simon replied.

"Fucking tragedy," Melson said. "I'm so sorry. If there's anything I can do..."

"As a matter of fact—"

"Hit me," Melson said, no hesitation whatsoever.

"I need a little background on a certain prominent citizen. Any suspicious activities, past investigations, anything connecting him to smuggling or anything else," Simon said.

Melson grunted. "Benjamin Ashman. I know for a fact you were told to stay away from that."

"What are they covering up, Greg?" Simon didn't bother denying it. Melson was a friend he could trust. Someone who'd understand.

"Truthfully, nothing I know of," Melson said. "The man's pretty clean. Oh there's always talk, especially about rich guys. Everyone suspects with money and power comes corruption, of course. But this guy seems like the genuine article. Far as I know."

"Can you dig around a little? Let me know if there's anything we don't know about?"

Melson paused a minute, thinking. Probably debating the risk and cost to him of being caught. Political or not, he valued his job and pension. And Simon knew having him there benefitted the rest of the straight, nonpolitical, dedicated cops like Simon who served underneath him. "Unofficially," the Deputy Chief finally replied, "I'll do a little looking. But I have to be very careful. No one can know. So it'll take some time."

"Understood," Simon agreed. "I appreciate it."

"Of course, John," Melson replied. "Hey, keep your nose clean. Don't go off the deep end over this. Bailey and Tucker are the best. They'll find what there is to find."

Simon nodded. "I know that. Doesn't make it any easier. Anyway, I got some suspicions about the evidence from that warehouse shooting."

"Thought they were returning it tomorrow?"

"They are," Simon said. "But I took a look this afternoon. It's hinky, Greg. Might be a mistake. I just want to be sure."

"Not much time. Good luck."

"Yeah, thanks." Simon kept the facts about confiscating some evidence to himself. No need to involve anyone else, put them at risk.

"You're one of the best, John," Melson said then. "You hang in there. I'll be in touch."

"Thanks, Greg," Simon replied, just as the Deputy Chief hung up. He sat in his chair for a while, thinking over all the facts and evidence he'd uncovered related to the warehouse, Ashman, Santorios.... He wondered what Oglesby might know. Dialed him up at his desk.

"Central Property. Detective Oglesby."

"Martin, it's me, Simon."

"Hey, John. Where are you? Boss is asking."

"Working from home today. Just needed some quiet."

"Gotcha. What's up?"

"Just wondering what you thought of them declaring those nanochips legit—the idea that you got the numbers wrong."

Oglesby paused a minute, then his voice got quieter, almost a whisper. "Bullshit. Those numbers were checked and double checked. They were reported stolen by Ashman Industries' shipping partner."

"Then what's going on?"

Oglesby grunted. "You tell me. Why would Ashman steal his own nanochips?"

"How could you guys get the numbers wrong? Didn't they send over a sheet?"

"Yeah, a scanned list but parts of it were fuzzy. They make the case that it's those numbers that are involved."

"Fuck me," Simon said.

"Fuck us," Oglesby corrected.

"Any chance he's not involved—his own people working behind his back?"

"Of course," Oglesby agreed. "But seems unlikely. We're quietly making some calls."

"Good. Let me know what you find, okay?"

"Of course."

"You gonna be at Santorios' funeral Saturday?" Oglesby asked.

It was a dumb question. He already knew the answer. Simon wondered what the fellow detective was really asking. "Yeah, I'll be there, of course. Supporting Andy. Paying respects."

"Have something for ya then, if I can. Meanwhile, keep your nose clean."

"'Kay, thanks. Tell Becker I took her advice and took a couple days off. Slept in. Forgot to call, okay?"

"She won't buy it," Oglesby chuckled.

"She won't be happy but she did suggest it."

"You got it."

Simon hung up knowing that now his only choice for the moment was to wait. Checking his watch, he saw that he needed to pick up Emma in an hour. Perhaps tonight he'd take her out for dinner and a movie—daddy-daughter date. It had been too long. She'd love it.

Picking up the check waiting on his table, he downed a last cup of coffee and stood, heading to the register to pay his bill.

SIMON DROPPED EMMA off at school forty-five minutes early, making her promise to study extra for her math test in fifth period that afternoon, then drove back to downtown Kansas City to headquarters. He'd promised to meet Lucas at the City Diner in thirty minutes but first, he wanted to see if he could beat the homicide shift in and get a look at their file on the investigation into Santorios' killers.

Homicide consisted of four squads on the 9th floor, each in cubicle farms with sergeants much like property. The homicide office was quiet, but Simon lurked outside waiting for someone to come by or leave. After a few minutes, a custodian appeared, pushing his cart out the key-carded door.

"They're not in yet, I believe," the custodian said as Simon held the door for him.

"Yeah, but the Sergeant said to meet him here in ten minutes. I was just gonna wait." Simon flashed the custodian his badge.

The man shrugged. "I suppose don't matter none. Good luck." Simon let him by and he kept on rolling his cart toward the next squad as Simon slipped inside.

Simon went straight to Bailey's and Tucker's cubicles which faced each other. He quickly thumbed through the files piled on each desk and found nothing with either the case number or Santorios' name, so instead he hurried over to file cabinets along one wall where he knew homicide detectives kept their active case files.

Yeah, Bailey had talked to him, but revealed nothing Simon didn't already know. He knew there had to be more. He'd done the same to other cops inquiring on cases they were too close to, so he suspected Bailey was holding back most of what he and Tucker had uncovered, and Simon needed to know what it was.

The cabinet was locked, but Simon had long ago learned how to pick basic locks. He looked around again quickly to make sure no one had come in or was watching him. Still clear. It took him only a few seconds with to open the file cabinet with two paper clips off a nearby desk. It was meant to deter snooping, not prevent it. Then he began flipping through the files labeled with Bailey and Tucker's team number—three. Nothing.

He was quietly shutting the file cabinet when someone cleared their throat behind him. He turned around to find Detective Jerry Tucker sipping a cup of coffee and watching him.

"Find anything good?" Tucker teased.

Simon sighed. "I was just looking for the daily logs. Melson said I could see them."

Tucker was chubby with a round face and white Santa Claus beard, his white hair cut short on top, his skin freckled from years of sun and beginning to wrinkle and show its age. Five years older than his partner at fifty-two, he looked like a wise, kind grandpa, which was ironic considering he'd been widowed a decade earlier by cancer and had no offspring. Still, being easy to talk to had served him well as a detective, but his normally soft green eyes focused on Simon in a hard stare now. Simon didn't feel like talking.

"Deputy Chief, eh? We were told you were to stay off this case," Tucker said, sipping again as he shot Simon a cockeyed look.

Simon cursed inwardly, putting on his best sheepish grin. "Well, worth a shot."

"Get outta here. We keep those files in the Sergeant's office, and you know his locks aren't so easy to pick."

Simon groaned. "Come on. She was my partner. Can't you at least tell me something? Who you're talking to? What you've got?"

Tucker shook his head. "I know how you feel, John. Really. I wish I could. But Deputy Chief Keller backed the order to keep you excluded for now. It's outta my hands."

"Shit." Simon nodded, his shoulders sinking along with his hope of keeping track of the case. He glanced at his watch—he had ten minutes now to meet Lucas. "Thanks, Jerry. Thanks a lot." And from his tone, they both knew he didn't mean it.

Before the other detective could respond, Simon shoved

his hands in his pockets and marched toward the hallway and the elevator waiting beyond.

THE CITY DINER was part of a large building on Grand at East 3rd, on the northeast corner, and you could find it from three blocks away in any direction just by following smell of bacon and grease. A local institution, it was located in a large, square cement building with neon lighting, signs, and checkered tile under the outside windows off the street. Inside, the diner had a long black and white counter surrounded by white tables with black, faux leather chairs and it served old style diner food. Burgers, steaks, chicken, sandwiches, soups, salads, and breakfast—most famously its giant, plate-sized pancakes. The walls were white brick, the menus laminated.

Simon ordered two of the monstrosities, like always when he made it to the City. Cheap, fast, hot, tasty food. It wasn't fine dining but it was a lot cleaner than most greasy spoon diners of the past. And the whole place smelled wonderful— a glorious mix of eggs, meat, oil, grease, toasting bread, and other flavors that made Simon's mouth water.

Lucas, when it was his turn, threw the waitress a curve. "Gimme a diablo sammich and a Dr. Pepper. And I'm in a goddamned hurry."

"What?" she asked, with a puzzled look.

"He'll have water," Simon said, shaking his head. "He doesn't eat."

"What's a diablo sammich?" the waitress asked.

Lucas leaned back, amused with himself.

"It's a line from *Smokey and the Bandit,* an old movie," Simon said. "He's being a smartass. Sorry. Just ignore him."

The waitress shrugged and left to place their order.

Simon glared at Lucas. "You think that was funny?"

"Yes, it is a very funny movie."

Simon rolled his eyes. "It's not nice to confuse people like that."

"Should I apologize?"

"No, when the food gets here you just shut the fuck up and take a few fake sips of water from time to time, okay? I won't be long."

"Ah, shut the fuck up again, your favorite phrase," Lucas noted.

"Anyone ever tell you that you talk too much?"

"No," Lucas said.

Simon rolled his eyes. In less than five minutes, the food came and Lucas did as asked, saying nothing further while making a good show of sipping at his water.

Afterward, they arrived at the gallery in ten minutes, right at nine as it opened for the day.

Simon led Lucas inside like they owned the place, ignoring the stares of a few employees who recognized them and heading straight for the nearest paintings.

"You remember these?" he asked Lucas.

Lucas nodded. "Some of them."

"I thought you had a camera in your head," Simon said. "Run it back or whatever you do. Check."

Lucas smiled. "I am. Some of them are in different places. Others are different."

Simon looked at him, wondering why he hadn't expected it. "Different how?"

"Not the same works."

Simon locked eyes with the android. "You mean some that were here the other day are gone?"

Lucas nodded. "They have rotated them, I suppose."

"The ones we saw at the evidence warehouse?"

"Yes, all of them are those we saw."

They'd covered their tracks. Simon cursed, then turned, spotting the stairs and hurried toward them, climbing up to look for the Degas he knew had a place of honor at the top.

It was gone, too. Replaced by a large, disturbing scene of dystopia, pain, horror credited to someone named Heironymous Bosch.

"Son of a bitch." Simon had never been a big art fan but this was one of the craziest, most disturbing images he'd ever seen. The crazy German was off his rocker. Probably killed himself for being so damn depressing. He turned and hurried back down to join Lucas.

"They hid them," he said as they stood together again, looking at more paintings.

"Why?"

"They knew we might catch on if we opened those crates," Simon said.

"But they are getting them back."

Simon nodded. "At noon today. But they had no idea if we'd opened them. It's a good thing I did."

"What will we do?" Lucas asked.

"Go see an old friend," Simon said, motioning toward the door. "Come on."

"Hassling my employees again?" a familiar female voice said.

Simon turned to see Stacey Soukup, the beautiful gallery manager. She looked even more stunning than he remembered. Simon coughed to cover the fact his mouth had fallen open as he stared. His heart threatened to burst from his chest with its pounding.

He recovered and smiled. "Actually, I was leaving them alone. We came to look at the art this time."

She gave him a quizzical look, not sure if she believed him.

"Look, I want to apologize for the other day," he added. "I was upset—"

"I read about your partner in the paper," Stacey interrupted, truly sympathetic. "I'm sorry. That must be hard."

Simon sighed. "Yeah, she was special. Real tragedy."

Stacey cocked her head toward the paintings nearby. "Find anything you liked? Had questions about?"

"Just getting a feel for it really," Simon said.

"There are some beautiful pieces," Lucas agreed, still examining several bright colored landscapes hanging on the wall nearby. He kept moving his head back and forth, scanning in a very odd, not very human way.

What the hell are you doing? Simon shot him a look and smiled at Stacey, hoping to distract her. "Is Mister Ashman in? I should apologize to him."

She shook her head. "No. Not today. Not sure if he'd be ready for that."

Simon laughed. "Yeah, well, fair enough. Asshole moment. My bad."

Stacey smiled warmly, accepting it at face value. "He's a good man. If you only got to know him."

"Maybe he is. Wonder if I'll ever get the chance. My boss likes him."

"Yes, Chief Keller is one of our finest patrons."

Lucas suddenly turned and looked at them. "You know we could show her the paintings, ask her—"

Simon shook his head harshly.

"What paintings?" Stacey asked, brightening with decided interest.

"She should be quite familiar with them," Lucas said.

"Familiar with which? I'm always happy to help," Stacey offered eagerly.

Simon elbowed Lucas in the side hard before he could say more.

Lucas stepped back, rubbing his side. "Why are you hitting me?"

Simon distracted Stacey with a different approach. "Can I ask you a question?"

"Of course," she actually seemed pleased that he would.

"We noticed some of the paintings we saw the other day are not here, or at least not where they were..."

Stacey stiffened a bit as her lips pursed in obvious frustration. "They were taken out for some special private exhibition the day after you were here."

"A private exhibition?"

"Yes," she shook her head. "I was given no notice. Mister Paulsen insisted on it. There was a memo from Mister Ashman. Something for a rich friend."

"You don't seem very pleased about it."

"They took out some of our prize pieces," she said, nodding. "Not only does it risk damage, but having so many gone at once has really hurt our number of visitors and public interest. Some people traveled far to finally come see the Degas and other key pieces, and they didn't enjoy showing up to find them suddenly gone."

"Don't galleries like this do private exhibitions often?" Simon asked.

"Sometimes, yes," she replied. "But we plan them in advance and give public notice. And we've never had so many key pieces missing at once. It's bad business to have most of our most popular pieces gone at the same time."

Simon grunted, giving her a heavy nod. "I'm sorry. I know this place means a lot to you."

She took a deep breath, recovering. Stretching her arms as if to shake off the frustration. "It means a lot to a lot of people. We've worked hard to make it a wonderful collection. We're very proud of that."

"It's wonderful," Lucas commented and Stacey smiled, but he never turned around.

"Your friend wanted to show me something?" Stacey asked, looking at Lucas.

"He was just curious about the missing pieces," Simon said quickly. "Photographic memory. He really liked them."

"I like them, too," Stacey said. Lucas turned and they exchanged a pleased look.

Before Lucas could say anything else he shouldn't, Simon cleared his throat. "Well, I better get out of here before one of Ashman's men sees me and gets the wrong idea." He turned and tapped Lucas on the shoulder. The android nodded to Stacey and turned for the door.

"It was nice seeing you, detective," Stacey said.

"Thanks. Nice seeing you, too, Ms. Soukup," Simon replied.

"You remembered my name?" She blushed a little, eyes sparkling.

"Well, it's on your name tag," he motioned to the plastic tag clipped on her blouse.

She turned redder, face falling. "Right."

Simon laughed. "You're cute when you blush. Don't worry about it. Detective's observation skills. You have a great day."

She managed to smile again, raising her hand and wiggling her fingers in a child-like wave as Simon turned and followed Lucas back outside to the car.

"Where are we going now?" Lucas asked as Simon clicked the lock open on the car with his keyfob.

"To see an old friend who knows his art," Simon said.

"Why did you not ask her about the paintings?" Lucas asked as Simon went around the car to get behind the wheel.

"Because no one's supposed to know we have them," Simon answered, shushing him.

"But if no one can know, how do we verify your suspicion

that they are forgeries?"

Simon opened his door and motioned for Lucas to get in the car. "Just trust me."

"That would be easier if I understood what's going on," Lucas observed as he opened the door and climbed into the Interceptor.

"Yeah, but less fun for me." Simon shut his door and turned on the engine. Moments later, they were pulling away, heading for Union Hill.

FOR MOST COPS, not a day went by that you didn't meet someone who could only be classified as one of a kind, unique. Murray Barber was one of those people. He lived in one of the city's oldest neighborhoods, Union Hill, in a restored house dating from the 19th Century. One of several on a short street not far from Crown Center, one of the city's leading entertainment complexes, Murray, as everyone called him, shared it with his two wives—one legal, one common law. It wasn't the only time Simon had seen such living arrangements in seventeen years on the Force, but Murray had been the first, when the detective first encountered him as a newly minted detective almost a decade ago.

Murray had become one of Simon's first informants, extremely knowledgeable and connected on the area of art and the arts. His specialty was forgery, because when they first met, Murray had been under suspicion of it himself. In fact, Simon had busted him and sent him to prison for several years. But it had been John Simon who also testified at his parole hearing and helped get him early release for good behavior. For while Murray was definitely guilty of forgery, he was also guilty of being one of the most charismatic, charming individuals John Simon had ever met, and he had behaved well in prison, but he'd also been one of those guys the detective learned quickly would be more use to him on the outside than locked behind bars.

So John Simon had gone to bat for him, knowing his crime had been minor in the larger scheme of things. He'd been convicted on solid evidence, but only once after decades with not so much as a ticket for speeding. Sometimes it was useful to offer good will to someone with hopes their gratitude would lead them to help you put away far more dangerous, damaging people. Murray was one of those, and Simon had never regretted helping him out.

Long brown hair braided with a bushy beard, Murray was the stereotypical hippie with a great set of Hawaiian shirts and loose dungarees or shorts suitable for any occasion. Simon couldn't recall a time he hadn't matched these with leather sandals. The informant owned several pair and they were his sole preference in footwear—winter, spring, or summer. Simon often wondered how his feet never froze, but then Murray stayed inside a lot, even in summer, so perhaps he just hibernated.

In addition to his patented look, his trademark was also that he never appeared in public without a fez bearing a helicopter blade that spun in the wind. He owned a variety, collected from years of attending fan conventions—science fiction being his favorite. Because, in addition to being a hippie, Murray was also a dedicated nerd, and one who couldn't give a shit about what anyone else thought of him. He knew who he was and he was comfortable with it so his attitude was "fuck you if you couldn't deal." Simon liked that most of all about him.

As he parked the Interceptor at the curb in front of the house, Simon ran Murray Barber's name through the KCPD system just to bring himself up to date of any recent activities. He was pleased to see the man had stayed good to his word and kept clean. Good. Simon could just deal with him for his expertise and not have him begging for favors. That would make this much easier.

He and Lucas climbed out of the Interceptor then went around to the rear, where Simon popped open the trunk and they removed the four paintings he'd confiscated from evidence. Shutting the trunk and locking the car again, Simon carried the large Degas and Lucas carried the others as they walked up the sidewalk and several cement stairs to the front porch where Simon rang the bell.

Jan Barber answered on the first ring, smiling as she saw it was Simon. "Johnny! It's been ages! How are you? Murray will be thrilled to see you."

"I doubt that," Simon replied as they hugged. Then again, Jan was that way with everyone—warm, welcoming, never met a stranger. Of mixed Asian and African descent, she had long dark, dreadlocked hair with tiny beads decorating the strands in rainbow colors. She was short but skinny, and her smile lit up a room. As usual when he visited their home, she wore a flowery sun dress that stretched down to her ankles.

Pulling away, she examined Lucas and asked, "Who's your friend?"

"This is Lucas George," Simon said. "Another one of my sources."

Jan chuckled. "Lucas George, eh? Mur will love that. Come in!" She stepped aside and waved them both past, making room for the bundles they carried, then shut the door gently behind them.

The inside of the house was as eclectic as its owners: trinkets, collectables, action figures, posters, art, and more decorated every surface, every spare length of wall, including two couches, three end tables, and a recliner. These included quilts, blankets, and Afghans of various sizes and colors which Jan had collected on their travels or made herself. Knitting was one of her favorite past times. And she seemed to become more and more skilled at it every time Simon visited. Some of her creations were so intricate they truly amazed him, especially knowing she made them from scratch out of her head with no patterns.

Murray's other "wife," Linda, Hispanic, round in body and face, poked her head out the door from the kitchen and waved. "Hey, John! He's in the cave as usual." That meant Murray was in the add-on out back, his workspace, hobby room, and office all in one. Simon had been there many times but Jan led the way anyhow.

"Good to see you, Linda," he called back, returning her smile. She wore hand embroidered tie-dyed clothing either from Africa or Latin America. She had a variety and they were her favorite casual wear for home.

Both women, like Murray, were in their fifties or sixties. Simon had never had occasion to check them for sure, just their husband. And they were too nice for him to invade their privacy. If he didn't have need of the information, he preferred to leave it alone, especially for such nice people. Murray had faced the consequences of his actions, including the attendant invasions of his privacy, background checks, interrogations, and more, but why should his wives suffer for his mistakes?

They passed through a dining room with a table that

could seat twelve but currently had barely three spaces left clear. The rest was covered in boxes filled with old magazines, documents, books, and more. Probably one of the occupants' latest sorting project in nostalgiaville. The three of them were not idlers, for sure, always keeping busy in one way or another.

After the dining room, they followed Jan down a short hall and into the add-on, a wide, open space which was all Murray. His prized collectables, books, and more filled every shelf, chair, couch, table, and space. Including a large, antique Oak desk that sat at one end. Murray himself was dancing around the room, smoking a cigarette, totally unaware of their presence, until Jan walked over and turned the music down—classic Bob Marley—and cleared her throat.

"Hey!" he protested, whirling around, and winked when he saw her, then spotted Simon and Lucas. "John Simon, you son of a bitch. Who let you in?"

Lucas looked taken aback, but then Murray just burst out laughing and Jan and Simon joined him, as Simon set down the Degas, leaning it against a nearby table, and the two men embraced.

"I busted in, used my gun and everything. Warrant," Simon said.

Murray frowned. "Son of a bitch, I knew I shoulda kept that cocaine in my hideaway."

Simon grinned, knowing he was kidding. The hippies smoked cigarettes of all types, but pretty much shied off other substances, even limited their alcohol. Murray claimed he was "too old for that shit," when asked. And Simon knew he'd had a triple bypass a few years back and probably been warned by his doctors and wives that he should take that mantra for real.

"You're too old for that shit," Simon teased.

Murray and Jan laughed.

Jan shook her head. "He knows you too well, Mur."

"Dear God, that he does. All my secrets. Poor bastard." The hippie winked at his wife and blew her a kiss.

She chuckled and waved at Simon. "I'll leave you to your business. Don't get him too excited. Heart can't take it."

"He lives with two wives," Simon replied. "Somehow I think I'm the least exciting part of his day."

Murray flapped his eyebrows and guffawed. "Great way to keep in shape. You should try it."

Simon grunted. "I'll take that under advisement."

Jan motioned to Lucas, meeting Murray's eyes. "That one's named Lucas George."

"No fucking kidding?" Murray chuckled. "Nice to meet you, sir. It's like a childhood dream come true."

Lucas accepted the proffered hand and shook it, even while shooting Simon a confused look. "Uh, thank you. You also."

Murray eyed the paintings, getting serious now and let him off the hook. "What you got for me?"

"I need you to look at these and tell me if they are originals or fakes," Simon said, cutting to the chase.

Murray nodded and grabbed the Degas, lifting it up onto the table where Simon had leaned it against, then began tearing off the shipping materials. "Where'd you get these?"

"You're better off not knowing," Simon said.

Murray raised an eyebrow. "And you say I'm the criminal."

Simon raised his hands in mock innocence. "I got the badge to prove it."

"Fuck you," Murray teased then pulled back the last of the covering and took in the Degas. "Wow. A Degas. Well done, too. This might take me a day or two."

"I need it faster," Simon said.

"Oh, like I got nothing better to do than wait for you to show up and drop everything."

Simon grinned. "Don't make me lock you up again."

"Can you give me overnight?"

"Yeah, but I'm gonna check in late afternoon, just to see what you turned up."

Murray made a face. "Slave driving capitalist pig."

"I've been called worse."

Murray snorted. "Hell, you've been called worse by me."

"Don't remind me," Simon said, shaking his head at the memories.

Murray nodded, then looked at Lucas. "You be careful out there with this guy. He attracts trouble like Wile E. Coyote, brother. Everywhere he goes."

"He does attract much action," Lucas agreed, clearly wondering what a Wile E. Coyote was.

Murray chuckled. "Poor bastard knows you well. Be safe, Simon."

"You, too," Simon said and turned for the door. He knew the hippie would want to get to work right away and further conversation would only provide a frustrating distraction, so he led Lucas back through the house.

They said quick "goodbyes" to Jan and Linda, declining the offer of fresh lemonade and cookies, then let themselves out and headed for the Interceptor.

"They seem very nice," Lucas said. "Are they not mad that you put the man in prison?"

"He was guilty and he knows it," Simon said with a shrug. "Besides, I also helped him get out."

"You are a perplexing man, John Simon," Lucas replied, pondering the meaning of this.

Simon nodded. "Now you sound like my ex-wife."

They climbed in the car without further discussion.

CHAPTER 12

NEXT, SIMON DROVE them south to Overland Park and Nichol Labs, where he had a friend who specialized in custom chip installs. Julia Liu was young, only a decade older than Emma, but she was a Korean American prodigy, having finished high school around Middle School age and then defeated college in her late teens. Now, she was a highly paid expert working at one of the top tech companies in the Midwest. Why there and not one of the coasts where she might make three times the money, Simon didn't know, but the one time he'd asked she'd told him: "My family's here—four generations, since we came over from Korea after the war. Where else would I wanna be?"

That pretty much settled it as far as Simon was concerned. Few white Americans kept such strong generational ties. He certainly hadn't, and he admired it. Sometimes he even envied her.

The receptionist out front was gorgeous, but it took two words for Simon to evaluate her as not the brightest apple of the bunch. She seemed out of place here in a world of intellectual elites like Julia, but someone had to answer the phone. She let them back without delay because Simon had called ahead and made an appointment. She offered to show them the way, but Simon had been there and declined.

Julia's office was in a small room with four cubicles in a back corner of the third floor. The building was one of those tinted glass monstrosities of modern architecture that rose into the sky like black ghosts, reflecting back light and images of everything around them to anyone passing within view. The inside smelled as sterile as the outside looked. Simon's nose found nothing of interest until he entered Julia's office and caught a faint whiff of fruity perfume.

A large, tinted window made up most of the wall behind the row of cubicles. Currently, the cubicles on either side were unoccupied—their occupants likely off doing various errands, eating, or in meetings. Julia waited in her middle cubicle, waving when she saw Simon enter from the winding halls and rising to give him a quick hug and a peck on the cheek.

"You look good," he said.

"You too," she responded, smiling.

"This is Lucas George, a friend," Simon said, motioning to his companion.

Julia offered her hand and they shook as well. "Mmmmmmmm, synthetic. You're working with an android?"

Simon groaned, while Lucas looked both disappointed and surprised.

"How did you know?" the android asked.

"I wouldn't be much of a tech expert if I didn't keep track of trends," Julia said. When Lucas still looked sad, she added, "Your body temp is too low for a human, sorry. It's a very good likeness. Most people would never notice."

"They don't," Simon agreed.

Lucas brightened. "There are twelve in my line. Others are

Paul, Anna, Susan, Judy, Mildred, Henry, Martin—"

"This is why we're here," Simon interrupted, pulling the confiscated nanochips out of his pocket and handed them to Julia. She unwrapped them delicately and began examining them.

"Hmmmm. High end stuff. Ashman Industries," Julia said, confirming what Simon already knew. "Very fast, probably like what he runs on." She nodded to Lucas.

"I believe they are," Lucas agreed, looking pleased.

"Where'd you get them?" Julia asked as she used tweezers carefully to pick up one of the chips and put it under a microscope on her desk.

"Confiscated evidence from a potential smuggling case," Simon said.

"Ooooooh, smuggling nanochips, easy to do," she commented as she closed one eye and looked through the lens, concentrating.

"The serial numbers were reported stolen, then not," Lucas added helpfully.

Julia looked up at Simon, puzzled. "What does that mean?"

Simon shot Lucas a silencing glare. "He's confused. I need you to check the serials, see if they hold any data, et cetera."

"Well, these types of chips tend to work as processors to speed up various functions, commands, et cetera. They are not memory chips so much as worker chips. But there can be some embedded memory." She squinted through the microscope. "Write this down."

She read off a sequence of numbers Simon knew was the serial number for that chip. He wrote it down in his notebook, then waited.

Next, she took the tweezers, pulled the chip off the scope and inserted it carefully into some kind of adapter which she then inserted into the computer terminal on her desk. Numbers and code began flashing across the screen for several minutes, until finally a beep sounded and a command prompt appeared in a window.

Julie typed in coded instructions and a directory of sorts opened.

"Hmmmm, this is interesting," she said. "A lot more in memory than I'd expect. This may be higher end than I thought, something new."

"Can we look at the data?" Simon asked.

She grinned. "Who do you think you're talking to? Gimme a moment." Her fingers moved across the keyboard like lightning as she typed seemingly endless sequences of commands and codes, then finally waited.

Windows began opening with various data. It took thirty seconds or so, but then the final of two dozen or so windows settled onto her screen. Flashing across the top in red text was: "National Security Agency-Top Secret-Eyes Only!!!"

"Holy shit," Simon said. His whole body tightened, a heavy feeling in his stomach. What had he stumbled onto?

Julia nodded. "Holy shit is right. This is government stuff. Stuff we shouldn't see."

She was right. This case had just become a lot bigger and more dangerous than he'd imagined. His skin tingled as he locked eyes with her. "I need to know exactly what it is, what's its purpose," Simon said. "What are these guys into?"

Julia sighed and leaned back cocking her head. "We can

both get in big trouble for this." She pushed a button and the screen flushed, the adapter holding the nanochip popping from her drive. "Call me tonight. At home. I'd better not do this here. But I'll do my best."

Simon nodded his understanding. "I owe you."

Julia rolled her eyes. "What else is new?"

He leaned in and gave her a quick kiss on the cheek then headed for the door.

"Don't be such a stranger," she called after him. "Lucas, nice to meet you. Love the last name!"

"Nice meeting you also," Lucas commented then followed Simon back out and down the hall.

As they got back to the car, the radio beeped.

"186."

Simon picked up the handheld from its Charger and clicked the transmit button. "Go ahead."

"Responding unit requesting your assistance at 287 South Arbuckle for shots fired," the dispatcher added. "Suspect is named Andy Harris."

"Shit!" Simon keyed the radio, "186, 1010," then looked at Lucas and motioned for him to hurry. "Let's go."

"What's going on?" Lucas asked.

"A friend is involved in a shooting and they want me there," Simon said.

"Probably someone you told to shut the fuck up," Lucas said. Simon shot him a look and realized that in spite of his straight face, the android had told a joke. Lucas looked pleased with himself.

"Shut the fuck up," Simon replied as he flipped on the

lights and siren and peeled out, heading for the highway.

PAUL PAULSEN HAD a small, almost closet-sized office just big enough for a desk, chair, and one file cabinet next to Benjamin Ashman's at the gallery. He was leaning back in his chair talking on a burner phone when Miles burst in.

"They took some of the nanochips and four paintings," Miles said, out of breath from running down the hall.

"What? Who? Hang on," Paul put his hand over the phone as an accented voice mumbled with impatient acknowledgment.

"The cops, man. We just finished inventorying the goods."

"Shit! You're sure?"

Miles nodded. "Positive."

"This could endanger everything. Get back on that fucking detective and follow him! The whole mission's at stake," Paul ordered. Miles grunted and turned, hurrying out as Paul took his hand off the phone. "We have a problem."

"I thought it was handled?" the South American on the other end said.

"So did I." Paul frowned.

"What happened now?"

"The cops kept some paintings and nanochips from the warehouse."

"Fuck! Find out who and get them back."

"Yeah, I'm pretty sure we know where to start. Miles is on it."

"Miles is an unbeliever."

"I know, but he's good at his job."

"I'm sending my people to help."

"We got this," Paul insisted, his lip curling back at the idea of direct interference. He ran his hand through his hair, scrunching his face. Thank God the contact couldn't see him.

"It'll be cleaner with my men," the South American replied. "Besides, you've said that before."

Paul cursed to himself. He didn't need his men to believe in the mission, just to fear and obey him. Or be greedy enough to like the good money he paid them. He made sure his voice was steady as he replied, "Whatever you want."

"You're goddamn right. You people have done enough to jeopardize the operation already." The caller slammed down the phone with a loud click and Paul hung up.

"Fuck you, too," he mumbled and wondered if the South American had just set in motion events that would make it worse.

A thought occurred to him and he leaned forward and picked up the phone again, dialing quickly from memory. He waited a few moments until a voice answered. "You still have access to traffic cameras, yes?"

"What do you need?"

"Can you track a specific vehicle?"

"I can give you recorded activity for the past month if you want."

Paul smiled. "Great but I just need the past day or two." He pulled a note from his desk where Miles had written down John Simon's license numbers for both his official and personal vehicles. He read them off.

"Give me two hours." The contact hung up.

And Paul leaned back in his chair and relaxed.

IT TOOK SIMON fifteen minutes, speeding with lights and siren spinning, to reach the scene—a construction site in a new development on the south end of the city, bordering Grandview. It was an area many cops lived, not far from where Blanca and Andy had their home.

A uniform lifted the yellow police tape, and Simon pulled the Interceptor to a stop behind the V of two black and whites. Four officers were there, including Sergeant Anthony Raymond and his partner Angela Peterson, whom Simon knew well. The other two were African American, both buff and tall, like linebackers, yet all four officers were cowering stiffly behind their vehicles, all but Raymond aiming shotguns. Raymond had a Glock 37 like Simon's.

Simon motioned for Lucas to stay down as they got out of the vehicle and approached, Simon loosening the clip on his sidearm as he walked bent over to join the responding officers.

"What have we got?" Simon asked.

"Fucking contractor went nuts, started shooting up the place with an automatic rifle," Peterson said.

As if prompted, Simon heard yelling and then several rifle blasts followed by splintering wood and shattering glass. The responding officers tensed, hands readying on their weapons.

"He's shooting up his own construction site?" Simon tried

to think of a motive and looked to Raymond for answers.

Raymond sighed. "Andy Harris."

Simon nodded. Santorios' husband. "Dispatch told me. Did you talk to him?"

"We tried," Raymond said.

"Just screams at us a bunch of gibberish about 'unfairness,' 'wanting her back,' and such," Peterson said, "then starts shooting again."

"He just lost his wife and child, Peterson," Simon said. "It's not gibberish."

Peterson shrugged. "People mourn in different ways."

"Who called it in?" Simon asked.

"Apparently he showed up while his own crew was working, had an argument with the foreman, then just started shooting up the frame, windows, roofing," Raymond replied. "They all took off. A few are down the block, waiting."

"He didn't shoot anyone?"

The sergeant shook his head. "Not yet."

Simon nodded and ran bent over back to his car, popping the trunk with a click of the key fob. He pulled out and began strapping on his black, Kevlar vest as Lucas appeared beside him.

"What are you doing?" Lucas asked.

"I need to talk to him," Simon said.

"Alone? Isn't it dangerous?"

"He knows me. I think I can talk him down," Simon said. "Just need to distract him, calm him down."

"Can I help?"

Simon thought a moment, eying the android. "You can't be in there. You're a civilian. Too dangerous."

"Bullets cannot kill me easily," Lucas said. It was an offer.

"Doesn't matter. You stay back."

With that Simon nodded to Raymond, slammed his trunk and hurried off at a run, bent over, moving around the black and whites toward the half-finished house.

"Cover the detective," Raymond ordered. "He'll try and talk him down."

"You got it, Sarge," the two linebackers replied in unison.

"Good fucking luck," said Peterson.

They all held their places behind the black and whites and watched.

Simon got to the edge of the sidewalk leading up to the front door and stopped. "Hey, Andy. It's me, John."

"John Simon?" a distraught voice he recognized called from within.

"Yeah."

"It's all fucked up, John, everything we worked for," Andy replied.

"I know. Totally FUBAR, pal, but you can start over."

Andy cackled. He definitely sounded off. "I had everything I wanted. Irreplaceable. There is no starting over."

Simon held his hands loose from his body, walking slowly up the sidewalk, ready to dive aside and pull his piece at any moment, but hoping it didn't come to that. He breathed slowly, staying calm. He'd done this before, and Andy was like family. He had to keep his head. Help his friend. Even after seventeen years, such situations could still control you. Shooters could force your hand. A cop had to stay focused and unemotional or it could all fall apart in an instant. He didn't want that happening. Blanca wouldn't want it.

"How about I come up and talk to you?" Simon called.

"You gonna shoot me?" Andy said with a chuckle.

"Hey. We're friends. I loved her, too. Of course not," Simon called back.

"Walk slowly, so I can see you," Andy said.

"Okay, but no more shooting while I'm coming up there."

"Yeah, yeah."

Simon took that as agreement and looked back at the other cops, nodding for them to stay put and keep calm. He'd handle it. They nodded back, resigned, but still on edge, ready.

Simon took a deep breath and stepped up onto the stoop, now fully visible through the open door frame where the front door would be. "You see me?" he called.

"Yeah," Andy replied. "Alone. Just you."

"I am alone," Simon confirmed, moving slowly into the framework of the house himself. He came into the middle of the front room before he saw Andy, standing two rooms back, cradling a black semi-automatic Adams Arms Evo rifle with two hands, currently aimed at the floor.

"You look like shit, Andy," Simon said, grinning, an attempt to put his friend at ease.

"I feel like shit," Andy said with no emotion, his eyes sunken, dark circles, his hair mussed. His clothes looked like he'd worn them for a week and he had several days' stubble on his face.

"You gotta take care of yourself," Simon added. "Get cleaned up for the funeral."

Andy coughed. "What's the point? I want my wife back, damn it." The last part came out with such pain, his voice cracking as he winced at every word.

Simon winced too, his heart aching inside. He wanted that, too. "I wish I could give that to you. I really do."

"We were finally getting there," Andy went on, "what we'd always worked for." His face tightened and his teeth clenched. "Then some assholes just take it all away. Motherfuckers! I want them to pay, John."

Simon nodded. "Yeah, me, too. But this isn't the way."

Andy shook his head. "I don't know what the way is."

"How about you put down the rifle and come talk to me?" Simon suggested.

Andy whirled, raising the rifle at beams overhead and firing multiple shots within seconds.

Simon ducked automatically, his hand grabbing for his sidearm, then he stopped. Andy wasn't shooting at him. It was venting. He had to keep cool. "Destroying someone's home is not the way either, Andy," Simon called.

"I fucking built it. I fucking designed it. It's not theirs 'til I get paid," Andy said, his voice acidic, bitter.

"Don't lose your business," Simon said. "You worked hard for that, too. This can be repaired." He motioned with a hand, panning the room. "But we have to stop this now."

Wood cracked off behind Andy to the north, and both he and Simon spun toward it.

Lucas was there, appearing out of nowhere, slowly stepping through a frame wall, approaching.

"Stay back!" Andy yelled, pointing his rifle right at Lucas.

"Have you ever fired a gun in the air and yelled, 'Aaaaaaaaaaaaaaaaaaaaaaaah,'" Lucas asked, clearly quoting some movie Simon couldn't remember.

Andy frowned. "What the fuck are you talking about? John, who is this?"

"Nobody," Simon said, glaring at Lucas. "Lucas, get outta here. I'm handling this." Simon turned to Andy. "He's not a cop. He's leaving."

"Badges? We don't need no stinking badges," Lucas said.

"Goddamn it, I told you to wait in the car!" Simon said, starting to lose it. He couldn't believe Lucas was doing this. He kept walking, slowly, one foot at a time toward Andy.

"Don't make me fucking shoot you!" Andy called.

"Why, Ed, are we cross?" Lucas asked.

"Ed? Who's Ed?" Andy looked around, paranoid, probably thinking there was another cop trying to sneak up on him.

"No one else is here, Andy, be cool," Simon said and glared at Lucas. "Lucas, get the fuck outta here! Now! Stop playing around!"

Andy fired three shots into a wood frame over Lucas' head. "Stop! I will shoot you!"

Simon started sliding north now, toward Andy and Lucas, afraid he might have to interfere.

"Dead or alive, you're coming with me," Lucas said, imitating *Robocop*.

Jesus Christ. What was the android thinking? Simon seriously wanted to shoot him himself.

"Okay, kid, let's do this. Come on, spread 'em," Lucas said in a tough cop voice, motioning to Andy. He was near the wall leading to the room the armed man occupied, and Andy's hands were shaking now as he pointed the rifle at the android's chest.

"I don't want to shoot you, man," Andy croaked out.

"I am the law!" Lucas said like *Judge Dredd.*

Simon looked back and forth between them. Andy's fingers were flexing on the trigger. He was pondering what to do. Whether bullets could hurt Lucas or not, he didn't want Andy to shoot him, to have to bear the burden of that. He didn't know Lucas was an android. He was scarred enough.

"Andy, look at me," Simon said, moving closer. "He's with me. I swear. He's a bit crazy, but harmless. He thinks he's trying to help."

"Is he quoting movies, man?" Andy asked, looking at Simon.

Simon nodded. "Cop movies. Emma taught him. Remind me to ground her for a month."

"Ahh fuck," Andy said and started turning back toward Lucas, but then the android was through the frame wall and five feet away, running, picking up speed, and he tackled Andy, taking him down. The Exo fell from the man's fingers, sliding just out of reach and Simon rushed them.

Andy struggled and yelled. "Get off me!"

"I am the law and the law is not mocked," Lucas said.

Simon grabbed Lucas by the shoulder and yanked him off

Andy, shoving him back while kicking aside the Exo with his right foot at the same time. Then he grabbed Andy by the arm and pulled him up, looking him over. How much did the idiot android weigh? Andy looked fine.

"You're all right," Simon said.

Lucas beamed. "I distracted him."

Simon shook his head. "Yeah, and me. You almost got shot. I told you to stay back. What the fuck is wrong with you?"

Lucas' face fell. "But I was helping. I want to help."

"That was a stupid thing to do," Simon growled, then he pulled Andy by the arm. "Can you walk?"

Andy mumbled in affirmation.

Simon led him back through the construction site toward the front door.

"We're coming out," he called ahead to warn the other officers. "Situation resolved."

Then he led Andy onto the sidewalk and down toward the official vehicles. The other officers visibly relaxed, lowering their weapons.

"Well done, Detective," Raymond said.

The other uniforms grinned. "What's up with your crazy friend?"

Simon glared back over his should at Lucas, who was standing in the front door frame, watching, a disappointed look on his face. "When I'm done with this, I'm locking him up," Simon said. "Gotta be a statute on public idiocy."

The other cops snorted, Peterson and Raymond coming forward to take Andy and cuff him.

"Take it easy on him," Simon said. "Cop's spouse. Killed in the line."

"How much damage did he do in there?" Raymond asked.

"Nothing that can't be put right," Simon said. "I think we can talk to him and avoid charges." His eyes pleaded with the sergeant.

Raymond nodded. "We'll work something out."

Peterson led Andy over and helped him into the back seat of their black and white.

Raymond motioned to the other uniforms. "Johnson and Johnson—get back out there." He was dismissing them back to the street.

"Johnson and Johnson, really?" Simon chuckled.

Raymond shook his head. "Field Sergeant thinks it's hilarious to put them together." He shook his head. "I gotta call this in."

"I'll meet you at the station," Simon said.

"See you at South," Raymond said, confirming they were taking him to the South Patrol Division nearby and headed for his car.

Lucas joined Simon, clearly confused about why the detective was mad. "No one was hurt."

Simon just ignored him and climbed into the Interceptor. Lucas climbed in the other side and Simon followed Raymond's patrol car up the street.

CHAPTER 13

A S SOON AS he made a left onto Bannister Road, Simon turned angrily to Simon. "You are *not* a cop! Not the law!"

"I was trying to help," the android replied, looking perplexed by Simon's fury. "The bullets cannot harm me like they do you."

"Doesn't matter," Simon said. "I'm already out enough on a limb bringing you along after my Sergeant ordered me not to, plus Shooting Team wants me on paperwork until I'm cleared. You putting yourself in danger time and again playing police is just going to make it worse!"

"I am a trained security guard. It's not the same maybe but I have some training," Lucas objected, almost as if he was insulted.

"Not the same thing, not at all," Simon said, looking for words to explain without insulting the android. Truth was, he'd grown to like him, even started thinking of him as a friend. But his refusal to let Simon do the police work, especially in front of other officers—including a veteran like Raymond—was pushing things too far. If Raymond reported it, Shooting Team or worse, Internal Affairs, might decide not to clear him and find more charges instead. He didn't care what the consequences were once he'd found Santarios' killers and brought them to justice, but he had to stay clear until then. Bringing them down was all that mattered to him right now. He'd deal with the rest later. He couldn't have Lucas calling attention to his rebellion against orders like that.

"Your friend with the gun was unharmed," Lucas said. "Is that not what you wanted?"

Simon exhaled loudly. "Of course, but I had almost talked him down before you jumped in." He stopped at a light, waiting, tapping his fingers on the steering wheel impatiently.

"I just want to help you," Lucas said. "I feel responsible."

The android had said he didn't have feelings. "You're not responsible. You did your duty. And in fact, your best course of action is to go back to the warehouse and do your job."

"They gave me something called 'personal leave' to recover from the traumatic incident," Lucas said. "Can I not choose to spend it helping you?"

"You helped, Lucas," Simon said. "But you've done all you can. Now it's time to let me do my job. You're getting in the way." Simon chose to ignore the fact that it made no sense to give property, especially an android with no emotions 'personal leave.' That could wait.

Lucas looked down, his eyes almost sad. But then androids had no emotion chips, right? "I understand."

"You belong to them, Lucas," Simon said. "You have an owner and an assignment. You can't stay with me forever."

Lucas nodded. "Of course. I am just property."

"In a way, yes."

Lucas' features took on a sad look as he nodded. "I have a

duty. I will do as you say." His smiled disappeared as he looked down again. "Even if I am a fake, like the paintings."

"What do you mean?" Simon looked at him as he pulled into the South Division's parking lot and looked for a space.

"I just quote cops, but I am a fake. I am not a cop."

Fuck. It was like talking to his mother. "Are you sure you have no emotion chip?"

Lucas frowned. "You already know this."

"Not even a guilt chip?"

"What is a guilt chip?"

Simon frowned. "You really know how to make a guy feel like shit, don't you?"

Lucas shook his head. "What do you mean? I am just stating facts, am I not?"

"Yeah, in a way. But you have many skills. A purpose. It's just as important as what I do in its own way, okay?"

Lucas thought a moment, then nodded. "Okay."

"But in a situation like that there's real danger," Simon said. "Your actions could result in someone getting shot— you or me or someone else. And that's unacceptable. I know you think you are doing the right thing but these situations are complicated and we have special training. You can't just improvise. Understand?"

Lucas still looked hurt but nodded as they pulled into the lot behind Central and Simon spotted an open parking space amongst the other units.

After he'd parked, Simon unhooked his seatbelt and opened his door to get out, then turned back. "I gotta go deal with Andy. Make sure he doesn't get burned for this. Wait for me here and I'll drive you home, or maybe that bench over there." He motioned to a cement bench beside the double glass doors leading into the back side of the station.

Lucas nodded. "Okay. I will wait."

Simon smiled and nodded, then climbed out of the car and hurried inside.

IT TOOK ABOUT ninety minutes to process Andy, including interrogation, checking ownership of the property, gun ownership, etc. Simon stayed beside him the whole time, making sure they gave him the best options available. In the end, because he owned the property and was building on it for resale, and because the weapon was registered to his wife, they let him off with a warning and confiscated the rifle.

Simon figured that was about the best they could hope for and then arranged for Sergeant Raymond to drive Andy home. Simon also promised to check in with Andy daily from now on.

When he got back out to the car, Lucas was waiting.

"I'm sorry I was so hard on you earlier," Simon said. "But it's because you scared me."

"I scared you?"

He nodded. "Yeah. You worried me."

"I am sorry," Lucas said.

Simon waved it off. "It's okay. I'll take you home now."

"You are late to pick up Emma," the android replied.

Simon looked at his watch. He was supposed to be picking Emma up right now. "Shit!" He started the Interceptor and began backing out of the space. "Okay, change of plans. We pick up my daughter, then I take you home."

Lucas brightened. "I will enjoy seeing Emma again."

"Yeah, she likes you," Simon said, hesitating as he remembered Emma had connected Lucas with the cop movies. What might she do next? He pulled out into traffic and headed for the nearest highway onramp to 435.

"Then you can bring me back to my car at headquarters," Lucas said.

Simon had forgot they met there that morning. "Right."

"I will try not to be a cop now," Lucas said.

Simon rolled his eyes. "Good." Simon almost missed the movie banter. Was there no in between with this guy? He turned up the radio as one of his favorite Styx classics, "Mr. Roboto," came on.

Lucas listened a moment then cocked his head. "They are singing about robots?"

"Well, kinda, I guess," Simon said.

Lucas grinned. "This is a good song."

The rest of the way Lucas listened intently as Simon pushed down the pedal and pushed the speed limit the whole way, weaving in and out of traffic. In total the drive took twenty minutes to Independence and another five to Emma's school.

As he pulled up in the circular drive he saw a few students waiting at the curb and one young couple making out on a bench but no sign of Emma. "Where the hell is she?"

he muttered, then scowled at the couple making out.

"They seem fond of each other," Lucas observed.

Simon growled. "They need better parenting." Then the couple broke it off for a moment, foreheads leaned together and giggled. Simon flashed back to the morning and realized the girl was wearing the same shirt his daughter had.

"Holy shit!" he yelled and slammed on the brakes, rolling down the windows as he glared at the bench. "Emma Amelie Simon!" He was in full on dad mode now. "Get your ass in this car NOW!"

Emma whirled, pulling away from another makeout session with the boy. She blushed. "Dad!" Then whispered loudly to the boy. "I gotta go."

He smiled at her as she stood and slung her backpack over one shoulder, then rushed for the car. The boy's eyes followed her the whole way, ignoring Simon's glares. Simon's hand went instinctually to his gun and he had to stop himself. *Fuck, just one shot in the foot to scare him...*

"Hey, Lucas," she said in sing song excitement at seeing her dad's companion.

"Would you like to ride up front?" Lucas offered.

"No, she can sit in back!" Simon snapped.

"But I wanted to drive, Dad," Emma whined as she opened the back door and slid in, depositing her backpack on the rear seat behind Simon.

"Simon says no!" Simon said, a phrase he always used with her when he was giving her an order and would accept no argument. He rolled up the windows as he glared back at her in the rearview mirror. "What...were...you...doing?"

Emma rolled her eyes. "Kissing, Dad. It's something

people do when they're attracted to each other."

Simon tensed and rocked in his seatbelt, trying to stay calm. "I know kissing, smartass. Why were you doing it?"

She shrugged as she slipped into her seatbelt and clicked the lock. "Because I like it."

Simon winced. "Jesus. Was that *that* boy?!"

"He's very handsome," Lucas said.

"Shut the fuck up! He was staring at your ass." Simon ignored Emma's "Thank you."

"He was?!" Emma said and looked away, waving to the boy as Simon pushed the accelerator and sped out of the drive way too fast.

"We made it clear you are not old enough to date, Emma," Simon said.

"I wasn't dating. I was making out," she whined, lips pursed, eyes hard with defiance.

Simon felt like his head would explode. "You're grounded!"

"From what? Dating?" She crossed her arms over her chest and stared out the window.

Lucas frowned. "You do not like this kissing? I find it most fascinating."

"You should try it sometime," Emma said and giggled.

"Simon says stop talking!" Simon said.

"God, Dad, you are such a sourpuss. Plus, you're the one who's late." She turned back to the window, not even glancing at him.

"I was dealing with a shooting call," Simon growled.

Emma's eyes widened. "Someone got shot?!" She looked back and forth between Lucas and Simon.

"It was a building," Lucas said.

"Shut the fuck up! She doesn't need to know that," Simon glared at Lucas as he turned the corner and dodged through traffic.

"You're speeding, Dad," Emma scolded.

"I don't care. I'm a cop."

"Cops do not need to obey the law?" Lucas asked, confused.

"Some cops do," Emma said. "And some do whatever the fuck they want."

"Goddamn it! I told you not to use that language!" Simon snapped.

Emma shot him dead with a look. "Whatever. You promised I could drive."

"My car, not the police vehicle."

"But I thought you were only fourteen? Is the law not that people drive at sixteen?" Lucas asked.

Simon groaned. "She means use the automatic computer on the car, to practice. She knows I hate that thing. It's not really driving, but I let her a couple times."

"Only when he's not being a dick!" Emma snapped.

"I'm your father! How about some respect?!" Simon replied.

"You get the respect you give!" she fired back.

Simon glared at her in the mirror again and turned the radio up again to his classic rock. Lucas nodded to the beat, listening intently and Simon began singing along to Bon Jovi's "You Give Love A Bad Name," aiming frequent glances back at Emma as he sang the words.

It was a long twenty-five minutes in early rush traffic to Union Hill, but Simon just ignored his daughter and kept the music on, until his cell rang, playing the chorus from a classic song "Rain" by Jars of Clay, a Christian crossover band he'd discovered in his younger days.

"Yeah," he said as he clicked the button to answer, turning the radio down at the same time.

He got the cell to his ear just in time to hear: "John Simon, you son of a bitch." It was Murray Barber.

"I was just about to head your way," Simon said. "But I have to take my daughter home first and drop Lucas off to his car."

"I'm pretty sure they are all forgeries," Murray said, without further preamble. "I want to run a few more tests, but they have all the markings." He began explaining. "The dating of the components, the canvas—"

"Murray, I trust you. You know your stuff."

"Yeah, okay, sorry."

Simon chuckled. "It's okay. I'll pick them up soon."

"Give me another day and I can probably tell you who I think made them."

"Which forger?"

"Yep."

"You can tell?"

Murray laughed. "Forgers have a signature just like artists do. The combination of materials, certain style and strokes.

They do good work, almost perfect in a lot of people's eyes, but I can tell. And these seem familiar."

"All right," Simon said. "Maybe I can pick them up tomorrow." There was a pounding sound and loud voices in the background.

"Cool, man." Murray's reply was interrupted by loud pops and a woman screaming. "What the fuck—

There were more pops then the phone went dead.

"Murray?!" Simon yelled. "Shit!" He dropped his cell in his lap and flipped on the lights and sirens at the same time as he pressed the accelerator. "Hang on!"

"What's going on?" Emma asked, attitude gone, her face filled with worry.

The Police radio lit up with shots fired reports. At the same time, the screen on the dash listing current calls refreshed as well and Simon recognized Murray's home address.

"What is going on?" Lucas asked.

"Someone's shooting at Murray's," Simon said and sped up even faster, pushing the accelerator to the floor.

He weaved in and out of traffic, racing through several stop signs and two red lights, then turned sharply onto Murray's street, tires squealing as he slammed on the brakes and drew his sidearm at the same time.

The front door of Murray's house was wide open, wood splintered beside the lock. A stream of bullet holes ran in a jagged line across it.

"Fuck! Stay here!" Simon yelled and climbed out, gun at the ready, racing toward the sidewalk.

As he stepped up off the curb, machine gun fire tore up

the lawn headed straight for him and he spotted a dark-skinned man aiming a classic Uzi at him, finger tight around the trigger.

Simon dove, and rolled back toward the car, yelling, "Get down!" to Lucas and Emma, even as he turned and fired two shots back at the man. The first missed. The second hit the man's leg, causing him to call out and turn so he was firing into some bushes.

Simon climbed in the car and slammed it into gear, hitting the accelerator, before he'd even finishing shutting the door.

Then more bullets tore into the rear of the car, cracking the windshield.

"Oh my God!" Emma screamed.

Simon accelerated and slid the car around a bend as he did, racing away up the street. Tires squealed behind him as two cars of armed men gave pursuit.

"They're chasing us!" Emma yelled.

"I see them, honey. Just stay down," Simon said, concentrating on his driving as he keyed the radio. "186, shots fired, officer needs help." He glanced in the mirror before continuing, "Being pursued by a blue BMW and a red Chevy van, unknown make. 31st Street at Gillham Road. Headed north."

"All available units, officer needs help," the dispatcher said then sent out a series of calls as Simon accelerated and ran two stop lights, hoping to lose the pursuit, but both cars followed, nearly colliding with vehicles entering the intersection from east and west. Tires squealed and metal crunched, but the pursuers kept coming. Then he thought about Murray, Linda, and Jan and said a silent prayer they were safe, knowing it was his fault they were in danger.

"How the fuck did they know about Murray?" he muttered.

"What's going on, Dad?" Emma said, her voice shaking as she cowered in the back.

Simon's focus turned back to eluding the pursuers and keeping his daughter safe. "Some people really dislike public displays of affection," he joked, trying to make her laugh.

Instead, she glared. "Not funny!"

Simon shrugged and spun the wheel, tires squealing as the back of the car fishtailed and he turned right onto 25th Street headed east. "186, on 25th headed east," he called to dispatch.

"Units responding, 186 headed east on 25th Street at Gillham," the dispatcher replied. Several cars responded in confirmation as Simon finally heard sirens. Men with guns leaned out the sides of the pursuing cars and fired at the Interceptor again.

Simon zigzagged, dodging the bullets, but a few struck home.

Suddenly, a large box truck turned right into the right hand lane ahead, slowing down the traffic and forcing Simon to apply the brakes as he looked for a way around.

"Get over!" he shouted, waving frantically at the rear window of the Volvo blocking his way with one hand.

In an instant, the Chevy was beside him, slamming into the side of his vehicle, the driver shooting out the passenger side front window with a Glock as Lucas leaned toward Simon, not knowing what to do. Sparks flew and metal and rubber screeched as Simon fought to keep the car from entering the oncoming lane.

Then there was an opening coming. Simon slammed on the brakes, hit the accelerator, and pulled out into the oncoming center lane and sped around two cars, zipping back over just before a head on collision with a honking cargo van that swerved and slammed on the brakes in an attempt to avoid him.

Now the tailing cars were trapped behind the box truck and a Volvo station wagon.

"No wonder Mom complains about your driving," Emma said.

"Nice! I'm trying to keep us alive," Simon said.

Gunfire cut off Emma's reply as Simon watched bullets tear into the Volvo through his rearview mirror. The driver served then accelerated until a tire blew out, causing the Volvo to swerve into the box truck and send both spinning toward the curb.

The BMW and SUV veered the opposite way, slightly encroaching into the opposite lanes until they'd sped around them.

"Stay down, Emma!" Simon warned.

"I thought you called for backup?" Lucas asked.

"They're coming!" Simon yelled as bullets tore into the back of the Interceptor again. The rear windshield disappeared in a shower of glass particles as Emma screamed. For the second time, Simon thought about giving Lucas the gun to return fire, but shooting from a moving vehicle was foolish and difficult even for practiced shooters, let alone someone who'd never fired a gun. And the men tailing them were mostly counting on luck, not precision.

He turned his focus back to driving and glanced in the mirror at his daughter. "You okay, honey?"

"No! I'm being shot at!" she yelled, shooting him a shocked look.

"You were curious about shootings—" He cut himself off as two cars stopped ahead at a light, leaving Simon little time to react. He grabbed the wheel hard and accelerated, slamming straight on into the back of one of the cars, a Ford Taurus, and pushing it into the intersection with the screech of tires and metal. The driver glanced back in fear and alarm, as Simon tapped the brake then hit the rear bumper again, spinning the car out of the way and swerving to continue on. Cars entering the intersection on each side, squealed to a stop, as one driver shook a fist and yelled his cursed outrage.

Then Simon finally saw the first black and white turning left and dodging past the crunched Taurus to join the pursuit behind the BMW and SUV.

"Finally," he mumbled.

"Go faster," Lucas suggested.

"There's too many cars on the road," Simon pointed out. The road ahead was growing busier by the second as rush hour spread to the streets from overfilled highways.

"Then we're going to die." Emma's voice shook.

Simon jerked the wheel left and swerved across three lanes, turning onto a bridge, then taking a sharp right onto the highway. "Fine. Maybe we can slow them down and lose them."

He merged into the moving but jam packed highway traffic, looking back as the BMW and SUV followed, with slight delay. Two black and whites followed thereafter.

Simon stayed in the far right lane.

"This is slower. Do you have a plan, Dad?" Emma whined.

"Sure. I do this all the time. Regular day at the office," he replied, then swerved right onto the next exit, forcing two cars to brake suddenly behind him as one rear ended the other, partially blocking access to the exit. "That should slow them down," he added.

"My God, you just made those people have an accident," Emma said, looking back, surprised.

"A fender bender. They're fine," Simon said. "Mayor gets the bill."

"What—do you get a ribbon for it?" Emma said, clearly offended by his nonchalance.

"Good idea. I'll suggest it to the Chief," Simon said and grinned.

Emma shook her head. "You're crazy."

Simon slowed as he approached a red light with several cars waiting at the top of the exit. He veered over to drive half on and off the shoulder and sped around them just as he looked back in the mirror to see the BMW and SUV following. One of the black and whites reported the shifting locations over the radio as other cars acknowledged.

Another black and white appeared at the top of the ramp, siren blaring, lights spinning. Simon motioned behind him.

The uniforms inside nodded back as Simon turned right and raced off. He watched in the mirror as the black and white waited for the cars Simon had passed to turn off the exit, then sped up, cutting off the BMW. Only the BMW plowed through, slamming into the black and white and sending it spinning into two passing sedans on the far lanes, as the BMW made a wide turn and sped off after Simon again. The SUV slowed and turned, following right behind.

"That worked well," Emma cracked.

"Simon says stop the commentary!" Simon snapped back, annoyed. He scanned the road ahead, looking for a way out. Then he saw another curve in the road and accelerated, turning the wheel so he was riding the center lane. The BMW and SUV raced to catch up, drawing nearer by the moment.

"They're still right behind us," Emma warned, ignoring his order.

"I see them," Simon confirmed. The SUV sped past the damaged BMW and was right on the tail of the Interceptor now.

A semi was coming toward him in the opposite lane and Simon had an idea. He slowed a bit as the SUV sped up, trying to come alongside.

"Hang on," he warned Lucas and Emma.

Simon pulled the emergency brake just as he and the semi both entered the intersection from opposite directions. He spun the wheel sharply and sent his car skidding, passenger side first, now pointed down the road to the left of the direction they'd been traveling. As the semi driver reacted, honking and swerving left himself, Simon released the emergency brake and slammed the accelerator down again, racing onto the cross street past a sign reading E. 23rd St. The smell of burning rubber and oil reached his nose as smoke poured into the air behind them.

Behind him, metal and tires screeched as the SUV tried to turn left and plowed head on into the semi at full speed, crunching up like an accordion.

The BMW slowed to avoid the sliding accident and then turned left to follow Simon.

"Oh my God, they're dead!" Emma said, horrified.

"They were trying to kill us," Simon said. He glanced back

to see tears flowing down his daughter's cheeks as she rocked on her seat, going into shock. *Shit.* He'd terrified his own child.

The passenger in the BMW opened fire on the Interceptor from behind again as passing cars swerved clear, slamming on the brakes to avoid the bullets.

Simon pushed on through another red light and kept going, the BMW in hot pursuit.

Cars sped across an intersection two blocks ahead as others waited at the red traffic light. Simon would have to stop.

Just then three more black and whites entered the chase from a nearby alley, one beside the BMW. Simon saw an officer run out and throw a spike strip across the street just behind him.

The BMW driver saw it too and slammed on the brakes.

Simon kept going, looking for an alley or something to get off 23rd.

Black and whites closed in on the BMW and the driver suddenly turned off, forcing incoming cars to swerve and brake, then accelerated into an alley as his own tires joined the squeals. Two black and whites managed to follow in pursuit. More burning rubber filled the air.

Simon slammed on the brakes and moved right toward the curb as the other black and white caught up and pulled alongside. Both Simon and the uniform in the passenger seat rolled down their windows.

"You okay?" the uniform called.

Simon nodded. "Shaken up but yeah. I gotta get back to where it started and check on some people."

The uniform nodded. "Ten four. We'll handle it here." He paused, having a thought. "Slow down though, will ya?"

"I drive a lot slower when no one's shooting at me," Simon said, pushing the button to roll the window up again.

The uniform laughed as his partner turned the black and white around and circled back.

Relief poured over him like ocean waves as he examined Emma and Lucas, realizing except for scrapes and bruises for the humans, they'd all three escaped injury. His heart pounded but began to slow as sweat dripped from his forehead and stung his eyes. He blinked to clear it.

"It'll be okay, baby," he called back to his crying daughter, doing his best to lock his eyes on hers with a loving, reassuring look.

"Simon says leave me alone," she whispered her voice cracking and just shook her head, curled up and shaking in her seat. He wanted to pull over and just hold her but he had to check on Murray and his wives, so he pulled out again when the light ahead changed and headed back for the highway again.

CHAPTER 14

B Y THE TIME Simon pulled back to the curb in front of Murray's house, there were two black and white units already there and sirens filled the air.

"Stay here!" he ordered Emma and Lucas as he climbed out and raced for the house, slamming the door behind him as he drew his Glock 37.

He entered calling, "Detective on scene!" and found four uniforms already searching the house. There were bullet holes in the walls, shattered windows, knickknacks in pieces on shelves or on the floor—the front room had been a shooting gallery.

"Is anyone here?" Simon called.

One of the uniforms, an Asian woman in her late twenties, peered back at him from the kitchen. "Clear. No bodies." Simon badged her and she nodded.

In moments, the three male uniforms joined them. The kitchen hadn't suffered as much damage—just a few bullets having made it through the door. There was no sign of blood in either place.

"No bodies, no blood," a white uniform said, blond, blue-eyed, with the physique of a college athlete. He probably had been. His name tag read: Wallace. The Asian's name tag read: Chang. The other two males were like Mutt and Jeff, the one named Doss—tall and thin—while his partner Pisani was shorter and rounder.

Simon relaxed and holstered his gun. "There should be a man and two women living here."

"You know them?" Chang asked.

Simon nodded. "Old friends." He motioned outside. "You guys wanna set up the tape and prep the scene. I'm going to take a look around real quick."

They nodded. Wallace turned back at the door. "Crime Scene's on its way."

There was a familiar buzzing outside and a drone appeared, flashing as its camera took pictures through the front door.

"Goddamn it!" Simon glared at it. "Keep the press away, will ya?"

Wallace stepped forward. "We'll do our best, sir." The drones were far worse than live reporters to manage, so Simon knew it was probably a losing cause and shrugged in understanding.

Simon made a quick run through the rooms and found no sign of the paintings he'd left. *Fuck. Did Ashman's people get them?* It did appear that Murray and his wives had gotten away somehow. He hoped that meant they were okay.

There were a couple chairs overturned and a tipped over card table in the back room, either from startled occupants or the gunmen's search. He wondered how many there had been—since four of them took off chasing him.

As he turned and headed back for the living room, he saw Lucas and Emma in the doorway.

"I thought I told you to wait in the car," he scolded. Then he saw Emma's red eyes and tear streaked face. She looked like a little girl for the first time in ages. As their eyes met, she ran into his arms and held on for dear life. He wrapped his arms around her and held on. His stomach fluttered as his chest warmed and his anger mixed with happiness and concern. He felt guilty for enjoying the moment because his baby was in pain. He just wanted to make her feel better, reassure her, but at the same time, he couldn't remember the last time she'd needed him like this.

"It's okay, baby," he whispered, brushing her hair gently with his right palm. "I'm so sorry."

"Is Murray okay?" Lucas asked.

"No one's here," Simon answered and their eyes met.

Lucas looked puzzled. "Their house has much damage. It is unfortunate."

"Yes, but if they're alive, that'll be enough," Simon said.

Emma sniffled against his chest, rubbing her tears on his shirt. "I love you, Daddy."

"I love you, too," he said, hugging her tighter again. "It's all going to be okay. I promise. The bad men are gone now."

Emma nodded and turned her head to the side, just resting there against him.

Simon heard commotion outside as more vehicles arrived, and moments later JoAnn Becker appeared in the doorway, frowning when she saw Lucas, taking in the room.

"Is everyone okay?" she asked.

Simon nodded. "Shaken up but we'll survive."

Becker's eyes met his. "You wanna tell me why you led four shooters on a destructive, volatile high speed chase through the city today?"

"Just lucky I guess?" Simon teased.

The Sergeant's eyes narrowed. She was not amused. "I can think of only one case you'd be working right now where a forger might be involved. And I know you can't be working that case because you were ordered off it by myself and Deputy Chief Keller. Yet here we are in a forger's house that's been shot up, we have two dead shooters and a wrecked semi, several vehicles involved in collisions, and more damaged by bullet holes."

"I was just consulting with Murray on a hunch, boss," Simon said. "He called me and I heard gunshots and the phone went dead. When I got here, men shot at the car and chased us off. I had just picked up Emma from school, I was trying to get her to safety."

"It's true. He drove *very* fast," Lucas said with all seriousness.

Simon shot him a warning look. *Don't help.*

Becker ignored him and nodded. "Are you okay, sweetie?" She looked at Emma.

Emma sniffled and turned to nod. "Yes, ma'am."

Becker looked apologetically at her. "Scary stuff. I'm so sorry." Then Emma turned back to embracing her Dad.

"I am also okay," Lucas assured her.

Becker forced a smile at him but then turned to Simon and nodded at Lucas, serious again. "What's he doing here?"

"I was going to take him back to Central and his car when I realized I was late to pick up Emma from school. Then

234

Murray called—"

Becker sighed. "What hunch would involve Murray?"

Simon paused a moment, searching for words. He needed to tell her what he knew without making more trouble for himself for taking the evidence. "A couple of the paintings and nanochips from the warehouse were in my car. I had some experts look at them, just in case..."

Becker scoffed. "They just happened to be in your car? Those were supposed to be returned this morning."

"I know. They needed more time."

"And what did these experts find?"

"The paintings are fakes, Sarge," Simon went on. "And the chips contain classified data, government data—the kind you and I aren't supposed to see; the kind that have nothing to do with an art gallery."

Becker stiffened. "You're sure about this?"

Lucas nodded helpfully. "Most certain. We saw the government data."

Becker shot Simon a look of disbelief. Why had a civilian been given access?

"Lucas, don't help," Simon said then turned to Becker again. "Positive. I'll have documentation as soon as I find Murray and call Julia at her Lab."

"These items wouldn't have anything to do with alarms going off over at Property on Holmes earlier this week?" Becker asked, making a face that said she knew damn well they did.

Simon raised his hands in innocent denial. "I don't know anything about that."

"We have caused no alarms," Lucas said.

"Stay out of this!" Becker and Simon both scolded at the same time.

Becker stared at Simon a minute, knowing he was lying. Crime scene techs entered and moved past them, working the scene. Oglesby and Dolby entered next and their faces filled with concern as they saw Simon and Emma.

"Holy shit, are you guys okay?" Dolby asked. Moving to hug Emma from behind lightly like a mother hen.

"They really did a number on your car, didn't they?" Oglesby said.

"We're okay," Simon nodded, gratitude in his expression. Then the other detectives noticed their boss's expression and shot him supportive looks but moved quickly on.

"Shit," Becker finally said, shaking her head. "I was just about to tell you the Shooting Team cleared you and you go and do this. Now I have to call the FBI."

"The Feds? Fuck! They'll just take over—" Simon replied.

Becker nodded. "Yeah, well, classified data is above our pay grade, you bet they will."

"What have Bailey and Tucker found?"

"They're interviewing witnesses, looking at bank records— they know what they're doing," Becker said, dodging.

"Yeah, thanks for having me shut out," Simon growled.

"You're lucky we don't write you up for that little stunt you pulled breaking into their files," Becker answered, glaring.

Simon knew better than to respond and just waited.

"You get back to the office and write up the reports on this incident and everything you've found. I want them on my desk by the time I get back," Becker said. "I'll have uniforms take Emma and Lucas where they need to go. I'll set a meeting with the Feds for as soon as they're available this afternoon or early evening. Tomorrow morning, latest."

Simon's cell beeped in his pocket. An incoming text message. He pulled it out and flipped to messages as she talked. The message read: *What the fuck did you get me into, you son of a bitch? Call me. — Murray.*

Simon exhaled. "Murray's okay. Thank God."

"He have news for you?" Becker asked.

"I have to call him," Simon nodded. "Did they ID the two shooters in the Taurus?"

Becker shrugged. "I came here first. Harris is covering that scene, I believe. They'll let us know."

"Don't hold back on me this time," Simon said.

She shot him a warning look. "All right, go," she ordered.

Simon grabbed Emma by the shoulders and gently turned her around, pushing her toward the door. "Let's go, baby."

"I want to stay with you," she whined, looking up at him with sad eyes that melted his heart.

"I have to work," he said. "You'll be safer at the house. I'll have someone stay with you."

Outside, cameras flashed from paparazzi drones as a news van arrived and the crew began setting up. Simon covered his daughter's face and led her to where Chang and Wallace were interviewing neighbors.

"I need you guys to take her home and hang with her for a bit," Simon said. "I'll get back there as soon as I can."

Chang nodded, smiling reassuringly at Emma. "We'll take good care of her." She pulled away and led them toward one of the black and whites. Once Emma was settled in the backseat with Chang standing outside, leaning over and talking with her softly, comforting her, Simon turned to Lucas.

"I'm sorry you got dragged into this. I really do appreciate all you've tried to do," Simon said.

"I keep searching my memory for more," Lucas said. "But it can be difficult with the regular memory wipes of temporary data."

"How do they wipe your memory and not erase who you are?" Simon wondered.

"There is a complex coding of dates and times," Lucas said. "Plus permanent memories like personality, operating software, etc. are stored differently."

Simon had never been a huge computer fan. He used them for work and correspondence but hearing technical details just left him in a haze. "I'll take your word for it. You'd think a security guard would need to remember some things."

Lucas nodded. "When I started it was once a month, but Mister O'Dell increased it recently to once a week. I am sorry I could not help you more with the Sergeant."

Simon grinned. "Actually, you backed me up kinda like a partner. I appreciate the effort. It's just that as a civilian—"

"Ahhhhh," Lucas pursed his lips with understanding. "I am not a cop."

Simon extended his hand. "You take care."

Lucas shook it firmly, his eyes almost sad. "It was good

meeting you, John Simon. Thank you."

Simon nodded one more time then released Lucas' hand and turned, heading back for the Interceptor. He had a ton of paperwork to get done in the next hour or two.

SIMON WAS CRUISING along Gillham Road headed back for headquarters when Murray texted him: *Liberty Memorial, 20 minutes. Come alone.*

He made a quick left onto Pershing and circled back to Main, turning right on Memorial Drive and heading up to the circular Liberty Memorial Mall that cut across the surrounding park and ran up to and back out to Memorial from the 1926 obelisk.

Finished in 1926 and built of limestone in Egyptian Revival style, the Liberty Memorial was a towering 265 foot tribute to the soldiers of World War I that sat atop a hill at the heart of the south end of downtown Kansas City. Its interior included stairs and an elevator to reach an observation point at the top, with great views, and it had been expanded in the year 2000 to include the National World War I Museum. At night, the top of the Memorial emitted steam with red and orange spotlighting—creating a flame affect.

The grounds were designed to create an open, very pleasant park popular as a place to walk, people watch, and meet. Sometimes street musicians and artists set up there and worked or entertained the crowds. Today, one woman was painting on a mobile easel—a beautiful landscape of the park that looked near completion as Simon cruised past. A few pedestrians stared at his bullet-ridden Interceptor with its shattered rear window, but he ignored them as he lucked into a parking spot along the curb and quickly took advantage. A black and white cruised through on a routine check and pulled to a stop, the uniforms also eying his vehicle as Simon climbed out. He nodded and flashed his badge then continued walking toward the Museum and Memorial at the north end.

Four teenagers were laughing and chattering as they flew toy drones in mock battles over the grassy lawn. As he stepped onto the curb near the descending cement steps that led into the Memorial and Museum complex, a light breeze tousled his hair and the peaceful lilt of birdsong filled his ears, clashing with the adrenaline and images still flooding his body after the chase and shooting. In seconds, Murray Barber appeared, climbing the stairs with his two wives in tow—the three of them managing to carry the paintings Simon had left with them and a satchel. They looked warily around as they approached Simon at a fast clip.

Murray stopped, facing him, and nodded. "You son of a bitch. You almost got us killed."

"They got poor Lucky," Linda said sadly, referring to one of the cats that roamed their property as she wiped away a tear.

"I'm so sorry," Simon said, meaning it, his eyes offering sympathetic apologies. "They traced me or followed me somehow—"

"Doesn't matter," Murray said, his eyes constantly scanning the environment around them—almost like an addict, but Murray was clearly not on anything at the moment, at least. "We know you had no part in it. They're all fakes. I documented it on the hard drive and some research there in the satchel."

All three set the paintings down on the sidewalk as Jan offered Simon the satchel.

"I can get you put away somewhere safe until this blows over—" Simon offered.

Murray raised a hand. "No thanks. We can take care of ourselves. Just get these fuckers, okay?" His eyes met Simon's with a look that could kill.

Simon grunted his understanding. Murray would kill them himself if he had half a chance. "If there's anything I can do—"

Jan quickly rushed up and gave him a warm hug. "We're all okay. Very lucky. We wouldn't have made it this far in Murray's business if we didn't know how to protect ourselves...and hide."

"They shot through the door," Linda added, her eyes glazed and intense as she remembered. "That saved us. Gave us warning."

Simon recalled the bullet holes in their front door. He didn't know what to say but wished he could think of something. These were good people, despite Murray's criminal past.

"I think the fucking cat's scream startled 'em," Murray said, chuckling in that "it's not funny but it is" way. "Gave us time."

"Poor Lucky," Linda said again.

"Name kinda seems ironic now," Jan said, her own eyes teary now.

Simon didn't smile. It wasn't the time. He'd buy them a thousand cats if he thought it would make up for what they'd been through because of him. He choked out, "Okay. You guys take care."

"Can you get stuff back to the car?" Jan asked.

"I got it," Simon said, motioning toward the black and white, which had just rounded the U to head back out toward Memorial Drive. "They'll help."

"Cool, dude. Later." Murray nodded once, a nod filled with meaning, then he turned and put his arms around the ladies, leading them hurriedly away.

Simon keyed his radio and called the black and white by number. The two uniforms returned and helped him load the items into his car. He explained it was evidence in a case, returned by an informant. They looked like they'd wanted to ask tons of questions but didn't.

He thanked them as he pulled away, then headed back for his desk at the office.

The next two hours were consumed by paperwork. Dolby stopped by as she checked out for the day to tell him Becker had set a meeting for her office at eleven the following morning. Simon actually found himself relieved. The reports and write-ups were taking longer than expected. His computer and typing skills had always been a handicap at such things and he missed Santorios especially, since he'd relied on her to take care of much of the paperwork while they were partners.

Later, he drove home and picked up Emma, taking her out to dinner and a nice motel for the night. Just to get her away from things, calm her down, make sure they had a quiet, uneventful evening. He even called in and took the night off—something Becker approved after a quick call as a onetime thing. His daughter had been in a shooting. She understood. Any cop would. Tonight he was all hers.

They ate burgers at Rock Star, one of the best local places down in the West Bottoms, then lounged around playing computer games on Emma's tablet and laptop, talked books, school, life—so many things. Both forgot all about the kissing incident earlier in the day. Simon only remembered after she fell asleep with her head in his lap and it was the last thing he wanted to bring up when they'd been having such a wonderful time.

He read for an hour or so, then gently lifted her and carried her to the king size bed and tucked her in. It had been a long time since they'd shared a bed, her being a teenager now, but tonight, he wanted her close, so he took a shower, changed into pajamas he'd packed from a dusty drawer he hadn't opened in ages, and crawled in beside her. She quickly rolled over to nestle against his arm and he fell asleep holding her, the warm contentment a kind he'd forgotten but remembered now as one of the best feelings on earth.

CHAPTER 15

A FTER PICKING UP his car at Central, Lucas drove back to his small apartment in a building off 4th Street near the River Market. An area just north of downtown off the highways and the Missouri River, the area had a rich history that included several name changes: River Quay from its 19th century founding through the days of much mob activity, prostitutes, car bombs, and various vices. The area dated back to the 1850s and contained the area where Kansas City itself was first founded. More recently, it had been revitalized with a thriving farmer's market, restaurants, shops, a steamboat museum, and more. It had become an active place for music, people watching, and shopping, especially on weekends and holidays, and from 2016 on, it had been serviced by Kansas City's revived street cars, allowing residents easy and cheap access to the entire downtown through the Union Station and Crown Center areas.

Lucas had been given the apartment by his maker, Doctor Livia Connelly because of its proximity to public transport as well as good opportunities for him to practice blending in and interacting with humans. He frequently went down to cruise the market area and buy what little provisions he needed—including decorative items for his one bedroom apartment, furniture, and even a couple of plants. He had made friends with a few regulars who called him by name, some of whom probably still had no idea he was an android, and he liked it. This was "his" neighborhood, his home, and he belonged there. He enjoyed spending time there when he was not working, and after being away so much with John Simon, it felt great to be back.

In fact, he had spent very little time exploring the area at night, so that night he took a long walk down 4th to Main Street and circled the Market which ran between Main and Grand on the West and East and 5th and 3rd on the South and North. It was not nearly so active at night, although restaurants were open, and a couple night spots. But he enjoyed the gentle breeze off the river, and the sounds of friendly chatter, play, and music drifting through the air around him. It created a nice steady drone that allowed him to think about the past few days and all he'd been through.

He hadn't meant to endanger anyone, so Simon's anger both surprised and hurt him, to the degree he could hurt anyway. His assistance to John Simon had started because he and Connelly thought he had a responsibility to do what was right and help the police—before his usual memory wipe took away the details. But as things had progressed and Lucas had learned more of the plot and activities, he'd come to feel more and more responsible for helping stop the criminal activities. He had never met Benjamin Ashman, but always been told he was a good, honest, decent man. Connelly certainly thought so. But in addition to Asimov's Three Laws, Lucas' programming also included instructions to obey all human laws and not participate actively in breaking them and for self—preservation. Unwittingly, he had been made an accessory to the illegal activities at the warehouse perpetrated by O'Dell and others. And in the process, when Simon and Santorios discovered them, Lucas had been shot. In essence, they had tried to harm or destroy

246

him, whether intentional or not, so his programming, his sense of ethics, and his logic processors had all led him to conclude he was on the side of the police in this, the side of setting things right. And helping John Simon seemed the best way to do so.

He had spent hours watching all the movies Emma Simon had uploaded for him. Learning how cops think, act, talk, move, etc. And he had used some of it—his best interpretation at least—in his work with Simon, although it did appear that he had gone too far at times and caused the detective concern. He was not officially a law officer, there were limitations—he understood that. But people had died because Lucas had failed at his duties to guard the warehouse, and he wanted to see whomever was responsible brought to justice. He wanted to help.

Plus, he had to admit: he liked John Simon. Tough, vulgar, and ill-mannered at times, perhaps, all those things came out of his passion to help people, care for people, and set things right. Lucas considered that honorable. It was not far from his own attitude, in fact. But the memory wipes had really put him at a disadvantage, so he'd tried making up for it in other ways, ways Simon seemed worried would cause trouble for himself, Lucas, and other cops. And now maybe even danger.

Now Lucas found himself frustrated and torn. He did not want to go back and work for Ashman if it meant being part of criminal activities. At the same time, he also was property and had obligations whether he liked them or not. The more he walked and thought, the more he realized he needed help to make the right decision. He'd circled the Market twice and almost reached his apartment again as he realized the one person who could help was his maker.

He found his car parked in the garage across from his

apartment where he had a pass and grabbed his keys from a compartment in his chest where he stored them for safe keeping. Then he got in the car and drove across town to Connelly's Leawood lab off Roe Ave and 127th Street and VOIPed ahead to let her know he was coming.

Connelly met him at the door in her white lab coat. She looked sleepy but clearly had not been asleep. She'd been working long hours as usual. He expressed concern for her well-being as always, and she brushed it off, ushering him into a lounge area with couches and chairs just off the lab before she asked, "What's going on that brings you here this time of night?"

For the next few minutes, Lucas explained his dilemma and all the activities which had led him there as best he could. Occasionally, his maker interrupted with questions to clarify details, but mostly she listened. Finally, Lucas ended with, "I don't know what to do."

Livia Connelly nodded and leaned back on the leather couch she'd sat on facing him, clicking her teeth in thought. "Mister Ashman paid a lot of money for you, Lucas, but I always intended for my creations to be as human as possible, including some elements of free will. Worked hard on that in fact, taking advantage of the best chips, components, and AI tech available to make it happen. In many ways, you are practically human with the exception of having flesh, blood, and requiring food and drink. So your feelings are natural, understandable."

Lucas brightened, warmed by the compassion in her face and voice. "So I am not a failure?"

Connelly chuckled. "Oh no, Lucas. Of course not! You are wonderful! I am very proud of you. Especially after what you've done to help Detective Simon. He was not very nice to us at the police station, but you have still acted with honor and respect in helping him despite that. No, you are not even close to a failure."

Then she paused and Lucas' face fell. He suspected he knew what she would say. "But I must go back to my job?"

Connelly sighed. "Actually, one of the clauses of my contract with buyers is that my creations cannot be used for any dangerous or illegal activities. It is why I included in your programming requirements for self-preservation and obeying human laws. So, if you are being included in illegal activities, even unwittingly, it technically violates the contract."

Lucas was pleased. "So I may quit."

She shook her head. "Not so easy. I can't just take you back. Not without returning a whole bunch of money that I have invested in further research and don't have right now."

Lucas frowned, shoulders sinking. "But—"

She raised a hand to stop him. "What I can do is tell Mister Ashman that due to potential violations of the contract, you cannot come back to your duties until the legal issues are resolved so that you are sure to have no part in them."

Lucas sat up straight again, nodding. "So I can help Detective Simon?"

Connelly shrugged. "Well, it will buy you a week or three at least from work. If Detective Simon has asked you to go home and not be part of the investigation, this won't change that."

Lucas hmmphed. He really wished he could do more. "If my temporary memories had not been wiped, I could be much more helpful. I wish that had not been done to me."

Connelly's face twisted in thought. "You haven't been wiped since the incident at the warehouse though, right?"

"Yes." Lucas looked at her hopefully.

"Have you tried recalling items from your optics?"

"My optics? Like what?" Lucas searched his memory, but came up blank.

Connelly laughed. "You were built with many special features but not all of them were explored in your training because many of the things I made standard are not required for performing your particular assignment."

"So I have capabilities I am not aware of?"

"You could use them if various circumstances arose. It would probably be automatic. But you would not apply them with free will yet because they might not occur to you." Connelly stood and motioned for Lucas to follow her through wide double doors into the lab. The doors were propped open and given the hour, Connelly's assistant, Steven, was gone, leaving the lab vacant except for Lucas and his maker.

She motioned for him to sit on a stool near a desk which contained three flat screen monitors and a keyboard. Bending down, Connelly retrieved a cable and approached Lucas. "Access panel please."

With a soft whir of hydraulics, he complied, opening an access panel in his arm.

She then inserted the cable into an opening and popped it into place, turned, and went back to the computers. "One example of the capabilities I am talking about is your optics."

"My optics? Vision?"

She nodded. "Yes. You say you were in a police chase, I

heard about it on the news. Did you get a look at the people chasing you?"

"Only from a distance," Lucas said, shaking his head. It was not enough to describe them or be of much use.

Connelly typed into the keyboard and images began flashing across the screen. "What day was that? Yesterday, right?"

Lucas nodded. "Yes, a few hours ago."

A data screen popped up, and his maker typed in the date and an approximate time of 3:30 p.m. A new set of images came up and Lucas recognized some of them included the Interceptor, Simon, and Emma.

"These are your optic memories from the chase," she explained. "Now, all we have to do is find where you were looking at—there!" She tapped a button and froze the screen to an image of looking out the shattered rear window of the Interceptor at occupants on the blue BMW, close on its tail.

"It is all blurry," Lucas said. "I still cannot recognize them."

Connelly tapped some buttons, narrowing the image in on the front windshield of the BMW and then focusing, pulling in, closer, clearer. Now he could make out faces. They were not men he had seen at the warehouse but they were familiar.

"I can do that?" he asked.

"Yes, you can," she said with a delighted smile. "I just have to talk you through it once. Better yet, we can print this." She tapped a button and a photo printer to the right whirred to life. In a few moments, two very good color images of the scene on the screen popped out. His maker grabbed them and set them on the desk where he could see them. "These might help the detectives find these men."

"My goodness!" Lucas was delighted too. "Can I search my memory to see if I have recall of where I might have seen either of these men before? I tried reviewing my saved footage but turned up little."

"If it hasn't been erased, yes," his maker said. "Just tell your optics to highlight their faces and run searches."

Lucas watched the screen even as he concentrated on his optic sensors, sending instructions. Suddenly the men's faces were surrounded by red dots on the screen. Then pulled out—extracted from the larger photo—and filled the screen as floating heads. He sent a search command and more images and data raced across the screens. In less than two minutes, he got an image of one of the men sitting in the car down the block the night he had gone to Simon's house and met his daughter; the night he'd uploaded all the movies.

"He was there! That's Detective Simon's house!" Energy filled him as he realized further: "They know where the Detective lives! Emma!" His friends were in danger. He had to help!

"There may be more," his maker suggested. "Keep searching."

Lucas first focused and clarified the image of the man outside Simon's house then made print outs. He found one more instance of one of the men in a car watching he and Simon at the Art Gallery on one of their visits there. He also found images of the other two men who'd chased them and died in a fire. Both were dark complected, with dark hair and features he'd seen in people with Hispanic backgrounds.

Next, his maker helped him extract audible memories of sounds he might have heard, and he got a little recording of the men yelling and talking in some foreign tongue and recorded that on a small chip to give to Simon. After a few hours, he was very excited.

"I am so pleased you have showed me this," he told his maker.

"I am so pleased it is useful," she replied, eyes sparkling.

"Now, I must find Detective Simon and warn him," Lucas said, standing.

"It is the middle of the night. Perhaps this can wait until tomorrow?"

Lucas shook his head. "What if he and his daughter are in danger? I must warn them."

Connelly grunted. "Okay, but be careful. I do not want anything to happen to you either. You are my child."

Lucas hugged her and she returned it. After a minute, as they pulled away, she added, "One more thing. Though there aren't really emotion chips per se, I did design you to learn from experiences, so you can learn to simulate the fondness and attachment humans often equate with emotions."

"So I can feel?"

"In a certain sense, over time, as your thoughts and understandings of certain relationships become complicated, you may develop something that resembles feelings, yes."

Lucas embraced her again, lifting her feet off the floor in his enthusiasm as his arms wrapped tightly around her. She cried out with surprise but not displeasure. He was pretty sure he was currently simulating what must be joy. "Thank you, Maker. I love you."

Connelly's eyes seemed to glisten a little as he set her down. "Thank you, Lucas. I love you, too," she whispered softly. She reached up to squeeze his hand and smiled.

Then he waved, turned, and hurried back to his car, determined to stay up all night and watch for trouble outside Simon's motel. He'd let the man sleep. Humans needed that after stressful days. When he saw the man the next day, Lucas could talk with him then.

PAUL FOUND MILES waiting for him in back corner booth at Denny's and slid in opposite him, nodding in greeting. "You order yet?"

"Just coffee," Miles replied. "Waiting on you." The restaurant wasn't crowded this time of day, so Miles had chosen a corner booth off by itself that might give them the semblance of privacy.

"Let's do it," Paul said and flagged down a passing waitress. She took their order and then hurried on to the table she'd originally been working. Paul ordered a big stack of pancakes. Miles ordered French toast. Paul ordered coffee, black, and they both ordered bacon on the side. Paul liked to eat well in the morning, so pancakes were a bit of a departure from his healthy routine. However, he ordered fresh strawberries on top and no syrup. That would help a lot on the calories. Miles, he knew, couldn't care less about such things. The man had no sense of style or refinement. He was pure, macho brute, which made him bad company at art events and society evenings but perfect for what Paul needed him for, and that's all he cared about.

Paul leaned back against the wooden booth, raising his eyebrows. "You have news?"

Miles nodded. "The fucking android."

"What android?" Paul searched his mind for the reference.

"From the fucking warehouse. The one Ashman bought for 'security.'"

Paul remembered. The android was just there to scare people off, call in strange intrusions. He'd actually been worried its presence would be problematic for their enterprise, but with O'Dell there, the android had followed orders and stayed away, kept to itself. "What about it?"

"It was in the car with the detective when we chased him from that house," Miles said.

Paul's brow furrowed. "Are you sure?"

Miles nodded. "Yeah, clear as day. I think he's been helping him."

"Helping him? I thought O'Dell told me his memory was wiped weekly."

Miles shrugged. "Why else is he hanging out with a cop? And I checked, he was given 'personal time' after the shooting and hasn't been in to work."

"Personal time?" Paul scoffed, shaking his head. "What the fuck does an android need with personal time?"

Miles chuckled. "Supposedly O'Dell thought having him out of the way for a bit would let them clean up easier, keep him from saying too much 'til he could wipe his memory."

"His memory hasn't been wiped yet?!"

Miles shrugged again. "Last I heard, no."

"Fuck!" Paul shouted, then saw staff and patrons turning to stare and looked down, avoiding their eyes. "I want him taken care of," he whispered.

"Taken care of how? Wiped?" Miles asked. "I don't know how to do that."

"Destroy him if you must," Paul said. "Or bring him to our people. They can take care of it."

The waitress brought their coffee, smiling. "Everything okay?"

They forced smiles back, doing their best to look friendly. "Sure. Sorry about that," Paul said. "Got a little excited."

She chuckled. "Woke everyone up." She winked. "Anything else y'all need while I'm here?"

Both men shook their heads. "Just the food, babe," Miles said in a flirting way.

She shot him a mock scolding look: *naughty boy*, then whirled and headed off again.

Miles leaned back and blew on his coffee, watching her ass waddle as she walked away.

Paul glared at him and snapped his fingers. "Hey!"

Miles looked at him. "Don't get too tense. People might wonder." He blew again then took a careful sip, savoring the taste. "Mmmm. They know coffee here."

Paul looked around and realized people were still looking over from time to time, curious about them. He exhaled, deliberately lowered his shoulders and leaned back against the bench again, pretending to relax despite the burning tension inside. "We have a mission here, Miles. I need you to stop being so casual about it and focus. There's work to do."

Miles nodded. "Right, saving the world."

"Yes, it's not a punchline," Paul said sternly, eyes narrowing.

Miles sipped his coffee again, savoring the flavor a

moment, then leaned back in his chair casually, but his eyes were focused, intense. "No problem. I've got this. Warehouse super says he has its address. Asked if we wanted to talk to it."

Paul shook his head. "No. We have no further use for it."

"What about Ashman? Those things are expensive. "

"We'll tell him it was damaged in the incident and get a new one," Paul said. "Let me worry about that."

Miles leaned forward with anticipation. "Never taken out an android before. Should be fun. Any suggestions?"

"Suggestions for what?" Paul sipped his coffee.

Miles raised his hands in question. "How to kill an android?"

Paul realized he had no idea. "I don't know. Google it or something. Maybe O'Dell had a manual. Ashman's never seen it. He just ordered it sent to the warehouse. O'Dell managed it."

"Fine," Miles said, after another sip. "I'll check his office. See what I can find."

The waitress arrived then with their orders, sliding a steaming plate of pancakes in front of Paul and French toast in front of Miles, smiling. "Syrup's there," she said, setting a carafe beside Miles' plate. "Need any more butter? Water? Juice?"

Miles shook his head. "Just your number, darlin'."

She shook her finger at him like a mother scolding a child. "You're a smooth one, aren't ya? Enjoy now!" Then she winked, spun, and hurried off.

"I think she likes me," Miles said, smugly. "I'll get it yet."

"Shut up and eat," Paul scolded. "You have business to focus on."

Miles' grin faded to annoyance. "Yes, sir." And then they both tore into their breakfast, conversation over for now.

CHAPTER 16

SIMON WOKE TO a beeping alarm around 6:15, cramped and uncomfortable in the recliner he'd moved to sleep in after Emma had chased him out of bed. She had no idea she was doing it but the girl was unpleasant to share a bed with—kicking, hitting, pushing—the worst kind of bedhog. So, after a few frustrating hours of trying to share and get sleep, he'd given up and moved. Now, he watched her sleeping peacefully, sprawled out across the king size. He used to spend hours just watching her sleep as a child—loving every breath, adoring every cute movement, the sheer joy of her existence. She was older now, more beautiful, more like her mother, yet still so young, and he hadn't lost that feeling watching her. He just didn't get to do it as often. Maybe he'd try more.

He sensed movement out of the corner of his eye and turned left to see a shadow outside the window. Their room was on the first floor looking out on a parking lot.

He stopped, paused for a better look through the curtains. A man stood in shadows outside in the parking lot nearby.

Grabbing his sidearm from the dresser, he threw off the blanket and stood, hurrying toward the front door. Opening it wide, weapon at the ready.

Lucas stood staring at Simon. His car was parked in the

space behind him.

"What are you doing out here?" Simon asked, relaxing, even as he took a cautious look around out of instinct—just in case.

"Waiting for you," Lucas replied.

"How long have you been standing there?"

Lucas shrugged. "About ten minutes. I was waiting in my car."

"Why didn't you knock? You're lucky one of the other guests didn't get worried and call the cops."

The android's brow furrowed. "You are the cops." Then he held up a stack of photos so Simon could see the one on top. It was a shot of two men in a blue BMW—the car that had chased them the other day!

Simon grabbed the photos and flipped through them. There was a shot of the men in the SUV as well as varied angles of the four men during the chase. "Where'd you get these?" He looked up at Lucas.

Lucas tapped his head.

"What?" Simon shot him a puzzled look.

"My optical processors recorded these memories," Lucas said.

"Then why didn't you show me this before?" Simon asked, irritated now.

"Because I did not know the full extent of my capabilities," Lucas said. "And I do not have a photo printer."

"What do you mean?" Simon motioned for Lucas to follow him into the motel room as he flipped through the photos again.

Lucas explained about his visit to Doctor Connelly and their discussion.

"Wait. You didn't know you could do this?" Simon asked, skeptical. "I mean, those would seem like handy talents for a security guard."

Lucas nodded. "I agree, but my maker said Wayne O'Dell requested that they not be in my training. I was only trained for the specific needs of the job."

Simon stopped, closing the door behind him as their eyes met. "You have capabilities you don't even know about?"

"Yes, not fully," Lucas said, as if it were common. He glanced over at Simon's sleeping daughter and lowered his voice. "Is this not the case for human beings who discover latent abilities in themselves?"

"Well, yeah," Simon agreed as he slipped back into the recliner and reviewed the pictures. "But your mind is a fucking computer. How can it not know?"

"It was programmed to ignore certain abilities at the request of my owner," Lucas said, still matter of fact, like it didn't bother him.

"Me? I'd be pissed," Simon said. "Fucking unbelievable. You could have images of the men in the warehouse."

Lucas held up a small flash drive. "I do. And audio."

"Audio?" Simon asked, intrigued, as he accepted the drive. "Audio of what?"

"The men in the SUV, and the warehouse," Lucas said.

"So if we voice ID the men...Holy shit! I can't believe you held out on me!" His mind raced with possibilities as adrenaline coursing through his veins woke him up better than his morning coffee ever had.

"You found this all out last night?"

Lucas shrugged. "I told you I want to help."

Simon beamed. "You have, in a big way. More now than before."

Lucas looked pleased, his eyes even sparkling. Simon wrote it off as his imagination. Or was it an electronic trick? "I will not go back to work until this is resolved."

"Why not?" Simon asked as he stopped reviewing the pictures and set them on the table in front of him.

"Because I was made an accessory to criminal activity," Lucas said. "Against my will. It violates my programming."

Simon nodded. "Some humans are programmed that way, too."

"Will your Sergeant change her mind?" Lucas asked, clearly meaning he wanted back on the case.

Simon sighed. "I don't know. But we can show her what you found first thing. You're still not a cop. I'm sorry."

"But you want my help?" Lucas said.

Simon shrugged. "You're not the worst partner to have around."

Lucas smiled again, bigger this time. "You think of me as a partner?"

Simon looked at his watch, wondering how soon to wake Emma. *I shouldn't have said that.* "You have your gifts, let's say."

Lucas started moving in a jagged way, circling, moving his arms and legs. Simon realized after a minute he was imitating something from a movie: some kind of touchdown dance perhaps?

"What are you doing?" he asked.

"Celebrating," Lucas said. "It is nice to make a friend who appreciates you. To my owner, I am just property."

Simon had never thought about the android's life from that perspective before. He felt sorry for him. "That would suck."

As the android continued his awkward movements, Emma chortled from the bed, sitting up and yawning. "You're doing it wrong."

Simon stood and showed Lucas the dance. Lucas watched carefully and adjusted his movements accordingly.

"Oh my God! What are you doing?!" Emma looked horrified. "Dad, you suck, too!"

"What? I think I've got it down," Simon said.

They kept dancing, Lucas looking pleased.

"Oh my God, you two are such geeks," she said, shaking her head, then giggling.

"Come on," Simon said, sidling over to the bed and taking Emma's hand. "Dance with us. It's time to get up anyway."

Emma shook her head vigorously. "No. I don't think so."

Simon rolled his eyes. "No one can see us. Just the three of us."

"Yeah, but still," she said, pulling her hand away and shaking your head.

"Okay then, get up and shower so we can eat before I take you to school, since you refuse to dance," Simon said in a fatherly tone.

Emma glanced at the digital clock on the bedside stand and groaned. "You guys woke me up too early!"

"I'd be waking you up in fifteen minutes anyway," Simon said. "Besides, you kicked me out of bed hours ago. I didn't get much sleep."

Emma looked horrified again, her mouth forming an O. "I so did not, Dad!"

"Kicking, punching, shoving—bed hog," Simon said as he danced back over toward Lucas, making a face at her.

"Oh my God, Dad, stop!" She got up and scrambled toward the bathroom, shutting the door behind her.

Simon shot Lucas a satisfied look. "Well, that got her going."

Lucas nodded. "We need music."

Simon looked at him and realized how ridiculous they both looked. He stopped dancing and shook his head. "No. We can stop now. Work to do."

Lucas stopped dancing with a shrug. "Okay, partner. What now?" His eyes widened as he bounced on his feet eagerly.

AFTER BREAKFAST AT a Denny's near the motel, where they left Lucas' car, Simon and Lucas rode together in the Charger to drop Emma at school, then went straight to Central Division and waited in Becker's office. The Sergeant arrived at 8:00 a.m. sharp, Starbucks cup in hand, and groaned when she saw them.

"I thought we already settled this," she said with a groan. "Can I get my caffeine on board before you start in on me?"

"It's not what you think," Simon said with an innocent look. "Take a look at these."

As she moved behind the desk and scooted out her chair, he tossed the stack of Lucas' photos across the desk. They landed in front of her and she picked them up. "What's this?"

Simon waited as she flipped through the photos. "These are the men who chased you all over downtown trying to kill you?"

Simon nodded. "See? You're sharp even without your caffeine, boss."

She glared. "To quote a certain detective: 'Shut the fuck up.'"

Simon grinned. Lucas laughed.

"Where'd you get these?" she asked as she sat down, spreading out the photos before her, then sipped her coffee as she examined them in detail.

Simon pointed to the android. "Inside his head."

Becker looked up at them. "What?"

"He has gifts," Simon said, his grin widening.

"I'll say," she replied, but her eyes demanded further explanation.

"He has capabilities he wasn't aware of by orders of Benjamin Ashman," Simon explained. "His maker showed him how to recall and edit optical memories so he could print them."

Lucas nodded. "We also have audio."

"You just now discovered this?" Becker scoffed. "You've been taking him around for three days."

Simon shrugged. "I had no idea. I've never met an android

before, have you?"

Becker took a long sip of her coffee and shook her head. "You'd think you would have asked."

"He could have," Lucas said. "I was unaware of my full capabilities."

Becker frowned. "How can a computer—"

"That's what I said," Simon replied, sitting on the edge of her desk.

"This could blow the case wide open," Becker said, shaking her head.

"I know," Simon said, "and I want to work it." He motioned to Lucas. "With him."

Becker's face changed from excitement to frustration. "We've been over this. A civilian—"

"He has some training for security, and he has special abilities we can use," Simon argued.

"He also belongs to one of the most powerful businessmen in town, who happens to be your chief suspect."

Lucas looked back and forth between them. "My unwitting involvement in criminal activities violates my programming. I cannot return to work for Mister Ashman until this question has been resolved."

"So instead you want to work for us?" Becker looked at Lucas. "Even if I wanted—there are policies."

"You know damn well exceptions can be made!" Simon argued.

"By the Chiefs, not me!" Becker replied, raising her hands to say it was out of her control.

"Fine. Then please ask," Simon said.

Becker leaned back in her chair and grabbed for her coffee again. After another long sip, "Let's start with the meeting. See how that goes. Keller and Melson will be there. I haven't even gotten permission for you to work the case yet."

Simon stood, groaning in protest. "I'm the only one who's connected the illegal activities with the murders, the forging—"

"One murder so far, with suspicions about others," Becker said. "And you did it by withholding evidence that was ordered returned."

Simon held up his hands this time. "Don't tell me you're refusing to back me on this."

"I'm with you so far, though more convincing at the meeting will go a long way. But the FBI is in this now, and homicide, the admin office—it's not just up to me."

Simon knew better than to argue with that. He just took a deep breath and nodded, exchanging a look with Lucas.

"While we're waiting, you said something about audio?" Becker said.

Simon motioned to the envelope. "On the flash drive."

Becker shot him a quizzical look, then dug the manila envelope from under the pictures and tipped it upside down, shaking it. The flash drive fell out onto her desk.

Simon beamed.

Becker took the drive and inserted it into the computer on her desk, typing some keys. A noisy audio began playing.

"We cleaned it up as best we could at my Maker's lab," Lucas offered.

The audio had the sounds of the chase—birds, insects, cars, tires squealing, some gunfire, as well as shattering glass, screaming pedestrians, etc. Then, through the midst, you could hear men yelling. Two in English. Those were the BMW guys, Simon figured. Then two more in some foreign tongue.

"Is that Spanish?" Becker asked.

"We're not sure," Simon replied.

Becker motioned to the squad room. "Get Correia in here."

Simon hurried over and poked his head out. "José!"

Correia and Maberry looked up from their desks. Simon pointed to Correia and motioned for him to come over. Maberry followed.

"Are you making trouble for us, man?" Correia joked.

"If this is about the guy José hit again, I hear Simon's chase will cost the city hundreds of thousands—" Maberry jumped in, defensively.

"Just shut up and listen, both of you," Becker growled.

The two detectives joined them in her office and she reran the audio.

"Is it Spanish?" Becker asked after the foreigners had chattered for a bit.

Correia shook his head. "It's Portuguese. Brazilian, in fact. Who are those dudes?"

"The ones that shot up the city chasing Simon," Becker said.

"Oh shit," Correia replied. "This case just got a whole lot bigger if South Americans are involved."

"There's something going on," Becker said. "We aren't sure what it is yet."

"You need our help?" Maberry asked, clearly hoping to get in on some action.

"No, that was it." Simon jerked his thumb toward the squad, quickly trying to herd them away.

"I'll let you know, okay?" Becker said.

Maberry and Correia exchanged disappointed looks then turned and headed back for their desks.

"I'm in charge, remember?" Becker said to Simon, a warning.

"Sorry, boss," he replied.

Becker shrugged it off, checking her watch. "We have two and a half hours 'til the meeting in the 9th floor briefing room. Go work it."

Simon felt a rush. Finally official sanction. He could work at his desk, use all the official resources. "I'm on the case then?"

"For now," Becker said. "We'll see how the meeting goes, but I'll push for it."

"Thanks, Sarge," Simon grunted. "Thanks a lot." He moved to her desk and she gathered up the pictures and slid them back into the envelope. Then turned and pulled the flash drive, inserting it as well, before handing the envelope to Simon.

"Just go so I can finish my coffee and wake up, all right?" she said, waving dismissively.

Simon and Lucas turned and exited into the squad, Lucas following the detective back to his desk.

"So what now?" Lucas asked.

"Just have a seat. Time to start running these images

through databases and see if we get any matches," Simon said. He pulled out the photos and flash drive and set to work. Finally, he was getting somewhere.

KANSAS CITY POLICE Headquarters, built in 1938 at 1125 Locust, was a nine story stone monolith in downtown Kansas City, Missouri. Located right next to the city detention center, it held offices for the Chief, his deputies and assistants, and various investigative units, including Homicide detectives, and had been remodeled internally in the early 21st Century to comply with the Americans with Disabilities Act using property tax revenues.

At 11 a.m., Simon, Lucas, and the others involved in the two cases gathered in Homicide's Briefing Room on the 9th floor. Sergeants Becker and Carter, two FBI agents, who'd introduced themselves as Falk and Stein, Detectives Bailey, Tucker, Oglesby, and Dolby. They were joined by Captains Hamil and Snapp of Homicide and Property, and Deputy Chiefs Kenyon Keller and Greg Melson, who nodded to Simon as he entered the room. The room smelled of sweat, dust, paper, and various colognes and perfumes of the officers who frequented for daily briefings throughout the day.

To Simon's surprise, Becker stepped to the podium to run the briefing. He'd thought homicide would have it for sure, given their case was a cop killing, but apparently Becker and Carter had agreed she'd run the show.

"Okay," Becker said. "Let's get this rolling. We'll start with Detectives Bailey and Tucker laying out their case of the death of Detective Santorios and go from there." Looking at the two homicide detectives, she nodded then moved aside as they stood and moved to occupy the space behind the podium where she'd been standing.

As Bailey and Tucker laid out their case, Simon paid close attention. This was his first chance to hear what they'd turned up. He only knew a scant few details and being blocked from their reports and files had left him frustrated, leading to his pursuit of the case on his own. He was curious if they'd come to similar conclusions to his own and how they'd gotten there.

They started with the discovery of the body at the Admiral by one of the employees and went from there. Santorios had clearly been tortured as evidenced from scars and wounds on her body as well as the coroner's report, which found she'd been subjected to such things as toenails being forcibly removed to electric shock and even waterboarding in the course of the few hours her captors had kept her alive. This was the first time Simon had learned of the extent of her suffering at her captor's hands. Clearly they'd wanted information. Since Santorios hadn't finished her reports prior to her disappearance and since they'd shown up at the warehouse following a tip and based on a resulting hunch, Simon wondered what she'd had to tell them. Or had the torture all been in an attempt to extract answers she couldn't provide? Thinking about that and the suffering she must have endured really pissed him off. He felt the heat rising as his body tensed and he leaned forward in his chair. *These motherfuckers will pay.* What kind of animals did such things to a pregnant woman?

Next they went over cause of death—which had been clear from moment one: a single bullet through her forehead into her brain. As common, the assassins had used a .22 to be sure the bullet ricocheted inside her skull and did the maximum damage, rather than flying out the back. This ensured it would be fatal, not survivable. Surviving direct bullets to the head was rare, for sure, but Simon had seen it once, and miracle though it was, it had been because the bullet entered and exited in a straight path, doing minimum damage.

When it came to suspects, Tucker identified Wayne O'Dell, the warehouse manager who was now dead, Garcia, his aide, also dead, and that was where the trail went cold. He mentioned Benjamin Ashman's possible involvement and Simon heard exhaling behind him and turned to see Deputy Chief Keller scowling, tensed at the mention of the businessman's name. They also had questioned Ashman's aide, Paul Paulsen, but both seemed to have alibis sewn up and had given them nothing, answering questions as if they were routine without any emotion. Simon knew that didn't prove innocence in either case, but it did prevent the detectives from having anything substantial they could use.

Forensics, Bailey said, had turned up very little—the bullet in her head had no fingerprints on it, nor did her skin. The hotel room had been virtually clean except for a few hairs in the carpet, and those were not a match to either O'Dell or Garcia, making it as likely they could be from any number of prior guests or motel employees who'd been in the room at various points. Useless, basically. There had been no note, no weapon. She'd been killed elsewhere and dumped there, so no powder either. It had been a professional job in every way. And the two homicide detectives had been working it hard but getting nowhere...so far.

"What about cameras?" Simon asked. "In the front lobby."

"Motel has them," Bailey answered, looking somewhat annoyed by the interruption. "But the person who rented the room came alone and kept his back to the camera the whole time. He clearly knew where it was. White, dark hair, jeans, flannel shirt, old boots, looks like a high school kid—nothing else distinguishing."

"And we interviewed all the employees—the clerk's description didn't match either of our known suspects and no one remembers seeing anyone go into the room besides the guy who checked it out," Tucker added.

"So we have a potential, unidentified third suspect," Simon said, wanting to confirm what he'd understood.

Tucker nodded. "Definite, not potential, but beyond the description of a tough kid who looked barely out of high school, cocky grin, thin, brown eyes—that's all we've got. And that could be a lot of people."

"Especially in that neighborhood," Bailey added.

Simon actually thought to himself that it described a minority of people in that neighborhood. Being just on the border between downtown and the poorest areas of Independence and Prospect Avenue in Kansas City itself, the area was known for its ethnic population—especially Hispanic and Black—and had been for years. The only kids matching that description who'd hang there would stand out. Still, the numbers might involve tens of suspects, a lot to interview. They didn't have anything specific enough to narrow it down, that's what mattered, and it was killing their progress. Simon had been there.

"What about traffic cameras?" Agent Falk asked.

"They got shots but no clear angles at suspects' faces," Tucker replied. The media and the public seemed to believe the traffic cameras and security cameras would solve such problems with ease, making identification of suspects in such cases fast and easy, but that rarely happened. The wide angle lenses captured whatever angle they were pointed at and nothing outside it, so even in cases where multiple cameras covered a location, images of suspects clear enough for ID were rare. Those who got sent traffic light citations and images would surely find this hard to believe, but then they only saw images when the system worked, not when it didn't. And cars moving at the speed the chase had occurred were particularly hard for the cameras to capture well.

The Deputy Chiefs and FBI agents asked a couple other questions then Becker introduced Oglesby and Dolby and asked them to lay out their case on the stolen nanochips. Simon's fellow property squad mates were as professional and confident as their homicide counterparts had been.

It had started with reports from companies, Oglesby began, including Ashman Industries and several shippers, of stolen shipments. They'd gathered descriptions, sample chips, shipping and receiving information, etc. And then the list. The list Simon had seen.

"The list they now claim was inaccurate," Simon commented.

Dolby nodded. "Except we don't know. It's fuzzy, impossible to read."

"With all the tech we have, they can't even generate a clear list?" Chief Melson asked, skeptical.

"Shippers blame shipping companies, shipping companies blame the shippers, customers blame them both," Dolby explained.

"We're caught in the middle," Oglesby added, stating the obvious. "And shipping companies are notorious for being slow to adapt to modern technology. Hell, some still cling to diesel rigs."

Melson chuckled. "Yeah, well, whatever cuts corners, I'm

sure."

The whole room nodded and grunted in affirmation.

"Anyway, the nanochips Santorios and Simon found at the warehouse were originally identified as matching the list, then Ashman claimed that was wrong and we can't verify it for certain with the blurred list."

"So we had to take their word for it?" Simon said sarcastically and looked at Keller.

Keller glared at Simon. "Benjamin Ashman is a personal friend to the Mayor and the Chief—"

"And yourself," Simon added, accusatory, fighting the urge to punch the smarmy smugness of the Deputy Chief's ugly face.

Keller scowled. "We've met on a few social occasions." He clearly wasn't about to admit anything further. "We had no proof those nanochips were stolen. They were in his warehouse and his company manufactures them."

"Except they were with forged paintings from his Gallery and the chips secretly stored classified government data," Simon said.

The room stopped as everyone except Lucas and Becker stared.

"What the hell are you talking about?" Keller demanded.

Simon looked at Becker. She nodded and stepped to the podium, motioning for Dolby and Oglesby to sit back down.

"This is where it gets interesting," Becker said. "Master Detective Simon has come up with another angle—new information that not only connects both these cases, but led us to call in the FBI for help."

FBI Agent Falk was tall, thin, and black with a tightly

trimmed mustache, the rest of his face clean shaven. He had strong green eyes, the penetrating kind and wore a long black trench coat over his button down shirt, tie and slacks. His partner was shorter, with a developing paunch, white, and fine tailored suit. His Eastern European facial features hinted at his Jewish faith, but then his last name, Stein, made that fairly obvious.

Falk nodded, "Tell us what you know, Detective." In other words, this is why we're here so get to the important stuff.

Simon cleared his throat, standing, and walked to the front of the room. "First of all," he said, looking at Bailey and Tucker, "I believe your boy from the Admiral is on the right of the BMW in these pictures." He nodded to Lucas, who stood and began passing around copies of the photos he and his maker had printed from his optic memories.

Everyone in the room eagerly grabbed their copies and began examining them.

"Who are the other two?" Agent Stein asked.

"Foreign. Brazilian, we believe, based on audio we can play for you in a bit," Simon said. "And they were killed in a car chase while trying to kill myself and two others."

Falk looked up from the photos. "Did your run them against databases?"

Simon nodded. "Miles O'Ryan is driving the BMW. Guy next to him is Andrew Helm. The two foreign guys haven't turned up yet, but we suspect they may be mercenaries."

"We? Who's we?" Captain Snapp asked.

Becker raised a hand. "Myself, Detective Simon, Mister Lucas George..." She indicated Lucas. "He was a witness to several activities and provided the photographs."

"Provided the photographs?" Bailey said, clearly annoyed as he got further into the photos of the men at the warehouse and a few other shots. "How come we're just getting these?"

"Because we didn't know we had them," Simon said.

Captain Hamil tipped his head toward Lucas. "This guy was withholding?"

Simon shook his head. "No. He didn't realize they were there." He looked at Becker, who shrugged. He would have to explain context now and searched for words that wouldn't offend Lucas or belittle him.

"How can a person have photos and not realize it?" Tucker scoffed.

"Truly. Explain this," Falk said, as everyone looked at Simon and Lucas.

Simon motioned for Lucas to join him at the front. Lucas strode up an aisle from the back of the room where he'd waited after handing out the photos.

"Gentlemen and ladies, welcome to the 23rd Century," Simon said. "The latest model android."

"What?!" Tucker almost yelled it, face filled with disbelief.

The others looked puzzled too.

"This guy's R2-D2?" Bailey said, shaking his head.

"Actually," Lucas said, helpfully, "I am more like C3PO—fluent in multiple forms of communication." He beamed.

Dolby grunted. "Cool." She clearly had no problem with the idea.

Everyone else but Becker and Simon looked at him like he was nuts.

"He's owned by Benjamin Ashman," Simon added. "Basic

level security for his warehouse."

"Your big case breaking evidence is coming from a machine? Some kind of AI?" Keller sneered, shaking his head. He didn't believe it at all.

"Yes," Simon said. "He has optical systems he was not trained in at Ashman's instructions. They were not necessary for his duties but are standard in his model."

"So he really didn't know he had images? And you didn't either?" Falk asked.

"Yeah, exactly," Simon said, nodding to the agent. It was that simple.

"You're trusting a machine that could have a virus on a murder case?" Keller scoffed, dismissive.

"I have no viruses," Lucas said, looking right at the Deputy Chief. "My systems are regularly checked and self-maintained and I do not maintain open or unsecure connections to any networks."

"He can access them when he needs them," Simon clarified.

"You cannot accuse a prominent, important citizen based on the ramblings of some robot!" Tucker said. He looked at Becker. "I cannot believe you bought into this."

"What about the fact that the paintings are forged? An expert verified it. I have detailed analysis. And a chip expert found the government data," Simon said.

"How did you get such analysis when those crates were ordered turned back over to Mister Ashman earlier this week?" Keller demanded.

"I pulled a few samples and took them for analysis," Simon said.

"Wait. You stole evidence?" Melson asked, frowning. "The alarms at Property—that was you?"

Simon kept a straight face. "I acquired samples before they were handed over. Planning to give them back if nothing turned up."

Keller tensed, standing up. "You broke the law! Captain, I want Internal Affairs—"

Captain Hamil frowned, glaring at Simon.

Simon cut Keller off, scanning the other detectives. "I was suspicious when Oglesby told me the list was blurry. Why would they do that? Why wouldn't they want us to have detailed data of the missing items we were searching for?" The FBI Agents and his fellow cops, including Melson, were clearly understanding his motives. Only Keller was pushing the issue.

"You broke into an official KCPD evidence facility—" Keller yelled.

"Actually, records show Master Detective Simon signed in before the incident occurred, Ken," Melson said. "There is no proof he was involved at this point."

"In fact, property officers reported no missing items," Becker added as everyone looked at the fuming Deputy Chief.

"But Ashman's people did, hours after the items were returned to them," Hamil said.

Simon glared at him. Hamil shrugged. He wanted no nonsense where the questioning of his men was concerned. Simon wished he'd kept his mouth shut but then Keller probably already knew.

"Sounds to me like there was probable cause for further

inquiries," Agent Falk said. His partner nodded beside him.

"Certainly sounds to me like it led to more information that will help your case," Stein added.

Keller exhaled and sat down, still fuming.

"Whatever the case, it has led to information that we can follow up on, maybe break these cases open," Melson said.

"And we do see a likely connection," Sergeant Carter of homicide agreed, speaking for the first time. "We'll all work together on this and see where it leads. But no one is to talk to the press or anyone outside this room about Ashman Industries or other details until we have clear evidence. If things need to be returned to Mister Ashman, apologies issued, let's keep it private—save everyone embarrassment. Okay?"

The officers looked around the room as everyone nodded and grunted in agreement.

"Where are the nanochips with the data?" Stein asked.

"Safe. With an expert." Simon said.

Both agents shot him distrusting looks. "Those need to be handled with great care. We must retrieve them, make sure that data is safe," Stein said.

"Fine," Simon said. "We can get them back today. Trust me. They are safe." He needed to check in with Julia ASAP, hoping she'd done as promised and secured the chips at home or somewhere else private that would be safer and hard for Ashman's goons to find.

"For now," Falk said. "Didn't someone try to kill you and your asset—" he checked his datapad "—a Mister Barber? An art forger, I believe?"

Simon nodded, eyes narrowing as he remembered. "And

my daughter and Mister George, yes. Those are the four suspects in the pictures."

"So how do you know the chips are safe?" Falk asked.

"Because my expert is in hiding and staying there until I tell her it's safe," Simon said. "And she knows how to hide." Julia actually did have good experience with that from her youthful days as a hacker and internet troll. He hoped she hadn't lost her touch.

"Then how can we reach her today and get them back?" Stein asked, clearly probing for the information.

"I have a way to communicate, don't worry," Simon said and his stare told them that was all they would get for now.

Both agents' faces flashed with anger and they started to argue.

Carter added, "O'Ryan and Helm have records, petty crime to assault. But based on a couple phone calls, their current addresses seem to be bogus."

"Yet they're out there somewhere, still a threat," Stein said. "So they could find this expert and get the nanochips back if we don't ensure their safety—"

Melson cut them off with a glare. "You will get everything you need and full cooperation from us. This is just an overview. Not everyone here needs the specifics, so we'll talk afterward."

Becker nodded. "Sergeant Simon and Mister George will be working this case along with Detectives Bailey and Tucker, Oglesby, and Dolby, and Agents Falk and Stein and their teams. Sergeant Carter and I will coordinate and keep the Chiefs informed." She and Carter made eye contact with everyone in the room for confirmation and acceptance then.

"A robot citizen is investigating this—" Keller objected.

"He is assisting Master Detective Simon as a consultant, only when it's appropriate," Becker said firmly.

Melson nodded. "She cleared it with me. I'll make sure all policies are followed."

Tucker scoffed and leaned back in his chair, fuming again, with his arms crossed over his chest.

"Oglesby and Dolby, see me for the expert reports on the forgeries and stolen chips. Carter, you and the Agents as well, the rest of you are dismissed for now."

Simon nodded to Falk and Stein. "I'll be at my desk when you're done."

The two agents nodded in gruff acknowledgment as Simon headed for the door.

CHAPTER 17

LEAVING THE BRIEFING room, Simon followed Bailey and Tucker back down the hall to the homicide squad room and their cubicles. He wanted to get his eyes on as much evidence as possible quickly before the FBI changed their minds and took away the case. Now that he had been granted official access, homicide was the place to start. He'd seen most of the robbery case files. In fact, he was responsible for the bulk of those that mattered for the Ashman angle.

Tucker and Bailey ignored him, chatting over the soundtrack of ringing phones, clicking keyboards and chattering voices that filled the large room as they stopped for coffee at an alcove. Tucker took sugar and cream but Bailey drank it black.

"Scott still pissed at you?" Tucker asked his partner, one of the few gay cops who had survived the department for so long. The reason was Bailey was tough, a former bodybuilder, great in a fight, solid sense of humor, and damn good instincts. He also was one of the top shooters with a handgun in the entire detective squad.

"What do you think?" Bailey said with a shrug. "'You work too much. You care about this job more than me. When are you going to keep a promise and make it home early for a change?'"

"Sounds like my ex-wife," Tucker said with a chuckle.

"He ain't going anywhere," Bailey said, amused. "He loves me, but he's my bitch all the way."

They both laughed as they finished stirring their coffees and turned back to head for their desks, spotting Simon.

"Thanks for stealing our case, John," Bailey said, frowning.

"I didn't steal it," Simon said. "Worked another angle. Trying to help you guys."

"Trying to help us?" Tucker grunted. "I think you just miss your days in homicide."

Simon had worked in homicide for five years when he first made detective. Later, they'd needed a senior man for a revamp of robbery and he'd been there since. He'd stayed not because he liked the work better, but because the hours were a bit less demanding, gave him more time with Emma, more time for life. "I miss your handsome face, Jerry, that's what I miss," Simon said. "Same reason Tom stays."

"I'd miss his ass actually," Bailey added.

Tucker stopped and bent slightly, wiggling his ass then slid into a chair. "Suppose you want to look at our files?"

"Yeah, before the Feds steal the case from all of us," Simon said.

All three glanced over to the briefing room windows where they could see the two Sergeants, the Deputy Chiefs and the FBI Agents in intense conversation.

"Melson won't let them, I'm pretty sure," Bailey said. "And

Keller has been riding us like ants on a picnic. He wouldn't like it either."

"Ants on a picnic, eh?" Simon grunted. "Sounds like Keller all right. Always leaves me itching."

They all laughed as Lucas came across the room to join them.

"What's up with the robot, Simon?" Tucker asked, skeptically.

"He's all right," Simon said. "Has my back. Some useful gifts, too."

"Gifts, eh? Technical skills?" Bailey asked, looking Simon over to confirm. "He sure has a pretty package."

Lucas stopped beside them. "Hello, I am Lucas George." He stuck out his hand, either ignoring or oblivious to what they'd been saying.

Bailey shook it, firmly. "Strong, too. You single, Lucas?"

Lucas looked confused. "Single? I partner with Simon..."

"Leave him be, Tom," Tucker said, shaking Lucas' hand. "He's harmless. Just annoying," he said, nodding to his partner.

Lucas examined Bailey's arm muscles and the large Glock holstered under his arm. "He looks highly competent to me."

The detectives guffawed.

"Yeah, in every way," Bailey said with a wink.

"Which files you want?" Tucker asked, looking at Simon again.

"Whatever you got," Simon said. "Anyone run financials?"

Tucker nodded, moving to a file cabinet behind his desk

and pulling out files. "Yeah, seems fairly clean and straight forward—for a rich guy. Wish I had some of his money, though."

"Don't we all," Simon agreed, accepting a stack of files from Tucker.

Tucker grabbed several more and motioned to an empty desk beside Bailey. "They're out for the day. Use that."

Simon carried the files to the empty desk and set them down, Tucker following. "Grab a chair, pretty boy," Simon said to Lucas. "We've got some reading to do."

He sorted out the files by subject and made two stacks, one for himself, one for Lucas as he fell into the chair at the desk. "Okay, you scan these financials. Look for anything unusual—names we've come across, odd transactions, etc. Anything that doesn't fit the routine patterns."

"How will I know the patterns?" Lucas asked as he opened the first file.

"You get those from the files," Simon replied. "You will catch onto their routines quickly. Especially with that computer head of yours. Look for anything that doesn't fit."

Lucas began scanning the pages and turning them within a few seconds. It was almost as if he was just flipping through, not really reading, but Simon knew it was his powerful optics.

"What is he doing?" Bailey asked.

"Speed reading," Simon said. "Special gifts."

Bailey shook his head. "Fuck, lucky bastard."

"Better not let the Sergeant see that," Tucker said. "Tom is barely literate and he's been squeaking by. Maybe they'll hire this guy."

Bailey rolled his eyes, leaning back in his chair like a man with no worries. "I read you pretty good. Knew the divorce was coming a year before you did."

"I was blinded by love," Tucker said as he slid back behind his own desk across from Bailey.

"How about you fill me in?" Simon asked, and multitasked as they broke down details, while he scanned his own set of files.

Altogether, it took about forty-five minutes of back and forth for Simon to feel like he had a decent handle on the files and their theories. And by then, Lucas had finished the stack of financial files and moved on to reading the ones Simon had finished and set aside.

"You find anything interesting?" Bailey asked, clearly figuring the civilian lacked the skills to offer decent analysis.

"There are several smaller accounts opened at various locations which have been receiving transfers of large lumps regularly for the past five years, a change in the pattern," Lucas offered.

"What?" Bailey leaned forward. He and Tucker clearly hadn't noticed that.

"Does it say who the smaller accounts belong to?" Tucker asked.

"Various businesses," Lucas continued. "One with the initials PRP Enterprises, others with similar names."

"We should run a trace," Simon said. "Could be subsidiaries of Ashman's companies."

"Or a vendor," Bailey added.

"Why didn't we notice that?" Tucker asked, looking at Bailey.

"The amounts vary and activity is scattered over many pages, a couple a month," Lucas said. "There are many transactions to follow..."

"Are you saying we overlooked it?" Bailey said, voice rising as he tensed and sat up in his chair.

"I was merely trying to offer an explanation—"

"Relax, Tom," Simon said. "He's trying to help."

"We didn't see anything in there that looked promising so far," Tucker admitted. "We were pursuing other angles."

"It's only been a few days," Simon said, an acknowledgment that he understood the complexities of such cases. Bailey relaxed a bit. "Did you check out Ashman's associates, friends, ex-employees?"

"Some, but we still have more on our list," Bailey said.

"Why don't you give us the list and let us get started?" Simon suggested.

"I thought the FBI guys were waiting to get those nanochips and paintings from you," Tucker said, cocking his eyebrow in question as he pulled a page from a file and offered it to Simon.

Simon smirked. "They can wait a little longer. Not sure I'm done with them yet." Simon accepted the page and stood, nodding to Lucas. "Let's go."

"Want us to tell them anything if they ask?" Tucker said.

Simon shrugged. "Tell them we have an active case to work. They can call me and arrange a time to meet later."

And he and Lucas hurried out, headed for the elevator, walking right past the briefing room as the two FBI Agents turned mid-sentence to stare curiously at them. But then someone else started in again and they returned to their argument.

INSTEAD OF HEADING west from headquarters, Simon took a right at 11th and headed east as Lucas looked over the homicide detective's list of Ashman's associates.

"The first one on the list is off 7th," Lucas said. "Where are we going?"

"We're going to check out those addresses on the two guys who shot at us first," Simon said.

"But you told Detectives Bailey and Tucker—"

"I know what I told them," Simon said. "And you can bet the FBI boys will ask them what I said and where I went. I want to be sure about those two shooters before the FBI take over this case."

"They seemed cooperative in the meeting—"

Simon shook his head. "You truly know nothing about human politics, do you?" He stopped at a light, trained eyes habitually taking in the pedestrians, drivers, vehicles, and buildings around them.

"Government? Elections?" Lucas asked, trying to infer Simon's meaning.

With the Interceptor in repairs, they were using his Charger, making them even less conspicuous than normal. Simon spotted nothing of interest, accelerating again as the light changed.

"Politics is the thing humans get very angry and fight about a lot, isn't it?" Lucas asked.

Simon grinned. "Yeah, you nailed it. And it's not just about politicians. Currents of politics interweave most human interactions in various ways." He turned right and headed down The Paseo.

"Why would humans permit this if politics makes them so angry?" Lucas asked.

Simon laughed again. "They don't have a choice. It just happens."

"You make it sound as if they cannot control it," Lucas said.

"Exactly."

Lucas cocked his head to the side, thinking. "This sounds more like a disease than ideological disagreements."

"It most definitely is, pal," Simon agreed as he stopped at a light and waited in the left turn lane. A few other cars drove through the intersection headed north and then he turned left onto 22nd and took a quick right on Flora Ave, looking for the apartment listed for Miles O'Ryan. On both sides, green trees lined the street, then the right side gave way to grassy lawns as the left filled with a chainlink fence surrounding the property of a very large AME church. Its brick structure looked shiny new, only a few decades old, with a tinted glass entrance and white stone at the base of the main building.

According to the GPS, the apartment in the database as O'Ryan's last known address would have been right across the street. But it was an empty lawn. Simon pulled to the curb, not surprised in the least.

"Well, one of them supposedly lives here," he said.

Lucas looked around. "In the church? He is a holy man?"

"Yeah, Jihadist with a gun but from AME," Simon quipped, smiling inwardly at the android's obvious confusion. "He lied, Lucas. Gave us a false address."

"Officers do not check this?"

"They don't always have time, depending on the crime," Simon said. "It was a minor arrest for erratic driving, suspected DUI. They gave him the tests and he resisted, so they brought him in to cool down," Simon added, recalling notes in the database.

"He does not sound like a nice man," Lucas said.

"What was your first clue—the bullets hitting our car?"

Simon pulled out again and took Flora south, turning right on 23rd to head back West again toward Main. As he did, he remembered Julia Liu and took out his cell, calling up her own cell number and hitting 'Call.' He raised a finger for Lucas to stop talking and listened through several rings before she answered.

"Julia, John Simon."

"Hey, John."

"How are we?"

"Finding some very interesting data. This is hot stuff. Not anything that should be passed around like this," she said.

"Well, we kinda knew that from the shooting," Simon said.

"Yeah. Is everyone okay? Are you okay? I saw something about a chase on the news."

"Fine. Just my official vehicle needs some work," Simon replied.

"Your daughter was with you?"

"Yeah, I'd just picked her up from school."

Julia made a sympathetic groan. "Oh, wow, she must have been scared to death, poor thing."

"Yeah, she was, but she's doing better now. How are you?"

"Oh, you asked before, sorry. One track mind," she replied. "I am fine. No one has bothered me. Though my boss is starting to wonder what project I have that's kept me at home the past few days."

"I'll probably be by later to pick them up, or meet you somewhere. Feds are here."

"Ah, the FBI is involved now? Fun," Julia said, knowing full well from his past stories what that meant for him.

"I didn't tell them where you are or give them your number," Simon said.

"How'd you manage that?"

"I escaped before they could corner me," he said, chuckling. "Anyway, they won't bother you until I can go with. So you hang in there. Call if you need anything."

"Sure. It's actually fascinating stuff."

"You know you shouldn't be reading it in depth," Simon said, a warning tone concerned with her safety not the legal implications.

"Oh, I skimmed," she said. "But in case you wanted my analysis..."

"Yeah, thanks. Talk to ya soon," he said and hung up as she uttered a goodbye.

By the time the call ended, he was turning left on Main and headed for 39th, the area around University of Kansas

Medical School, where Helm's last known was. Dating from the 1950s, the Valentine neighborhood and surrounding area, including the Med School grounds, was filled with history. Historic homes lined quiet residential blocks. Along main thoroughfares like 39th, Southwest, and Broadway, storefronts of brick often had apartments or storage upstairs. The area had a popular nightlife on those busy corridors, too, and Andrew Helm supposedly lived in an old family apartment above a spice shop a few doors down from Prospero's Bookstore, a Kansas City landmark on the block between State Line Road—which marked the border between Kansas and Missouri—and Bell Street, one of the residential zones.

Simon got lucky and found a spot right beside the curb in front of the bookstore. "He lives above that spice shop there. Come on," he said to Lucas as he opened his door carefully and climbed out.

Lucas followed and they headed into the shop.

"We're looking for Andrew Helm, your tenant," Simon said as he badged an older Asian woman behind the counter.

Her face screwed up in real or fake confusion. "I know no person named Helm."

"He's wanted for questioning," Simon said. "We need to take a look." He stepped past the counter, looking for the stairs and she objected in some Asian language Simon didn't know, but he suspected it was Chinese, and moved to block his path. Given her diminutive, under four foot frame, skinny as a rail, he fought the urge to laugh.

"You do have an apartment upstairs, right?" he said again.

"Yes, my daughter live there," she said.

"No boyfriend? Friend? Andrew?" he said again, this time

flashing the photo he carried of the BMW and its occupants.

She shook her head vociferously. "No man. That my daughter!" she insisted, as if he'd insulted her daughter's purity and honor.

"If we find out you're not telling the truth, we will be back," he warned, stepping back to the other side of the counter as he and Lucas looked around. The place stank of mixed incense scents, spices, and clove cigarettes, though it was impossible to make out anything specific in the cornucopia clogging the air.

Simon turned back for the street, more than ready for some fresh air as Lucas followed.

"What do we do now?" Lucas asked.

"We show his photo and ask around," Simon said, turning right and heading up the block to Prospero's, a two story bookstore, mostly used, that occupied the corner for decades and was a place any local booklovers would stop in from time to time. They'd know people who frequented the neighborhood. So Simon headed for the counter, amidst the dusty smell of the old books and packed shelves that surrounded him in every available space.

He badged the counter guy, one of the owners he thought, and then set the photo on the counter. "You ever seen either of these two in here? Younger one supposedly lives in the neighborhood."

The counter guy picked up the photo and examined it carefully. "You know, we get a lot of people in here, man, but neither of these guys strike a chord."

"Yeah, well, last known address of the younger is two doors down," Simon said, matter-of-fact, not pushing.

The counter guy smiled. "Hell, if that were the case, I'd

know him. He certainly hasn't been around in a long time, if he did live there. Above the spice shop, right?"

Simon nodded.

"Yes," Lucas jumped in. "The woman said her daughter lives up there."

"Oh hell," the counter guy scowled, "that place has been a dump for ages. I hope not. We renovated ours finally about twelve years or so ago and it needed a ton of work. That place hasn't seen any work in decades."

"So you don't know for sure?" Simon replied.

The counter guy shook his head. "Nah. Not my business, you know, man? But I certainly wouldn't want my daughter living there. Who knows?"

Simon nodded. "Thanks."

"Sure," the counter guy said as Simon moved over to a nearby shelf where Lucas was now browsing.

"You shopping or working a case?" Simon asked.

"Books are fascinating," Lucas said. "But very dusty and space consuming."

Simon shrugged. "Well, that's why computers and nanochips are replacing them. But some people collect data the old school way."

Lucas smiled. "I like that."

Simon chuckled. "Glad you approve. Come on." He headed for the door and the android followed.

Just as they'd almost reached the sidewalk, a familiar kid walked past—brown eyes, cocky sneer. Simon realized it was Helm.

"You there!" he yelled and hurried forward, adrenaline

pumping as his body automatically tensed and he started to run.

Helm turned, saw him, and took off racing along the sidewalk to the west.

Simon and Lucas pursued on foot.

"Come quietly or there will be...trouble," Lucas called after Helm as they ran.

"Don't shoot him, Robocop," Simon teased. "We need to talk with him."

"I am unarmed," Lucas said, confused.

They followed Helm across State Line, dodging horns and swerving cars as the light changed, and chased him down the block. He was fast, in great shape. Lucas surged ahead, but the kid jumped off the sidewalk and raced in front of cars, straight across toward the Med Center. Lucas ignored the cars and followed, causing people to swerve, slam brakes, tires squealing. A few cursed.

Simon followed more cautiously, flashing his badge. "Police business, sorry," he yelled. None of the angry drivers looked appeased.

They ran left onto the Emergency Entrance lot and then Helm disappeared through double doors. Lucas entered after him, then Simon followed two minutes later. The Emergency Room lobby was crowded and bustling—people chattering, nurses, orderlies, and doctors checking in, working, asking questions, circling, injured people moaning or crying. But Helm was nowhere in view. Simon made his way through as quickly as possible and found Lucas in a hallway, head turning as he looked around, searching.

"You lost him?" Simon asked.

"He came in but I cannot find him," Lucas said.

"Yeah, well, we'll never find him in here," Simon said, stopping to catch his breath.

"But I was not far behind," Lucas said, disappointment in his voice.

"It happens to all of us," Simon said. "Come on. We'll get someone to stake out the neighborhood. Find him later." He turned and headed back for the doors.

After a couple of seconds, Lucas followed.

CHAPTER 18

AS HE DROVE up Main Street, headed north again, Simon made a few calls, inquiring about Benjamin Ashman's associates. He made appointments with a few for that afternoon and early the next week. Then he answered a call from the FBI demanding to know where he was.

"I'm working the case," he replied, not even attempting to hide his annoyance.

"We need those nanochips," Agent Stein said. "And you knew that. You should have waited so we could arrange it or at least left us the information."

"My other expert got shot at," Simon growled. "I'm not taking chances with my friends' lives. You didn't need to know until you were ready and you were in a meeting with command when I left." Fucking Feds thinking they own the whole world. He hated working with them.

"Well, we're ready now!" Stein shot back.

"Okay, let me set up a meeting after lunch," Simon said. "I'll call you back." He hung up before the Agent could even argue and dialed Julia Liu.

"Still alive," she answered with a teasing tone.

"And in good spirits," Simon said. "Look. The Feds want

those chips. Can you meet us somewhere this afternoon and hand them off?"

"Sure. River Market, in front of the Steamboat say around 2?" she answered.

"Perfect," Simon said. "It'll be me, Lucas, and two assholes in suits."

"Assholes in suits? Ah, that's why I left the corporate world for a lab," she mock whined.

"Isn't your lab owned by a corporation?"

She chuckled. "Don't try and entrap me with technicalities, Detective."

"See you at two," he said.

"Yep."

He hung up and called Stein back, setting the meeting. Then turned right at 15th and headed for Broadway.

"Who we looking for first?" Lucas asked from the seat beside him.

"Ashman's ex-protege, Mia McGuire—now one of his chief critics and rivals," Simon said, while waiting at a light in the left turn lane at Broadway.

"I thought when you called she wasn't in the office," Lucas said.

Simon nodded. "Yeah, but her assistant said she was at lunch with Japanese clients, Woo Song." He made the turn on Broadway and began scanning the right side for the restaurant.

"Really? What is that?"

"It's a restaurant, karaoke. I don't think the slip was intentional."

"What's karaoke?"

"People singing along to favorite songs," Simon said. "Crazy human antics. You'll love it."

Lucas pursed his lips and mumbled, "Hmmm."

Simon pulled into a small lot and found one of two open spaces, parking the Charger. Woo Song was to the north. He and Lucas got out and headed for the doors.

"Look, it would help me out if you can distract her clients somehow, while I talk with her," Simon said. "We don't want word spreading around about investigating Ashman any further than it already has."

Lucas nodded as Simon grabbed the door handle of the glass front door. Lights fluttered inside from the dance floor and pounding music leaked through to the street.

"I'll see what I can do," Lucas said.

"They're Japanese," Simon suggested. "These people love robots. Improvise."

Lucas shot him a quizzical look as Simon opened the door and they stepped inside.

The place smelled of Chinese food buffet and exotic spices. Half the tables were empty, but Simon immediately spotted two Asian men dancing and singing to Madonna on the stage. They didn't look like "Material Girls," but they were enthusiastic about making the claim.

Scanning the room, he found a dark-skinned woman in an expensive, tailored business jacket and skirt, sitting with three other Asians at a table on the right side, two away from the stage. There were six plates filled to the brim with Chinese food. The three Asians were eating with chopsticks and laughing. The woman—Mia McGuire, he hoped—was using a fork and watching the performers on the stage with amusement. The woman looked to be in her early forties, about right for a person who'd started with Ashman in her twenties and been pushed out a little over a decade later. Now they were rivals and she had her own company, smaller, but still competitive. Her lips were full, round, her eyes intense, focused, very blue, and she wore just enough makeup to highlight her features well but not seem obvious. She was important and she dressed and acted like it.

As Simon headed for the table, Lucas stood to one side, watching the stage with curiosity. The two Asians performing weren't awful as karaoke goes, and Simon had to admit he loathed karaoke, especially when it involved people with voices like cats serenading an alley. The Asians wore business suits and ties, like their three companions, but that didn't stop them from awkwardly moving enthusiastically to the rhythms in some kind of attempt at real choreography. Their voices were far better than their moves.

Simon stopped beside the table and smiled. "Mia McGuire?"

She looked up, surprised. "Yeah. Who's asking?"

Simon was reluctant to flash her a badge in front of her clients. "I need to talk with you about something important."

She frowned. "This is important. I'm with clients." She panned the table with her hand.

"Yes, but *official* business," he said, emphasizing the third word and locking his eyes on hers, trying to get the message through.

"Official like what? You an agent or something?" She shifted nervously in her chair, looking at the Japanese, who had quickly gone back to watching their friends and ignoring

Simon as soon as they realized he wasn't talking to them.

"Yeah, something," Simon said.

The Madonna song ended, and the three Japanese applauded their friends vociferously and stood, bantering in Japanese—obviously deciding who would be next—as the others stepped down from the platform and came back to the table.

McGuire had kept her stare focused on Simon, even as she put on her best smile and joined the applause from her clients and others at nearby tables. "This isn't a good time," she said through clenched teeth.

Before any of McGuire's group could get to the stage, Simon heard the familiar strains of Styx and turned to see Lucas standing before the microphone. The Japanese businessmen brightened with recognition and began conversing, then Lucas launched into:

"*Domo arigato, Mr. Roboto, Mata au hi made... Domo arigato, Mr. Roboto, Himitsu wo shiri tai...*"

The android's Japanese sounded perfect, incredibly so. Then he did the best Robot Dance Simon had ever seen. The Japanese businessmen enthusiastically raced to the stage to cheer him on and Simon found himself alone with McGuire.

He badged her. "It's about Benjamin Ashman."

McGuire scowled at the name then looked toward the stage and her clients. She sighed. "Can we make it quick?" Her gaze found his again with a look that said: *not in front of the clients, please.*

Lucas launched into the verse now with the Japanese handling the echoes: "*You're wondering who I am (secret secret I've got a secret)...*"

Simon nodded and sat down beside her in one of the vacated chairs. "You were Ashman's protégé, yes?"

"You clearly know that or you wouldn't be here," McGuire said. "My guess is we have about three minutes. Is that really the stuff you want to ask me?"

Simon grunted, accepting the challenge. "In your time with Ashman, did he ever involve you or himself in anything that pushed boundaries?"

McGuire raised a brow. "That's what his business is about—pushing boundaries, getting there first."

Simon clarified, "Legally."

She chuckled. "Ah, of course." She thought a moment. "Actually, he was pretty clean. In fact, shockingly so for one so rich and powerful in my experience. Didn't even make lewd comments, hit on me—like the others did. In fact, he called them out for it a time or two."

"Really?" Simon knew that wasn't always the case, even in the 21st Century, despite all the progress society had supposedly made. "So, he wouldn't be involved in illegal nanochips, data, forged art..."

McGuire turned back from the stage, stiffening and straightening in her chair. "Are you saying he is?" She seemed totally shocked at the idea.

"I'm saying someone might be," Simon said.

"At Ashman Industries?" she asked, clarifying.

Simon nodded.

She shook her head. "Wow. That would blow my mind if it's Benjamin. I mean, I am pissed at the guy for the way I got tossed aside and written off, and he's a tough competitor, doesn't make it easy for me going out on my own like this, but—" She paused, thinking a moment.

Simon waited, not wanting to interrupt her and break her train of thought.

Lucas and the Japanese hit the chorus now: "*Domo arigato, Mr. Roboto, domo...domo, Domo arigato, Mr. Roboto, domo...*"

"You know, most of it was Paul," she said then.

"Paul Paulsen?"

She nodded, her eyes darkening at the mention of his name, flashing a bit of anger. "Yeah, he's the one who really pushed me out. Ashman hired him out of college like me. Supposed to be his next big protégé."

"*Thank you very much, Mr. Roboto, For doing the jobs that nobody wants to. And thank you very much, Mr. Roboto. For helping me escape just when I needed to...*" Lucas sang.

"*Thank you, thank you, thank you,*" McGuire's clients sang in pronounced accents. "*I want to thank you, please, thank you...*"

"But Paul hated me from day one," McGuire continued. "Hated women, I think. But he resented me for sure, and I thought he was a cocky, smartass kid who should have respected my position and accomplishments and let me teach him. It started that way, too. Ashman encouraged it." She took a sip of her soda and leaned back in her chair. "But Paul worked on him, earned his trust, his ear, had a couple of impressive successes that didn't involve me, showed me up once or twice—and that was it. I was out, he was in."

"So he replaced you?"

"In Benjamin's favor, yes...and then eventually in my job, too," she agreed. "I wasn't asked to leave. I felt I had no choice. I wasn't going anywhere in Ashman's company anymore, you know? And I had ambitions, goals...I was almost as good at what Benjamin does as he was, and everyone knew it. Maybe Paul targeted me because of it..." Her voice trailed off as she looked down, lost in sad memories.

Simon watched Lucas dance for a minute, amazed by the android's well designed choreography. They'd heard the song on the radio the other day but where did he get that?

"The problem's plain to see: Too much technology."

"Your friend isn't bad," McGuire said with a chuckle.

Simon nodded. "Yeah, I had no idea."

"My clients love it," she said and sounded pleased.

"So if I look at illegal activities, you think I should start with Paulsen?" Simon asked, getting back to business as the song entered repeated choruses, winding toward the end.

"Domo arigato, Mr. Roboto, domo...domo..."

"Yeah, I would," she said, sounding sad. "Hell, for all I know he could have corrupted Benjamin by now. We don't see each other or interact much and haven't for years now. But I know who he used to be, and the old Ashman wouldn't risk his hard work with such crap. But Paulsen...yeah, he's capable of anything."

She grew silent then, watching her clients dance and cheer as Lucas finished the song. Then they all gave him high fives as the android stepped down from the stage.

"Purrfect," Simon heard one of them yell.

Lucas thanked them as they followed him back toward their table and McGuire. Simon stood.

"Get what you needed?" Lucas said softly as he stopped beside his partner.

Simon laughed. "Yeah, for now."

The Japanese men were chattering and circling round Lucas like he was a celebrity.

Lucas shrugged. "You wanted them distracted."

"Where'd you learn that dance?" Simon asked.

"The Robot? It's in my programming," Lucas said *sotto voce.*

Simon thought it was a joke but couldn't tell for sure. "Really?"

Lucas winked.

It took a few more minutes and some quick introductions from McGuire followed by handshakes to extract themselves, but the two men finally did and headed back for Simon's car.

AS THEY LEFT Woo Song, Simon reflected on the interview with Mia. She'd actually been quite helpful and he wished someone had gotten to her sooner. Of course, it wasn't Bailey or Tucker's fault. They had a lot of interviews to do, and the trail the killers left was not very clear either. But Simon had had a feeling when he saw her name that Mia McGuire, an ex-protégé, would actually offer a lot of insight that could be useful, and she had.

Simon hadn't liked Paul Paulsen since they'd clashed at the Gallery in Ashman's office, but he had seemed like a typical weaselly assistant, wannabe tough guy, not the kind who could mastermind any kind of plot with top secret data, technology, and forgeries. But then sometimes you were wrong. Paulsen needed more checking into. Perhaps even his own interview. Simon thought he'd rather enjoy that. If he had pushed Mia out and won Ashman's ear, he probably still had an immense level of trust, maybe even bordering on blindness. As soon as he had a chance, Simon intended to find out—prod him and see what came out.

An hour later, Simon and Lucas met FBI Agents Falk and Stein in a broad, long plaza outside the Steamboat Arabia museum at the River Market. It was bustling with people, though not as crowded yet as it would be over the weekend. People shopping the farmer's market stalls for various fruits and vegetables, spices, meat, and more, plus others people watching or just hanging out. A young man leaned against a tree with his guitar case open at his feet for donation and belted out his renditions of the latest pop tunes. The air was clean and clear despite the muddy, mossy smell of the river nearby layered over everything.

Simon greeted the agents matter-of-factly but they ignored him, instead offering annoyed, impatient stares. He had not played by their rules, followed their plan, and so he was contemptible. Simon simply waited, amused.

"Where is she?" Falk demanded.

Simon looked around. "She'll be here. Don't worry."

And no one said anything further as they searched the crowd and waited. This was all business, nothing but. The air between them tense.

In a few minutes, a fresh wave of museum goers poured out the glass doors onto the plaza, and Simon spotted Julia Liu amongst them.

She smiled as she saw him and hurried over. She had only a black leather laptop bag slung over one shoulder. "Sorry, I'm late," she said.

"No worries," Simon said, smiling back.

"The chips please?" Stein demanded, unfriendly and extended his hand.

Julia frowned, looking at Simon. Rude. Then she grabbed the strap and slung the bag off her shoulder, handing it to Simon. "I need that bag back later."

"Sure," Simon says.

"It's part of evidence," Falk said coldly as he grabbed the bag from Simon's hands and the two agents turned and hurried back for their cars.

"What the fuck, John?" she asked, scowling as she watched them go.

"Federal boys, see why we love them?" Simon replied.

Julia shook her head. "Yeah, assholes."

Lucas nodded. "We're Police officers. We're not trained to handle this kind of assholes," he said.

Simon and Julia laughed.

"You got that right, Lucas," Julia agreed. "You two be safe. I'll email the reports they took in the bag, make sure they don't keep them from you."

"Thanks," Simon said.

"Later." With that she whirled and disappeared into the crowd, and Simon and Lucas headed back to the parking lot a block away where they'd left the Charger.

They parted ways for the night in headquarters' parking garage and Lucas headed for his own car and home. Simon went back up to the ninth floor to read through more homicide files, planning to add summaries of the day's events to the case, and also decide which elements of his own reports needed to be shared at this point formally.

The homicide squad was fairly quiet, most day shifters having gone home and the night shift detectives either out on calls or working existing cases. He made his way through the cubicles, ringing phones and humming computers and electronics piercing the silence around him, headed for the briefing room where Carter and Becker had decided to set up shop for the case—because the number of people involved demanded more coordination and more room to work. It also centralized filing, reports and other key information, so that people wouldn't have to run around constantly chasing down what they needed.

As he neared the briefing room door, Deputy Chief Keller stepped out, shutting off the lights as he did, his eyes widening with surprise upon seeing Simon.

"Chief," Simon said in acknowledgment, without any warmth.

"I was just looking over the files," Keller said, sounding oddly nervous, like he'd been caught at something. "Monitoring this one very closely."

"You made that clear, Chief," Simon said. Privilege of rank, he figured. He had no authority to question it.

"Yeah," Keller said quickly, confidence returning, and nodded, hurrying off toward the elevators.

The whole thing just left Simon curious. Stepping into the briefing room, Simon flipped on the lights and tried to figure out what Keller had been looking at. Various files were spread across the long table, some in stacks, a few closed but in front of chairs. Someone's black Galaxy S17 cell had been left there next to an almost empty cup of coffee.

Simon couldn't see anything that identified where Keller

had been working, so he began looking for the files he'd wanted to review.

Then the table began vibrating and the cell beeped. Simon looked over and saw the screen flash with a return number—another cell, and the name Paul Paulsen. He stopped.

Paulsen was calling someone working the case? It made him immediately think of the leak that revealed Murray Barber's ID.

He walked over to the phone and took a look, sliding his finger across the message to try and open it for any more details. It was locked. But he debated whether to pick it up and try and look at it.

Then he heard someone coming, footfalls on the carpet, and Keller returned, looking frustrated. He saw the phone call and his shoulders relaxed. "Ahh, left my phone."

Simon stepped back out of the way as Keller hurried over to pick it up. "I, uh, think someone called or sent a message."

Keller looked at the screen. The notification had disappeared when Simon touched it. "I'll figure it out and call them back."

Simon shrugged and went back to his files, his mind racing. Keller—the leak? Why the hell was he talking to Paulsen? It could just be Paulsen calling to inquire about the case for his boss. They already knew the Deputy Chief was watchdogging them and trying to protect Ashman from a witch hunt or potential false accusations.

Simon thought about calling Becker, but he knew she'd just tell him he didn't have enough. But he could watch Keller. Look for more. After the way Keller treated him, singling Simon out as a bad seed, he'd love to see the asshole disciplined or even fired. Simon would take pleasure in finding dirt on the man. He'd never seemed right to him anyway, not that he relished finding dirty cops. That was a tragedy for everyone, especially prominent administrators and would just hurt the department's community relationships and citizens' trust. But someone was helping the shooters find Simon and his snitches. It was the only explanation for all the shootings, the way they stayed ahead of the investigation and seemed to manipulate things.

He decided he'd keep it to himself for now but do some checking. See what he could dig up.

Pulling out a chair, he slid down and opened the file he'd been searching for, digging in while also pondering how to phrase his own reports as he did.

CHAPTER 19

SIMON FINISHED REVIEWING the files around 8 p.m. and called to check on Emma. Her Mom would be home Sunday so she was still with him. But Simon had arranged a ride through one of the teachers who also happened to live on the Kansas side. Emma was fine, claiming she'd finished her homework and was now streaming her favorite TV shows she'd missed that week.

"I'm fine, Dad," she insisted. "I don't need a babysitter. It's quiet."

Simon thought for a moment about calling Dolby or a couple uniforms to keep an eye on her 'til he got home. But things had been quiet, and he thought she'd be fine for a while. He reminded her to call him if she needed anything and also left Lucas' number and Dolby's just in case.

"I love you, sweetheart," he said.

"I love you, too, Daddy," Emma replied, he could almost hear her grin. "Sap!"

Simon chuckled. "Damn right, and always will be about my baby so get over it."

She made a raspberry into the phone. "Be careful, okay?"

"Yep. Be home as soon as I can." He hung up and left his desk, heading for the garage. On his way, he called a friend at Central Patrol and asked them to request someone from Kansas City, Kansas patrol to make several drive-bys at his house throughout the evening until he got home. It was a common courtesy extended between departments that worked so closely together by virtue of sharing the same metro area, so his friend assured him it would be taken care of.

Sure, Simon trusted Emma, but after all they'd been through this week, he wasn't taking chances. She wouldn't likely ever know and he felt a release of tension knowing there'd be cops around looking in on her, at least from nearby.

He'd picked up quite a bit from the case files that he hadn't really grasped before—little nuances that might shed light on various suspects and activities and were at least worthy of looking into. Paul Paulsen had a lot of influence in Ashman's organization, which matched what Mia McGuire had told him. In fact, he seemed to almost be functioning as de facto head of operations, executing Ashman's instructions and desires, while Ashman focused more on strategies and overarching concerns. As a man known for both his business and social acumen, that surprised Simon. Ashman seemed like the type to be more hands on, and according to McGuire he had been when she worked for him. What had changed? Why was Paulsen given such free reign? He didn't seem that smart or savvy to Simon. More like muscle and a shield for his boss—not qualities top executives usually had.

Simon decided if anyone might know, it was Stacey Soukup, the Gallery manager. Of all the people he'd talked to in Ashman's organization, she'd seemed the most surprised by what happened at the warehouse and that the investigation would cast any suspicion on her beloved boss. She'd defended him as a good man, multiple times, and she'd been willing to talk to Simon honestly about that the couple of times they'd met.

There'd always been a mutual attraction between them. It had been a while since Simon had dated anyone, even casually, but maybe he could make use of the attraction to get a few answers that might put things in perspective for him, if he approached it the right way. At the very least, talking to a beautiful woman who liked to flirt with him wasn't the worst way to end his day. She was the first woman in a long while he'd even had such thoughts about.

He still had the forged Degas in the trunk of his Charger. He'd turned the others over, but held onto it wanting to ask a couple more informants about it. But then he hadn't had time and the FBI had yet to ask about it. So he'd take it to the gallery and show Stacey. She'd said Fridays was one of the nights she often worked late, the gallery open 'til 9 most weekends, so he figured he'd wait until she locked up and was headed out to catch her and ask about it.

He drove down Main and arrived at the Gallery twenty minutes later. Every space along the curb was full so he had to either look for a spot in a nearby garage or use the police credentials on his sun visor and park illegally. He decided he'd rather not call attention to himself and found a space a block away in a garage.

Grabbing the large, wrapped painting, he carried it with him and headed back for Ashman's Gallery. It being the Crossroads Art District, this was not all that unusual a sight and drew him only a few glances. People bought art at all hours down here. Granted, his was big, so big he had to hold it against his chest with both arms stretched wide to balance it as he walked, but nonetheless, no one acted as if it was anything but routine.

As he crossed Main at a light, passed the trolley tracks, and reached the Gallery was, he realized the large, open main room was packed, and instead of the usual classical music, the vibrant beat of New Age and soft pop was vibrating the sidewalk and building as he approached. Apparently, the Gallery was having an event. Looking through the panoramic front window, he could see art everywhere, more tightly spaced than it had been on either of his prior visits. People of all colors, shapes, sizes, and sartorial tastes were moving around with beer and wine glasses and plates of cheese, crackers, and fruit, chatting as they examined the various pieces. Even the double-wide stairs to the second floor were packed. A major event of some sort was happening.

He stood outside, debating whether to leave and come back another time, when he spotted Stacey across the room near the base of the stairs, laughing as she chatted with a couple in their thirties who were dressed fancily in a cocktail dress and tux respectively. Their hair was immaculate, their faces clean and smooth as a baby, and they carried themselves with the confidence of wealthy, successful people used to the world parting like the Red Sea before them as they conquered it one step at a time.

As she laughed, Stacey tossed her hair back with a flip of her head, making a silly reply of some sort that got the couple chuckling, then she glanced over, panning the room, and her eyes met Simon's. They held for a minute, and he nodded his head in acknowledgement. He was in his work suit, a bit rumpled from the day, but not totally under-dressed.

The gallery manager looked back at the couple, politely excused herself and turned, eyes glued on Simon again as she wove through the crowd toward the door, apparently intending to either greet him or chase him off.

The warmth of her smile left him hoping for the first.

As she opened the doors and stepped out onto the sidewalk, a colorful sculpture caught Simon's eyes— surrealist, odd, a figure of some sort—a woman he thought.

"Good evening, Detective Simon," Stacey said with genuine warmth, her eyes meeting his with genuine interest. "We're having an exhibit tonight to honor one of Mister Ashman's oldest friends who's celebrating a 60th Wedding Anniversary this weekend."

Simon smiled back. "Wow. The place is packed. Must be a popular guy."

Stacey nodded. "He definitely is. Were you looking to sell something?" She motioned at the wrapped painting he'd set at his feet on the sidewalk as he waited.

"Uh no," Simon said. "Something I wanted to show you actually. I thought I'd wait 'til you closed for the night, but looks like that might be a while."

She grinned. "A few hours longer than normal for sure, but the buffet makes a great supper, and the company is a delight." Her eyes examined the wrapped piece beside him. "What is it?"

Simon looked around. "Is there someplace I can show you?"

Stacey paused a moment, thinking, as she glanced inside at the crowded showroom. "Well, if you don't mind taking it around through the alley, then we can get to the storeroom. Awfully crowded in here."

Simon nodded. "I don't mind."

Stacey pulled a radio from her pocket and keyed it,

instructing someone to open the storeroom door and meet them there. "It's locked, of course. Right this way." With a wave of her hand, she headed for a narrow run between buildings.

Simon had to twist and maneuver the painting, leaning its bottom against the tops of his shoes and holding it with both hands at the top as he walked sideways to get it through, but he did it. She glanced back and watched him a few times, amused.

"Sorry about that," she said as they finally reached the wider alley behind the gallery.

Simon shrugged. "Glad I could entertain you. Meant I get to see more of that great smile."

She blushed a bit, looking away then gave a muffled giggle. A woman giggling at his compliment? It had been a while, and he liked it. Then she reached up and ran her hand through her hair. He'd read somewhere that was a good sign. His heart beat a little faster as he tried to keep his cool.

"Besides, cops get to haul all kinds of stuff through crazy spaces," Simon said as nonchalantly as he could manage. "After seventeen years, I'm used to it."

She stepped back as the double steel doors to the storeroom squeaked open nearby and one of the employees Simon recognized from his other visits to the gallery greeted them, looking them over.

"Thanks, Neil," Stacey said. "I'll take it from here."

He nodded, turned, and headed back to the crowded front again without a word.

Stacey led Simon inside, then closed and locked the double doors behind them, turning to motion to a large metal table nearby. "You can lay it out there, if you want."

"Okay." Simon carried the forged Degas over and did exactly that. Then he began slowly and carefully unwrapping it. "Do you have gloves we can use?"

Stacey smirked like it was obvious. "Of course." She stepped over to nearby shelving and grabbed two sets of rubber gloves out of a Kleenex-style box on the second shelf, carrying them back and offering one set to Simon. He let his hand brush hers as he accepted a pair and she made no move to pull away. Damn.

"Thanks," he said as they both slid them on. Usually he carried his own in his inside suit pocket but he'd taken them out when he'd had this suit dry cleaned the week before and forgotten.

Simon finished unwrapping the painting in silence as Stacey stood by eagerly waiting. Finally, he pulled back the strip of brown paper covering the painting itself and her eyes widened with shock.

"Oh my God! Where did you get this?" she asked.

"You recognize it?"

She nodded. "Of course, it's our prized Degas. The one on loan at the moment thanks to Paul."

"I thought you said Ashman sent them out?"

She chuckled. "If it comes from Paul, it is from Ashman. Paul is his right hand. He receives the instructions and makes sure we handle them." That confirmed what Simon had suspected after talking to Mia McGuire.

"You don't interact with your boss much?"

Stacey shook her head as she ran gentle fingers along the frame and examined the painting. "This is the wrong frame, it's way too modern. Cheaper too. Why in the world would they switch it out?"

"Because this is not your Degas," Simon said.

Stacey stepped back like she'd heard a gunshot, her shoulders sinking in dismay, her head shaking. "What are you talking about?" Her eyes met his.

"It's a very good, top quality forgery," Simon said. "The one we found at the warehouse the night of the shooting."

"Wait. I thought all that had been returned," Stacey said.

"It had. Except for a couple I kept to have examined a little more closely," he said. "Suffice it to say, I know someone I once arrested for similar activities. Now he evaluates art for value and authenticity. He wrote up a full report on the elements that clearly demonstrate this is fake, including the frame."

"Son of a bitch!" Stacey said, then blushed a little. "Sorry."

Simon chuckled. "No apologies necessary to me. It is very well done, but not yours. Any idea why it would be in Ashman's warehouse being moved around by a team led by Garcia and O'Dell?"

Stacey shook her head, her mouth slackening as she rubbed an eyelid. "I can't believe it..."

Simon waited, giving her time to process the information.

She looked right at him. "Whatever the reason, I'm sure Benjamin Ashman would be appalled. He loves art too much. It thrills him, energizes him. We already know O'Dell was involved in something shady that Benjamin knew nothing about. This must be part of it."

"You really trust your boss, don't you?" Simon asked.

Stacey nodded adamantly. "I've known him for years. Yes, I do."

"Well, I wanted you to know. He won't talk to me, so that's why we've been asking so many questions. Seems odd that forged paintings and stolen nanochips would be moving around his facilities without him having any knowledge."

Stacey grunted. "A few years ago, I'd have agreed with you, but since Paul started moving up, it's changed a bit. Ashman is getting older—taking more vacations, more time with family and friends. And he really trusts Paul, you know? So more and more, he has let Paul handle the day to day execution of many decisions."

"And is this Paul worthy of such trust?"

Stacey shrugged. "Ashman seems to think so."

"What about you?" Simon watched her closely with every question to catch her reactions. So far, he could tell she was being completely open and was deeply confused and surprised by the new revelations.

"Paul is a bit demanding," she said. "None of the people skills of our boss. But he's quite competent, and he gets things done, that's for sure. He has been nothing but respectful of me. The gallery being Benjamin's passion project, he probably interacts with me the most of any of his managers."

Simon leaned against a nearby pillar. "I just wanted you to know I wasn't all bad. See what your take on this was. I've been asking a lot of questions, yes, and I know it's bothered you, but hopefully now you see my reasons."

She nodded. "I always assumed you were just doing your job. I'm sorry you've been unable to have a decent conversation with Mister Ashman." She thought a moment then nodded toward the painting. "He really should see this."

Simon shrugged. "I need to take it with me. Evidence."

Stacey nodded in understanding. "But he's here. Maybe we can get you a moment with him?"

Simon hadn't expected that. Was she really willing to stake her job and relationship on bringing in a cop who'd been regarded as harassing the boss to an event? "Is there somewhere I can stash this? Don't want it disappearing." He began carefully re-wrapping the painting.

Stacey nodded. "Yeah, I know just the place." She turned for the shelves again and grabbed two rolls of packing tape then moved in to assist. They worked side by side in silence for a bit as Simon played out scenarios in his head, trying to devise the best approach to Ashman.

PAUL PAULSEN MET Miles and Helm outside his closet-sized office on the second floor of the Gallery. When they'd called to tell him they were on their way, he'd told them to take the back stairs. Concealed behind a swinging file cabinet that appeared to make up the wall outside Paul's office, only a few people knew about the secret exit, but Paul's people used it a lot.

"What's going on?" he demanded as they stopped in front of him in the corridor.

"That Detective and the robot showed up outside my place," Helm said, clearly rattled. His eyes were red and watery and he was tense.

"Down by the bookstore?" Paul asked, trying to remember where the kid lived.

Helm nodded. "Yeah."

"How'd they find you?"

Miles shrugged. "They were showing photos around—of both of us. Traffic cams or something."

Paul shook his head. "My source said we were clear after the chase. He took care of it."

"They're getting too close," Miles said, a warning tone in his voice.

Bile rose in Paul's throat. He despised weakness. "Don't tell me you're scared, too?" His mouth tasted sour, his lip curling. The two men averted their eyes, embarrassed.

"We need to take him out," Miles said.

"You were told to do that days ago," Paul said. "You're the ones who keep screwing it up. And now the FBI has come in on it."

Miles' eyes widened with alarm and found Paul's again. "What?!"

"They kept some nanochips and searched them. Found the data. And they know the paintings are forged. Feds are all over it."

"Fuck," Miles replied, shoulders falling.

"So tonight's the night," Paul said. "We've got help. We've got targets. Take care of all of them." He pulled out his phone and hit send on the text he'd been preparing before they arrived.

Both men's phones beeped in their pockets, lighting up as they reached for them.

"Coordinate with our friend's people as needed, but get it done," Paul said, dismissively. "He's as tired of screw ups as I am."

Miles nodded just as a tall, thin employee came down the hall, hurrying, eyes locked on Paul. He was in his mid-twenties, just out of college and totally naive. His face bled hope and positive thinking. He hadn't lived enough to know that was all bullshit.

"What is it, Neil?" Paul asked.

"That Detective's here," he said.

Paul frowned. "The one who assaulted me? Made a scene?"

Neil nodded. "With Miss Soukup. On the security feed, I saw them in the storeroom looking at the Degas."

"The fucking Degas is not here," Miles said and his eyes met Paul's. They both knew what it meant.

"Son of a bitch!" Paul said, patting Neil on the shoulder. "Thanks, Neil. Get back to the party, okay?"

Neil nodded. "Sure. Did I do good?"

Paul pulled a fifty dollar bill from his pocket and slipped it into the employee's hand. Neil pocketed the cash with a satisfied look, then turned and hurried off.

"Take care of him," Paul said, looking at Miles and Helm.

"What about the party?" Helm asked.

"Take him elsewhere, as quietly as you can, but deal with him," Paul said and turned, hurrying after Neil toward the party. He stopped at the end of the hall and turned back. "And get that fucking painting." Then he turned and was gone.

"What do we do?" Helm asked.

Miles rolled his eyes. "Fucking find him and kill him, dumbass."

And he led the way down the back stairs.

STACEY LED THE way from the storeroom into the gallery itself. People milled about as waiters and waitresses worked the room with trays of hors d'oeuvres and drinks. Some were just chatting, others took in the art. A few stumbled around, clearly on the verge of overdoing the free wine. Groups of men ogled the ladies and discussed them with leering looks. And in other places, Simon spotted small groups of women doing the same thing to the men. Takes all kinds.

"How much do people pay to attend something like this?" Simon asked, looking at the crowd around him.

"Two hundred dollars," Stacey replied, as if it were nothing.

Simon scoffed. "Two hundred dollars a person?!"

She nodded. "A plate."

Rich people. Simon hated them. "Just for hors d'oeuvres? For two hundred dollars they ought to each go home with a Picasso!"

"Picasso's are worth far more than that these days," she said with a chuckle. "You like Picasso?"

"Yeah, women with three breasts," Simon said, "I was all into that in college." He grinned.

Stacey laughed again, leaning her head to one side and shook her hair as they continued on through the crowd.

"Where's Ashman?" Simon asked, still trying to locate the owner amidst the crowd.

"He's over by the Picassos, actually," Stacey said.

"Of course, I should have known," Simon replied, and

then saw she was serious.

Benjamin Ashman stood at the center of a circle gathered around several Picassos in one corner of the room. He looked warm, inviting, and totally in his element, clearly a man used to being the center of attention, who loved every bit of hosting such extravagant events.

As Simon and Stacey started weaving their way toward him, Ashman suddenly turned and raised a glass, clearing his throat. "Ladies and gentlemen!"

The room stirred as people turned and Ashman said it once more before all voices quieted and all eyes focused on him.

Stacey and Simon came to a stop at the front of the circle facing her boss as he continued.

Ashman raised his glass. "To great art and great company!" he said in a toast then drank from his glass.

The crowd raised their glasses and drank, some repeating his words.

"I hope you are enjoying the evening, my friends," Ashman continued. "Creating this gallery and sharing it with you has been one of the greatest joys of my life, and truly, tonight is for making memories!" He raised his glass in toast, then sipped again and the crowd imitated the gesture.

Simon saw people to the right parting as Paul Paulsen and a couple tuxedoed security men with ear pieces pushed gently through, eyes locked on Simon.

A waiter appeared nearby carrying a fresh bottle of champagne, preparing to uncork it and refill glasses.

Simon grabbed it and turned with it toward Paulsen and the guards. "Allow me," he said and started shaking it.

The waiter and Stacey shot him confused looks. Then Paulsen and the guards reached the front of the crowd. Paulsen whispered and motioned toward Simon. The guards started for him just as Simon popped the cork. It shot across the room and hit one of the guards in the nose, causing him to groan and reach for his face. Champagne showered the other two and the crowd mumbled, stepping back, clearing the area.

"What is the meaning of this?!" Ashman demanded, his voice changed from warmth to fury. He glared at Simon and Paulsen, looking back and forth between them.

"You don't remember me, Ben?" Simon said then, stepping forward. "I'm so hurt. And after all that talk of good company, too." He flashed his badge. "Master Detective John Simon. You remember now? The one from the warehouse."

Ashman looked embarrassed, but motioned for Paulsen and the security men to stay back and let him handle it. "Ahh, Detective Simon, of course," Ashman forced a smile. "You must learn to be careful when opening champagne. It can be difficult to handle."

Simon nodded looking at the guard with the bloodied nose. "Yeah, sorry about that, pal. My aim's better than my touch."

"I hope you're enjoying the evening, Detective," Ashman said, acting as if Simon were just another invited guest.

"Oh yes, I am, especially all the authentic pieces," Simon said. "Much better than the forgeries at the warehouse."

Ashman's smile faltered and he glanced at Paulsen, confused. "I really don't know what you're talking about. We deal only in legitimate pieces. You must be confused."

"Nope," Simon said, looking at Stacey, who had stepped

away, embarrassed and wanting to disassociate herself from him. "Tell him, Stacey. You saw it."

Stacey shook her head sharply, but Ashman turned toward her. "Miss Soukup? What is he talking about?"

Stacey starred at Simon—was she angry or just shocked—then cleared her throat as Ashman's narrowing eyes met hers. "It's true. Almost an exact replica of our Degas. The frame was wrong and a few other things. He says he had it analyzed by an expert."

"Murray Barber," Simon said. "You know the name. Your men tried to have him killed." He smirked. People in the crowd mumbled around them.

Ashman frowned. "I don't have people killed, Mister Simon. But yes, I know Mister Barber is an authority in the area, though I've never employed him."

"Well, trust me," Simon said. "Paul here had his buddies shoot up Murray's house and everything."

The mumbling in the crowd grew louder as people stared at Ashman, less warm and more suspicious now.

Ashman saw he was losing the crowd and his eyes glistened as he stiffened in panic. "I can assure you, Detective. Whatever happened to Mister Barber, I am most sorry to hear it, but I had nothing to do with it."

"Then why did we find crates of forgeries at your warehouse in the Bottoms, Ben?" Simon said, staring at Ashman, unwavering.

Ashman shook his head. "I already told you and the Chief, I apparently had some rogue employees. I had nothing to do with it and I fully support your request to find whoever's responsible and punish them to the fullness of the law. I won't stand for it." He said the last with a resolved look as he panned the crowd, playing to them, seeking support. Only a few responded positively.

"If y'all bought pieces here," Simon said scanning the faces of the crowd now, "I'd have them evaluated before you pay. Just in case."

"Detective enough!" A familiar voice shouted, and Simon turned to see Deputy Chief Keller stepping out of the crowd. "Your harassment of Mister Ashman is an embarrassment to the department. You will leave at once!" He pointed toward the door.

Ashman's brow creased and he glared now, furious. "I will not stand for these slanderous allegations, Detective. All evidence was returned to us. We know nothing of these activities as your own Chief is fully aware. I have been cleared of all charges. Now please, this is an evening of friends—"

"No one's cleared 'til an investigation's over, Ben," Simon answered. "And this investigation got my partner killed. She was pregnant. So yeah, I'm still here and I won't stop 'til I find those responsible."

Ashman motioned to Paul and the guards who began moving in again.

"Expect to report to my office for charges first thing in the morning," Keller said, raging at Simon's defiance.

Simon ignored Keller, staring at Ashman. "I'll take that as a warning. But you should see the painting for yourself. Come over and talk to me tomorrow. Fifth floor. I'll show you the evidence. It's within your rights as the accused."

He flipped Keller the bird as the guards began surrounding him and one swung at Simon with a right cross. He dodged it, whirling and kicking the man in the groin, spotting a second guard closing. That guard tried to grab his leg as he wound around but Simon slipped away and grabbed the first guard, who was bent over, propelling him into the second guard. A third guard grabbed Simon from behind and Simon stomped his foot, freeing himself, then kicking back with his foot into the man's knee.

As he faltered, Simon turned and the crowd cleared all the way to the front door. Simon raced across the space in large strides, made it to the door and grabbed the handle, pulling it open just as two more guards charged. Simon slammed the door in their faces and ran across the street, cutting off traffic. Tires squealed as two cars swerved and the stench of burning brake pads filled the air.

Simon hit the sidewalk on the opposite side, sweat slickening his forehead, and raced up an alley, glancing back as the two guards followed, a street-width behind. As he passed two green trash dumpsters, Simon stopped, pushed one from the wall and rolled it back out across the guards' path then the other, effectively blocking most of the alley, then turned and ran again.

Metal scraped behind him as he left the alley—the guards had reached the dumpsters and were clearing their path.

He ran down a sidewalk and reached the garage where he'd left the Charger. Racing through a metal door left propped open, he took the cement steps two at a time to the second level, retrieving his key fob from his pocket as he ran, and then clicked the button to unlock the Charger, its lights flashing a yard ahead of him as he raced up and opened the driver's side door, sliding into the seat and inserting the key in the ignition in one fluid motion. The car vibrated as he started the electric engine, and then he was backing out and taking off, headed for the street.

As he did, he pulled Stacey's card from a stack between the seats and called her cell. "Hello?" she answered, distraught.

"Sorry about that," Simon said.

"Oh my God, you asshole," she replied. "I cannot believe you did that."

"Just meet me out back with the painting, please," he insisted.

"You probably just got me fired," she yelled as Simon stopped at a light, looking back as the two security men rushed out of the alley toward the garage and looked around, clearly having no idea where their prey had gone.

"I need that evidence. I promise I'll make it right, if needed. Please meet me."

Stacey looked away. "Just leave me alone."

"I will once I get the painting," he promised.

"Fine," she said and hung up.

The light changed and Simon accelerated normally, not wanting to draw attention from the security men as they argued behind him on the curb. He drove down the block and then made two more turns, crossing Main to find the alley that led behind the gallery. He turned in and drove slowly forward, stopping as he saw Stacey dragging the painting out the back door from the storeroom.

Simon pulled to a stop, slamming the car into park and popping the trunk, then got out and hurried around to help her.

"Thanks," he said, taking the painting from her.

She put her hands on her hips as he lifted the trunk lid and began working the painting inside. "Why did you do that?"

Simon shrugged. "I had to get his attention before Paulsen threw me out."

"In front of the whole crowd?" Stacey said, exasperated. "You humiliated him and me. God knows what kind of damage this will do to the gallery!"

"I'm sorry, Stacey," Simon said. "If Ashman's innocent, I'll make sure he's cleared in the press. I promise. But he's stood in the way of this investigation, and if he's unaware of the connections, I need him to start asking questions." The painting situated, he turned to face her.

"Asking questions?! All he's questioning now is the same as I am: your sanity!" she said, glaring.

"Look. Do you really think with you backing me up he isn't going to start looking at the evidence we returned to see for himself what we have? Asking questions? Wondering what's going on?"

She sighed, thinking a moment. "No. He's hands on with issues. He will care, of course."

Simon nodded. "Exactly."

At that moment, Paul and two security men appeared in the doorway behind her, guns raised and aimed at them.

Simon slammed the trunk lid and grabbed Stacey's hand, pulling her behind the car. "Come on!"

Paulsen and the men fired, bullets bouncing off the Charger's roof, one shattering a back window.

Simon pushed her toward his open driver's door. "Get in and slide over." He drew his own service weapon and fired back.

"Why are they shooting?!" she demanded then screamed

and ducked as bullets tore into a telephone pole just behind her. She slid into the car and Simon dove in after her, slipping it into gear and slamming the door as he pounded the accelerator.

Paulsen and his guards fired at them from behind as Simon raced off, shattering the back windshield and making popping sounds as bullets sunk into the Charger's metal body.

At the end of the alley, tires squealed as Simon spun the wheel and turned the car violently onto the street, taking off again.

"My God! Why were they shooting?" Stacey said, still in shock.

"They kill people," Simon said. "I wasn't lying about that."

Stacey shrunk down in her seat, looking at him with disbelief. "These are business people..."

Simon softened, sympathetic at her fear. She'd surely never experienced this kind of thing before. He knew how alarming it could be. "We're all right, Stacey. Let me take you home, okay?"

She nodded, saying nothing as she reached back and grabbed the seatbelt, sliding it over her and fumbling with the latch.

"My daughter does that, too, when I drive," Simon said, smiling. "Something about a lead foot."

"You really think this is a time for jokes?" She sounded exasperated again.

Simon stopped smiling and focused on the road. "No. Sorry. It's how I deal with being shot at." Experienced at it or not, his own heart was still pounding hard and each breath was work.

They continued on in silence, until he realized he had no idea where he was taking her. "Where do you live?"

"Huh?" She looked at him, confused.

"Driving you home," he reminded her with a shrug.

"Oh." She gave her address and he nodded.

"Okay. Just relax. I'll get you there safe, I promise."

She only nodded back, then sat in silence, wrapping her arms around herself as she shook. Simon looked her over as best he could. She appeared unharmed and he felt relief. She'd probably never speak to him again but that happened. Some people just couldn't handle the things that came with the job. They weren't cut out for it. There were days when he wondered if he really was, too.

The intersection ahead was clear so he ran the red light and turned left on an onramp to I-35, accelerating to highway speed and heading for her home in Leawood as he keyed the radio to call in the shooting.

CHAPTER 20

THE SCENE DETECTIVE John Simon had created was bad enough to chase away a few guests, but then gunfire out behind the gallery in the alley had scared off even more, effectively shutting the party down. Benjamin Ashman was furious. He stormed into the storeroom to find Paul Paulsen and two security men holstering weapons and discussing Simon's escape and he lost it.

"What the *fuck* are you three doing shooting at a police officer?" Ashman demanded through grinding teeth, his brow crinkled as heat flushed his body.

"We thought he was stealing art—he loaded something into the back of his car," Paul said, silencing the security men with a look. "Stacey helped."

"Stacey Soukup?" Ashman asked, momentarily thrown off track. He had no idea what the detective had been ranting about but he knew Stacey Soukup. She was one of his most loyal, trusted, and honest employees. Whatever was going on, if it involved illegal activities, Ashman was certain she had nothing to do with it. "You just scared off potential donors, old friends—"

"The detective took care of that!" Paul snarled.

Ashman recoiled. His aide had never dared yell at him

before. It just wasn't done. Not that his employees feared him nor did he want them to but he was a man of wealth, power, and influence. He had made many careers. Working for him was a privilege and those lucky enough to do so always regarded him with appropriate respect. Paul had been his most trusted protégé for over a decade. But lately he had taken on a distractibility, a distance, an attitude, and now he was yelling at Ashman himself? That was the last straw. Intolerable.

Ashman tensed, glaring at his aide. "You *do not* yell at me *ever*, Paul! Is that clear?"

Paul started protesting, but Ashman cut him off with a raised palm.

"No. Unacceptable. And what was that Detective saying about forgeries in my warehouse? Something Stacey Soukup saw and backed him up?"

Paul turned to the security men. "Go see to your duties."

The intimidated men nodded and left.

"I wasn't done yet," Ashman said.

Paul turned back to him and shook his head. "We are not discussing that in front of them. You want to scold me, fine. But not in a way that undermines my authority with the employees I manage." It came out as both a statement of fact and a warning.

Ashman was having none of it. "I will discuss whatever I want, whenever I want with you, Paul, make no mistake. You work for me, period. Owe me your career, in fact. Or have you forgotten?"

Paul turned red, stiffening, his breathing slow and deliberate. "I have forgotten nothing. But perhaps you need a reminder of how loyal I have been. What I have done for *you.*" He punctuated the last word with a raised finger he aimed and pointed at Ashman's chest.

Ashman ignored it, raising his voice back in his own warning. "Whatever this is—I want those responsible fired and their names turned over to the police, Paul. Period. We are legitimate businessmen. We do *not* engage in illegal anything. My entire enterprise may be at risk. Certainly my reputation, after tonight."

Paul snorted. "You have no *fucking* idea what I do for you, Benjamin. What it costs. What it takes."

Ashman frowned. "Are you admitting to knowledge of this? Illegal activities using my name, my resources, right under my nose, Paul?!"

Paul's expression changed not a wit. Instead, he narrowed his eyes at his employer. "I admit nothing. I am telling you. I run this company now. Not you. Not for a long while. And you may have your name on the letterhead, but you owe me everything for its continued success. There is a plan—your plan—and I have followed it to the letter. Everything we do, everything this company is about serves the future of the planet, the public—making a better world. Sometimes, that takes foresight and vision that you seem to have lost, but I have not!"

Ashman couldn't believe his ears. He shook his head, not knowing what to make of the implications of his aide's words. "What are you saying to me?"

"I am saying that sometimes, things happen for the best interests of our goals—by us or our associates—that you might not always see as the correct way but they are the *only* way. Times are changing. And for this company to survive, for it to continue leading the way, sacrifices have been made."

"Paul—"

"I am handling it, Benjamin. As you asked me to. As you wanted," Paul said sternly. "Don't you threaten or scold me again. I am *handling it*." With that, Paul turned and marched toward the doors leading to the lobby.

"Are you admitting—"

His aide whirled, stopping just inside the doors, glaring. "I admit nothing. And you will say no more about this. Detective Simon has nothing. Can prove nothing. And his accusations will go nowhere. I have it under control, whether you trust me or not. But the one thing you will not do is embarrass me like this again." Then he turned and slammed through the doors, palm first, disappearing and leaving Ashman alone.

Ashman was floored. He didn't know what to say for the first time in a long while, but he knew that clearly things had gone terribly wrong, and it must be his fault, his responsibility. Ultimately, that's how anyone else would see it. Whatever it was—he had to find out and put a stop to it. And he had to do it on his own if he could, minimize the damage, or it might cost him everything.

For the first time in his life, Benjamin Ashman was actually afraid.

STACEY SOUKUP LIVED in a well-appointed, modern two bedroom house on a cul-de-sac off Roe Avenue in Leawood, a small suburb in Johnson County, Kansas. The home had false shutters and columns to give it a faux colonial look, an attached two car garage, and a circular drive that led to the garage on one side and then curve around past the front door and out to the street again to the right of that.

Simon pulled the Charger to a stop on the drive in beside the concrete stoop that led to the bright red double front doors.

"You okay?" he asked his passenger who had stopped shaking but sat in silence most of the way.

She shook her head. "They were shooting at us."

Simon nodded. "Yeah, we covered that."

Her eyes were frightened. "I could have died."

"I'm sorry," Simon said, "but you didn't. You're okay."

She sighed then nodded. "I didn't want to believe—"

Simon put a gentle hand on her arm. "Look. Bad people hide themselves well. You didn't know. I get that. And from his reaction, maybe Ashman didn't either. I'm not sure."

Stacey shook her head harshly. "It's that Paul Paulsen, the son of a bitch. Most of us never liked him, never trusted him."

Simon grunted. "Me either." Then serious again, "He's clearly involved but it's not just him. And I promise you, we will find out who and we're going to take them down."

Stacey grunted. "I imagine I lost my job tonight." Her eyes widened with realization. "I have no car! We left mine there! Great..." She was clearly trying to figure out how she'd get around in the morning.

"Want me to have some uniforms drive it over?" Simon asked.

"You do that?" She seemed surprised.

They did, but not for everyone. "If I ask, they will. But I'd need your keys."

Stacey thought a moment. "Let's not worry about it right now, okay?"

Simon shrugged. "Okay, sure."

Stacey looked at her house, thinking, hand reaching for the door then pausing. "That was the most scared I think I've ever been in my life."

"For most people it is," Simon agreed.

She whirled her head around, meeting his eyes again. "I—can you come in for a bit? Not sure I'm ready to be alone yet."

Simon nodded. "Sure, if you want." He reached over and opened his door, and she did the same.

They got out and met by the stoop, taking the steps together as Stacey fumbled in her pocket for the keys.

"My boss probably hates you now, at the very least," she said.

Simon shrugged. "I get that a lot, too."

Stacey chuckled. "I'll bet. You have some way about you." She opened one half of the glass doors and slid her key into the lock on the red door, turning. The door opened and she led the way inside.

As Simon stepped in behind her, she flipped a switch on the wall and the corridors lit up—light yellow painted walls, a staircase up to the bedrooms straight ahead. He spotted a family room and office to each side and a kitchen and dining area straight back through a hall beside the stairs.

"Forged paintings," she mumbled. "I should have known."

"They didn't do it where you could see," Simon said. "How would you know?"

She frowned. "Well, I run the place, when paintings were taken in and out I always knew. They didn't do them in isolation. The work's too good." Someone had taken them out to do the work right under her nose and it bothered her. Simon would feel the same.

"Do you want anything? Coffee? Beer? Wine? Water?" she said as she turned to face him.

He shook his head, but before he could say anything she threw herself into his arms and kissed him passionately. Simon didn't resist, though it took him a moment to return it as he felt a stirring, desire kindling. She tasted delicious—red wine, cheese, some kind of fruit.

After a moment, she broke away and put her cheek to his, lips near his ear. "I don't want to be alone tonight."

"The shooting team won't be available for a while. I suppose I could stay for a little bit," he mumbled. It had been a long time for him and he was nervous, feeling a bit like a high schooler again, which seemed silly.

She leaned back and kissed him again and he got over it.

Their hands explored each other as he reached back and swung the door shut. Then she took his hand and led him up the stairs.

MILES WATCHED WITH binoculars as Julia Liu worked in her lab alone. He watched as the lights in surrounding offices and floors slowly extinguished, one by one. He was fairly certain after a couple hours that she was alone on the floor. The only other people he'd seen inside the building had been three security men—one at the front desk, the other two on rotating patrols around the floors every hour or two.

He'd parked his car in the parking lot of the building one lot over. Now he silently climbed out and made his way through the shadows across the lot toward Nichol Labs. His plan was to climb a fire escape that went up the side of the building, then break in the door and hit the target, getting out before the guards responded. He'd done it before. From what he could tell, the fire escape landing on Liu's floor entered the building very close to her office, too. That made it easier.

He could have shot her from the car with a rifle if he'd wanted to. But he had to be sure she was dead. He had to send a message. This was about John Simon and silencing his persecution of the men and their mission.

He took a deep breath and slid around the side of the building, deep in shadows, too close for the spotlights' omni rays to touch him and yet close enough he had to move rapidly in case one of the guards randomly looked out one of the nearby office windows. From what he could tell, the entire bottom floor was administration and office workers. The labs like Julia Liu worked in were higher up.

Reaching the fire escape, he climbed the black metal stairs as quietly and rapidly as possible, headed for the third floor. If it had been higher, he might have had to revise his plan, but her location made it easy—a simple in and out. Despite the adrenaline rush, he felt a lightness in his senses, a heightened awareness of everything around him—the insects' and night birds' songs, the breeze whistling through grass and leaves, traffic on nearby roads, even a jet engine somewhere in the distance overhead.

He made it to the third landing in a matter of thirty seconds and examined the door. Picking the lock would be simple for a man of his skills, but he didn't care to waste the time. Instead he pulled his pistol, and shot it out quickly, then pulled the door open as the alarm blared and rushed down the hall.

Seconds later, he reached the lab, raised his Sig Sauer and shot Julia Liu four times, twice in the forehead. She hadn't even had time to scream before falling to the floor in a heap, blood pooling around her.

Miles was out as quick as he'd come, holstering his pistol, and took the fire escape stairs two at a time. Gotta love these old buildings, especially labs and their fire code requirements.

He slipped through the same shadows he'd used on his approach as he headed back for the car. Inside Nichol Labs, lights flipped on as the security men went into action. Two rushed up the stairs for the third floor, while the other worked the phone with the security company. He watched the man at the desk a moment as he slipped back into the BMW and sneered. *Amateurs. Too fucking late as always.*

He took off his gloves, tossed them on the right hand seat, started the engine and sped away. More teams were working other targets. He had just enough time to back up the main team and ensure they got the key target this time.

Soon, it would all be over.

He turned up the rock station on the radio and enjoyed Sammy Hagar Group's newest hit—the result of his and Michael Anthony's latest collaboration since they'd both told the Van Halens to shove their arrogance up their stupid asses. "I'm Over You, Get Over Yourself" was one of his favorite new tunes and he blended his voice with Hagar's seamlessly, he thought, as he drove away headed for the Kansas-Missouri Border.

LUCAS HAD GONE to Ashman's warehouse in the Bottoms to look around for any clues that might lead them to new evidence in the case. He still had his credentials to get in, and no one had thought to change them, so after poking around the warehouse itself for a bit and finding no suspicious crates—he hadn't expected to; they'd surely moved their operations elsewhere after the shooting and police investigation—he headed for the office to look at files. Primarily he was hoping to find addresses for other warehouses the criminals might use. Breaking into the file cabinets had been easy. Then he grabbed a file at a time and flipped through them with his thumb rapidly, almost like fanning himself, letting his cameras record each page instantly as it sped past before refiling it and taking the next file to repeat the process.

To his surprise, he encountered no one: no security android or human, no workers, etc. It was late at night, yes, and he knew the warehouse staff worked mostly days, but still, he'd expected to be replaced at the very least, yet no one was there. He was in and out in a little over an hour and headed for Fairway, Kansas to show Simon what he'd found.

There were several alternate warehouses and storage facilities on record. That didn't mean the criminals used any of them, of course. They surely were working harder to hide their activities now. But it was information he didn't think the police had before, and it was a place to start. So he wanted to share it with his friend and partner as soon as possible and see what he thought.

Emma was home alone, doing homework in between bouts of dancing around to her music. Lucas rang the doorbell as he heard the dance beats coming from within loud enough he felt them under his feet on the stoop and waited. The volume decreased a bit first before the door opened and Emma appeared.

"Lucas!" she said cheerfully, smiling so wide he thought her face might break. Then she hugged him.

He hugged her back and returned the smile. "Hi, Emma. Is your father home?"

She pulled away and motioned for him to come in. "Not yet. I'm waiting for him."

Lucas scrunched his face in surprise. "I wonder where he is."

Seeing his look, Emma frowned. "Did something happen to him?!" Her eyes widened and she stiffened, looking worried.

Lucas stepped inside and shook his head, then patted her shoulder as he shut the door. "No, I'm sorry. He just hadn't mentioned working late."

Emma's shoulders sank and she exhaled, noticeably relieved. "Don't scare me like that."

"It was not my intention."

She moved back to the couch where several books lay open and her laptop occupied the coffee table. "Wanna do my math for me?" She winked.

Lucas shook his head. "I do not believe that would be helpful to your learning process."

Emma rolled her eyes. "Yeah, yeah, worth a shot, though."

Lucas took a seat in a recliner opposite her, shifting around until he settled in comfortably.

"So...what happened today?" she asked. "Anything exciting?"

Lucas hesitated. Was it appropriate to discuss this with her?

She groaned. "Come on, Lucas. My dad talks to me about stuff."

"I am not sure what it is right to tell you," he replied. Then he had a thought. "Do you want to see an amusing video?"

She squinted her eyes, brow furrowed. "A video of what?"

"I just need to connect to your flat screen." He motioned toward the nearby TV.

She stood and hurried over, grabbing an extra cable from behind. "You can use this," she said as she lifted it and offered it to him, "or you can use WiFi to connect directly. The password is 5172012."

Lucas set to work on his internal computer, preparing to connect, then considered the number. "Your birthday?"

"Yeah. How did you know that?" Emma smiled, though her eyes showed surprise.

"Your dad must have told me," he said as he used his own WiFi band to connect to the TV. "Auxiliary channel, please."

Emma turned the flat screen on and flipped the channel manually, then headed back to her chair.

Rewinding his memory to the right time, Lucas found the video of the karaoke bar and set it just as he started his song, then let it roll.

Emma's eyes widened as she saw what was going on. It

was all from Lucas' point of view with Simon at a table talking to the business woman and the Japanese business men scattered around while other patrons ate at various tables and wait staff moved in and out, working the tables.

Emma laughed as Lucas started singing. "Oh my God! That is the perfect song for you!"

Then the camera began moving as Lucas did the robot dance choreography and the Japanese men imitated him.

"They're doing the robot!" she said, tickled.

Lucas nodded. "Me, too."

"Oh my God, I have to see that!"

Just as Lucas stood, preparing to demonstrate the dance, the front bay window exploded inward under the staccato rhythm of streams of machine gun fire.

Lucas flipped, grabbed Emma as she screamed, and pushed her to the floor.

Bullets tore through the couch, with whooshing poofs, as fabric tears appeared and stuffing popped out in the holes, the flat screen stopped and smoked, falling over under a barrage. Lucas grabbed Emma and began spider walking over the top of her to get her into the hallway, behind more walls.

"What's going on?!" she yelled, terrified.

"Just stay with me," Lucas said, calm and soft in an attempt to keep her from panicking. "I can shield you."

They cleared the couch and crawled across the foyer then onto the carpeted hallway and laid down, Lucas on top of Emma, in the hallway, listening as bullets streamed again, bedroom windows exploding, bookcases and furniture splintering and more.

"We have to call Daddy!" Emma said through sobs.

"Don't worry," Lucas was dialing 911 over the WiFi using VOIP even as he spoke. He'd try Simon after.

Whoever was shooting circled the house and started firing into the back windows now too as others continued firing at the front. The house was turning into a mess. Lucas reported shots fired and asked for police and ambulance response to the address, then tried Simon, but no one answered. Shifting, he hunkered down to keep Emma safe, mind racing for ideas what to do if the gunmen came inside. Surely Simon had guns at home.

"Emma, I need to know where your Dad keeps guns at home."

"In his bedroom and the garage," she whispered.

"I have to try and get one," he said.

She nodded. "Bedside stand, gun safe. I have the combo."

"Okay, you stay put. Give me the combo."

She told him the numbers. "Don't leave me!" she added, her voice shaking.

"I'll be right back," he promised and crawled again, headed for Simon's bedroom.

SIMON AND STACEY had made love passionately, twice in a row, over the course of an hour. They'd both thrown themselves into it in a way Simon had almost forgotten, emotional, senses heightened—both wanting to escape the memories of earlier that night and so much more.

Later, Simon dozed, his mind fighting to keep him awake with thoughts of the case and Santorios. But somehow he managed to drift off a little because it was a good half hour after 11, the last time he'd glanced at a clock on the bedside stand, when the ringing of his cell awoke him.

He moaned, rolled over and checked the caller ID—it was Sergeant Becker. Stacey slept soundly behind him as he flipped open the phone and softly answered. "Simon."

"John, JoAnn. Where are you?" Becker asked, her tone all business.

"At a friend's," he replied, feeling suddenly more alert as he wondered why she'd called. Did she need him at a scene? Had something broken with the case? Had the Chief heard about the incident with Ashman and called her?

"There's been a shooting," she said and paused. "At Nichol Labs."

It took him a moment before Julia Liu's face popped into his mind and he froze. "Oh no..."

"Oglesby said you know her," Becker continued, not saying the name. His tone had said it all.

"Shit. Goddamnit. Yeah," Simon said, sitting up and fumbling for his clothes in a new rush of adrenaline and energy.

"What is it?" Stacey mumbled, sleepily and rolled over on her back, squinting at him. Her skin still glistened with perspiration from their lovemaking. He caught a whiff of its scent mixed with her perfume and shampoo. He loved the way she smelled.

"There's something else," Becker said.

"What is it?" Simon asked, repeating Stacey's question.

"I got a call from a computer tech on seven, Michael DeMarco," Becker said. The name meant nothing to Simon and he waited for more, hoping there was a payoff given the urgency of her voice. "He called about a special request he'd gotten from the second floor. Earlier this week. Relating to your case."

Simon found his pants and slid them on—first boxers, then slacks. "What about it?"

Becker swallowed before she spoke again. "Deputy Chief Keller asked for special access to his own feed."

"Of what?" Simon found his socks and began slipping them on. What had Keller done now?

"Traffic cams and the KCPS that tracks the cars."

KCPS stood for Kansas City Police Positioning System, the department's own high level GPS system that could track all department vehicles and tie into traffic cams, allowing authorized personnel to pull up surrounding traffic feeds and watch if an emergency or key incident required it.

"What the fuck?" Simon mumbled as he reached for his shoes.

"He was tracking your every move, and watching the camera feeds," Becker went on.

"What?!" Simon stopped dressing and stiffened. Could this be tied to how easily the gunmen had been finding Simon and his contacts? Tracking their activities? "That son of a bitch! Can you track dates, times, and locations or something?"

Becker sighed. "Maybe. They can reconstruct it with some time and effort, but the system is heavily used just from ordinary monitoring. It will take time to see how much they can identify of what Keller was doing."

Radio chatter broke out in the background and Keller went offline a moment to talk with others wherever she was.

"Sorry about that," she said after a few minutes when she returned.

"What now?" Simon asked.

"A shooting—but over in Fairway, Kansas side. Different MO. Machine guns. Residential."

Simon stood, panicked. It was suddenly very hard to breathe. "Did you say Fairway?!" Becker didn't know about the house he'd inherited. Few did. Emma was home alone!

Just then the sliding glass doors on the far side of the bed where Stacey was sleeping burst and sent a shatter of glass on Stacey, the bed, and Simon as gunfire erupted from outside.

Simon saw the muzzle flashes as he fell to his knees, calling for Stacey. She screamed and rolled over as Simon heard Becker calling for him on the phone. His skin tingled with bits of pain where he assumed bits of glass had bitten into him as they flew.

In moments, Simon leaned over the sheets, more glass cutting into his chest as he reached for Stacey, trying to pull her to safety. But then her body jumped as bullets tore into her and he saw blood flowing as the mattress popped and holes filled with stuffing appeared there, too.

He dove down, grabbing his Smith and Wesson and then popped up, firing back at where he'd seen the muzzle flashes outside.

Gunfire came back at him as he rolled and twisted, landing on one knee beside a desk at the foot of the bed and firing again.

This time, gunfire erupted but the muzzle flashes curved upward as someone outside fell.

Simon leaned to one side, looking out the window, and then there were more pops and flashes as someone fired a pistol straight at his head. He ducked as bullets splintered the desk beside him.

"Stacey!" he yelled, still hoping she was alive somehow.

"John!" he heard Becker's faint voice calling over the dropped cell. Sirens sounded in the distance, approaching. Simon fired more shots outside then leaped, diving back behind the bed as he reached for the phone.

This time, no one returned fire. The sirens were growing louder by the second. The first responders would arrive in moments.

"John?!" Becker shouted again as Simon slid the phone back to his ear.

"Ambulance, gunfire, machine guns," he said, giving Stacey's address. "At least two down."

"Uniforms are arriving now," Becker said, as Simon smelled the iron of Stacey's blood and noticed she hadn't moved from lying on her back, her eyes open and glassy as her head tilted toward him. There was no life there. He winced, his shoulders sinking with his heart as he just stared at her lifeless form.

"Goddamnit! I gotta go, JoAnn!"

He stood and grabbed his shirt off the back of a chair, stuffing his left foot into the remaining shoe and grabbing his holster as he ran for the door and out down the corridor.

"Wait for the uniforms," Becker said. "We need your report."

"No! Emma," Simon said as he pounded open the front door, startling two uniforms with guns drawn who'd started up the stoop. "In the bedroom!" he called, hurrying past.

"Sir! Stop!" one of the uniforms yelled, turning with his sidearm aimed.

"Simon, Property, Central," Simon mumbled, then threw his shirt over his arm and fumbled for his wallet, stopping and badging the man.

The uniforms relaxed then and hurried inside as more cars arrived and pulled into the drive.

Simon saw another uniform leaning over a dead gunman in the yard as his partner looked on, talking into a radio.

"John, talk to me!" Becker demanded.

"Emma's in Fairway," Simon said as he reached the Charger and opened the driver's side door, slipping into his seat and fumbling for the keys.

"I'll call you back," he said as he hung up and started the car, peeling away with squealing tires as he raced for home. His heart pounded so hard he thought it might explode from his chest. His limbs shook as he held to the wheel for dear life and kept accelerating. After his eyes blurred, he gasped, realizing he'd been holding his breath.

"God, please let her be okay," he mumbled as he slipped onto an onramp and raced onto the highway headed north. It was all he could do to keep focus as he zipped in and out of traffic, switching lanes constantly, his sole focus getting to his baby and protecting her.

"You motherfuckers!" he yelled, punching the steering wheel with his right hand. First, Santorios, then Stacey. His chest tightened with a mix of anger and fear. If anything happened to Emma, he'd kill them all.

CHAPTER 21

S IMON MADE THE fifteen minute drive from Stacey Soukup's house in Leawood to his home on Canterbury in Fairway in under seven minutes. He'd popped the magnetic light on top of the Charger and hit the siren, accelerating through every light and intersection and using opposite lanes as necessary to speed around other traffic.

He screeched to a stop at the curb in front of his neighbor's house and ran across the lawn in wide strides, headed for his house. Flashing lights filled the night air as several Kansas City, Kansas police vehicles and an ambulance encircled his home.

Simon badged the uniforms guarding the scene and two detectives who glanced over from the lawn as he ran. He found Lucas and Emma sitting on the back of the ambulance in the drive, as Emma was examined by Paramedics. Across the lawn, a few yards away, he saw the dead gunman, a machine gun dropped where it fell a few feet away.

"Daddy!" Emma cried as soon as she saw him and lurched to her feet, pushing the Paramedic aside as they rushed to embrace each other. Simon felt his heart relax instantly, tension leaving his body. His baby girl was all right.

Lucas stood and smiled at Simon.

"Where were you?!" Emma demanded.

Simon looked at Lucas. "I was out working a case. I'm sorry."

Emma's brow furrowed, her eyes tightening as her nostrils flared. "You should have called me."

It was look she'd inherited from her mother. "I know, honey. It was last minute. I forgot."

Emma shook her head. "Unacceptable. You know how you'd feel if that was me."

She had him dead to rights. "I know. I screwed up."

Emma looked at him as if she had more to say, but instead, she buried her head in his shoulder and just hugged him and cried.

"I got one of the men," Lucas said. "The other two drove off in a BMW."

Simon took a deep breath. "Thank you."

Lucas nodded.

"What are you doing here?" Simon asked the android.

"I got some information at the warehouse I wanted to share with you."

Simon hugged Emma one more time, leaned back, wiping her tears with his thumbs, then lifted her back up to sit on the back of the ambulance. "Let the man finish, baby." He stepped aside and motioned to the Paramedic, who moved in to continue dressing a few cuts and abrasions on her arms and face, mostly, Simon assumed, from broken glass like his own.

"The house is a mess," Emma mumbled.

"Don't worry about the house, babe," Simon said gently and tousled her hair then turned to Lucas. "What information?"

"I went back to the warehouse where we met to look around," Lucas explained.

Simon nodded. "Right. I figured you meant that warehouse."

"I found no evidence of nanochips or forged art, but I was moving quickly," Lucas continued. "What I did find were addresses of other warehouses and storage facilities on shipping orders."

Simon frowned. "Really? And you were able to just walk right in?"

"No one had changed my security pass," Lucas said with a shrug. "The file cabinets did not have good locks."

Simon chuckled. "You seem to have picked up some bad habits."

Lucas grinned. "Yes, I have been spending time with some bad influences it seems." They both chuckled. "I came to show you and then the shooting happened."

Simon extended his hand and Lucas shook it. "Thank you. For watching after my baby," Simon said.

Lucas nodded. "We were watching the karaoke, and I was about to do the robot dance when—"

Simon shook his head. "She doesn't need to know everything we do when she's not around."

Emma made a face, punching her dad in the arm. "It was awesome. How did you keep a straight face?"

"I was working," Simon said. "No dancing on the job; it's department policy."

Emma and Lucas chuckled.

"How many were there?" Simon said, taking a deep breath

as he relaxed further, his thoughts focusing again after the stress and panic as he'd raced over.

"Three at least," Lucas said, knowing he meant the gunmen.

"You get their faces?"

Lucas nodded. "I believe at least two, but they were outside, in shadows." He had video but he didn't think it would be helpful.

"We'll take a look soon," Simon said.

An approaching siren made them all turn as a KCPD sedan pulled to the curve behind Simon's Charger. Sergeant Becker and Anna Dolby got out and flashed their badges, hurrying toward the ambulance. Simon stepped out to greet them and noticed they both relaxed significantly at seeing Emma was okay.

"What brings you here, Sergeant?" Simon asked.

"A shooting involving one of my detectives," Becker replied. She motioned to Dolby. "Go inform KCKPD we are here and offer to coordinate, Anna."

Dolby nodded and hurried off, but not before hugging Emma quickly and patting her hair.

"Who lives here, Detective?" Becker asked.

Simon and Emma exchanged a look. If he told Becker his secret, he knew he could trust her, but she'd probably prefer not to know in case it ever came up with administrators. He stumbled over what to tell her.

Lucas stepped forward. "Me, Sergeant."

Becker looked puzzled. "I thought I read a report that had you in an apartment near River Market?"

Lucas nodded. "Well, I just got the house. It was time for a change. Since I am seeking new employment."

Simon and Lucas exchanged a look, Simon offering a silent thanks. Becker would find out when KCKPD sent over the reports, of course, so he'd have to tell her. But now was not the best time. He wanted to do it when he was calmer, collected, not just recovering from shootings involving his house, his lover, and his daughter.

Becker pursed her lips, looking at Simon. She clearly had deduced the truth but she simply grunted. "Well, sorry about your home then, Mister George."

Lucas sighed. "I have insurance."

"What exactly happened here?" Becker asked.

Lucas ran it down for her in a few minutes and answered a couple questions, then motioned to the KCK Detectives. "I am waiting for a formal interview, but that's what I've told them so far."

Becker stepped up to rub Emma's back. "Glad you're okay, sweetie." Then she turned back to Simon and Lucas. "I'm going to go see if we need to coordinate since this seems to be related to our case. John, I want a report in the morning. We'll also get a statement from Mister George for the files."

"Of course," Simon said as Becker turned and hurried off to join Dolby and the other detectives.

Simon's head fell back. Thank God he had a boss who liked and trusted him. The Paramedic had finished with Emma as his partner eyed Simon.

"You want us to clean up those wounds?" the medic asked.

Simon had forgotten about the cuts. "Yeah, okay." He took a seat beside Emma on the back of the ambulance. "Thanks."

And he thought about Keller. Keller had helped them trace his movements, find his home, remove his security, the safety of the Barbers, Julia Liu, everyone who trusted him. Because of Keller, his friends were dead and his daughter's innocence stolen. Simon could have gone another decade before having Emma realize the realities her father dealt with every day. Now that dream was over. The car chase, now a shooting at his house, shootings at the Barber's, the Lab, Peter Green, Santorios—Keller was going to pay. Simon would see to it. But before he went after a Deputy Chief, he knew he had to clean up a few loose ends, make sure his own ass was covered, because Keller would fight back hard. Despite his long dislike for the man, Keller was no fool. He knew how to play the game; knew how the department worked, and he would use every bit of his knowledge and resources to save himself and his career no matter who he destroyed in the process.

The KCK Detectives and Becker were interviewing Lucas and Emma now as Simon waited on the ambulance, watching. He fought the temptation to go check out the damage to his house. Crime scene techs wouldn't want him there. He had to wait for later. He could tell from the bullet holes and broken windows he saw just on the front that the damage was likely extensive. He had insurance, of course, but the agents would sure love this—especially from a cop. Not to mention the neighbors who'd been friendly so far but might now not feel so happy having a cop living in their midst.

He sighed. So much he'd have to deal with later. For now, he had to wait until the KCKPD was through then find a safe place for himself and his daughter for the next few days.

Santorios' funeral was in the morning, but after that, Simon would be stepping things up to red alert and pushing the FBI and others to hit back hard—searches, interviews, anything and everything to solve the case and put the gunmen and their bosses behind bars. He wouldn't rest until that was accomplished. They'd threatened his family twice. That made stopping them his number one job.

PAUL CALLED THE South American from his Lexus, parked outside Ashman Tech in a dark parking lot in Overland Park. The Brazilian answered right away.

"Hallo?"

"Ashman is becoming a problem," Paul said without preamble.

"Benjamin Ashman? I thought you were handling him," the accented voice said.

"So did I, but that Detective showed up at the gallery tonight and now he's not handled," Paul replied.

"John Simon?"

"Yeah. Ashman's furious. And he knows I'm involved somehow."

"*Merda!*" The Brazilian shouted, then coughed, calming himself a moment before continuing. "I can come."

"Keller says they know someone from Brazil is involved," Paul added.

"Como?"

"Audio," Paul said. "No idea how they got it."

"*Filho de puta*! I will be there Monday."

Paul grunted. "The sooner the better. We took out a bunch of them tonight. But with the FBI involved—"

"You made a mess," the Brazilian said.

"The mistake was letting them live long enough to investigate," Paul said. "Simon is like a rabid dog. Killing his partner only pissed him off."

"Not killing him makes it worse."

"We've tried," Paul said, irritation seeping into his voice at the accusation. His jaw tightened, his arms and legs twitching involuntarily. "Your men have been no help." If anything the sloppy foreigners had made things worse. Their hits had failed even more than his men's had. "At least we got the snitch."

"Do not attempt to shift blame," the Brazilian said, his voice tightening in warning. "There is too much at stake to argue. Monday. Be ready."

"No problem," Paul said.

With a click, the line went dead.

"Asshole," he mumbled and noticed someone running toward the car through the shadows.

Moments later, there was a knock at the driver's side window. Paul rolled it down.

"Here," Ray Stanford said, passing a small box through the window.

Paul accepted. "How's it work?"

"Get within fifteen yards and turn it on," Stanford replied. "Jumbles his memory. And the nanochips, too."

Paul knew his company had made the tech that made Lucas George possible. What he hadn't known until calling Stanford was that they'd also developed a way to disable it when necessary. With a few enhancements, Stanford had even extended the range. "Excellent."

Stanford simply nodded, turned, and hurried back into the shadows again.

Paul rolled up his window, setting the package beside him in the seat. He'd open it later. It contained a remote control-like device that would shut the android down. It was time for a reckoning for all of his enemies. He hadn't heard from all of his men yet, but it appeared John Simon had once again survived the hit, and they weren't sure about his daughter. Lucas George was also undamaged, something Paul feared. Taking androids out with bullets was next to impossible. The scientist and Stacey Soukup should be dead. The forger, if alive, was in hiding. Keller would confirm soon.

Monday would be the day. None of the others would make it through the week. Paul would take them all out if necessary. The mission was too important. The world needed men like him more than men like Simon; needed the checks and balances; needed the tests. A man like Simon couldn't begin to understand. He could, however, be a royal pain in the ass. Paul was tired of his ass aching.

SIMON HAD GROWN up as religious as anyone else in his small hometown of Lindsborg, Kansas. Hardy people with strong cultural ties to the Swedish immigrants who'd named the town, residents were farmers and craftsmen and their work often centered around sustaining cultural traditions like Dala horses, handcrafted trolls, and culinary delicacies like Swedish Rice Pudding and Swedish meatballs, amongst others. Just south of Salina on I-135 in a valley surrounded by agricultural fields, Lindsborg was a town of under 4000 residents, which grew by several hundred the nine months a year that Bethany College, a respected private local university was in full swing. The students' presence is what had saved Simon from feeling like a total oddball. Being a minority as a brunette, having students and workers around kept him from totally standing out amongst his blond, blue-eyed friends.

Like their Swedish ancestors, most Lindsborgers were Lutherans or Catholics, those who practiced at least. Simon's parents had been seasonal attendees—Easter, Christmas, and a few other holidays throughout the year. The Catholic priest's words at Santorios' funeral reminded him much of the traditional Lutheran liturgy he'd heard as a child. Being Blanca Santorios' partner, Simon had a seat up front, on the second row, behind family—just behind Andy, in fact. Almost a thousand people had shown up for the funeral—cops, civilian KCPD staffers, friends, family, and even sympathetic members of the public. Blue dress uniforms like Simon's own surrounded them like a wall, but the strength of support didn't keep Andy and other family from emotionally tearing up during the funeral. Simon reached up and grabbed his friend's husband's shoulder to squeeze from time to time, managing to contain his own tears, but Emma sniffled softly beside him.

The service was held at The Church of the Holy Martyrs on East 79th Street at The Paseo, near where Blanca Santorios had grown up, just on the edge of the barrio. A solid rectangular structure of brick, the outside facing The Paseo had a concrete statue of Saint Mary facing the street over the side door. It led through a gated fence to a sidewalk next to a blue city bus stop. The inside altar was sky blue with marble arches and podium and another, full color painted statue of Mary that looked out at parishioners. Beside this on a tripod, an enlarged 3-photo spread of Blanca Santorios showed her in uniform at her Academy graduation, in her wedding dress, and in civilian clothes—that beautiful, warm smile, bright welcoming eyes staring out at the audience as the priests presided over her earthly goodbyes.

The few times he'd let himself take in the photos had brought Simon closest to tears, so he looked away quickly, steeling himself, trying to remain strong for the support of Emma and the others around him. Sergeant Becker and several Central Division detectives sat together on a long pew a few rows back across the aisle. The Police Chief and several Deputies occupied the row opposite Simon, just behind family. Simon and Emma shared their pew with neighborhood friends and an older couple, all of whom became emotional themselves when Blanca's father stepped up to say a few words. Andy looked as if he wanted to but couldn't pull himself together, but Jaime Santorios showed the strength often evident in Latino patriarchs and spoke movingly and well about his daughter's career, the family's pride in her accomplishment, and their dashed hopes for the future. He ended with a hope that her killers would be brought to justice. Next, the Chief himself spoke followed by Sergeant Becker—both talking about honor, service, dedication, and sacrifice.

Simon glanced over at Deputy Chief Keller during those remarks but the man kept a tightly controlled look and stared straight ahead, not even acknowledging Simon's stare. Simon fought the urge to approach him when the service ended and the crowd filed toward the back. "What do you think about that talk of honor, service and dedication there,

Keller?" he wanted to demand. But he knew better. Tipping off the Deputy Chief would be a huge mistake that might endanger their entire case. But watching the man's smugness as he paid respects to the family and silently stood beside the coffin briefly in tribute, made Simon's muscles harden enough that he felt a jab of pain from his old back wound and had to quickly turn away and engage Emma and Becker in conversation to distract himself.

After the service, the motorcade following the hearse and family limos stretched over a mile long as they drove from the church in South Kansas City to the cemetery off East 83rd at I-435, Memorial Park, where the Santorios family had their plots.

After a brief burial service, Simon joined friends, family, and fellow officers in paying respects at the casket one more time before it was lowered into the ground. Simon distinctly noticed Keller had not followed from the church—not entirely unusual given that KCPD still had to operate while burying its own, yet definitely a sign that his priorities were elsewhere. Santorios' family likely wouldn't notice or care, but to Simon it was just one more slap in the face from the man he now believed was in large part a conspirator if not outright contributor to the deaths of Blanca Santorios, Julia Liu, Peter Green, and several others.

After the funeral, Simon stood with Emma and Becker as people filed for their cars. The Police Chief stopped briefly to shake their hands and offer condolences, then moved on with his entourage. Finally, it was just Simon, Emma, Becker, and Andy standing at the casket. Even the rest of the family had moved off toward the limos now. Andy just stood there staring at the shiny top of his wife's final resting place.

Simon wanted to say something, his mind searching for the right words, as he cleared his throat.

He never got the chance. Hearing him, Andy Harris turned and his eyes narrowed as they locked on Simon's. "Tell me you got the bastards, John. Tell me you made an arrest."

Simon shook his head. "We're close, Andy, I promise. But you'd have been the first to know if we had."

Andy turned and marched over with large steps, grabbing Simon by the lapel. "You fucking better get them, John! You fucking better kill them like they killed her! Or I will, I swear!"

Simon nodded. "I know, Andy. I want them, too."

Emma started sobbing beside him, clearly overcome by Andy's strong emotions as Becker put an arm around her and motioned to Andy. "We're doing all we can, Andy. I assure you."

Andy scoffed and stared at the Sergeant. "All you can?! My wife and son are dead! Forever, Sergeant! Don't fucking talk to me about all you can, okay? I want my family back!"

Andy balled his hands and started pounding his fists into Simon's chest. Becker tried to step forward and pull him back but Simon gently raised a palm and motioned her away. He just stood there for a few minutes, letting Andy hit him, letting him release the terrible pain and anger until he exhausted himself. And slowly, softly, tears began flowing down Simon's cheeks, too.

Finally, the grieving man's punches weakened then petered out and he stood, arms dropped to his sides and whimpered before his wife's partner and friend. "God, I loved her."

Simon locked eyes with him. "I loved her, too, Andy." With that, Andy collapsed against him and the two men embraced. This just made Emma sob more and Becker wrapped an arm around her.

They all four stood there, letting the tears and sorrow out, holding each other for several minutes. Then Andy finally sniffled, pulling away. With a final nod to the men waiting to lower his wife's casket, he turned, stiff, almost like a soldier, and marched away toward the waiting family and limos as Simon went to embrace his daughter, his Sergeant beside him, watching the man go. He saw from her face they both felt as if they'd betrayed him somehow. Even though both knew they'd done everything they could.

On the way back to Central, Becker rode with Simon, sending the other detectives who'd driven her on ahead.

"You two okay?" Becker asked gently after they'd driven a bit in silence.

Emma nodded. "I'm so sorry about Blanca."

"Me, too, sweetheart," Becker said, scrunching her eyes in sympathy before turning back to Simon.

"Me three," Simon choked out, focusing on his driving as the tears dried on his cheeks.

"From now on, I'm tightening the reins," Becker said. "Soon as we get back. Falk and Stein will be waiting for us, and I've asked Carter, Bailey, Tucker, and Melson to join us along with our key people. No one else can be in on this until we've dealt with Keller. Only people we trust."

Simon nodded. "I'm not even sure I trust all of them." He slowed to a stop at a light in the left turn lane and flipped on his signal, waiting to enter the on ramp for 435.

Becker scoffed. "Come on, these are the good ones."

Simon grunted. "Yeah, sorry. Just not at my best."

"It's not your fault, John," Becker said, reading him perfectly. "Andy's grieving. He didn't mean it."

"He didn't even say that," Emma said, confused.

"He didn't have to," Simon replied, checking traffic as he turned the Charger onto 435 and headed north. "I'm the senior partner. It's my job to look after her."

"She's not a child, John," Becker said. "She's a qualified KCPD veteran who knew the risks and knew how to handle herself. Old fashioned sentiments aside, you know it's not on you."

But Stacey was on him. Goddammit. "Fuck what I know," Simon snapped. "I feel like he did. I want them dead." He stared straight ahead as he said it, embarrassed at the emotional outburst, especially in front of his own daughter.

Becker took a deep breath and looked at him. "I want the bastards, too. So let's fucking go get them, okay? But together, the right way."

Simon grunted. It was all she needed. He was fully onboard, as she'd known he would be.

"We gotta talk with some people at the office, baby," Simon said. "Do you want to go back to the hotel and wait?"

"Can I wait with Lucas?" Emma asked.

"He'll be with us," Becker said.

Emma frowned. "I can't listen, too?"

Simon shook his head. "No. Police business. Not a place for you, sorry."

"Then I'll use your desk and listen to music. You have internet, right?"

Simon and Becker chuckled, exchanging a look. Whatever

did parents do before the internet for instant entertainment in such situations?

"Yeah, sure," Simon said. "But no looking at porn, okay?"

Emma blushed, her mouth forming a horrified "O" as Becker stifled a laugh. "My God, dad, of course not!"

"She's at that age," Simon said to Becker, shooting her that bewildered look parents of teenagers often shared when their kids were slipping out of control.

"Dad!"

"Mine went through it, too," Becker said, sighing. "Better watch her credit card bill carefully."

"I had to take it away," Simon quipped.

"You did not!" Emma said, punching his arm, her face turning beet red now.

Simon and Becker exchanged knowing looks as he took the ramp from 435 to 70 and headed west toward downtown. Emma suddenly realized she'd been played and blushed.

"I hate you guys," she muttered.

CHAPTER 22

SIMON, BECKER, AND Emma arrived at Central to find the place busier than usual for a Saturday. Oglesby and Dolby were talking at their cubicles, stacking files; a computer tech was installing a card-key entry system on the door to the squad; and several clerks, some of whom Simon recognized as week-day only, were working phones, filing, etc.

"What's going on?" Simon asked the Sergeant as they wound their way through toward her office.

"Gotta couple things to talk about in my office, and then everyone will be here for a case meeting and I'll lay it all out," she replied.

Simon turned to Emma and motioned toward his desk. "Over there, honey."

"I need the computer," she reminded in a sing-song voice.

"Yeah, I'll be there in a sec," he said, and continued following Becker to her office.

Once inside, she motioned for him to close the door.

"Card-key for the squad?" he asked as he watched maintenance men arriving with dollies containing three very large file cabinets and rolling them into the squad.

"Limited access. Files, too," Becker said. "From now on,

this stuff is eyes only and we keep them secure."

"Keller?"

"Bingo," she said, nodding and pulled a form from a stack on her desk where it had been buried, offering it to Simon. "Sign on the dotted line, Sergeant."

"What's this?" he asked as he accepted it. He looked it over—a chain of evidence form detailing how he and Santorios had removed several paintings and nanochips from the evidence at the warehouse for purposes of testing by experts the night of the shooting. It had already been filled out and signed by the Sergeant. He shot her a questioning look.

"If we're going after Keller, we have to cross our T's and dot our I's," Becker explained. "He'll hit back hard, with everything he can find. It's not your fault the form got buried, and I forgot to send it to evidence after you filed it."

Simon caught on, smirking. "You are a devious woman, Sarge."

She smirked. "Yeah, yeah, yeah. Don't expect me to cover your ass every time."

He set the form down on the top of a nearby file cabinet, withdrawing a pen from his pocket and signing in the appropriate space. He hadn't expected the move, but it made him grateful and appreciative of his great supervisor even more. "Thanks."

She nodded as he handed it back. "I'll make sure this gets scanned and filed correctly with the appropriate explanation after the meeting. In the meantime, go get Emma situated," she motioned toward the squad and Simon glanced through the window to see Emma leaning her chin on her fists, looking totally annoyed and bored.

"She always has that look," Simon said, shrugging. "Comes with the age."

Becker chortled. "Yeah, I used to get it from Noah and Caroline, but still, we may be a while."

Simon chuckled and turned, reaching for the door. "Yeah, I'll get that porn going for her."

They both laughed as he opened the door and headed out into the squad toward his desk. A loud commotion was coming from the far end of the room near the interrogation rooms.

"Get in there!" Maberry shouted from somewhere in the corridor.

Correia appeared at the end of a row of desks, motioning. "Hey Simon! You know this asshole?"

Simon looked over and saw the detective wanted him to look in an interrogation room." I know a lot of assholes. Comes with the job." Correia's eyes had an urgency in them.

"Dad!" Emma called as he turned away again.

"Be right back, I promise, babe," he said to her as he went down an aisle between cubes, winding his way toward Correia.

They went into the corridor together and stood outside a door marked 'three' with a small window where Maberry was waiting. "Guy says he has to see you. Made a real scene downstairs."

Simon stepped forward as Maberry moved aside and peered through the window. Mister Information, the railyard bum was pacing the room, muttering loudly to himself, his limbs animated, agitated.

"Says you promised him protection," Correia added.

"He gave me a good lead on Ashman's people," Simon said, stepping back from the door. But too late, as Mister Information's scraggly face appeared in the window now, close up, and his eyes squinting at Simon.

"Hey, man!" he yelled. "Someone's following me! I saw the news—how all your witnesses being shot at. You gotta protect me!"

Simon rolled his eyes. "Throw him in a cell a night or two. He'll be safe enough."

Correia and Maberry shrugged.

"Made a real scene in the lobby," Maberry said. "Insisting to see you. If we hadn't happened by, he'd probably already be there."

Simon sighed. "Have them shower and shave him, too. Looks overdue."

The detectives grunted. "Yeah, he stinks. Glad we didn't have to drive him in our car," Maberry said.

Simon turned and headed back for the squad, shaking his head, as the two others turned back to the room and opened the door.

"You won the lotto, big boy," Correia said. "A night in holding."

"What?!" Mister Information screamed as Maberry stepped in behind his partner. "You told them to lock me up, Simon? I helped you!"

"I'm putting you somewhere safe," Simon called as Maberry released his hold on the door. The door swung shut cutting off further protests as Simon headed across the squad room again to join Emma.

As he typed his login info into the computer on his desk

for her, a clerk approached and motioned to some files on his desk. "Any of these belong to the Ashman-Santorios matter? Sergeant wants them all secured in the cabinets."

Simon finished logging on and stepped aside so Emma could get to work. She clicked and tapped with the mouse, opening a browser as he faced the clerk. "Maybe a couple. I'll bring them over. The rest are in my drawers."

The clerk nodded. "We'll move those."

"Careful with the order, okay?" Simon said as the clerk moved off. "I have a system."

The clerk chuckled, shaking her head. "Yeah, yeah, they all say that."

Simon really did have a system but he knew some of the others were pretty mishmash about their filing. He let her go without further objections and looked up to see Falk and Stein arriving with a couple more FBI types and Deputy Chief Melson, moving through the cubicles to find space. Oglesby and Dolby rolled out some extra chairs and Simon knew the meeting was about to start. Then Lucas appeared, nodding to Simon as he made his way past the file cabinets lining the outside wall and came to hover near Simon in his cube.

Simon tipped his head toward Emma. "Turn your music up and don't listen." He pulled out a drawer and motioned to some change inside in a cup. "That's for the machines. Don't talk or interrupt."

Emma was too busy on the internet to even nod. "Gotcha," she mumbled and kept staring at the screen as Simon slipped her earbuds into her ears, turning on her IPad. He rolled his chair out of the cubicle at the same time as Carter, Bailey, and Tucker arrived from homicide, standing against the wall outside Becker's office.

The last to arrive were Maberry and Correia, who shut the door behind them as Becker stood outside her door beside a bulletin board. Carter took a seat, clearly deferring to Becker.

Simon looked at Lucas, who turned to him with a sympathetic look. "Sorry I did not make it to your partner's funeral. I was not sure if I was welcome."

Simon frowned. "Of course you would have been."

"I have never been to a human burial rite before," Lucas said.

"Funeral, Lucas," Simon whispered. "We never call it that."

Lucas shrugged. "Okay, I'll remember."

"Gentlemen, ladies," Becker said. "From now on this case is need-to-know only for the people in this room."

"What about Keller?" Maberry asked. Simon figured everyone had heard rumors by now but Maberry wasn't the only one at the table who sat up and turned toward Becker at that question.

"Deputy Chief Keller is *not* on this list," Becker said. "In fact, his status has been changed on the case."

"Changed to what?" Dolby asked.

Becker looked at Melson and then Simon. Deputy Chief Melson nodded. "Suspect," she said and waited for the reactions breaking out all around her.

"Keller's a suspect?!" Maberry repeated.

"What the fuck?!" Correia asked.

"I never liked that guy!" Dolby muttered.

Becker raised a hand to silence them. "We have evidence that Chief Keller has been feeding location information on our officers and this investigation to the other suspects." Her lips settled into a grim twist, her limbs close to her body as she stiffly scanned the room.

"Jesus Christ," Agent Falk said.

"Your CIs?" Oglesby asked.

Simon nodded. "Amongst others."

"That fucker!" Dolby said.

"When are we going to arrest him?" Maberry asked, all too eager. All of them had had past run-ins with Keller.

Becker held up a palm to stop them. "We're working it. Together. We have to act very carefully because if we arrest one, the others may disappear."

"They shot at my daughter," Simon said, panning the room and meeting each person's eyes in turn. "They don't get to walk on this."

The others grunted or nodded in agreement, then Becker continued.

"From now on, all internal files, communications, etc. related to these cases will be secured in this room and these file cabinets," she motioned to the three cabinets occupying the rear wall behind her. "No one gets in here, and no one has passes except those authorized, and you share them with *no one*." She pulled a dozen key cards from her pocket and fanned them out like playing cards, then tossed them on the table, where everyone began reaching for the card with their pictures, some trading with others 'til everyone had theirs. "If you need a file or place to work, we have extra space you can use either the spare cubicle or down the hall."

"Even our Captains are need to know," Carter added.

"Where'd Keller get the info?" Bailey asked.

"Traffic and GPS technology," Lucas answered.

"Fuck," Maberry said.

"Does the Chief know?" Dolby asked, referring to Chief of Police Weber, everyone's boss.

Melson cleared his throat. "Yes, a little. But we're keeping details close to the vest, too, for now. And the Chief had no complaint. He doesn't want Keller's friends in his office leaking while we're preparing search warrants, subpoenas...." His voice trailed off as the others grunted and mumbled in understanding.

"He fucked with my family, I'd probably just shoot him," Correia said, looking at Simon.

"Correia!" Becker scolded.

Melson looked at Simon and nodded. "Master Detective Simon has showed excellent restraint, considering." Even the Deputy Chief reacted like he agreed with Correia.

Becker shook her head. "We do this the right way, and we do it so it sticks. High jingo has interfered enough." High jingo was a cop term for situations frought with politics that attracted a lot of interference from higher ups and politicians, etc. "And once we go after Keller, you know he'll fight back—dirty, whatever it takes." She locked eyes with them each in turn again, waiting as each acknowledged it.

"The Bureau can handle things if you need—" Stein started to say.

Simon's head turned sharply and he glared. "Fuck that. You're not cutting us out now. We've lost too much." His fellow KCPD backed him up, all staring at the FBI guys.

Stein raised his hands in surrender, shooting Falk a defeated look. "Just an offer," Stein said.

"Let us know what we can do," Falk said.

Becker smiled, disarmingly. "We're in this together. In fact, FBI will take the lead on any searches involving Chief Keller or other KCPD personnel if it leads there. We're not taking any chances of false accusations about evidence tampering et al.."

Falk and Stein nodded in agreement.

"We'll lead searches on existing suspects and Ashman," Becker continued.

"We can bring in as many people as you need," Falk said.

Becker nodded. "And we'll ask that. KCKPD will also be assisting."

"Kansas? Why?" Dolby asked.

"Because they came on the case when two shootings bled over into their jurisdiction," Carter said, speaking for the first time, "and because their people are less likely to leak as long as we act quickly." Most Kansas City officers knew each other to some degree across departments. In a city with invisible borders, cooperation and bleed over was all too common, but Carter was right. KCKPD rumors would take longer to reach Keller and give them an advantage.

"We need a couple days to get the paperwork and warrants in order, then we hit Monday morning and we hit hard. All hands on deck," Melson said. "But no discussing this case over the air or outside this room as long as you're in the vicinity of any KCPD properties. And don't forget about the cams in your cars."

"Well, we're gonna need telepathy then," Correia cracked, shaking his head.

"If only you had WiFi in your heads," Lucas joked and everyone stared at him—not getting the android humor. Lucas paused then narrowed his eyes. "Keller's a scumbag and scumbags see the judge on Monday morning."

This time, the room laughed.

"*Robocop*, nice," Maberry said, correctly identifying the quote despite Lucas' modifications.

Lucas sat up, looking pleased with himself. Simon winked at him. The kid was getting the hang of those quotes.

"Just pay attention to who might overhear," Carter said, and Becker nodded.

"We're going to act quickly," she said. "Close it down and arrest them all within a few days."

Everyone mumbled agreement, the excitement palpable. Oglesby, Correia, and Maberry leaned back in their chairs, ready and raring, others like Dolby and Becker looked somber, tense. The two FBI guys kept their expressions blank, reserved, showing no emotion—all business. Typical Feds.

Melson just looked resigned. "People, this whole situation with Chief Keller makes me sick. It's really unacceptable. But I want you to know, the Chief and I, we are behind you. We've got your backs. So just do your jobs. Keller will never bother you again when this is over."

The relieved, grateful looks from everyone around the table matched Simon's feelings but he stayed reserved, worried. Keller would not go down quietly, as Becker had warned. And Simon was one of his favorite targets. He'd be watching his back for a long time to come, no matter what assurances came from the second floor.

Becker motioned and Carter began handing out a stack of forms.

"These are our targets, people—search warrants,

subpoenas, etc. Break them up and start working them," Carter said as the papers made the rounds around the table. "We've already notified Judge Shoemaker to expect us. Sergeant Becker and I will go with Chief Melson to get them signed. You just have them ready and solid by tomorrow mid-day."

The cops and FBI agents grunted and mumbled acknowledgment again as they began looking over the stack of forms.

"Okay, enough, get busy!" Becker ordered, motioning for the door, and chair wheels skidded on carpet, hands slapped desks and cubicles as people scooted back, stood, gathering their things and heading for the door.

Simon stood and walked to the doorway to stand beside Becker, watching Emma at his desk. "Do you need me here?"

"You got something to do?" she asked.

"I can't go home, they know where I live," Simon said, assuming Becker already knew about the Fairway house.

"Yeah, why don't you and Emma take a weekend away, have some fun, but be back Monday first thing," she said, eyes softening with concern.

"Her mother is back tomorrow night and she'll be going home anyway," Simon said. "Thanks, boss."

"Take Lucas," Becker suggested. "They're after him, too. Not sure he knows how to make himself scarce."

Simon chuckled. "Yeah, I've noticed that. Emma really likes him, too." They exchanged a look of agreement, then Becker headed for her office and Simon headed for his cubicle, where Emma was chatting with Lucas.

EMMA HAD ALWAYS wanted to visit the Jesse James Home Museum in St. Joséph, Missouri, since reading about it in school, so Simon checked out of the Overland Park Hotel they'd used the night before and drove with Lucas and Emma the seventy-five miles north on I-29 to St. Joséph. He'd gotten out of the office around 2, so they made it in plenty of time, hitting first the Patee House, where Robert Ford killed the outlaw Jesse James on April 3rd, 1882, and then the Pony Express Museum nearby.

The Jesse James House was a small, white one-story house with black shutters in the middle of downtown St. Joséph. Restored with period furniture, including items reported to have belonged to and been there when James occupied the house and was killed, the house consisted basically of a couple small bedrooms and the kitchen/main room. It was fascinating more for the event that made it famous than for anything architectural or otherwise. It had the musty, old smell nineteenth century restored houses often had. The wallpaper was decorative like art though faded, and they'd even hung the painting James was supposedly straightening when Ford shot him in the back that famous day. Altogether, Simon found it interesting more for atmosphere than anything else, but Emma and Lucas went through it with rapt fascination, asking lots of questions of Simon and the Museum staff, and Simon was more than content to mostly follow along and listen in.

Next door, St. Joséph's only National Historic Registered site, the Patee House, had once been both a hotel and the founding headquarters of the Pony Express. It had now been made into a museum with fascinating period artifacts of all shapes and sizes. Almost three times the size of the James

Home, they spent a good two hours there while Emma and Lucas again asked tons of questions and chattered happily as they explored every inch.

They ate dinner that night at a Mexican Cantina not far from the museums then checked into a Red Roof Inn downtown and chatted a while before Emma fell asleep reading a book. Simon finally turned the light out himself after discussing the case with Lucas. Lucas himself simply plugged his power into a socket and stationed himself by the door on lookout. Simon found it a mix of amusing and sad, but then it also made him rest easier and he got the best sleep that night he'd had in months.

The next day they headed southwest on State Highway 59 to Atchison, Kansas, where a bemused Simon took Emma to some of the so-called haunted houses the area was famous for. Again, Emma and Lucas were quite rapt and intrigued by the whole experience, while skeptical detective Simon choked back laughter multiple times to avoid offending the tour guides. The three houses they visited seemed dated but normal Middle American to him. He never once saw anything that even remotely resembled haunting, nor did he feel the odd presences or cold breezes the guides claimed were ever present. Even the crooked paintings that could never be straightened and broken mirrors that were broken as quickly as they were replaced—so they claimed—seemed the kind of things easily explained by simple effects—wires or electronics and such—not supernatural beings. Still, Emma smiled the whole day, bouncing on her feet with excitement at times, and just watching that, especially after all they'd been through the past few days, was more than enough to get Simon smiling, too.

He was also amused at watching Lucas' reactions as well. Lucas listened to the guides unquestioning, as if what they said must be completely factual and beyond question. Sure, he was not a trained detective like Simon, but after the time they'd spent together, Simon found himself disappointed. He thought he'd taught the android a few things, but apparently skepticism wasn't one of them. Later, Emma expressed more doubts as they drove away than Lucas did. Still, she'd loved the day, especially the escape from city life and worries about the case, and Simon had to admit getting his own mind off it for a few hours here and there had also left him feeling recharged and fresh, with renewed energy for the days ahead.

They arrived back in Independence that night at Lara's house around seven-thirty and found her watching a cabby unload her bags from his trunk. Lucas waited in the car while Simon escorted Emma up to the door, carrying her small suitcase.

"Lara," he said, nodding to his ex, who looked as pleased as usual to see him—or was that a permanent scowl? He almost couldn't remember what her smile looked like.

"John," she said as the cabby returned from depositing the last suitcase in the entryway and she paid him in cash.

The cabby returned to his car and pulled away before either of them said anymore. Emma hugged her mom and chattered about their little away trip.

"Really? You did a lot in a short time," Lara said. "You must be exhausted."

"We are," Simon and Emma said simultaneously, then they both laughed. Lara showed concern for her daughter while somehow managing to simultaneously glare at her ex.

"Well then, come on inside," Lara said. "Thanks for taking care of her," she added as an afterthought.

Even after all these years, the coldness cut through his heart like a dagger, but outwardly he just shrugged it off. "You're welcome. Thanks for the advance notice."

She looked annoyed. "It was last minute. Boss' orders." She tossed it off like it was unavoidable, but when they were married she'd always known her schedule several weeks in advance and she'd done this to Simon several times in the several years since their divorce. Then she turned and followed her daughter toward the house.

Emma paused in the doorway turning back. "Be careful, dad." She said it with such a worried, somber look that her mother raised an eyebrow more from curiosity than concern.

Simon carried Emma's forgotten suitcase to the door and handed it to her, leaning forward to kiss her forehead. Instead, she pulled him into a tight hug.

"I love you, dad," she said.

"I love you, too," he replied.

"I wish you could stay," she said, eyes meeting his.

Lara looked shocked. "For God's sake, Emma, you stopped asking for that ages ago. You know he can't."

Emma ignored her mother, eyes communicating a lot with no words. She was worried she'd never see him again, about the case, what might happen.

Simon winked and tousled her hair. "It'll be fine, I promise."

Emma frowned at him. "It better. You know I hate when you lie to me."

With that, Simon laughed, Lara's continuing glare showing she had no idea what the joke was.

"I've got him, you know," Simon teased, motioning

toward Lucas in the car.

"You keep him safe, too," Emma said, waving her fingers at Lucas, who smiled and waved back. Then his daughter hugged him again quickly, turned, and hurried inside with her suitcase. Simon closed his eyes in the moment, enjoying every hug he could get. There'd never be enough. It had been a helluva week for them but he was relieved to know that as they upped the pressure full throttle on the case and sought to close it and make arrests, Emma would be away from him in a safer place, less likely to draw unwanted attention that might get her hurt. That alone would make it far easier for Simon to concentrate on the case.

Lara stood there a moment, watching him watch his daughter go with a puzzled look. "What was *that* all about?" she asked.

Simon dismissed it with a wave. "Just a case. Usual stuff. Good night." He didn't wait for her to reply, instead turning and walking back toward the car knowing she probably wouldn't. He wondered if looking at him ever hurt her the way he hurt when he looked at her.

Her answer was closing the door and locking the deadbolt loudly behind him. Simon grunted to himself then got in the car and drove away.

CHAPTER 23

SIMON AND LUCAS arrived at Central just before 8 a.m. after another night in a hotel. On their way, they'd stopped by Simon's Canterbury house in Fairway just to check things over and so Simon could grab another suit. Andy Harris' men had boarded up all the broken windows and sliding doors and secured the house for him after the KCKPD crime scene techs cleared the scene. He hadn't been back himself since he left the scene but was glad to see the place undisturbed. Andy would be getting him an estimate on repairs soon, and he planned to start work as soon as the case was over.

The raids began at 9 a.m. as soon as Ashman's businesses opened for the day. FBI teams led by Stein and Falk raided Ashman Industries' corporate campus on south Broadway while Simon and Lucas led a team to raid the Ashman Gallery once again. Correia and Maberry, Oglesby and Dolby, Bailey and Tucker, and each of the Sergeants led teams raiding various storage facilities revealed in Lucas' search of files and the KCKPD teams raided anything on their side of the state line—all simultaneously.

They'd decided to hit the businesses and storage facilities first before the suspects' homes because they thought it more likely they'd find solid leads there. The apartments and houses would be covered on a second set of raids after they'd served search warrants and put teams to work at the offices and warehouses first.

Benjamin Ashman was nowhere to be found during the first round of searches, but Paul Paulsen was in, and Simon took special pleasure in personally patting him down.

"Spread 'em," he ordered as soon as they located Paulsen in a small, closet-like office on the Gallery's second floor.

"What are you doing here?!" Paul demanded.

"Warrant," Lucas said and held the paperwork up for Paulsen to see. Simon just grinned. The asshole stood and actually read it over.

"This is starting to become harassment, Detective," Paul said with a sneer. "I think our lawyers will have something to say about this."

Simon grabbed him and whirled him around, shoving him against a wall and pushing his legs aside as Paulsen surrendered and raised him arms. Simon made sure the pat him down slowly and as obtrusively as possible.

"Oh! What's this?!" Simon said as he found a holstered Glock G41 strapped to Paulsen's back, under his suit jacket. "Is this a loaded weapon?"

"That seems suspicious for a businessman," Lucas added.

"Some of our pieces are worth millions," Paul growled. "Concealed carry permits are legal and on file."

Simon clicked his teeth and shook his head, dropping the Glock in the evidence bag Lucas was holding ready. "Bag it."

Lucas sealed the bag with a "My pleasure," and set it aside atop a nearby file cabinet.

"Yeah, well, we'll see if you get it back once we run ballistics from all the 'legal' shootings you've set up lately, okay?" Simon added. He searched more pockets. "Ah look, a phone."

He handed the cell to Lucas, who pulled a cable from a socket under his sleeve and plugged the phone in, uploading data—lists of calls, address book, tracking data, etc.

"You can't do that!" Paul protested.

"Covered under the warrant," Simon lied. They'd get a real warrant later and redo the search so it would stick.

"He likes to call South America," Lucas commented as he internally began analyzing the data.

"Weren't two of those men who chased us from South America?" Simon asked Lucas, just taunting Paulsen. He already knew they were.

"I believe so," Lucas replied.

"I don't know anything about those men. That's a client. Legitimate business." Paul's brow furrowed and he shook his head.

"Where's Ashman?" Simon asked.

"I have no idea," Paul said. "Am I his keeper?"

"Actually, I was told you were—his keeper and chief asshole," Simon replied.

"Fuck you," Paul said.

Simon smirked and punched Paul in the right side, causing him to hit his head as he bent forward, doubling over in pain. Simon yanked him upright again and threw him against the wall. "Where you going? Not done."

"Oh, I think you've felt me up enough, Detective," Paul said and spun to face him. "And now we'll be talking about police brutality."

Simon grabbed Paul by the throat with one hand and

shoved his back against the wall, lifting him onto his tiptoes. "You sent men to kill me and my teenage daughter. You haven't even *begun* to see the brutality I am capable of yet, asshole."

"Hit me again then," Paul said smugly. "You're just setting up my lawsuit."

Simon kicked him in the groin with a knee then cracked his elbow hard into Paulsen's back as the man bent over with pain again. He motioned to Lucas. "Hand me the cuffs. We're taking him in."

"For what?!" Paul choked out.

"Questioning," Lucas said.

"You don't have shit on me," Paul said. "You're not even a cop." He glared at Lucas.

"Then you shouldn't have anything to worry about, should you? Now, shut the fuck up." Simon cuffed his hands behind his back and shoved him toward Lucas. "Take him down to the car, will ya?"

Lucas smiled and nodded, grabbing Paulsen by the cuffed hands and dragging him away so fast, the man stumbled, struggling to stay on his feet.

Then Simon set a team to work searching the offices, while he went exploring for anything obvious that might provide leads. It quickly became clear that any criminal activities had been well hidden and covered under routine paperwork and daily business activities. If there was anything there to uncover, it was going to take a lot of man hours and digging through files and computer files to uncover it and make those connections. Simon wasn't surprised but he was frustrated. He wanted these guys nailed now, off the street, and prevented from any more assassination attempts on himself or others he loved.

"Son of a bitch," he cursed as he left the Gallery and walked to his car.

"Maybe he'll tell us something," Lucas said hopefully.

Simon looked at Paulsen, sitting handcuffed in the back of his car with a scowl, staring straight ahead. "He won't, but we still have to try. And if he has that CCP like he says, we don't have anything to hold him on but suspicions right now. His lawyer will get him kicked in a few hours."

Lucas frowned. "No wonder your work makes you angry so much."

"Who me?" Simon scoffed. "I'm not angry."

Lucas narrowed his eyes. "Flush it down the pipe and see if it comes out on my end, alright? That's what we do first, we narrow it down."

"What the fuck movie are you quoting now?" Simon asked.

"*The Departed*, I believe," Lucas said, looking satisfied.

"Scorsese can go fuck himself," Simon said, "He writes better mobsters."

"I thought he was a director," Lucas said as they headed for the car.

"Whatever, Hollywood wannabes," Simon said.

"A wannabe with many Oscars?" Lucas asked.

"Just shut the fuck up, okay?" Simon said and climbed in the car.

Lucas remained silent as he climbed in the passenger side and shut the door. Moments later, they pulled away.

SIMON AND LUCAS left Paul Paulsen in a holding cell across from the Desk Sergeant to stew and checked in with Becker, who was headed out to lead a search of Ashman's residence. She agreed that waiting for results from other searches and searching Paulsen's apartment first were good approaches to his interview, so Simon and Lucas headed out for Mission Hills while Becker put a uniform on the door to guard Paulsen.

Paulsen lived in a twenty-six hundred square foot house on two acres south of the Mission Hills Country Club off Oakwood Road. The house was Colonial Modern with an attached two car garage and a heated swimming pool in the back. It was a big place for one man to live alone, Simon thought, but the maid, who was working, said Paulsen was the sole occupant. She did, however, report a series of relationships with both men and women, many of which were volatile and none of which lasted very long. For a guy who seemed to be on top of the world in business success, Paulsen's personal life was the opposite. In fact, while decisive in business, it seemed in personal relationships, Paulsen had trouble making up his mind. The maid, a Guatemalan immigrant, dismissed him as being a "crazy gringo." Simon found it ironic how close to truth she was. Her boss was a sociopath for sure.

The house was laid out with a balcony down the middle—the upstairs containing a partially open space used as an office next to a large master bedroom with walk-in closet and full bath, then an extra bath and two more bedrooms on the far end. The balcony looked down upon the entryway and a large family/dining area that stretched the entire length of the house—front to back. Beside that was a large kitchen then a smaller family/living room area on the north end of the house with a laundry room between that and the garage.

Bookshelves and display cases were arranged strategically between pods of couches and chairs with everything looking neat and tidy, almost like something out of a magazine. Paintings decorated available space, some familiar, others by lesser known local artists. Paulsen clearly prided himself on his taste. Many of the novels were leather bound collector's editions, both classics and best sellers, and he had various handcrafted art pieces from around the world mixed in and displayed on extra space in front of the books along the middle row of each shelf. The dining table was fancy dark wood, shiny and polished, with engraved highlights matching the chairs. The kitchen was so clean it sparkled, everything in its place—so much so that Simon was beginning to wonder why the man wasted money on a maid. Or then again, maybe she was that good at her job.

As he and Lucas meticulously searched the house with gloves and evidence bags in ready use, the maid simply sat down at the kitchen table for a long break. Simon questioned her long enough to determine that Lupe had little awareness of what her employer did outside the home and cared very little for what he did in it. Then Simon went back to supervising evidence teams and helping with the search.

While he was in Paulsen's master bedroom, where he'd just uncovered a gun cabinet, Becker called. "We found some more crates of possible forgeries and nanochips at one of the warehouses on Lucas' list," she said. "And by the way, Paulsen's CCP checks out. So we can't hold him on that."

"Shit. I was afraid of that," Simon admitted. "Nothing here so far either, but surely something will turn up. We can at least hold him for forty-eight and sweat him."

"Yeah, but his lawyer will be down there raising the roof soon," she said. "I'm on my way back shortly."

"Well, tell the lawyer 'hi' from me, eh?" Simon teased, chuckling.

"You guys take all the glory and leave the fun stuff for me," Becker fired back.

The phone beeped with another line but Simon didn't recognize the number and stayed with Becker. "What have the other teams turned up? Any weapons?"

"Yeah, a few, in the warehouse," Becker said, "and some in trunks or under seats of vehicles. Have to wait for ballistics to see if any of them match the slugs we've pulled from the shootings."

"We're always waiting on those assholes," Simon said, faking annoyance, but knowing the score.

"Yeah, well, those assholes also save your ass in court half the time, so be nice to them," Becker warned.

"I wasn't going to say a thing," Simon said. "That's fun stuff I leave for you."

"Fuck you," Becker said. "Gotta go. See ya."

And she hung up. Simon saw the message signal blinking on his phone and clicked the button to check his messages. What he heard almost made his head explode.

"What the fuck?!" he yelled, tensing so hard he stumbled from his position crouching and had to catch himself with a hand.

"What's going on?" Lucas asked, sticking his head in from the next room.

"Some moron let Paulsen go," Simon said as he dialed back the unknown number and stood, pacing.

"Officer Pantazis," a young male voice answered.

"Pantazis—where's my fucking suspect?!" Simon yelled, then took a deep breath trying to calm himself and failing.

"Hello? I'm sorry. Who am I speaking with?" the uniform asked with uncertainty.

"Master Detective John Simon, asshole. You let my suspect go?! What the fuck?"

"Uh...Deputy Chief Keller told me to," the uniform said, fumbling for words. "Guy's lawyer was throwing a fit, yelling at me, and he got Keller on the phone. Keller asked for the evidence. I read what we had in the file outside the door. Said we didn't have enough to hold him, that he could come back in later if we got more."

"Come back in later?! Jesus Christ, he'll disappear! The man's a murderer!" Simon couldn't believe his ears but inside he knew that taking it out on the young uniform wasn't right either. What would a three year uniform know about standing up to a Deputy Chief? Even Simon would have to think long and hard about that.

"I'm sorry, sir. Orders," Pantazis said again.

"You stay right there. I'm coming back now," Simon said and hung up, hitting speed dial for Becker. He motioned to Lucas, who stood in the doorway watching with a concerned look. "Car, now!" He said as he ran. "They let fucking Paulsen go!" Simon said as Becker answered.

"Who? What?" she said, trying to take it in. "When? Why?"

"I think you covered all the basics there, Sergeant. Keller," Simon said, taking the stairs two at a time with Lucas close on his heels.

"Son of a bitch," Becker said. "I'm almost there. I'll get on it. Maybe we can catch him before he leaves."

"It was ten minutes ago," Simon said. "Uniform left a message while I talked with you. He's gone."

"Just get back here and we'll find out where he went," Becker said as Simon and Lucas raced across the driveway toward the Charger.

"Believe me, I'll be coming full siren and lights," Simon said and hung up as he slid behind the wheel. Seconds later, his tires burned as he spun out of the driveway and flipped on his siren and lights, pounding his fists against the steering wheel as he sped up the street.

SIMON STORMED INTO the squad room on 5th with Lucas trailing behind and headed straight for Becker's office where Becker, Carter, Agents Stein and Falk, Sergeant Anthony Raymond from Patrol, and Deputy Chief Melson were in heated discussion.

"Can you believe that rookie uniform, man?" Maberry said as Simon moved past.

"Sorry, bro," Correia added.

Simon nodded to them but said nothing as he opened Becker's door and stormed on into her office. Lucas hesitated, waiting outside.

"John—" Becker said calmly as Simon entered, tense and fuming.

"What the fuck?!" Simon said.

"Our guy screwed up," Raymond said. "I'm sorry, John.

We have a BOLO issued and all units looking for Paulsen and his vehicles." Be On the Look Outs were the modern incarnation of APBs.

Simon threw up his hands. "We had him *in* custody. Right where we want him. Where we *need* him. This is inexcusable!"

"We kept this case limited, John," Melson said. "How is a patrol officer going to fight a Deputy Chief?"

"He should have called someone to check," Simon said.

"He called you," Carter replied.

Simon shook his head, pacing. "No, he left a message that Paulsen had already been kicked. He should have asked before he did that."

"Well, it's too late now, John," Becker said. "We just have to find him again."

Simon turned, stopping and facing them. "Yeah, and hope no one else gets killed while he's loose." That statement gave everyone pause. They'd probably thought of it but hearing Simon state it bluntly painted scenarios none of them had wanted to think about.

"Jesus Christ! What a fuckup," Simon said, surprised the FBI Agents had remained silent so far. The FBI loved to blame the locals for incompetence on joint cases. What was their angle?

There was a knock at the door and everyone turned to see Lucas standing outside, smiling.

Becker raised a brow at Simon.

Simon strode to the door, opening it a crack. "This isn't a good time, Lucas."

"But I have information that might help," Lucas said.

"We'll talk about it when I get out in a minute, okay? This is important," Simon said dismissively and started closing the door.

"Okay, but I have located Mister Paulsen," Lucas added nonchalantly. In fact, it was soft enough, it took a moment to register.

Simon swung the door wide, grabbed Lucas by the arm, and pulled him inside. "What did you say?!"

Lucas beamed. "I plugged into the traffic system. Detective Maberry assisted me."

Becker nodded. "Okay, you did that here?"

Lucas nodded. "Detective Maberry called someone and asked for access to search for Mister Paulsen."

"How can you be sure you found him?" Agent Falk asked, urgently. All eyes were on Lucas.

"Because he emerged onto Locust at 3:24 p.m. and got into a blue BMW with plates matching a car that chased Detective Simon and I earlier this week," Lucas explained, impressing them all with the details. "Would you like to know the plate number?"

"No, no, where is he?" Falk urged.

"He is currently in the blue BMW headed north on I-35 right now, near exit 8A," Lucas said, nodding.

Everyone started talking at once as Becker picked up her phone and dialed. "Yeah, this is Sergeant Becker at Central Property, I need tracking on a Blue BMW..."

"I can search very fast," Lucas said by way of explanation and shrugged.

Simon and Becker grinned, Simon patting him on the back, excited. "Give the Sergeant that plate number."

Lucas read it off and several of the others jotted it down.

"Wait! Do we want to detain him or follow him?" Simon asked, looking at the two Feds.

Stein and Falk exchanged a look.

"Good point," Agent Stein said. "Let's see where he goes."

"Right, but get someone on him now!" Melson said.

Becker was nodding into the phone. She covered the mouthpiece with her hand. "They have a chopper closing in."

"Okay, but have them keep far enough back not to spook him," Simon warned.

"We can send an unmarked FBI chopper," Falk suggested.

"Fine, call it in and we'll swap out, but we're not losing him in the meantime," Carter said as the others nodded in agreement.

Stein was already dialing a phone. "We have one at the airport downtown."

"Son of a bitch!" Simon said, grinning at Lucas. "I could kiss you right now."

Lucas shrugged. "That would be my first kiss."

"No PDA on duty, Detective," Melson teased. "We appreciate your assistance, Mister George."

"We'll make him an offer he can't refuse," Lucas said in a gruff voice.

Several of the others chuckled.

"That was a mafia guy, not a cop," Simon said.

Lucas shrugged. "It seemed appropriate."

"Chopper'll be there in two," Stein said, hanging up his

phone.

Becker nodded and spoke into her phone again, "Tell them an unmarked FBI unit is going to take their place shortly...yeah...thanks." She hung up and motioned to the door. "All right, let's get some units out after them. Why are we standing around?"

"We have to go. Somewhere there is a crime happening," Lucas said.

Simon rolled his eyes. "Stop being cute and get moving, partner," he said and gently pushed Lucas toward the door.

Suddenly, Correia appeared in the door, wide eyed. "You guys might want to get out here."

"What?" Becker asked.

They all hurried out into the squad and stopped, stunned in a circle outside Becker's door. Across the room, standing just inside the entrance from the elevators, stood Benjamin Ashman and an older blonde man with graying hair in an expensive three-piece suit.

"My client has come to offer information," three-piece said, clearly Ashman's lawyer.

Becker and Simon exchanged curious looks. Then they all moved at once.

Simon headed for Ashman, with Lucas, Melson, and the Feds close behind as Becker motioned to Maberry and Correia. "José and Art, get out to I-35 and coordinate with the Fed's chopper in tracking those suspects."

"I'll send Bailey and Tucker to help," Carter offered as he picked up his phone.

"You got it, boss," Maberry said as he and Correia grabbed their coats and keys and headed for the elevators.

Becker and Carter hurried toward Ashman and the others. "Greg, we need to find Keller and keep him away."

"I'll handle that," the Deputy Chief said and hurried for the elevator. "You guys get started here. And by the book." He shot Becker and Simon a warning look.

"Yes, sir," they both answered.

"I'm Isaac Buchanan of Buchanan, Baerg, Chase, and Wayne," the attorney said. "Mister Ashman is here voluntarily, not as an admission—"

Simon cut him off. "We'll read him his rights as per procedure, but we understand that. Let's go into a room where we can talk." He motioned toward the hallway. Simon had the feeling that everything in the case had just changed dramatically. Maybe Stacey had been right about her boss? He couldn't wait to hear what Ashman had to say.

Buchanan nodded and Simon led the way, the whole crowd following toward the interrogation rooms.

CHAPTER 24

U SHERING ASHMAN AND BUCHANAN into an interrogation room was easy—six was wide open. It took another ten minutes of maneuvering and haggling for the law officers to agree who would go into the room with him and do the questioning and who would watch from the observation booth next door. In the end, Simon, Falk, and Becker went into the room, while the others filed into the booth.

Simon waited a few minutes for someone to turn on the recording equipment. They'd agreed he would lead the questioning but that Becker and Falk would jump in as needed.

"Mister Ashman, Mister Buchanan," Becker said with a nod, "I am Sergeant JoAnn Becker, this is Master Detective John Simon and Agent-In-Charge Ray Falk of the Federal Bureau of Investigation."

Ashman and Buchanan stood and shook hands with each in turn before sitting again on the far side of the table from where Simon, Becker and Falk took chairs.

Simon read Ashman his Miranda rights. "Do you understand these rights as I have explained them to you?"

"I do," Ashman said.

Buchanan cleared his throat. "I want it clear from the start that my client has come here of his own free will to cooperate with your investigation. He's doing this because he believes he's discovered illegal activities by some of his employees that are tied to his companies and resources. These are activities he has no prior knowledge of and was not aware of until only recently. And he confesses nothing. He has had no part in any of this, which is why he is coming forward. Benjamin Ashman is an honest man who does business as he lives his life: with integrity. He is as appalled as you are at discovering these criminal activities amongst his employees and he only wishes to offer assistance to you, now that he's become aware of the truth of some of your prior suspicions, to make sure they are brought to justice."

Becker, Simon, and Falk nodded.

"We understand," Becker said.

"I assume you're recording this?" Buchanan said.

"That is standard procedure," Becker agreed.

"All right, well, Mister Ashman wants to clear his good name but, as I said, he denies any involvement in criminal actions and his cooperation today is intended as an act of good faith to disavow you of any suspicions of involvement on his part. The moment we suspect that you are wishing to use his testimony here to entrap him or further suspicion or potential slander of his good name, this interview will be over." Buchanan looked at them all in turn.

"We make no promises," Simon said. "We have reason to be suspicious of the activities surrounding Mister Ashman's businesses—"

"But we are willing to listen and be convinced," Becker jumped in, shooting Simon a look. Buchanan and Ashman had begun shifting nervously at his words.

Simon nodded. "Of course."

"If you had evidence to prove Mister Ashman's guilt, you'd have already arrested him," Buchanan said, eyes on Simon. "Correct?"

Simon smiled. "Of course."

Buchanan leaned back in his chair and looked at his client. "Then let's keep that in mind as we begin." With that, he nodded to Ashman, who took a deep breath and looked at the law officers across the table, ready.

"Sergeant Simon will be leading the interview," Agent Falk said. "We are here to support him as necessary and oversee."

Simon shot him an annoyed look for the "oversee" part, then turned back to Ashman. "Do you wish to make a statement before we start with questions?"

Ashman thought a moment, shifting restlessly. He rubbed his hands down the legs of his slacks as if smoothing them over, eyeing the law officers again, then cleared his throat. "It might be easier to tell you what I know and let you direct your questions thereafter."

"All right," Simon said, full on snark. "Go ahead." He leaned back in his chair, listening.

Ashman bit his lip, avoiding eye contact for a moment, then looked at Buchanan, who nodded with an encouraging look, telling him to go ahead.

Ashman crossed and uncrossed his arms, then leaned forward, resting his elbows on the table and looked at Simon. "I believe the man responsible for the activities you have been investigating is Paul Paulsen, my senior associate and Executive Vice President," he finally said.

"It has come to my attention that he is involved in activities which I would never have agreed to, including possibly the shipping of forged artworks and stolen nanochips, and that men in his employ, men I trusted as security, custodial, and shipping personnel, are working for him in these activities without my knowledge. This has probably been going on for some time, although I was only made aware of this when Detective Simon began asking questions and I started asking questions myself. They denied it, of course, and at first, I believed them, but when Detective Simon was being shot at by Paulsen and those men as he left my gallery the other night, and then..." He faltered a moment, his voice weakening as he stared down at his hands, sullen as he continued, "...when I heard Stacey Soukop had been shot and killed..."

Simon gritted his teeth at hearing Ashman speak her name and thought, *It's your fault, you son of a bitch. You're responsible.*

After a moment, Ashman took and deep breath and continued, "I detected that they may not have been truthful with me, that they were hiding things from me, and I did a little investigating of my own that seemed to confirm my suspicions."

"What were they hiding?" Simon asked.

"Well, for one, I was unaware that Paul himself was carrying a concealed weapon. I'd never asked him to do so. We employ security, of course, for our gallery and some of our warehouses. We deal in valuable commodities and we have had nanochips stolen for another company we own, as we reported a month or two ago," Ashman said. "There are things needing protection. But I see no reason for my executives to arm themselves, and it strikes me as both unnecessary and disturbing that he felt the need to do so."

"He tried to rough me up the day we met," Simon reminded him, memories of the confrontation in Ashman's gallery office flashing through his mind.

"You stormed in, aggressively accusing me," Ashman replied. "He was being protective."

"But you don't think he was armed?" Falk asked.

"Not by my authority," Ashman insisted then shrugged. "I suppose he could have been. But I didn't know about it, and I would not have approved. We have security men for that."

"Not a fan of guns?" Simon asked, with a doubting tone. He was still looking for Ashman's angle on this.

Ashman swallowed and met Simon's gaze. "Guns have their place, I believe, although I rarely use them myself. My father was an avid hunter. I just haven't had time for it. But I am not opposed to the occasional skeet shooting or target practice and even inherited some of his rifles. I store them at my house in a very secure gun safe, as I'm sure the men who searched my house earlier today discovered." He looked at Becker, who had led the search at his residence.

Becker nodded. "We did. We opened it in your presence, in fact."

Ashman nodded back. "And everything was in order, was it not?"

"All the guns were legally registered and properly secured, yes," Becker said. "Although we did take samples to run ballistics tests for some of the shootings we believe are tied to recent events related to illegal activities."

"Yes, yes, I understand," Ashman said. "You will recall I raised no objection."

"Of course," Becker agreed.

"I also found on my private video feeds and computer files, transfers of money to accounts that were undertaken on my behalf by Mister Paulsen but that seem irregular and I don't remember authorizing. They seem suspicious and unusual. And it appears that Mister Paulsen makes an appearance on video just before men broke in and stole nanochips from one of our warehouses."

"He does?" Falk looked at Becker and Simon.

Simon shrugged. He thought Oglesby would have subpoenaed all footage. "Did we not look at video?"

Becker nodded. "I thought we subpoenaed it all."

"You subpoenaed video from the warehouse and security feeds, not from Mister Ashman's private feed," Buchanan corrected.

The law officers exchanged surprised looks.

"I don't think we knew Mister Ashman had a private feed," Becker said.

"It was not—"

Ashman raised a hand to cut off Buchanan, shooting him a look that said he'd handle it. "Knowledge of my private feeds is held very closely by me. Not even Paul Paulsen is aware of the extent of it. It is a security feature I had installed years ago as extra insurance but rarely use. I had not even looked at it until Paul raised my suspicions. Your investigators were given the feeds we felt at the time were relevant. I was unaware my own feed would provide a better view or I would have provided it. You have my apologies." He motioned to Buchanan, who reached into his suit and pulled out an envelope, which he slid across the table to Simon.

"These are videos of relevant feeds from Mister Ashman's

own office that actually show Paul Paulsen in closeup in the shadows," Buchanan said. "I believe you will find he seems to have allowed the thieves access to our facilities."

"Son of a bitch," Simon said. He knew Paulsen had been involved, suspected Ashman too, of course, but proving it had been the difficulty. Was Ashman really here offering to hand them that very evidence no strings attached? He could hardly believe it.

Becker accepted the envelope. "We will look at these as soon as possible, Mister Ashman. Thank you." She smiled across the table at him.

Ashman nodded, returning the smile. "There's more. The videos of other dates show other suspicious activities involving Mister Paulsen, my former warehouse manager Mister O'Dell, a man named Garcia, and several others that I believe relate to shipping and receiving of forged artworks as well as stolen nanochips. I believe you will also see them concealing said nanochips in the frames of paintings."

"Bloody hell," Falk said.

Simon shook his head, feeling a jolt as his pulse quickened, his stomach tingling. "That's how they hid them to get them past searches. Very smart. Those nanochips were so tiny, they'd be hard to detect." Ashman had just broken the whole thing open for them it seemed.

Ashman nodded again. "Yes, Paul Paulsen is most certainly clever. After all, he fooled me and I am no fool."

Ashman certainly was being calm and nice, showing no resistance. Not what Simon had expected. But what would he ask in return? Simon decided to approach it directly. He was actually starting to believe a man he'd never thought he would like or trust. It threw so many things about the investigation into question. He didn't want to be convinced.

"We've been after you pretty hard," Simon said, eyes boring into Ashman. "Why are you helping us?"

"Because I am no criminal, Sergeant," Ashman said. "I want no part of such activities. I may object to public humiliation and attempts to damage my reputation which I believed were without cause, but I am not going to stand in the way of justice when my own people are betraying me and threatening years of good work and hard labor with such activities. You have my sincere apologies for the harm that has come to your partner and others as well as the shooting at yourselves and others."

"Provided you prove that Mister Ashman's people were involved with it," Buchanan added, ever the lawyer.

"Yes, well, we certainly can prove some of that already, and if these videos are what you say they are, that will go a long way toward proving the rest," Agent Falk said.

"They shot at my daughter, Mister Ashman," Simon said, watching the businessman for a reaction. "My fourteen-year-old daughter. And I believe they killed my partner, too. She was pregnant."

Ashman's eyes turned sad, his shoulders hunching, as he slouched in his chair. "I am so sorry, Detective. I promise you, I would never have given my approval—"

Simon opened his cell and pulled up photos of Miles O'Ryan and Andrew Helm. He showed them to Ashman, one at a time. Ashman took the phone and examined them.

"Do you know these men?" Simon asked.

Ashman nodded. "I believe they work security for Paul."

"Do you know their names?" Simon added.

Ashman thought a moment. "One of them goes by 'Miles,'

I believe, but the other, no."

Simon accepted the phone back. Ashman actually looked sad about Blanca and Emma, worried even. Like he cared. It was pissing Simon off. He wanted to hate him. He took a deep breath. "One of them is dead. But the other is still out there. Do you know where we can find this Miles?"

Ashman shook his head. "I have thousands of employees, of course. I can't possibly know where all of them are at any given moment. I don't even know who sits at every desk or location, of course."

"Realistically, no one could expect him to," Buchanan said.

Simon knew they were both right, but this was too easy. "And you want nothing in return for telling us this, giving us footage?"

"I want to clear my name," Ashman said.

"As we said, he is here to fully cooperate, but this is not a confession of any wrongdoing on his part," Buchanan reiterated.

Fucking lawyers. "Yeah, we got that the first two times," Simon said.

"Do you know why Paulsen has been calling South America?" Agent Falk asked. The FBI had subpoenaed full phone records over the weekend and apparently they'd gone through some of them.

"We do business all over the world," Ashman said, leaning back in his chair with a thoughtful look. "But no, I couldn't say for sure."

"No one has approached you from Brazil or another South American country with business propositions about nanochips or art?" Simon asked.

Buchanan laughed. "They do business all over the world—nanochips and art—of course someone has probably inquired—"

Ashman cut him off, leaning forward. "Actually, a year ago, we had a particularly troublesome contact from a Brazilian named De Sousa, I forget his first name, but I could probably look it up in records. He was wanting things we don't ordinarily provide."

"Like what?" Simon asked.

"Nanochips with special data already loaded, lesser artworks, even some prints—"

"What kind of data?" Falk asked.

"We never got that far," Ashman said. "I turned him down."

Simon and Falk exchanged a look.

"But if Paulsen went around you..." Simon said.

"He may have, it seems," Ashman admitted sadly.

"We need whatever information you have on this De Sousa," Falk said. "Contact information, background, company, address, phone numbers..."

"I can make a call to my office," Ashman said, nodding.

There was a knock at the interrogation room door, then Carter stuck his head in. "We have confirmation of Paul Paulsen and another man meeting a flight from São Paulo, Brazil at the airport five minutes ago—"

Simon's and Falk's chair legs scraped the floor loudly as they scooted back in unison and stood.

"Get us that information as soon as you can!" Simon called as he headed for the door.

"Where are you going?" Becker asked.

"The airport," Simon said. "If you have any more questions, feel free." He and Falk raced for the door, Buchanan, Becker, and Ashman watching them go.

PAUL HAD JUST left the airport with João De Sousa when his phone rang. As Miles stepped around the BMW he'd parked at the curb and opened the back door for their guest, Paul noted the caller ID was from Keller's cell and answered.

"Yeah."

"Benjamin Ashman is in here with an attorney talking to Simon and the FBI right now," Keller said without preamble.

Paul shook his head, trying to unscramble his thoughts and understand what he'd just heard. "He's what?"

"What's going on?" Miles called from the back as he finished putting De Sousa's luggage inside the trunk and slapped it closed loudly.

Paul raised a finger to silence Miles as Keller repeated what he'd said. "Son of a bitch!" Paul said. "You need to stay on this, let us know what he tells them."

"They moved the files, changed rooms, I don't know," Keller said. "I'd have to find them and it's getting hot around here. I don't know if I can."

Paul's jaw tightened as his body temperature rose. He hated dealing with fucking politicians. "You get that information. I don't care what you have to do. Or we're all dead." He said it straight, without raising his voice, but every word came out with edge like a knife.

"I fucking know that, okay? Jesus Christ," Keller replied. "Let me see what I can find."

"You do that," Paul said. "And call me as soon as Ashman leaves." He hung up without waiting for a reply and turned, seeing De Sousa shut in the car, waiting for them, Miles standing on lookout nearby.

"Ashman's at the fucking Police Station?" Miles asked, having gathered a few details eavesdropping.

Paul nodded. "Fucker decided to protect himself. Typical."

"Son of a bitch. Want me to wait for him?"

"No. We're going to the hotel to drop De Sousa, then we'll get to his house," Paul said. "He has to sign a statement and that could take time."

"Do we tell the Brazilian?" Miles asked as they separated and moved toward the car, Miles headed for the driver's side.

Paul clicked his tongue, thinking, then shook his head. "No. We handle it for now."

"I don't know," Miles said, pausing with his hand on the door handle. "Taking out Ashman's a big thing."

"That will depend on what he told them," Paul said.

"Oh fuck. If he's talking to them, we've lost him."

Paul grunted. "Yeah, but we kill him and our operation's over. There's so much at stake. We're doing this to protect the greater good, remember?" It was a mission Paul had never doubted from the start, but he wasn't sure Miles had done more than follow orders. Had he ever bought in for real?

Miles chuckled. "One man's greater good is another's evil, brother. We can start over somewhere else."

"Only if we have no choice," Paul said. "The lost time matters."

"Whatever you say," Miles said with a shrug and opened the car door.

Paul knew then that Miles wasn't a fellow believer, which wasn't a problem for now but would be some day. As long as he was useful, Paul would ignore it, but he'd keep a closer watch. He opened his own door, climbed inside, and began chatting up the Brazilian as if everything was according to their plans as Miles pulled the car out from the curb and headed for the Interstate.

SIMON HAD JUST turned onto I-35 when Maberry came over the radio: "We lost them."

"What?!" Simon shouted into the mic. "You've got to be kidding."

"Hey! They lost us in traffic out by the airport construction," Maberry said. The nightmare that had become of Kansas City's airport expansion had quickly spread from the immediate surrounds of the airport terminals and runways to nearby highways, streets, and beyond and it seemed to be dragging on for years and years.

"God damn it!" Simon said, slapping the dashboard with the flat of his palm as he shifted in his seat. "You let José drive, didn't you?"

"Hey!" Correia said into the mic. "That's not funny, bro."

"Hit another old man?" Simon said.

Maberry and Bailey's laughter came in over the mic as

Simon turned his car around and headed back for headquarters.

"Go find him," Simon added.

"I hate you guys," Correia said.

Simon parked the Charger in his usual spot and headed with Lucas for the elevators.

"Did he really hit an old man?" Lucas asked.

"Oh yeah. Brazilians are crazy drivers," Simon said. "I can't believe he ever passed the test."

Lucas laughed, but Simon wasn't joking.

They reached the corridor and headed for interrogation to find Becker and Melson chatting alone in room 6.

"What happened to Ashman?" Lucas asked.

"His lawyer had a statement ready," Becker said. "He signed it and left."

"They lost Paulsen," Simon said.

"Fuck!" Becker replied.

"Let's get another BOLO issued," Melson said.

As he turned around to lead the way back to the squad, Simon spotted a familiar face ducking around a corner at the far end of the corridor.

"Son of a bitch," he whispered. "I think I just saw Keller."

"You two go around," Becker replied softly. "We'll go this way." She motioned down the hall.

Simon nodded and led Lucas around the hallways to approach from the inside as Becker and Melson moved straight toward where he'd seen Keller.

Just as they reached the far end of the corridor, Simon heard Melson's voice: "Ken, is that you?"

Footsteps ran toward them and Keller swung around the corner, bumping right into Lucas. Simon's partner reached out and grabbed him by the shoulder. "No running in the halls. It's dangerous," the android said deadpan.

Simon stifled a laugh as Keller stiffened, scowling and struggling to pull free.

"Get your hands off me! I am the Deputy Chief in charge of investigations!" Keller said, his face crinkling with anger, but his eyes showing fear.

"What do you need, Chief?" Becker said as she and Melson came around the corner, surrounding Keller from behind.

Lucas released his shoulder and Keller shifted for balance, straightening his jacket as he turned toward the Sergeant and his fellow Deputy Chief.

"I want an update on the Ashman investigation," Keller said, blanching and wrinkling his nose with indignation. "And I want to know why you haven't kept me informed."

"Chief's orders," Becker replied.

"I'm a Chief!" Keller snapped.

"Chief Weber," Melson said, squaring off with Keller.

"You're telling me the Chief said to shut me out?" Keller scoffed, shaking his head, but at the same time maneuvering himself into position to slip free of them and head for an exit.

"You wanna tell us about your private traffic and GPS feed?" Simon said, shifting position to block Keller's way. Lucas countered, reaching for the Deputy Chief's shoulder again.

"I don't know what you're talking about," Keller said, voice shaking a bit as he tried to dodge.

"We need some answers from you, Ken," Melson said as Lucas and Simon grabbed him.

"Starting with where Paulsen and his Brazilian friend are headed now," Becker added.

"How should I know?" Keller said, his voice suddenly rising as he avoided eye contact.

"Give us your cell," Simon said, holding out a hand. "Let's see who the last person you called was."

Keller sputtered, shaking his head. "You have no right to treat me like this."

"You're under arrest for suspicion of aiding and abetting, accessory to murder, and illegal use of department resources," Melson said.

"The fuck I am!" Keller said, suddenly squirming hard to jerk free of Simon and Lucas.

Simon punched him hard in the stomach, doubling him over.

"Assault on a superior officer!" Keller croaked out.

"Resisting arrest," Melson replied, nodding to Simon.

Simon and Lucas grabbed Keller by the arms again and dragged him back toward interrogation.

"Let me go!" he demanded.

"You may feel a slight sting. That's pride fucking with you," Lucas said.

Simon recognized the quote from *Pulp Fiction* and laughed.

"He's not even an officer! Get him off me!" Keller said.

"I am making a citizen's arrest," Lucas countered.

"You're getting much better, partner," Simon said, as he and the others laughed. Simon took great pleasure in dragging Keller's hands behind him and, not at all gently, slapping on the cuffs.

CHAPTER 25

MILES GOT THEM to Ashman's mansion in a gated cul-de-sac near Country Club Plaza in record time—less than half an hour. The vans carrying De Sousa's guards arrived fifteen minutes later. Having them leave the airport separately had turned out to be a wise decision, as Paul had been able to use them to run interference when he discovered KCPD officers tailing the BMW. The two vans had driven erratically, jamming their brakes and causing larger, slower jams in a construction area, bringing traffic to a virtual crawl for almost twenty minutes, while Miles sped ahead in the BMW and then took side streets the rest of the way, losing their tails. The guards then followed separately and no one was the wiser, at least not the cops.

Paul sent Miles to the gate to enter the pass code and admit the two vans, while he let himself and De Sousa into Ashman's house. Ashman's wife, Lee, had been surprised to see them, especially when Paul pulled his Glock and shot her in the forehead before she'd hardly said three words. He left her there, lying in the foyer, while he and De Sousa settled on couches in the nearby living room.

Ashman's mansion had seven bedrooms, three living rooms, two dining rooms, an industrial-sized kitchen with appliances made for entertaining large crowds, both an indoor and outdoor pool, a full office cum library and an indoor game room that had a large movie screen with several rows of seating, a two lane bowling alley, and pool, foosball, and Ping Pong tables. It was insane that only two people lived there now, and the house looked immaculate—with museum-quality art decorating every room in various appropriate themes to expensive linens, drapes, and carpets as well as tile, real wood, and marble flooring. The place had been in *Better Homes & Gardens* five times over the years, and it was an obscene display of the Ashmans' wealth and success, however hard earned. They'd raised five children here, several of whom Paul knew well. He'd been two years ahead of Ashman's oldest son all through school, in fact. Ironically, none of the five had followed their father's footsteps into the family business. All now had different careers and their own families elsewhere—the nearest being the youngest son in St. Louis.

Tonight not being an entertainment night, no one else was expected except for Ashman himself, so Paul ordered Miles and the guards to hide their vehicles behind the house near the servant's entrance and position themselves to keep a good lookout—both for security and advanced warning of the owner's arrival. When the deployment was finishing, Miles returned to join Paul and De Sousa waiting in the living room just off the foyer.

"What's the plan, boss?" Miles asked.

"The plan is eliminate our biggest problem," De Sousa replied casually, as if it should be obvious.

"To me, that's the cop," Miles said.

"Ah, but Benjamin has been talking to them, so he must go as well," Paul said.

Miles shrugged. "Hell, the guy's a weasel. Ask me, he's

been standing in our way for years anyway. You want me to pop him in the drive?"

Paul shot him a look of distaste—as if the mere suggestion were an insult. "No, I want to talk to him first. I'll handle it."

Miles grinned and leaned back into a recliner. "Fine. I'm here if you need me."

Paul found himself feeling an unexpected emptiness, despite the anticipation of a long expected confrontation with his mentor and employer. It was as if he'd already resigned himself to the outcome, which he had in a way, yet part of him kept raising the idea of hope: maybe somehow Ashman would surprise him and join their cause.

He supposed it didn't matter. He'd known getting into this, from the moment he stepped outside Ashman's authority and made moves to utilize his property and resources without consulting him, that a confrontation day would arise at some point. But he'd also told himself that Ashman could be sold on it, brought around to Paul's way of thinking gradually, and the fact that he'd failed in that endeavor left him numb, not sad as he'd have expected. Ashman had gone from an asset—a means to an end, really—to a liability, so there was no choice.

They'd deal with Benjamin Ashman, and then they'd deal with John Simon and the robot. And anyone else who got in the way.

Because the information they were disseminating was making a difference—data deemed secret and held closely by various governments and business entities to maintain superiority and advantage over others. When properly shared, this information evened the playing field and let others into the game in ways that kept any particular player from gaining an overwhelming, unique advantage they could lord over everyone else. It wasn't about Paul or João De Sousa wanting power for themselves, it was decentralizing power from the hands of the few to the hands of the many. Fuck the elite ten percent who'd long ruled the world. The other ninety percent wanted and deserved their place in the sun, and in gaining it, new ideas, new approaches, and new opportunities would come to be and push out many of the old, tired traditions that continued holding everyone back all in the name of "status quo"—the fear of change.

Paul had discovered his mission in college and taken years finding others of like mind with whom he might collaborate. De Sousa, despite his own family's tradition of wealth and influence, was one of those like minds, and he had found Paul and a small, close knit network of others. Then there were the staff they used to bring about their mission—men and women like Miles, who couldn't give a shit about the larger picture, but were easily manipulated and useful in their simplicity. They were also expendable and would be easily gotten rid of when the time was right. These people kept few ties to friends or families, used to their work requiring them to stay off the radar, assume names and identities, and generally disappear from ordinary life. That made them all the more easily erasable and Paul had already erased several over the decade since he and his cohorts set their plan in motion.

Miles yawned from his recliner and Paul stared at him in embarrassed annoyance. He shot De Sousa an apologetic look that the Brazilian returned with a knowing smirk. He was used to having such clueless but useful people surrounding him, used to their poor manners and nature—it didn't bother him.

Paul pointed a finger at Miles. "Who's watching the cameras?"

Miles sat forward, waking from almost a nap. "Oh. Yeah. I can do that."

Paul raised a brow, urging him to hurry, and Miles nodded, standing, and heading off for Ashman's security room nearby. The servants were usually only on duty at certain hours and situations. Right now, with things quiet, Benjamin had asked Paul to lay them off temporarily. And Paul knew there'd be no one to interfere with his plans this night. He had everything covered simply by luck and Ashman's careless attitude.

Less than five minutes later, Miles hurried back. "He's pulling up to the gate now."

Paul nodded. "Make sure the driver doesn't see our people until they come inside. We don't want them changing their minds."

"On it," Miles replied and hurried back to his station, already keying the radio to coordinate the other men.

Paul took a deep breath and smirked at De Sousa, and the two men relaxed, waiting patiently for Ashman's arrival, his reaction to his dead wife, and the long awaited confrontation that would ensue.

IT TOOK TWENTY minutes for Keller to confess what he knew and ten more for him to admit that he'd just called Paulsen about Ashman being in interrogation. From there Simon knew where Paulsen and De Sousa had gone: they'd be at Ashman's house, waiting for him.

"Someone try calling Ashman on his cell," Becker ordered

two clerks as they all raced out of the interrogation room. "Tell him not to go home! To come right back here!" She raced into the office as everyone else scrambled for keys, guns, etc.

In another five minutes, Simon and Lucas were headed that way with Oglesby, Dolby, Bailey, Tucker, Maberry, Correia, Becker, Carter, and the FBI following, along with Tactical Response Units from both KCPD and the FBI and several squad cars. Everyone went Code One—lights and sirens. Simon pushed his pedal to the floor and drove the Charger as fast as it would go, despite the fact he and Lucas had to wait to enter until the others arrived and set up. Regardless, he wanted to be there, holding out a small hope that he could somehow still beat Ashman and stop him outside the gate.

When he pulled up outside, he saw Ashman's car parked in the curved drive in front of the mansion and his heart sank.

"We're too late," Lucas said.

Simon didn't have to respond. He already knew. He took a deep breath, focusing on what he had to do and wondered if Benjamin Ashman or his wife were still alive.

PAUL ENJOYED WATCHING Benjamin Ashman squirm. He probably should have killed him shortly after the man fell to his knees, sobbing beside his wife's body, but instead, he'd watched and waited as Miles strapped him to a chair with rope and stepped aside. Paul and De Sousa had taken their time and enjoyed every minute of questioning him. They'd even broken a few of his fingers, just for fun. Ashman wasn't holding back. He confessed everything. Took all the fun out of it really.

"Cops!" Miles hollered from the window.

"What? How many?" Paul asked.

"How did they find us?" Miles muttered, then saw Paul's stare and replied, "A lot. More still arriving. Is that a SWAT team? I think there's two SWATs. Jesus."

"Motherfucker!" Paul said through grinding teeth, his pulse pounding as he drew his weapon and aimed it at Ashman's forehead.

"We done with him?" Miles asked.

"Yes!" Paul and De Sousa both replied in unison as Miles shot him twice between the eyes, Ashman's nose disappearing in chips of blood and flesh, disintegrating under the onslaught of the bullets. His head dropped as blood ran down his chest and legs to the floor.

"We might have needed a hostage, dumbass!" Paul said, frowning at Miles.

Miles shrugged. "We can still get out of here if we hurry."

"We're splitting up. Hold them off for a bit," Paul ordered Miles as he grabbed De Sousa and ran for the lower floor and the servant's entrance.

"I'm not coming with you?" Miles shouted after him.

Paul didn't answer. Miles had also outlived his usefulness. Having the cops kill him would just save Paul the hassle.

SIMON AND LUCAS went in with Becker, Maberry, and Correia, hoping to scout it out, maybe get Paulsen talking. They still worked it as a team, covering each other's backs, Lucas at the center, unarmed, ducking, rolling, sliding, one after the other, then trading positions for cover.

Ashman's mansion was just as imposing as the gate and ten foot high walls surrounding and protecting it. It somewhat resembled a Southern plantation house with a symmetrical facade, large, white stone Greek columns, a covered porch and balconies, all with ornate, hand-carved highlights, gables enclosing the roof, and an attached garage that was double story and half the size of the house, with a curved drive leading down to the bottom entrances. It was rumored Ashman collected classic cars and now Simon knew where he must store them.

But as they made their way past a Greek fountain lined on each side by rose bushes, fire from automatic weapons tore up the ground around them and they all dove for cover.

"Son of a bitch!" Maberry said as a ceramic planter beside him and Simon exploded and shards covered their skin and clothes. Maberry brushed at them with annoyance.

"They brought reinforcements," Becker commented.

"A *lot* of reinforcements," Correia added.

Simon cringed as he pulled a ceramic splinter from his cheek with a sharp pain.

"You're bleeding," Lucas warned.

Simon nodded and shot him an *I know that* look. "All right, Correia, you take the lead."

Correia scoffed. "Are you fucking kidding me?"

"Just keeping a promise I made to Madolyn Rayas," Simon said, deadpan.

"Who's Madolyn Rayas?" Lucas asked.

Becker and Maberry burst out laughing as Correia scowled.

"The wife of the man he ran over," Simon explained.

Then Lucas laughed too, even as they all ducked to avoid another round of gunfire.

"Jesus, Simon, we're being shot at. This is not the time for jokes," Correia said.

"You're the one who needs practice at aim, Correia," Simon said. "You shoot, we joke."

The others busted up again as Correia grunted, stood and fired several shots from his Glock at a gunman occupying a second floor balcony nearby. The man fired back, then fell with two shots in the chest, his stream of bullets arcing up to tear into the gable overhead as he fell.

Correia shot Simon a smug glare. "Shut the fuck up, all right?"

Simon chuckled as he and the others stood, aimed, and fired at other gunmen. They were diving for cover seconds later as the dead man's friends fired back with much better aim this time.

"Christ, I think you inspired them, José," Maberry said.

"You shut the fuck up, too," Correia said. "God damn partner's supposed to have my back," he mumbled.

"José, less cursing more shooting," Becker scolded.

They waited for a let up in the automatic fire, and Lucas

motioned. "I can distract them. Bullets do less harm to my exoskeleton."

Simon started to tell him to stay put, but his partner stood and yelled, "Come quietly...or there will be trouble." He really had the *Robocop* voice down, Simon had to admit.

Bullets tore up the ground around Lucas' feet then rattled his body as a couple hit his chest and he dropped into a crouch again. Simon was glad he'd made him wear Kevlar just in case.

"It didn't really work," he said.

"No fucking shit, moron," Correia said, shaking his head.

"Hey, he's hurt one hundred percent less innocent civilians than you!" Simon snarled.

"He's not even a cop!" Correia protested.

Then, at a letup in fire from the shooters, they all stood and fired back as a line.

"Did anyone try to get them on the phone?" Becker wondered.

"Forward team, this is AIC Falk, we're sending in tactical," Falk said over the radio.

"So much for talking first," Simon said.

"You think they want to talk first?" Lucas asked.

The others guffawed as Simon grinned.

PAUL AND DE SOUSA made it to the servant's entrance quickly, and Paul had De Sousa wait while he poked his head out to look for cops. No sign of any yet.

De Sousa waited while Paul checked the vans for keys, but found them locked. He motioned to De Sousa and pointed toward Miles' BMW.

De Sousa came out and they ran to the car where Paul climbed in behind the wheel. He found the keys above the visor where Miles always kept them handy and started the engine, De Sousa settling into the passenger seat beside him.

Paul buckled his seatbelt. "Sorry about this. The problem has gotten bigger than expected."

De Sousa frowned. "I should have handled it myself the minute it arose. But it hardly matters."

"The mission is all that matters," Paul said, repeating a mantra the leaders said often. He started the BMW and accelerated toward the gate as De Sousa's seatbelt clicked beside him.

"They will pay," Paul promised.

The gate opened and he slammed the pedal to the floor, speeding past several black and whites and unmarked cars with armed men lining up beside them before any could respond. He saw several reaching for shoulder radios and sneered, then headed for the airport.

He pulled out his cell and hit a number on speed dial. "Paulsen. Get the jet ready. We're on our way...Away from here. We'll file a flight plan later...I don't give a shit about the FAA..."

The hangar chief continued arguing.

"Just fucking have it fueled and ready!" Paul ordered. "Tell them Rio." And he hung up, focusing on his driving as he took a sharp left and headed for the Plaza. They had to switch vehicles. The cops would be all over this one.

"FUCK ME!" MILES said as the bay window in the Ashman's front living room exploded, shards of glass flying through the room like daggers, and he dove for cover behind a nearby pillar. He raised his Sig Sauer and fired back, but then wished he'd brought the AR15.

Paulsen had abandoned him, that son of a bitch! He understood getting De Sousa to safety, had even agreed with it. De Sousa was too important. So was Paul, but now he realized: they'd sacrificed him in leaving him behind. The Police had come in siege numbers. The fuckers had probably taken his car, too.

For just a moment, he thought about surrendering, telling everything he knew about Paulsen and his "mission." But he'd killed a police officer and shot at several others. They'd probably shoot him on sight. Besides, he wasn't cut out for jail. And he wasn't about to get a rep for not fighting to the end.

"Fuck this, too!" he said and looked toward the nearby stairs. He could still get out of this. He'd get himself out. Let De Sousa's men do the dying. Miles O'Ryan would live to fight another day. And maybe he'd even show Paulsen what sacrifice meant.

He took one more glance out the bay window and saw that bastard cop and his goddamn robot. If he waited for the right moment, he could hit them both.

SIMON HEARD THE call over the radio as he and the others continued exchanging gunfire with the shooters on Ashman's lawn. He and Lucas had taken cover behind a row of tall shrubs with a good view of the front of the house.

"Two suspects fleeing in blue BMW," an FBI agent reported then read off the license plate number.

"That's Paulsen," Simon said to Lucas, his attention off the shooters as his mind raced. It had to be Paulsen. And the South American, too, he'd bet. "Let's get to the car." He turned and fired three more shots at the nearest gunman, making sure he was clear, then whirled toward the gate, Lucas following.

Just then shots rang out from the house behind him. Simon turned, raising his gun and Lucas tackled him to the ground as several rounds flew over their heads. Looking back, he saw Miles O'Ryan aiming his Glock out the window and sneering.

Becker, Maberry, and Correia stood and riddled the asshole with bullets, his chest breaking out in red polka dots of blood, his sneer turning into a scowl as he wiggled and vibrated then dropped to the floor.

Simon realized Lucas had saved his life.

"Are you okay?" Lucas asked.

"You saved my life," Simon said, surprised, letting it sink in.

Lucas rolled off him and nodding, climbing to his feet then offered Simon a hand to help him up. "Partners have each other's backs."

Simon accepted the hand and they both crouched and ran toward the gate.

"They will be hard to catch," Lucas said.

"I'll call in help," Simon said.

"Where are you going?" Falk asked, stopping Simon near the gate.

"Paulsen's getting away with the South American," Simon said.

"You'll never catch 'em," Falk said.

"I'll call the FAA and hold all flights," Stein said as he dialed his cell nearby.

"I have to try," Simon called as he hurried past. "I know where they're going." He wasn't positive but he thought he had a pretty good idea.

Falk stiffened and turned. "You do?"

"Just get your chopper to follow me," Simon called back as he disappeared through the gate.

As they rounded the corner and headed for the Charger, Simon tossed Lucas the keys. "You drive."

"Me? I don't know the city." Lucas stopped, confused.

Simon opened the passenger door and motioned for him to hurry as he pulled the cartridge from his Glock and began reloading it. "I'll give you directions if I have to. I'll be busy."

"You like shooting, don't you?" Lucas said as Simon headed for the passenger side.

"Depends."

"On what?"

"If some assholes killed my girlfriend and then tried to kill me or my daughter today," Simon said and climbed into the car, gun resting on his knee while he reached for the seatbelt.

Lucas climbed in behind the wheel. "They shot me, too."

Simon motioned for him to drive. "I'll give you my extra gun. Go!"

They both slammed their doors and Lucas shifted the car into gear, pressing the accelerator. Simon figured with his computer brain, his partner might actually be able to drive faster and more daringly than any human. He hoped that was the case. He reached over and flipped on the siren, then plugged in the magnetic light at the center of the dash. "Don't stop for lights or signs."

"What about other cars?" Lucas asked.

"That's why we're Code One," Simon said, then keyed the radio. "186, traffic. Need a trace on a blue BMW." He read off the license plate numbers.

"Tracking," came the reply.

"Where do I go?" Lucas asked as they approached an intersection, the Charger increasing speed every moment.

"Take the next three rights and head towards the Plaza," Simon instructed.

Lucas shrugged and turned the car so sharply at the corner, Simon was jerked forward then back again in the seatbelt and the tires squealed so loud, Simon thought they could be heard over the gunfire at Ashman's house.

"Jesus," Simon mumbled. "Be careful that the tires don't slide into a curb."

Lucas took the next left even faster, taking out a street sign and bouncing the tires up over the curb and lawn of a house as he cut off a taxi and two Mercedes going the opposite way, their horns blaring.

"Driving is fun," Lucas said.

"Dying is less fun," Simon said and grabbed the handle over his head.

Lucas slowed for the final turn which took them out onto 46th, headed south.

"186."

"Go ahead," Simon said into the radio.

"186, suspect vehicle is on 47th headed east," the dispatcher reported.

"Take a right," he told Lucas.

"Which one?"

"Any one," Simon said.

Lucas swerved, then turned, the back wheels spinning east as he simultaneously directed the Charger's nose south into an alley. The car bounced and scraped as it shot over the bumps and potholes, Lucas narrowly missing two dumpsters and trash debris flying up under the wheels.

"Stick to the streets, not alleys," Simon said, shaking his head.

"You said any," Lucas replied, eyes locked on the road ahead, then he executed another sliding left onto 47th, two cars swerving to miss them and crunching into parked cars at the curb with the sound of screeching metal and breaking glass.

"Maybe I am too old for this shit," Simon muttered, as he bounced and banged around in his seat. Lucas just kept staring straight ahead, steady and focused, hands never leaving the wheel. "Okay, a little slower," Simon said as he keyed the radio. "186, patch me through to air support."

"One moment," the dispatcher replied and Simon scanned the road ahead, looking for the BMW.

PAUL HEARD THE thump of helicopters overhead. Just a couple blocks to go and he'd be at the garage where they had a vehicle stashed. He pushed the accelerator and sped up, weaving around Plaza traffic and scattering startled pedestrians at a crosswalk across Central and 47th as the BMW shot straight through.

"I thought we were going to the airport," De Sousa said in his heavy accent, holding onto a handle over the door as he shot Paul a worried frown.

"They know this car," Paul said. "I have another nearby. We gotta lose the choppers."

De Sousa looked out the window and turned, looking up at the sky behind them. "Hurry."

Paul made a face, knowing De Sousa could see but kept the vulgar response to himself. *Another time, asshole.*

"ALL UNITS, SUSPECT vehicle, Blue BMW, from Ashman residence is crossing Wyandotte," the dispatcher announced over the radio.

"We're headed down Main now," Falk said to Simon's surprise.

"You're after him, too?" Simon said as he hit the button to roll down his window, gun ready in his left hand.

"Thought you needed backup KCPD 186," Falk replied.

Lucas shot through a crosswalk at Central where angry pedestrians jumped clear, shaking fists at the damn reckless driver.

"Hey! We're walking here, asshole!" an angry man called.

Simon smiled and waved, then turned to Lucas. "Don't hit people."

"Against my programming," Lucas replied.

"He should be a block or two ahead," Simon said.

Cars did their best to pull over for the lights and sirens but as usual the streets and parking spots were crowded, so most just slowed and even stopped so Lucas could go around them. Simon was thankful for that at least.

He spotted tail lights and the blue of a BMW ahead. "There!" he pointed. He leaned out the window, taking his best aim and waited until he had a clear shot, then fired off several rounds at the fleeing BMW.

"SHIT!" PAUL CURSED as the back windshield exploded and he heard popping as more bullets struck the body of the car. He and De Sousa ducked as Paul swerved, trying to keep the chase car from lining up more shots.

"*Filho de puto!*" De Sousa shouted.

"Shoot back if you want," Paul suggested, annoyed that the Brazilian was not trying to do anything to defend them.

De Sousa scowled, shifting in his seat, sweat glistening on skin as tight as his posture at the moment. "Such a crowded place. It is only helping them."

"It's the nearest car we have stashed," Paul said.

De Sousa mumbled something in Portuguese that sounded awfully close to "idiot" or "stupid."

If he didn't have to drive, Paul would have shot him.

THE CHARGER SHOT past Baltimore and Simon saw the four horsemen and shooting streams of water as the JC Nichols Memorial Fountain loomed ahead.

He leaned out and took aim, firing at the BMW's tires now. Pedestrians ducking behind parked cars or scattering into stores, some screaming, at the boom of the gunshots.

The BMW swerved to avoid the fire, and then a black Ford Escalade with tinted windows shot out into the intersection at Main, headed south, blocking the BMW. FBI.

Paulsen over compensated, tires spinning, car twirling and crashed right into the fountain with a huge splash, metal and glass screeching, rubber still turning.

Lucas slammed the brakes and squealed to a stop as the Escalade slowed and turned back.

Simon tossed Lucas his backup gun from under the seat, a Smith & Wesson he'd preferred until the department insisted on the switch to Glocks. "Here."

Then he was out the door and running toward the fountain, armed FBI agents soon following.

PAUL RELEASED HIS seatbelt, blood running down his nose from a cut on his forehead and pulled his Glock, unlocking the safety as he glanced over. De Sousa was unconscious or dead, his bloodied face nodding against his chest as the BWM rocked in the fountain.

Paul opened his driver's side door and climbed out, aiming and firing at Simon and the FBI agents as he came.

"Drop it now!" Simon ordered. "And stop right there!"

"The mission is all that matters," Paulsen mumbled, firing off two more rounds as he splashed through water, seeking cover behind one of the black metal horsemen as the law officers fired back. The horseman pinged as a bullet ricocheted off its surface.

"It's over, Paulsen," Simon said.

Paul saw the android approaching, a gun in his right hand, kevlar over his chest and felt with his left hand for the remote in his pocket. "It'll never be over," Paul yelled. "It's too important."

"Would you like to know your Miranda rights, Mister Paulsen?" Lucas called and even Simon gave him a puzzled look. "I have memorized them."

Paul sneered. "I don't need anything from you, robot. You're not even a cop."

"He likes shooting people," Lucas said, matter-of-factly. "He told me."

Paul said, "So do I." Then he raised the remote and pressed the button.

"I'm trying to save your li—" Lucas' voice cracked, rising

and falling like a jammed cassette, then he fell to his knees.

Simon glanced at his friend and then Paul holding the remote. "Stop! What are you doing to him?"

"Killing him," Paul said and laughed, pressing the remote another time. His chest exploded then, pain arching out from the bloody hole just above his heart. The remote fell as Simon fired again, and Paul hit his knees, gasping for breath. "Fuck you, John Simon," he wheezed.

Blanca Santorios, Stacy Soukop, Peter Green—the names of all the dead flashed through Simon's mind as he aimed again. "Fuck you, too," he said and fired one last time.

Paul slumped, grabbing the statue to hold himself up, his Glock splashing into the water.

Two Feds were there then, hopping up onto the fountain and splashing through the water to kick at the gun and remote as Simon ran back toward the robot. Two more Feds converged on the BMW, guns ready.

"Lucas? Are you okay?" he heard Simon say, concern filling his voice.

Paul scowled as his eyes lost focus and he slid down into the water.

LUCAS WAS FROZEN on his knees, the Smith & Wesson still clasped in his hand, but it was like a light had gone off on his face.

Simon crouched, examining him. No bullet wounds, no other obvious damage. "What's wrong, pal? Talk to me."

Lucas' only response was a high pitched whine, almost a mumble.

"What did he do to you, pal? I can't understand," Simon said, his chest tightening into a ball, painful. He patted his partner on the shoulder, trying to breathe, keep calm, even as Lucas didn't respond further.

He slipped his Glock into the shoulder harness, grabbed Lucas under the arms, and began dragging him back toward the Charger. "I gotta get him help!" he called to Falk and the agents surrounding Paul.

Falk turned back. "The Brazilian's dead. And Paulsen probably won't last long."

"Good fucking riddance," Simon called back as he dragged Lucas' limp form across the pavement, headed for the Charger's passenger door.

"Is he shot?" Falk called.

"I don't know," Simon said as he began working Lucas into the seat, butt first, then moving him limb-by-limb, using the seatbelt to strap him in.

"You need me?" he asked, looking at Falk, his eyes moist, pleading.

Falk shook his head. "Go!" He motioned with a hand.

Simon slid across the hood of his car and raced into his seat, behind the wheel, strapping on the seatbelt, then slamming it into gear. Lucas hadn't even turned off the engine or lights. Simon accelerated, flipping on the siren as he keyed the radio. "Officer down, officer down. 186 in route to medical."

"186, which facility? Confirm please?" the dispatcher called, wanting to confirm and offer assistance as per usual practice in officer-involved shootings.

"Leawood," Simon replied.

"Repeat 186?" the dispatcher asked, confused.

"Leawood, Doctor Livia Connelly," he said.

"St. Luke's is closer," the dispatcher started to say.

"Fuck it. Inform Deputy Chief Melson and Sergeant Becker to meet me at 18678 W. 135th," Simon replied, then dropped the mic and accelerated, headed south onto Ward Parkway at top speed.

"Don't die on me, pal," he said to Lucas, not knowing what else to say. He wasn't about to lose another partner on this case. Especially a man who had just saved his life. He had no idea what Paulsen had done to Lucas, but surely Connelly could fix it. She had to fix it.

He wove in and out of traffic like Mario Andretti, stealing glances at his partner whenever he could and saying a silent prayer.

CHAPTER 26

LIVIA CONNELLY'S AIDE, Steven, met Simon at the car and helped him get Lucas quickly inside her lab, where she worked on her creations. Steven, science fiction TV show shirt, jeans, odd hairstyle, pointy glasses—looked the definition of a grad school geek, which it turned out he was. For Simon time had slowed to a crawl, the world around him moving at a snail's pace. He didn't remember the rest of the drive to Livia's and he only realized they'd finished carrying Lucas inside when they laid him out on the table.

After her initial exam, Livia was just as puzzled as Simon. She calmed him down with a soft voice and then had him repeat the story again, asking detailed questions about the device Paulsen had used and Lucas' reaction to it.

"He just shut down?" she asked after Simon finished.

He nodded, throwing up his hands and exhaling. "Fell to his knees and froze. All I got from him after was some kind of high pitched mumbly, almost scream."

Livia looked at Steven. "If we had the device," Steven said, leaving it unfinished but they all knew the rest.

"I can go back and get it," Simon said, "but it went in the fountain. It's probably ruined."

"We still might be able to analyze it and see what it did," Livia said, looking at Lucas' prone form sadly. She reached out and gently caressed his forehead like a mother caring for a sick child. "Oh Lucas. What have they done to you?"

"I suppose the man who did this is—" Steven said.

"—dead, probably," Simon cut him off. "I left before he actually died but I shot him multiple times in the chest."

Steven shook his head, giving Simon a look like he was the criminal. "Men and their guns."

"Hey, fuck you!" Simon snapped. "He's my partner! I wanted to save him and the guy kept pressing the button."

"You gonna shoot me, too?" Steven snarled, glaring at him.

Livia slapped him on the shoulder. "Enough! He cares about Lucas, too. Let's just focus on figuring out how we can bring him back. Please." She grabbed an Otoscope off a nearby table and used it to look at Lucas, but not in his ears like Simon usually saw it used but at his skin.

"*If* we can bring him back," Steven said.

"Steven!" she scolded. "It shows me the cells," she added, explaining to Simon. "A close up look, almost like a microscope. Handy, though not its intended purpose."

"Yeah, well, if you need to see what's between his ears..." Simon trailed off and she laughed.

"A lot more than you thought when you met him," she said, smiling and her eyes met his.

Simon cringed. "I know. I discovered that. He's my friend."

She nodded, her eyes offering sympathy, concern. "I know. He's hard not to love, once you give him a chance. He thought highly of you as well." She shook her head, looking sheepish. "I mean, thinks. We're not giving up on him yet."

Simon pulled out his cell phone and dialed Falk.

"What are you doing?" Steven asked as he grabbed another Otoscope and begin examining Lucas on the opposite side from Livia. "Contusions, some kind of entry wound here on his right arm, just below the shoulder."

"He was shot," Simon said as the phone rang. "Getting you that remote," he added to Livia as Falk answered. "Did you get that remote?"

"Simon, how's your partner?" Falk asked.

"We need to know what they did to him," Simon said. "The remote might help."

"Your Sergeant took it and she's on her way," Falk said. "We're pulling for him. Good luck."

"Paulsen dead?"

"Yeah, didn't last long," Falk said, not sounding sad at all.

Neither was Simon. "World's a better place. Thanks." He hung up. "Remote's on the way."

"All right, well in the meantime, let me see if these other injuries had any effect," Livia said, moving around to where Steven had pointed out the wounds.

"He didn't act any different after them, not 'til—" Simon just stopped midsentence, pained by the memory.

Livia nodded, offering him an encouraging smile. "Doesn't mean it didn't do a little damage. We want him good as new, so we'll fix everything we can."

Simon nodded. He just wanted his pal back. He sank into a chair, feeling as if he couldn't stand any more, his eyelids heavy. He barely noticed when Becker arrived a quarter hour later and delivered the remote. Or realized that Livia and Steven were analyzing it until they'd taken it apart and a computer started beeping.

"Fried his chips," Steven said.

Livia shook her head. "I don't think so or he'd have completely fallen. His suspension worked enough to keep him upright at an odd angle. I think that's what it was supposed to do but it didn't work quite as planned."

"Let's hope so," Becker said, standing beside them with a worried look, like Lucas was one of her own.

Simon realized he was now.

"This may take a while," Livia said, nodding toward Simon.

Becker nodded. "We have reports and some interviews about the shootings."

"I'm staying," Simon insisted before she even asked.

She kept walking toward him and put a hand on his shoulder. "You have duties, Master Detective. And orders."

Deputy Chief Melson arrived and stormed inside with a grave look on his face. "Doctor, I want that man restored, whatever it takes. The department will lend you all of its resources."

Livia replied with a grateful look. "Right now, we just need to sort it out, but thank you."

Melson handed her a card with his name and private numbers. "Call me anytime and keep us informed please."

She nodded, setting the card on the counter nearby. "We will. For now, we just need to work."

Becker helped Simon to his feet, taking his arm. "We'll drive you."

"You can both ride with me," Melson suggested. "I need an update on what happened out there from each of you."

Becker nodded. "Clean shoot. Straight forward."

"Yes, but the press will be all over it with Ashman dead," Melson said, then added, "amongst others" as he glanced at Lucas on the table again.

Simon relaxed and let Becker lead him toward the door. "You have my number?" he said, stopping to turn back and look at Livia again.

She remained focused on her work. "Yes, don't worry. I'll do everything I can." Her eyes met his and she squeezed them shut a moment, as if to make a promise.

Simon nodded at her and then Steven and left with the two administrators, heading for Melson's car.

BACK AT CENTRAL Patrol, the Shooting Team's questions were routine. There had been plenty of officers on hand to witness, and everything was straight forward. Simon got a bit of guff for taking Lucas along, but Becker and Melson went to bat for him on it. To his surprise, Falk and Stein backed him, too. In the end, after forty-five minutes of mostly routine questions, he was done and waiting to be cleared, which usually took a day or two barring complications.

Ballistics tests would also take time, but they'd found weapons on Miles O'Ryan and others that matched the caliber and make of those used in the shootings and murders against Simon, Lucas, Emma, Blanca, Stacey, Julia Liu, and Peter Green. Everyone felt confident a match was imminent. And Simon hoped so. He wanted a definitive match that would allow them to tell the public they'd caught Blanca Santorios', Julia Liu's, Stacey Soukop's, and Peter Green's killer. Benjamin Ashman's, too.

Meanwhile, there had been no word from Livia and Simon couldn't keep his focus. He thought about calling her, but an hour was being pushy, and he didn't want to be *that guy*. Instead, he thought about Lucas and how he'd spent his final hour looking out for everyone else. From standing up to call out the shooters in a manner the cops thought was naive or a joke to saving Simon, Lucas' every move had been about protecting others. Even when Simon had given him a gun and Lucas faced Paulsen, he hadn't used it; had acted like he didn't even want to—extending an olive branch to the villain. And that had cost him his life.

Did robots have life?

Lucas didn't even seem like an android anymore. To Simon, he had become real, a living and breathing partner and friend. He'd stopped thinking of him as an outsider and let him in, started caring about him, and never imagined how hard he'd take the loss. As much as he'd found the idea of an android silly—he'd always been skeptical about technology, especially in law enforcement; Emma called him a "troglodyte"—the truth was, he'd come to value Lucas' skill set and his heart. He'd gone from trying too hard, almost like playing cop was a fun game, to stepping back, observing, and really helping, letting Simon take the lead. If Lucas were a cop, and they became partners, Lucas would take the lead on his own cases and they'd work together only when needed, like Simon and Blanca, but unlike when they met, now Simon actually thought it could be possible. If Lucas wanted it. If Simon could convince the Academy and powers that be to give an android a chance.

"Are you okay?" Dolby asked, appearing beside his cube with Oglesby.

Simon forced a smile, looking up at them. "Yeah. Just tired."

"It's been a long day," Oglesby agreed.

"It's been a long fucking week, pal," Simon said and they all chuckled.

Maberry and Correia arrived then, sipping cups of coffee that had probably been reheating in the maker across the squad since around noon.

"Any news?" Maberry asked.

Dolby shook her head.

Maberry reached out to squeeze Simon's shoulder. "Hang in there, man."

"We're rooting for him, bro," Correia added, then they headed to their cubicles at the end of the row, opposite each other.

"Hey! Don't we all have reports to write?" Becker's voice boomed across the room from her office and they looked up as she approached. She took one look at Simon and her face changed to concern. "You need sleep, John. Why don't you go catch a nap? Paperwork can wait 'til morning."

Simon leaned back in his chair, groaning. "I can't even concentrate."

"I'll call you as soon as we hear anything, if Doctor Connelly doesn't call you first," Becker promised.

"My house is a mess," Simon muttered, realizing he hadn't been back to the house since Paulsen's men shot it up. He could probably sleep there and he definitely needed to check on it...or he could just lay his head down on the desk here.

Becker tilted her head, puzzled. "I thought that was Lucas' house."

Simon grinned sheepishly. "Yeah, right. Lucas' house."

Becker read him and shook her head. "We'll discuss this tomorrow. Dolby and Oglesby will drive you." She looked at the two Detectives. "One of you take his car for him, okay?"

They nodded and Dolby patted Simon on the back. "Come on."

Simon took a deep breath and scooted out his chair as they cleared the way, stumbling to his feet. Oglesby reached over to steady him.

"I'm all right, thanks," Simon mumbled. Oglesby let go, watching him.

"Get back here as soon as you can," Becker added, her eyes meeting Simon's to impart one last burst of sympathy and concern. Then, she added to the others, "I need all hands on deck" and headed for her office.

Simon followed Dolby, Oglesby beside him, and headed for the parking lot.

AT HOME, Simon slept like he hadn't in days. He'd laid down just to get a catnap and didn't wake again until six a.m. the following morning. The first thing he did was check his phone for messages. There was one text from Becker saying he'd been cleared on the shootings, but beyond that...nothing. So he started dialing Livia Connelly and then looked at the clock on his dresser and stopped. If she had gotten any sleep at all, it might be right now and she'd need it just as much as he did. He wanted her at her best working on Lucas. He'd call later.

He went to the kitchen, turning on more lights than usual because of the plywood boarding up all his shattered windows, and fixed himself some toast, poached eggs, and a glass of apple juice. He ate in silence at the table, the silence haunting. His memories of the house the past week all included Emma and Lucas. They'd really spent a lot of time together there, at least the times he was home. Being here now, alone in silence, just made him miss them both more.

After breakfast, he went outside and started examining the damage to the house in the daylight better than he'd done before. Becker had also told him in her text to "take the day" if he needed it. He certainly had plenty to do around here. He went back inside, opened the garage and then set to work filling bullet holes with putty and making a pile of debris that could be hauled away. Later, he'd call Andy and ask him to come do an estimate for any rebuilding or repairs they'd need.

He'd been hard at work for a couple of hours when he heard a car in the drive. Currently working on the back side, he slowly came around the house to see who it was.

As soon as she saw him, Emma rushed into his arms, hugging him, tears streaking her cheeks. "Daddy!"

"Hey, baby," he said, then saw Lara walking along behind her daughter with a mixture of anger and worry on her face. "Hey," he said to her as he hugged Emma tighter.

"We saw the shooting on the news," Lara commented,

coldly.

"Which one?" Simon asked casually. She looked annoyed by his lack of emotion.

"The Plaza," Emma said. "But we heard about Ashman, too."

Simon grunted. "Yeah."

"I'm so glad you're okay," Emma said, pulling back so she could look him in the eyes, but keeping her arms around him at the same time.

"I'm so glad it's over," Simon said.

"Emma told me about Blanca, John, I'm sorry," Lara said, actually sounding like she meant it. He saw a softness fill her eyes he hadn't seen in years.

"So those men won't be bothering us anymore, huh?" Emma said.

Lara looked around. "My God! What happened to your house?"

Emma and Simon exchanged a look and laughed.

"Machine guns did a number on it," Simon said.

Lara's mouth dropped open and she stepped toward her daughter with a worried frown. "My god, were you here, Emma?" She reached out and gently caressed her daughter's hair.

"I'm fine, Mom," Emma said, as if it were nothing. "The car was worse."

"They shot at you more than once?!" Lara's voice rose in pitch and volume 'til she was yelling. She glared at Simon. He almost laughed. For just a moment, it was like they were having a normal married couple fight again and it felt good.

"I'm fine," Emma insisted, hugging Simon again then releasing him and turning to her mom. "He has this great new partner, Lucas. He helped keep us safe."

"No one should need to help keep you safe from shootings, my God!" Lara whirled to Simon, her face red, lips curling, nostrils flaring. She bared her teeth with every word. "Why are you taking her around your job? Can I not even trust you for one week—!"

"Mom!" Emma yelled back. "Chill!"

"It was not my fault," Simon said. "We stumbled onto something. They went after us. If I had known, you know I would have kept her in a safe house."

"After, we were in hotels and stuff until you came home," Emma added, nodding to back up her dad.

Lara pulled Emma close and shook her head, at a loss for words. "Next time you can stay with friends. You don't need to be around this."

Simon stiffened, fighting to control his rising anger, taking deep breaths to stay calm.

"I love you both, Mom, and I need my dad. Just stop," Emma scolded, glaring at her mother.

"But—"

"No buts, Mom. Dad and Lucas kept me safe," Emma smoldered. Then she looked around. "Where's Lucas?"

Simon winced, having hoped to avoid the topic and took a step back involuntarily, gathering his thoughts. First Santorios, now Lucas. He couldn't bring himself to tell her.

"What?" Emma asked, her face switching to worry and fear. "Tell me, dad!"

Simon hesitated, then said, "He didn't—"

Just then a car door slammed and they turned around to see a Chrome Mitsubishi Outlander parked at the curb. Lucas had a car like that, seeing it made him sad again.

Then Emma grinned and yelled, bounding toward the car. "Lucas!"

The android had stepped from behind the car and was striding across the lawn toward them, beaming. He looked as if nothing had been wrong, shiny, like new.

"Hey, Emma," Lucas said as they embraced. Lara and Simon turned and walked over to join them.

"Hey, partner," Lucas said. And Simon realized he thought of Lucas that way too now, like it was totally natural.

"He looks great," Emma said, then shot Simon a curious look. "I thought for a moment you were going to tell me something bad happened."

Simon did his best to recover from the shock and force a smile, shaking his head. "To Lucas? Nah, come on, he's fine. See?" He motioned to his friend as he looked the android over to verify the truth of the statement.

"Lucas, this is Lara, Emma's Mom," Simon said, motioning to Lara.

Lara actually gave Lucas a warm smile and nodded. "Emma's gone on and on about you. Thank you for taking care of them both."

Simon couldn't believe she'd included them both but he hid a grin as Lara glanced his direction.

Lucas reached out and shook her hand. "You're welcome. They've taken care of me, too."

Lucas turned to Simon then, and their eyes met as they

looked each other over. Emma stepped back beside her mother and the two women just watched them with curiosity. Neither said a thing for several moments.

"Everything okay, pal?" Simon finally asked, breaking the awkward silence.

Lucas nodded, swinging his right arm around a bit like he was trying it out. "Shoulder's a little stiff, but I think they can oil it."

"I thought I lost you," Simon said, ignoring the joke as a mix of emotions flooded him. "You saved my life."

"Ah, don't take it so hard. Even Oedipus didn't see his mother comin'," Lucas said.

Simon crinkled his brows, confused. "What?" He hugged Lucas for a second or two, then let him go.

"It's from *Basic Instinct 2*," Lucas said, "an interesting movie."

"That movie's a piece of crap," Simon said, frowning.

"The first one's better," Emma agreed.

"You let her watch *Basic Instinct*?!" Lara was angry again.

Simon turned and shrugged. "Let her watch? Are you familiar with the Internet? They don't have to ask anymore, just type and search."

Lara crossed her arms over her chest. "At my house, I keep a close eye."

"It's like living under Hitler," Emma said, scowling.

"Hey! I am not some racist dictator!" Lara said, scowling back at her.

Emma made a face.

"Don't call your mother Hitler," Simon scolded, looking at Emma. "She's more like Mussolini or Idi Amin." They both chuckled.

Lara scoffed but he thought he saw the hint of a smile. "You are a bad influence, John Simon."

"You used to think I was exciting and dangerous," Simon said, quoting words she'd told him after her father questioned her choice years ago.

"Yeah, well, I was young and foolish," Lara said. "I can raise Emma smarter."

Lucas nodded. "She's very smart."

And with that they all started talking at once—Lara trying to argue with Simon, while Lucas and Emma traded notes on movies, music, and more.

Everything was back to normal, it seemed. And Simon had never been happier.

LATER, AFTER EMMA had settled down and Simon thought he'd convinced Lara to let their daughter return to his house on the usual schedule, Simon drove Lucas to Central Patrol for an interview and to start his paperwork. He'd taken half the day. That would be enough for now. He was too energized knowing his friend was alive and well. He had his focus back, and staying home fiddling was just a distraction from what he really wanted to do: the job.

"You know, I'd like to be a police officer, I think," Lucas said from the passenger's seat as Simon cruised down Ward

Parkway, headed east.

"Oh yeah?" Simon asked.

"You think I could be?"

Simon patted his partner on the back. "This is America. That's what it's all about—possibilities."

Lucas beamed now, his eyes almost sparkling. "No shit?"

Simon laughed. He'd been a bad influence on the poor android. "Yeah, no shit. I might have use for a good sideman." He turned left onto Troost, headed north then asked, "So what happened? Last time I saw you—you were a mess."

Lucas nodded. "My Maker fixed me."

"Right, but what was wrong?" Simon replied.

"Ah," Lucas nodded with understanding. "My circuits got scrambled by that remote. Apparently a failsafe went into effect that froze and shut me down, but she said there's no permanent damage."

"Damn, I was hoping you'd forget some of those quotes," Simon cracked. They both laughed.

Lucas looked satisfied, his eyes scanning off in the distance for a bit as he thought about something. "I was wrong about you, John."

"About what?"

"You're not too old for this shit."

Simon chuckled and punched Lucas in the arm. "Shut the—"

"—fuck up." They finished together.

"But you really should let me drive," Lucas added.

"It's my car, pal," Simon answered.

Lucas shrugged. "Some of us just have more skills."

"Oh! Is that right? Don't worry, I was driving before you were itching in your daddy's pants," Simon said.

Lucas nodded. "*Lethal Weapon*, nice. But I don't have a daddy."

"I figured it was some old toaster or something," Simon replied, smugly.

"Please, toasters are far too simple."

Simon rolled his eyes, thinking up another comeback as he squeaked through an intersection just as the light changed and continued on. He might actually like it if Lucas became a cop. Sometimes, it was good to have a partner.

Especially one with a decent skill for banter.

Lucas flipped on the radio and they both began singing along...

"*Shot through the heart, and you're to blame...*"

THE END

ACKNOWLEDGEMENTS

There are always a lot of people to thank when writing a book like this, but first and foremost I want to thank the men and women of the Kansas City Police Department who assisted and hosted me on ride alongs, showed me around their stations, and walked me through their jobs and various cases, answering any and every question patiently and thoroughly and even introducing me to others who could shed more light on things. First and foremost, Training Officer Gil Carter, to whom the book is dedicated, took me on over half a dozen ride alongs. Officers Andy Hamil, Lance Lenz, and Doaa El-Ashkar also shared their knowledge with me, during either ride alongs or exploring stations. I did everything from witness shooting scenes to chat with murder suspects, escort shooting victims to E.R.s, witness detoxing meth addicts, witness an officer involved violent incident, and get interrogated later as a witness. It was a real education. It's truly an honor to call you friends. My respect for Police Officers and the KCPD itself is much greater for knowing you.

Thanks goes to my friends who rallied around me to help me launch the new enterprise with Boralis Books. Fellow author Peter J. Wacks provided editorial input along with Ginjer Buchanan, Kent Holloway, Andrew Mayne, and Audra Crebs helped with marketing, business plan, and cover art, Guy Anthony De Marco and David Pederson helped with book design and conversion, Anthony Cardno and Guy also did the proofing, and several author friends took the time to make blurbs and introduce the book to their core fans.

Research assistance was also provided by Robin Wayne Bailey, tuckerized herein alongside Bob Tucker (originator of the term) as a homicide detective, who took me on a narrated driving tour of Kansas City to help me get familiar with its history and neighborhoods on a level I never had before. Tim Hightshoe from Colorado Springs P.D. for a trip to the range to fire every weapon mentioned in the book.

Thanks to the friends who generously allowed me to borrow their names, even combine them, for characters: Julia Soukop, Ken Keller, Gil Carter, Jonathan Maberry, Larry Correia, Elizabeth Gooch, Carol Doms, Corey Barber, James Murray, Martin L. Shoemaker, Jan Gebhardt, Linda Rodriguez, Robin, Christie Pisani, Allie Doss, my sister Lara McCullough, and I probably forgot a few so thanks to them too. Any resemblances are purely accidental because, believe me, I factionalized the hell out of these people just for fun. If we can't laugh at our friends, what the hell fun is there?

As always, Louie and Amelie are my heart, my beloved dogs and bosom companions, plus the newcomer Lacy the cat, thanks goes to them plus my parents, Ramon and Glenda.

Any inaccuracies or errors are mine and mine alone. I thank you for reading and truly hope the book entertained you and maybe taught you a bit more about the police and the important work they do and the sacrifices they make on our behalf. Seriously, thank them for their service. They earned it, even when they give you those traffic tickets we all hate.

AUTHOR BIO

Bryan Thomas Schmidt is a national bestselling author editor and Hugo-nominee who's edited over a dozen anthologies and hundreds of novels, including the international phenomenon *The Martian* by Andy Weir and books by Alan Dean Foster, Frank Herbert, Mike Resnick, Angie Fox, and Tracy Hickman as well as official entries in *The X-Files*, *Predator*, *Joe Ledger*, *Monster Hunter International*, and *Decipher's Wars*. His debut novel, *The Worker Prince*, earned honorable mention on Barnes and Noble's Year's Best science fiction. His adult and children's fiction and nonfiction books have been published by publishers such as St. Martins Press, Baen Books, Titan Books, IDW, and more. Find him online at his website www.bryanthomasschmidt.net or Twitter and Facebook as BryanThomasS. He lives in Ottawa, KS with his canine bosom companions, Louie and Amelie and a cat named Lacy.

Coming in February 2020

THE SIDEMAN

JOHN SIMON BOOK 2

For a sneak peek at the first two chapters,
visit
http://www.BryanThomasSchmidt.net/TheSidemanPreview

CPSIA information can be obtained
at www.ICGtesting.com
Printed in the USA
LVHW110718141019
634115LV00004B/17/P